SERIAL

CSI REILLY STEEL #1

CASEY HILL

ALSO BY CASEY HILL

FOREWORD

This book was written, produced and edited in the UK, where some spelling, grammar and word usage will vary from US English.

PROLOGUE

'Go on, I dare you.'

'Forget it, Jess– I'm not doing it, OK?' Reilly Steel trundled along the path on her way home from school.

Her younger sister skipped along in front of her, her fluffy blond pigtails bouncing with every step.

She hated collecting her sister from school – all her friends got to hang out at the mall, but no, she had to go get Jess, take her home, give her a snack, make sure she did her homework. 'You know Dad says we should stay away from him,' she muttered.

Twenty yards ahead, an old man walked slowly back and forth across his yard, raking leaves. Dressed in an old flannel shirt and dirty overalls, he had a pronounced stoop, thin silver hair raked across his head, and large gnarled hands wrapped round the handle of the rake. It was fall; the leaves were turning on the trees, the sun sinking lower in the sky with each passing day.

Jess looked at Reilly, her clear blue eyes shining with mischief. 'Go on, say something to him.'

'Didn't you hear what I just said? We're not supposed to talk to that guy.'

'But why?'

Reilly exhaled in annoyance. 'Why what, Jess?'

'Why aren't we supposed to talk to Mr Reynolds?'

She glanced at the older man and shivered. Randy Reynolds they called him – word was he had a taste for little girls. Jess was staring at him, her eyes wide with fascination as though she half knew the truth.

'He's a bad guy. He ... does things to little girls,' Reilly said, finally. She gave her sister a nudge. 'Come on, let's get going.'

Jess didn't move. 'What kind of things?'

Reilly sighed. She knew her sister well enough to recognize that look – Jess wasn't going anywhere until her question had been answered. 'Well, he likes to ... touch girls—'

'Touch them?'

'Touch their bits, you know ... like their private parts,' she continued, uncomfortably.

Understanding suddenly dawned in Jess's eyes. 'Eeew! Why would he want to do that?'

How to explain to a wide-eyed ten-year-old when in all honesty Reilly didn't get it herself? 'I don't know,' she mumbled. 'I guess some guys just do.'

Jess looked thoughtful. 'He's not supposed to do that though, is he?'

'No. Like Dad always says, nobody touches your private parts except you.' She nudged her again. 'Come on, let's go. We've got lots of homework, and you know Dad'll get mad if it's not done before he gets back from work.'

Not only that but Reilly also had to make dinner and clean the house, all the things a mom should do.

But not their mom.

She and Jess started walking again, closer to Reynolds' house. As they passed, the old man stopped raking. He looked up, his eyes glistening as he watched them walk past.

'Hi girls.' His voice was a low croak.

Reilly said nothing and kept her head down, but Jess stared right back, insolent, looking him straight in the eye. 'Jess, I'm warning you,' Reilly muttered out of the side of her mouth.

'You're a pretty one, aren't you?' Reynolds said, his mouth breaking into a grin. Jess stared back, a defiant look in her eyes. Reilly grabbed her hand and tried to haul her along, but she pulled free. 'You like little girls, don't you?' Jess challenged. She stepped forward. 'You want to touch my private parts, right? Go ahead then.' And with that, she lifted her skirt and flashed her pink cotton Snoopy pants at him.

'Jess!' Reilly cried, flabbergasted.

Reynolds stared transfixed – evidently torn somewhere between surprise, lust and shame. Then just as suddenly, Jess dropped her skirt, picked up a stone and hurled it with all her strength. Caught off-guard, the man stumbled backward and landed in a crumpled heap on his lawn.

Jess turned and ran, grabbing Reilly's hand as she raced past. 'Come on!'

They didn't stop running until they were around the corner. Breathless, Reilly looked at her little sister. 'What the hell were you doing, Jess? You don't flash at people ... Don't you ever do something like that again!'

Jess was wide-eyed. 'Why not?'

'Well ... because it's just not the thing to do.' Reilly struggled for words. 'We were told to stay away from him. You could get yourself in serious trouble.' She shook her head, amazed but also faintly impressed at her brazenness. 'I can't believe you did that.'

Jess looked back at her with innocent eyes. 'But you said he's a bad guy, and bad guys are supposed to be punished, aren't they?'

1

Reilly's head shot up off the pillow and she stared around her, momentarily forgetting where the hell she was. She took slow, deep breaths in an attempt to calm her heart rate and let her eyes gradually adjust to the shadow-filled room.

Lying back down, she stared up at the ceiling, the lights of the passing cars creating abstract patterns as they slid by in the rain-slicked streets below. Her thoughts wandered in a random, half-asleep manner and wound up back with Jess.

It had been a while since she'd dreamt about her sister. Maybe a year or more, which was good; Dr Kyle, her shrink back home, would have been proud of her. The less she dreamt about Jess and the less she thought about Jess, the better.

Because thinking about her, about *it* had never got Reilly anywhere. Although Dr Kyle would probably argue that thinking about Jess had had a profound influence on Reilly in every conceivable way. In fact, the doc had implied more than once that if the whole Jess situation had never happened, then she might well have decided to follow a very different path. But he was a shrink so of course he *would* say that.

Her thoughts had brought her full circle, wide awake in a dingy Dublin apartment in the middle of the night. Sleep was gone for now so pulling back the covers, Reilly got out of bed and headed for the bathroom.

She switched on the light and gasped at the sight in the mirror. A bright red scar ran along one cheek and she rubbed furiously at it, hoping the seam mark from the pillow would go away. Her eyes were glassy and swollen from lack of sleep and her fair hair was tousled, knotted and badly in need of a trim. A quick wash and shampoo would just have to do for now she sighed, stepping into the shower.

A few minutes later, she wrapped herself in a towel and padded barefoot into the kitchen. Or at least that's what the cheery real estate guy who'd rented her the place had called it – as far as Reilly was concerned, it was nothing but a glorified broom closet. But apparently in this town, a broom closet for a kitchen was all you got for the best part of a thousand bucks a month, and for that, Reilly had also been blessed with a 'modern open-plan living area' and a 'cosy bedroom'.

If you considered coffins cosy, she'd wanted to reply. But at least the place was in better shape than anything else she'd seen, and at the time she'd needed to find somewhere to live – fast. By then the hotel bills had started to mount up, and her employers were bitching about the expense.

Dublin had come as a shock to her – no strike that – *Ireland* had come as a shock to her. Growing up back home in California, her father used to love telling her and Jess colorful stories about the country of his birth; it sounded almost magical – a land full of green open spaces and welcoming, friendly people. She never tired of hearing tales about Mike

Steel's childhood before the family's eventual emigration to California.

But upon her arrival four months before, Reilly quickly realized that the slow-paced, easy-going picture of Ireland her dad had painted didn't fit at all with the Dublin she found.

Instead of the laidback and carefree natives he'd described, Reilly was faced with a population of supremely confident, well-educated and ambitious go-getters, even though like the rest of the world, Ireland had recently suffered its fair share of financial turmoil and unemployment.

While Reilly was under no illusion that working in Dublin would be a holiday, she was already taken aback at the level of serious crime in the country, particularly one with such a small population.

She fixed herself a coffee and turned her attentions to the day ahead. Although it was already 7.30 a.m., it was so dark outside it still felt like the middle of the night. It was days like this she really missed the sun coming up over San Francisco Bay – that she missed the sun, period.

She closed her eyes and pictured the view from the headland back home where she usually parked her car – the wide sweep of the bay, the breakers rolling in from left to right, the sea that deep, dark green that she loved, whitecaps calling to her as she hauled on her wetsuit and unloaded her surfboard from the top of her car.

By contrast, winter here was oppressively bleak and miserable – at first, Reilly couldn't understand how people even managed to rouse themselves from their beds, let alone summon the energy to work as hard as they did through those dark, gray days. But despite being starved of sun, Ireland was now Reilly's home and, sixteen weeks in, she was just about beginning to get used to it.

Not that she'd had the opportunity to spend all that much time outside, though. Since moving to Dublin, she'd been practically chained to the lab, which she supposed was a good thing. Labs tended to be the same all over the world and the one place in which Reilly felt most at home.

'Or the one place you feel most in control?' Dr Kyle had suggested, and maybe he was right. In the lab, surrounded by familiar equipment and implements that always did her bidding, she felt at peace.

Albeit temporarily.

Reilly shivered and, pouring the last of her coffee down the sink, she returned to her coffin-cum-bedroom and began to get ready for work.

THE SPARTAN OFFICE was lit by two lines of fluorescent lights, which cast a harsh light on the long table. Reilly spread a collection of evidence bags across the table and watched as her team wandered in, coffee cups and notepads in hand. They jostled each other, raced for the prime seats like kids in school, then finally settled and looked up expectantly at her.

'OK, what have we got?' she asked, glancing at the array of bagged and labelled items on the table in front of her. There was a bloodied T-shirt, a broken beer glass, a half-eaten burger and some fries – or rather, 'chips' as they were listed on the inventory.

One of the lab assistants, Gary, cleared his throat and peered at the report. He was the most confident of the bunch, in his late twenties with shaggy brown hair and small wire-framed glasses. 'According to the report, it's from an assault in Temple Bar.'

A popular tourist area of the city Reilly knew, full of restaurants and pubs.

'Yeah, it can get a bit rowdy down there at the weekends.' Lucy said quietly. Lucy was the only other girl in the group, a honey-pot the guys constantly buzzed around. 'Big groups of people out of it, not to mention all those hens and stags.'

'Hens and stags?'

Lucy flicked her blond hair back from her face and Reilly immediately caught a scent of her perfume. One of those celebrity-endorsed ones she figured, trying to place it; *Lovely* or *Amazing* – something like that? 'You know – last night of freedom before getting hitched?'

'Ah, bachelor parties, you mean.'

'Yeah. They usually get pretty wild.'

'Pity it's gone like that. It used to be such a nice area, all cobbled streets and old buildings.' They all looked at Julius. He was the only one older than Reilly, a career lab tech with the social life to prove it. She hadn't memorized all the details of his personnel file, but she did remember that he was forty-two, unmarried, and had worked at the forensic lab for over fifteen years. *Now there was an unusual profile for a lab tech*, she thought, sardonically.

These gatherings gave her a good feel for the team; their individual personalities, who excelled in certain areas and who didn't. Because this job wasn't just about collecting evidence and analyzing it to death, it was about spotting the small things, the tiny, seemingly insignificant threads that could suddenly bring an entire investigation together.

It was that great feeling, the immense thrill of chasing – and eventually finding – that crucial piece of evidence which had kept Reilly going all throughout her studies at Quantico, and later during her time with the police department in California.

Her determinedly hands-on approach was one of the reasons the Irish Police Commissioner had offered her the job of 'dragging the technical bureau into the twenty-first century' in the first place. And if Reilly was going to get the brand new Garda Forensic Unit operating like a well-oiled machine – as per her brief – she knew she needed to keep its employees stimulated and interested in the evidence, rather than have them locked away carrying out mindless analysis in the recently built, state-of-the-art crime lab.

Hence this morning's gathering.

'There were some witnesses,' Gary went on, 'but apparently it all happened very fast ... most of them were trashed, so they can't tell for sure who clocked him. The cops'll need a solid description before they can charge anyone.'

Reilly wasn't personally familiar with Temple Bar and made a mental note to go down there and take a look around. Since taking the job, she had spent much of whatever free time she did get walking through different parts of the city getting to know the surroundings and could now easily differentiate between the cobblestones at Dublin Castle to those situated around Trinity College – knowledge crucial to their work.

'Anyway,' Lucy grabbed the report from Gary, and continued reading, 'according to the cops, there was a bit of aggro, two men got into it, it quickly got nasty, and now one of them is unconscious in James's Street Hospital after being glassed with a beer mug. The bloke who attacked him legged it before the police got there.'

Reilly nodded, translating Lucy's slang as best she could. 'OK, what else? CCTV?'

'Hold on ...' Lucy quickly scanned through the report. 'Nope. They've got some, but they can't make the bloke out. Footage is blurred and there were too many other people around.'

'OK,' Reilly turned to the others. 'Anyone got any thoughts?'

'Well, we can test the blood on the T-shirt,' Gary ventured.

'Which tells us what exactly?'

'It'll tell us whose blood it is for one.'

'But we know whose blood it is,' Julius pointed out. 'Obviously it belongs to the guy who was injured.'

'Yeah, but it was a two-way fight, remember?' Rory, as usual, had bided his time before speaking. 'Maybe the attacker bled too, which means there might be two different samples on there. If there is, we can get a comparison sample from the victim, eliminate him, and then we're left with the sample from the guy who did it.' Rory was a rugby player, with a big build and dark, intense eyes. With his huge hands and crooked nose, he looked as though he himself knew a thing or two about street fights.

'That still won't help us identify the attacker, though, will it?' Lucy said, turning to Reilly who had remained silent, content to let the team figure it out amongst themselves.

'OK, so it won't help us identify him *now*,' Rory conceded, 'but it will give us something for later, won't it?'

'Good point,' she agreed. 'But is there anything else here that could help us identify him, something we could use to give the police some kind of a definite description of him right now?'

There was a brief pause as the team contemplated this.

'Fingerprints from the pint glass,' Gary suggested, eventually. 'Although, I suppose that's only good for a comparison too, isn't it?'

'How about the burger?' Lucy's tone was studied. 'It says here that the attacker was eating a burger just before the fight, so we could analyze his saliva for DNA.'

'Still no good – wouldn't he have to be already in the system for us to find a match?' Julius pointed out and they all looked at Reilly for affirmation.

'Correct. So again we're only talking about comparative evidence. All of your suggestions are great, and would certainly help mount a case against this guy if or when he's caught, but in the meantime, how do we help *catch* him? Come on, surely there's something among all this?'

The set of faces before her looked blank as they each raked through the evidence, and took yet another look at photographs of the scene.

Deciding to put them out of their misery, Reilly picked up the bagged burger.

'You were half right, Lucy,' she announced, holding it aloft. 'This is the single most important piece of evidence relating to this case. Not as Lucy pointed out, for DNA collection – although of course that too is important – but mostly because this innocent-looking cheeseburger can give us lots of information about this guy. His height, facial appearance, right down to whether he snores in bed or snuffles when he's awake.'

They looked at her, puzzled.

'In fact,' Reilly went on, studying the bag more closely, 'I can tell from just looking at it that our guy has got a thin, pinched face ... probably narrow too. And he seems to be missing a couple of wisdom teeth—'

'His bite mark,' Julius muttered, the penny finally dropping.

'Exactly. Now, a forensic dentist would have to give us specifics, but when time is of the essence and the cops are sure their attacker was the one eating the cheeseburger, we can at least confirm that it's a guy with a long, narrow face.'

Rory shook his head in wonderment. 'I would never have thought of that,' he admitted.

'Well,' the department's new specialist forensic investigator said with a smile, 'by the time I'm finished with you guys, there's nothing in this world you won't think of.'

2

At Harcourt Street station, Chris Delaney was putting the finishing touches to a written report when it happened again.

At first he tried to ignore it, putting the faint but all-too-familiar tingle in the joints of his first two fingers down to repetitive strain or sheer tiredness – he hadn't been to bed in over twenty-eight hours so it was only to be expected that his joints would be fatigued. He shook his hand to try and shake the pain, carefully turned the page on his report, put it neatly on the pile of finished papers, and picked up his pen again.

But then, as if to prove him wrong, the throbbing surged from his fingers through his left arm and upper body, almost sending him into spasm. Dropping the pen, Chris winced as the ache overwhelmed him, and when Pete Kennedy approached his desk, he struggled to remain impassive.

'What's up with you?' his fellow detective asked, eyebrows raised.

He tried to ride it out. 'Nothing, just got cramp – from all this bloody writing, probably,' he said through gritted teeth.

'Writing?' Kennedy sniffed, unconvinced. 'From all that

pumping iron if you ask me. I don't know why the hell you bother.'

Although Kennedy was a towering six-footer and well able to carry some additional weight, he still had a bit of a paunch, something he had no interest in doing anything about. Chris, on the other hand, enjoyed his regular workouts at the gym. It helped him cope with the demands of the job and he welcomed the physical endurance aspect too.

Based out of the Serious Crime Unit, he and Kennedy spent the majority of their time working city homicide. For a country that barely ten years ago reported one incident of murder every few months, the newer, affluent and decidedly more bloodthirsty citizens of Ireland seemed intent on making up for lost time. And as resources in their division were gradually becoming more and more stretched, things seemed to be getting progressively worse. Their latest case was an especially puzzling one.

A week earlier, a headless and dismembered male torso was found floating in the city's Royal Canal by a man out walking his dog. The Sub-Aqua Squad had spent hours in the murky, heavily polluted waters searching for remaining body parts and forensic evidence but so far had found nothing. Until they did, it was virtually impossible to identify the victim.

Following recent, similar episodic killings associated with sections of Ireland's growing ethnic communities, it was tempting for the authorities to explain it away as yet another ritualistic killing and while the murder certainly bore some of the hallmarks – such as dismemberment – Chris wasn't convinced. Some more sensationalist sections of the Irish media were only too eager to pin the incident on immigrants, but for him there was nothing definitive in the evidence so far that pointed the finger at any

particular group. Not until they found the head, at any
rate.

He swiveled round in his chair and looked at his watch.
'Well, seeing as all's quiet at the moment,' he said to Kennedy,
'I might head home for a few hours this morning – try and
grab some sleep.'

He stacked his papers in a neat pile and put the pen away
in his drawer, the thought of a couple of hours sleep sounding
tempting. Not that it would make a blind bit of difference to
his now almost continuous fatigue. Maybe he should pick up
some of those multivitamin things on the way home – seeing
that he hadn't been eating properly, something like that might
make the difference. And if it didn't, well, then he'd have to
think about getting himself checked out properly. He ruffled
his dark hair in a desperate attempt to rouse himself. Not to
mention organize a bloody long-overdue haircut.

'Detectives?'

Chris was already slipping his jacket on when one of the
uniforms put his head around the door, his tone agitated.

'What's up?' Kennedy growled from the depths of a bacon
sandwich.

'O'Brien wants you both next door for a briefing – right
away,' the uniform told them. 'And he looks pissed off.'

Chris and Kennedy exchanged looks. So much for sleep.

'What's it about?' Kennedy asked as they followed the
younger man down the hallway toward the Inspector's office.

The uniform shrugged. 'Not a clue.'

Kennedy looked at Chris and winked. 'Let me guess – the
Sub-Aqua Squad finally found that poor bastard's flute.'

O'Brien's office was a mess of papers, boxes of files stacked
against the walls, folders strewn all across his desk. But the
Inspector himself was sharp, his round, red face and flyaway
gray hair notwithstanding.

'I wish it was something on the floater,' he muttered. 'But it's something else entirely.' His expression was grim. 'Double shooting, possible homicide/suicide south of the city, in Dalkey. One male, one female, both pronounced dead at the scene.'

'Domestic?'

'Unlikely. They're only kids, college kids, the girl barely in her twenties, apparently.' He ran his fingers through his hair, messing it up even more.

'Shit.' Kennedy shook his head.

'Too bloody right.' The Inspector leaned back in his chair, looking like a man with the weight of the world on his shoulders.

'In Dalkey, you said?' Chris was taken aback at the victims' age and profile. Dalkey was a decidedly upmarket part of the city and shootings were an unusual occurrence.

'Maybe they stumbled across Daddy's hunting gun?' Kennedy said, evidently on a similar train of thought.

'Could be. I don't know what the weapon of choice was; to be honest, I don't know that much at all,' O'Brien replied. 'There's a unit from Blackrock already down there; they were first on the scene and as far as I know the Technical Bur—' He paused mid-sentence, and rolled his eyes. 'Sorry, I mean the *GFU* should be there by now too. It will take a bit of getting used to that one, although at least it rolls off the tongue a bit easier. Anyway, I need you two to get over there and see what you can make of it.' He shook his head. 'First the gangs, then the foreigners, and now we have posh kids shooting one another too – I'm telling you, this country's gone mad altogether.'

.   .   .

CHRIS STEERED the unmarked Ford toward a vacant parking space and looked up at the modern apartment block. Limestone walls, aluminum balconies, well-tended gardens, sea views ... Whoever owned this place had money.

'That's a hell of a vista,' he observed. Even in winter, the view out across Dublin Bay was spectacular, the rolling gray waves stacking up one by one as though impatient to crash against the shore.

'Hell of a turnout too,' Kennedy said, indicating the mass of vehicles parked outside. 'I wonder would there be the same interest if the crime scene was on Sheriff Street?'

'Guess not, but there are some pretty powerful neighbors around here who need reassuring things are under control,' Chris replied, looking up the hill in the direction of Killiney, Dublin's own Beverly Hills.

'So, I wonder what kind of mood Miss America will be in today?' Kennedy mumbled, nodding toward Reilly Steel's GFU van. He lit a cigarette and leaned on the bonnet of the car, admiring the surroundings. Chris climbed from the car, trying not to groan at the ache in his legs. 'No point rushing in if she's still there. What do you make of her?' Kennedy asked.

Chris shrugged. 'Too early to say.'

'Oh come on – don't give me that. An FBI-trained crime tech brought over here to bring us country bumpkins up to date and you don't have an opinion?'

It was true that eyebrows had been raised at the appointment and when a photograph of the blond, blue-eyed American had been passed around, there had been some skeptical comments. But far from being a wide-eyed bimbo, the latest addition to the force had trained at the FBI facility at Quantico and had expert knowledge and considerable field experience, as well as valuable exposure to the workings of the institution's state-of-the-art crime lab. Steel had also apparently worked with some of the best forensic investigators in the world and was held in high regard by her peers. How the hell she had been lured to Dublin, Chris didn't know, but either way, he was glad to have someone with her credentials on board.

He waved a hand as Kennedy's smoke drifted toward him. 'I reckon the head brass knew what they were doing when they brought her in – the old Technical Bureau was thirty years behind the times and we need all the help we can get.'

Up until then, they'd had little to do with the American. She tended to stay in the lab, apparently preferring working on the evidence than working the scene – something Chris could certainly relate to. But today Steel had had no choice but to attend as Jack Gorman, the field investigator their unit normally worked with, was away on a Caribbean cruise with his wife – some big anniversary celebration apparently.

'Come on, let's go,' he said, starting toward the building.

His partner stubbed his cigarette out on the ground and heaved himself up off the bonnet.

Going inside, they headed for the fourth floor, Kennedy huffing and puffing all the way. A uniformed officer guarding the scene directed them to the bedroom where the shooting had taken place.

'Ah, hell,' Kennedy whispered as he entered the room.

The place was beautiful; a neutral color scheme, beige carpet and white walls, light-colored bed linen, and tall bay windows opening out to a stunning view of the bay – in fact everything was idyllic except for the crimson blood splattered across the bed and up the wall.

The victims lay together on the bed, both fully naked. The girl's eyes were closed, her dark hair fanned out prettily on the pillow, looking for all the world as though she was having a post-coital nap – apart from the gaping hole low in her chest and half the contents of her companion's head sprayed across her cheek.

They were achingly young, in their early-twenties at the most. Chris's stomach turned over. Their boss was right – what kind of country was it that a kid barely out of his teens could get his hands on a gun? And a posh kid at that. Judging by his lightly tanned skin and toned rugby-player physique, he suspected that the boyfriend wasn't some malnourished scumbag the girl had taken up with to piss off her well-to-do parents. And he had one of those stylized oriental tattoos on his upper right arm, not the Celtic cross favored by the working classes.

His eyes quickly scanned the area. The murder weapon lay on the sheets – a 9 mm. It must have fallen out of the shooter's hand.

He briefly exchanged nods with state pathologist, who was conducting her preliminary examination of the bodies before their removal to the morgue. He gave an involuntary shiver. Sometimes Karen Thompson unsettled him more than the victims did. A serious woman with oversized dark eyes, Roman nose, and an exceptionally long neck, Chris figured she was perfectly suited for the strain of medicine where the absence of a bedside manner was a good thing. Briefly noting the arrival of the detectives, she resumed her examination of the bodies.

Several uniforms were busy around the apartment, some taking notes, most simply observing and helping guard the scene – a crime like this always drew a crowd. The GFU crew, dressed head to toe in white dust suits, were wandering around the area; dusting for prints on surfaces, gathering material and trace evidence, bagging everything as they went.

One of the forensics squatted low against the bed as he pointed and flashed his camera at the victims. And although he hadn't yet spotted Reilly Steel, Chris knew she had to be somewhere amongst the mix.

'Christ,' Kennedy muttered. 'What age were these two – fifteen?'

'College students according to Reilly, so they've got to be older than that.'

'But not by much. Bloody hell.'

Although in the course of their work they came across young victims on a regular basis, they were usually junkies or fledgling gang members who'd come from such troubled backgrounds it was almost impossible to imagine them ending up any other way. These kids, though – healthy, educated, middle class – could just as easily have been Kennedy's own son or daughter and for those reasons alone, it made it different.

'What the hell was he thinking?'

'Where the hell did he get the gun is what I want to know,' Chris ruminated.

Illegal weapons were increasingly finding their way out of the hands of paramilitaries and onto the city streets and, while any criminal worth his salt would know how to get hold of a gun at short notice, it should be a different story for a middle-class college kid.

He turned to the uniformed officer standing in the bedroom doorway. 'Who was first on the scene?'

'A unit from Blackrock,' the man replied, indicating a group of officers gathered in the living room – one of them decidedly shaky-looking. 'Young Fitzgerald is not long out of training,' he added with a slight shake of the head. 'Talk about throwing him in at the deep end.'

Chris cursed inwardly. He'd spotted Fitzgerald as soon as he'd stepped into the living room – he looked as young as the victims, he'd probably only just started shaving.

He stepped into the living room. Like the bedroom, it had tall French windows opening out onto a balcony with a sea view. A massive plasma TV screen filled one wall and a deep fireplace dominated the other. The whole place smelled of money. Chris wondered if there had been a robbery of some kind, but judging by the valuable objects scattered around the place, they obviously hadn't taken much.

He called the rookie over, who marched up to the two detectives, snapped to attention and straightened his uniform.

'Officer Fitzgerald,' Kennedy began, 'take your time and tell us what you can remember.'

Somewhat surprisingly, the younger cop was calm and articulate as he outlined what had happened when he first reached the apartment. 'The 999 was logged at 6.03 a.m. from this building, apparently by another resident who'd heard a gunshot coming from the apartment,' he informed the detectives.

'OK.'

'Our unit responded quickly,' he continued, 'and arrived at the scene at precisely 6.18 a.m.'

'Six-eighteen a.m. precisely?' Chris echoed, amused by the young man's certainty.

'Precisely, sir. I checked my watch just to be sure.'

The detectives exchanged a surreptitious look. 'All right. And then?'

'Well, at first we were ordered not to penetrate the building in case the perpetrator was still at large.'

Despite himself, Chris was tickled by the younger officer's terminology – it was something the training colleges instilled with vigor into new recruits. Personally, he wasn't a fan of this 'Robocop' talk and whenever he gave a radio or TV statement, he purposely spoke in layman's terms so the public could be assured that if they did come forward with information, someone in the force might actually be capable of understanding them.

'Then, at 6.45, we got word that the building was secure and they gave us the OK to go in,' Fitzgerald continued. 'So in we went.'

'Please tell me you didn't use the lift to get up here,' Kennedy remarked.

Looking faintly hurt, Fitzgerald shook his head. 'Of course not. The perpetrator may have used the elevators, so we made sure we entered via the stairs in order to avoid contaminating evidence.' He paused. 'I might be new, but I'm not stupid, Detective,' he added, pointedly.

Chris had begun to draw the exact same conclusion. 'So this is how you found them.'

'Yes, sir. It was obvious as soon as we arrived that both victims were dead, so we called it in as a homicide and possible suicide and made sure not to touch a thing until the forensic people got here.' He added the last part with emphasis, looking directly at Kennedy.

The kid could stand up for himself. Chris was impressed.

'Did you find out who called in the 999?' Chris asked.

Fitzgerald nodded and flipped open a black notebook. 'The woman living in the apartment next door, a Mrs Maura McKenna. Now, she doesn't remember everything exactly as it happened.' He sounded vaguely disappointed that his only witness wasn't up to his own high standards. 'According to her statement, she was fast asleep in bed when she heard a sound that quote – nearly lifted her out of her skin – unquote,' he said, reading from the notebook. 'The second shot came soon after, although she's unable to remember exactly how soon, but she believes it could have been four or five minutes. Then she rang 999.'

'OK.'

'She was also able to give us a possible ID on one of the victims. The girl living here is – or rather, *was* – Clare Ryan. She's a student at UCD. The old lady said that the girl's parents bought this apartment for her a couple of years back, when she first started at university. She doesn't know anything about a boyfriend, though.'

'Anything else?'

'That's it, sir,' the younger man said in conclusion.

'Thanks, we'll have a chat with the neighbor later,' Chris said, dismissing him.

Just a quick scan of the room confirmed that the dead girl was indeed Clare Ryan – there was a long white sideboard in the living room dotted with framed photographs of a smiling brunette. Chris picked up a photo, taken on a beach somewhere – Thailand, maybe? The sand was pure white, the sea azure. The girl's happy grin and lively eyes were a sad and stark contrast to the pale, lifeless cadaver in the bedroom.

'Any photos of the guy?' He looked up from his reverie and saw Kennedy watching him.

His gaze scanned the photographs for any sign of her companion. 'Who can tell?'

It was difficult to match any of the males in the photos to the dead guy, given that most of his head had been obliterated.

Kennedy studied the photos with him. 'Once her ID is confirmed, it should make it easier to identify the boyfriend – he was probably a student too.' He wandered over to the window, gazed out across the bay. 'Who'd buy a college kid a swanky place like this?'

'Good investment for the parents and they know their kid is living somewhere safe – or at least that's what they would have hoped.'

He and Kennedy would need to talk to Clare Ryan's college friends and fellow students. Hopefully they'd be able to shed some light on who the guy was and maybe why he had done what he did. The obvious theory was that he was the jealous type. Clare had been a good-looking girl, that much was evident from the photographs. Slim, with big brown eyes and an engaging smile, chances were the pretty brunette had turned more than a few heads on campus and that might have pissed off Prince Charming.

Or perhaps he'd been a previous Prince Charming and the guy had taken the break-up very badly. There were a few scenarios but no point in surmising at this stage, Chris thought, at least not until they found out more about Clare Ryan and her dead companion.

The detectives headed back toward the bedroom, but found their passage blocked by one of the uniforms.

'Sorry, I can't let you in,' the officer said, his tone apologetic. 'No one's allowed in for the moment.'

'What?' Kennedy frowned. 'What are you talking about? Of course we're going in.'

The officer looked uncomfortable. 'There's nothing I can do for the minute,' he said, giving a quick glance over his shoulder. 'She'll murder me.'

'Who will?' Chris asked. 'Dr Thompson? She should be finished by now – she was almost done when I saw her a few minutes ago.'

'No, not her,' the uniform answered, 'that new one from the crime lab – the American. She ordered everyone out and warned me not to let anyone into the room until she's finished.'

'Finished doing what?' Kennedy asked, straining to see past him. Then his eyes widened as he caught sight of something through the doorway. 'What the hell?' he spat, turning to Chris in astonishment.

They peered inside. Reilly Steel was standing in the

middle of the bedroom with her eyes closed and her arms wide open.

'Looks like she's doing some kind of yoga chant or something,' Kennedy snorted in derision.

'That's not it,' said a young female crime tech standing nearby. Her voice dropped to a whisper. 'She does this all the time, draws on her instincts, uses her senses to see if she can recreate the scene in her mind.' As she spoke, there was admiration in her voice.

'Touchy-feely crap,' Kennedy rolled his eyes.

'I don't think it *is* actually, Detective,' the woman replied. 'In the States her solve-assist rate was over 80 per cent.'

Chris had read this somewhere too. While Reilly Steel evidently had some unorthodox methods, her investigative record spoke for itself. Still, he thought with a grin, there was no getting away from the fact that this 'touchy-feely crap' would raise a few eyebrows in this neck in the woods, and it clearly wasn't going down too well with Kennedy.

'Yeah, well,' his partner muttered, 'if she thinks the rest of us are going to *sniff* our way through this investigation, she's got another bloody think coming.'

'I wouldn't dream of it,' a female voice replied from behind him. 'Besides, I doubt that whiskey nose of yours can detect much these days.'

Realizing that Steel had left the bedroom and overheard him, Kennedy's neck reddened and his face instantly turned a brighter shade of puce.

'Yeah, well ... we couldn't get in ...' he babbled.

'Sorry about that,' she said, extending a hand. 'Reilly Steel, GFU. I take it you're the assigned detective?'

'We both are,' Chris replied. 'This is Pete Kennedy and I'm Chris Delaney. Pleased to meet you.'

'Pleasure,' she said with a bright smile.

OK, Chris thought, so he'd seen the press release photos and heard all the blond jokes but bloody hell ... Considering her unglamorous occupation, Reilly Steel was a stunner. Her huge sea-blue eyes shone with a bright intensity and her lightly bronzed skin stood out in marked contrast to the white clinical cap she was wearing. Beneath it, he knew there was a mane of honey-blond hair, but despite her obvious beauty, or perhaps because of it, he could tell instantly that she was sharp and uncompromising.

'Well, I've pretty much finished my erm ... touchy-feely stuff,' she said, a glint of amusement in her eye, 'and the ME's done her thing, but we've still got a bit of work to do in there.' She moved back to the bedroom. 'You guys can come in – as long as you don't get in my way,' she added, looking sideways at Kennedy.

'No problem.' The older detective remained uncharacteristically muted as they followed her back inside.

'Have you found anything out of the ordinary?' Chris asked.

She moved to the foot of the bed. 'We won't know for sure until autopsy, but judging by the entry wound ...' she indicated Clare Ryan, whose body was now being carefully zipped into a black polythene body bag, '... the girl was shot in the chest from less than two feet. Point-blank range.'

She moved around, re-enacting the crime as she did. 'It looks like he was standing at the foot of the bed when he fired the first shot, and then lay down beside her before finishing himself off. Chances are she was still breathing at the time.'

Chris agreed. The amount of blood that had pooled beneath the girl suggested that she hadn't died instantly. 'He seemed to do a much better job on himself, though,' he added, his tone grim as he glanced at what was left of the young man's head. 'Not exactly Romeo and Juliet.'

'No.' Reilly bent down and picked up her forensic toolbox. 'We'll do a tox screen on the blood – see if it's a case of a trip gone bad or something.'

'Thanks, we'd be grateful for anything you could give us,' he said, ignoring Kennedy's disapproving gaze. His partner – like much of the force – was still largely skeptical about forensics, preferring instead to rely on good old-fashioned detective work and let the lab people back up *their* findings instead of the other way round.

'Chances are it's drug related, though. What isn't these days?' Kennedy grumbled.

'Well, I'd rather reserve judgement until we know more,' Reilly replied. 'I'll take a closer look at what we've got when we get back to the lab, though I'll be honest, it doesn't seem to be all that much. Of course, we've got a couple of cartridges to process, along with the weapon. Speaking of which ...' She snapped on a fresh pair of latex gloves and moved toward the gun, which could be safely retrieved now that the victims' bodies had been removed.

A gaggle of police officers had gathered in the room, grateful for the chance to be around something more interesting. Bit by bit, the majority had drifted back in once the pathologist had left and the victims' bodies were removed.

'Hey, can you guys stand back and give me some room?' Reilly asked, impatiently.

Realizing what she was about to do, Fitzgerald, the younger officer with whom the detectives had spoken earlier, quickly reached inside his pocket. 'Here,' he said, proudly presenting a pencil to her, 'you'll need this.'

Kennedy chuckled. 'What? Is she supposed to draw a picture of it or something?'

The younger man looked at him blankly. 'But don't you have to pick up the gun without handling it?' he asked, no longer quite so confident. 'In order to ... you know ... protect fingerprints and that?'

'You've been watching way too much TV,' Reilly said indulgently, taking the pencil and putting it aside. 'If I used your pencil to pick it up, I might disturb any gunpowder deposits or dirt lodged in the barrel. Dislodged dirt could alter striation markings on test-fired bullets and we don't want to do that, do we?' she added, in the manner of someone speaking to a 5-year-old.

'Um, no, I suppose not.' Fitzgerald looked almost sorry he'd asked.

'But you're right, of course, we *are* worried about protecting prints,' she went on, beckoning him forward to observe what she was doing, while the others kept out of her way. She knelt down by the bed and indicated for the officer to kneel beside her. 'But if I hold the weapon there,' she pointed to the butt of the gun, 'see the checkered part of the grip?' The rookie nodded, his attention firmly fixed on the weapon. 'Now, this part has such an uneven striation that it won't retain any identifiable prints, so it's fine to handle it here. Not to mention that it's the safest way to do it – I don't want the damn thing to accidentally discharge on me, either.' She slowly and cautiously lifted the gun up off the bed. Lesson over, she beckoned one of the others to help her safely prepare the gun for processing.

Fitzgerald looked at Reilly Steel with something approaching pure adoration. Chris smiled. Whatever the older guys in the force might think, the latest member of the GFU clearly had a set of fans amongst the younger generation.

3

R eilly sat at her desk, her features screwed up in an expression of intense concentration as she studied the crime-scene inventory for the Clare Ryan case. It was a couple of days after the shooting and nearly all the staff had long since left for the day.

To most people, the clinical setting and the oppressive silence – broken only by the low hum of the machinery – would feel eerie and discomfiting. For Reilly, however, the peace and quiet of late evening was her preferred time to work.

Now that everyone had gone home, she was free from the noisy distractions of twenty or so laboratory staff laboring all around her. The silence allowed her more time to work, more time to think, and tonight it might allow her to uncover what it was about this shooting that had been niggling at her for the last two days.

She'd sensed from the start that something wasn't right but so far had found nothing out of the ordinary amongst the evidence to back this feeling up. The two things she trusted most during an investigation were evidence and instinct. And since leaving that scene, Reilly's instincts were screaming that something was seriously amiss.

Gorman would have laughed if she'd tried to explain this to him. The long-time incumbent, he was head of the old forensic department and hadn't exactly been over the moon about her appointment, or the setting up of the new unit in general. She was glad that the old man would be away on vacation for a while; it gave her an opportunity to run this case the way she wanted – the way she was trained to do back home.

Since she'd arrived at the GFU, he'd tried to put her in her place, inferring that her job was just to oversee work in the lab, and that she should have little or no interference in what he was doing, or had done, up to now. While this was true to a degree, from what Reilly had seen, the older man's current methods were pretty half-hearted and pedantic considering it was such an important role, and the old dog had no interest in new tricks.

On top of it, Gorman had an unbelievable ego – something she'd at least been forewarned about before she got here. Like many traditional scientists, he seemed to operate under the belief that his word was gospel and he was also a condescending old chauvinist – something she could handle were he not such a sloppy investigator with it. Still she resented the way he spoke to the female staff, particularly Lucy, who was a real sweetie and Reilly knew was routinely wounded by her superior's dismissiveness.

But, office politics aside, Reilly also had to deal with the force's natural resistance to an 'outsider', to say nothing of the inevitable dumb blond jokes. She shook her head, recalling how, on her very first day at the office, she'd come out of a morning meeting to find a crimson Baywatch-style swimsuit laid out on her desk. No doubt the culprit and his buddies found it hilarious but it was water off a duck's back to Reilly; she'd had to deal with a lot worse back in her FBI student days.

She looked again at the evidence for the Ryan homicide. This was one of the first scenes she'd managed to co-ordinate entirely on her own, outside of Gorman's interference. Without him breathing down her neck, she'd had as much time as she wanted to run the scene in as much detail as possible. And plenty of time to apply her 'touchy-feely' techniques, she thought, biting back a smile as she recalled the reaction *that* had gotten.

It was something she'd learned and perfected at Quantico. Her lecturer, Rob Crichton, one of the best forensic investigators in the business, had drilled into his recruits the importance of the three-dimensional crime scene. She smiled fondly, recalling the now deceased Crichton – an anti-personnel device at a perp's apartment having put an end to the life of one of the best criminalists she'd ever had the fortune to work with. Although his death was a tragedy, she figured that Rob would have appreciated the irony of his body being blown to smithereens. He himself finally becoming the physical evidence he'd spent much of his life collecting.

'Your senses are there for a reason, people,' he used to say. 'Never, *ever* discount them.'

While Reilly had initially been skeptical, she soon discovered when she applied Rob's painstaking methods that she had an unusually keen sense of smell – something that had been invaluable in almost every case she worked. For some reason, she was particularly attuned to perfume and could draw easily on her inner database of various fragrance brands and body creams. For example, she knew that the ME, Karen Thompson, favored Red Door by Elizabeth Arden, and that Carol, the GFU receptionist, routinely wore CK One. Oddly, she'd noticed that Chanel No. 5, the American woman's favorite had a far less fervent following on this side of the Atlantic.

Either way, her instincts had served her well in the past and she wasn't about to discard them just because some red-nosed Irish cop thought they were dumb and irrelevant. All mouth and little substance; Reilly could eat a guy like Kennedy for breakfast – not that she wanted to, she thought, shuddering at the notion. He seemed OK, just old school. She'd heard his partner's name mentioned a few times over the last couple of months; Chris Delaney seemed to have a good reputation within the force, and unlike some of his more conservative colleagues, also seemed to be well disposed toward the GFU. She figured that those dark, almost Mediterranean looks must work well when it came to extracting information – particular from the female side of the population – although from what little she knew about him, he didn't seem the type to play on that. And in contrast to Kennedy, he certainly hadn't given her any attitude that morning, and seemed happy to take on board anything significant the lab might come up with.

Which, at the moment, wasn't exactly much.

They'd sent blood samples off for a toxicology screen which, if they came back positive, might – for the shooter at least – go some way toward explaining his actions. However, with the speed the labs worked at, who knew when she'd get those back.

They'd also collected the usual – fingerprints, trace, and fibers – which were now being analyzed. Ballistics were in possession of the gun and cartridges, and Reilly was planning on calling down there the following morning to see if they'd come up with anything of interest.

In the meantime, she was doing what she did best, going

over the scene in her mind, trying to recreate the kill, taking into account the evidence they'd uncovered, and hoping for something, anything, that might just help move this case forward.

But so far, all Reilly could come up with was that something didn't feel right.

She sat forward in her seat and for the umpteenth time picked up the photos of the victims taken at the scene before their removal. Again, she studied the blood and brain spatter on the headboard; much of the gray matter had spewed over the dead girl's face and hair – some even landing as far away as the pile of books on her bedside table. The blowback blood droplets on the headboard and wall behind were to be expected, traveling in the opposite direction to the path of the bullet. Her gaze moved downward to the gun's resting position on the bed where it had ended up after falling out of the dead shooter's hand.

What was it? she thought, kneading her forehead in the vain hope that the answer might somehow be released. What was it about this whole situation that was bothering her? Given the gun's caliber, trajectory and shooting distance, as well as the residue found on the guy's hand, the results all looked consistent, yet there was something telling her that there was more to this, that she was missing something. Something important.

But what?

Chasing evidence, hoping to find answers – sometimes Reilly felt it was all she'd been doing her whole life.

For some reason, Chris always felt like a naughty schoolboy talking to the state pathologist. Karen Thompson was typically so brusque and business-like (and so damn creepy) that he felt intimidated in her presence.

When he stepped into her office, she was just finishing up a phone call and waved at him to sit down. Lowering himself into a chair, he looked around. Everything was immaculate, orderly, organized – he'd bet even the books were alphabetized.

The dead girl had been positively identified as Clare Ryan. She was twenty-two years old, in her final year studying psychology at UCD, and as far as her distraught parents were concerned, was 'way too busy with her studies' to have had time for a boyfriend.

'Too busy studying. How many times have I heard that one?' Kennedy muttered when they'd finished interviewing the parents the day after the shooting. 'And what kind of numbskull parents would believe that a looker like her wouldn't have guys sniffing round her?'

Chris shrugged. 'So, they didn't know everything that was going on in her life – it's not that unusual. Not everyone has the same approach to parenting as you do.' Kennedy had two teenage daughters and, from what Delaney had seen over the years, was a strict taskmaster. 'Anyway, all we've established so far is that they didn't think Clare had a boyfriend. And if she did have one, her college friends will likely know who she was seeing.'

He and Kennedy had arranged to conduct interviews at the university that morning but following a call from Karen Thompson, Chris had taken a quick detour to the medical examiner's office at the opposite end of the city.

'There were signs of sexual activity between our two victims,' Karen said, bringing him sharply back to the present.

'What?' He hadn't actually noticed that she'd finished her phone call. As usual, she was straight down to business. 'So if

it is a boyfriend, we can rule out robbery or a sexually motivated attack?'

'Not necessarily. I said there *was* sexual activity – Clare's
vaginal fluid was found on our mystery guy, but there was a
complete absence of semen. And no signs of trauma – no
vaginal damage or tearing.' He started to say something, but
she cut him off. 'Detective, you and I both know that doesn't
necessarily prove anything.'

Chris did know this, but it didn't stop him from wishing it
did. Forcible penetration would have meant that they were
dealing with a clear-cut rape case, which somehow might
have been easier than an apparently motiveless murder/sui-
cide. Not to mention a case of missing identity.

'So what you're telling me is that there was sex, but it's
likely it wasn't rape, and might not even indicate a sexual relationship?'

'That's about it.' Karen sat back in her chair.

'Right. What I wouldn't give for a clear cut case,' he
muttered, hoping that Clare's college friends might be able to
shine some light on what was going on.

'Sure, Clare was a bit, like ... you know, a flirt, but she wasn't
seeing anyone, you know ... like, exclusively or anything,'
Clare's 'very best friend' Melanie told the detectives between
sobs when they called to interview her on campus. 'I just can't
believe she's dead,' she added, before bursting into tears yet
again. 'This is so, like ... massive.'

Chris saw Kennedy's expression and suspected his partner,
like himself, was wondering how on earth this American high-
school jargon had so entrenched itself into the lingo of Irish
college students.

'I know this is very difficult for you, Melanie, but when you say that Clare wasn't seeing anyone exclusively, does that mean that she might have been seeing a number of different guys?' he probed.

'No way. She wasn't, like, a slut or anything. How can you say that?'

'We're not saying that,' Kennedy soothed. 'All we're trying to do is figure out who might have hurt Clare and, as her very best friend, you're possibly the best chance we have of doing that.'

'Look, all I know is that she didn't, like, go out with lots of different guys. They digged her but really, she was just as happy on her tobler.'

The detectives both looked blank. 'Her tobler?'

Melanie rolled her eyes. 'Happy on her own? Tobler*one*?'

'Christ,' Kennedy moaned afterward. 'I'll tell you one thing, if my two ever end up talking like that I'll send them straight off to elocution lessons.'

'Man – that's so, like, harsh,' Chris jibed.

Melanie was insistent that Clare hadn't been seeing anyone since her previous boyfriend Paul, a fellow student. When the detectives interviewed him, Paul seemed shell-shocked by what had happened but was helpful and courteous.

'We went out for a couple of months, but when Clare started studying for her finals, we kind of drifted apart,' he told them.

Now, only days into the investigation, the detectives were fast approaching a brick wall. Everyone they'd spoken to had painted Clare Ryan as a normal, happy-go-lucky girl who was close to her family, had lots of friends and, according to her lecturers, was an extremely diligent student.

Having interviewed everyone in Clare's immediate circle, they still had no clue as to who the dead man might be, or why he had ended Clare's life as well as his own. And because most of the guy's face was missing and there was no chance of carrying out a reconstruction job, there was little else to help identify him.

While the funeral would normally be held soon after the body was released from the morgue, it hadn't yet taken place because the parents were having problems locating close family abroad. Chris was certain that when it did, there would be a pretty impressive turnout.

In the meantime, because of the victim's profile, the media frenzy had already begun in earnest. While it was almost expected that inner-city scumbags would go around shooting each other, violent deaths in so-called 'polite society' was simply not acceptable to the general public, and the demands for answers were coming as fast as the hysterical headlines. Which meant that O'Brien was leaning even heavier on the detectives for a breakthrough that wasn't easily apparent.

So far, not one person had a bad thing to say about Clare Ryan, or could give a single reason why anyone might want her dead. Which made the bizarre circumstances of her death all the more sinister.

4

'Reilly? Do you have a minute?' Reilly looked up from her desk to find Lucy in front of her, a worried expression on her face.

'Sure. What's up?'

The lab tech chewed uncomfortably at her lip. 'Something really weird.'

'So tell me.' She continued writing, giving Lucy only half her attention – she was busy and not in the mood to play guessing games today. Lucy needed to learn to think for herself and trust her own intuition more often. While she reminded Reilly a little of herself when she was starting out in forensics, there was this slight insecurity about her that she hoped would be erased over time.

'This I think you really need to look at.'

Something in her tone of voice caught Reilly's attention this time, and she put the pen down. 'What is it?'

'Can you just come and take a quick look?'

Following Lucy into the lab, they approached the light microscope. 'Just take a look and tell me what you see.'

Reilly bent over, looked through the eyepiece and adjusted

the magnification to 400X. 'Weird ...' she remarked, studying the specimen on the slide. She looked away for a moment, trying to make sense of it.

'I'm glad you think so too,' Lucy said, quietly. 'To be honest, I wasn't sure whether or not I should say anything ...'

'No, you were right. This is important. Important but weird,' Reilly added, almost to herself.

'So what do you think it is?'

'Looks like some kind of animal hair,' Reilly said. 'Human hair is much finer, and the scales along the shaft are a give-away.' She moved away from the microscope. 'Can't say which animal it is though, at least not until we have a comparative sample.'

'Which we do – in a way,' Lucy said, looking tentative.

Reilly breathed out deeply. 'Not exactly the kind of comparison we want, though, is it? Can I take a look at that paint sample again?'

'Sure.' Lucy duly prepared a second slide, this time using another piece of material evidence listed on the inventory.

Reilly quickly examined it under low magnification. 'Both paint samples will need to be analyzed further – and sepa-rately – using microspec,' she said, referring to the process of microspectrophotometry which involved electronically studying the wavelengths of energy absorbed and released by a single paint sample. 'That will tell us if they are indeed the same sample. But if I were a betting girl – which I'm not – they look pretty alike to me.'

'That's what I thought,' Lucy said. 'And seeing as this and the hair were both found at the Ryan scene ...'

'It means that one way or the other,' Reilly finished grimly, her head spinning, 'we've got a major problem.'

The hair and paint specimens she and Lucy had just examined were not the samples taken from the Ryan scene a few days earlier – they'd been collected the previous day from the home of a man who'd apparently committed suicide.

Now, back in her office, and reluctant to draw any hasty conclusions, Reilly decided to contact the unit dealing with the suicide.

She grabbed her coat and headed out the door. The station was just a few blocks away – she could use the fresh air to clear her head, and knew from bitter experience that it was always better to deal with the cops in person whenever possible.

Harcourt Street was always busy, but Reilly seemed to have chosen the rush hour. She was directed to the relevant room by a harried-looking female cop, then left to fend for herself. The room was a mass of scruffy desks, outdated computers, and busy officers. An older officer at a nearby desk noticed her lost expression.

'Who you looking for, love?'

'Jones,' she said, hesitantly.

He pointed her toward the back of the room. 'Over by the wall – see the lad in the blue sweater?' She spotted a thirty-something man with dark hair and thick eyebrows tapping away busily at a computer.

'Got it, thanks.' She weaved through the desks, finally reaching Jones' workstation. 'You Jones?'

He looked up slowly. 'Who wants to know?'

Reilly offered him her hand. 'Reilly Steel, GFU.' He looked surprised and she launched into her story without preamble. 'We're analyzing evidence collected from a suspected suicide your unit is handling. I'd like to ask you a couple of questions about that if I may.'

Guess you must have enjoyed that garlic dinner you ate last night, she added, silently, reeling back a little at the overpowering stench emanating from him. At times like this, her trusty sense of smell was a real disadvantage.

Like many of his colleagues, Jones was naturally wary of any interference from GFU and she readied herself for the inevitable defensiveness. 'Is there a problem?' he asked.

'Not exactly. As I said, I just wanted to clarify a couple of things for the file. You investigated a death in Donnybrook – a Jim Redmond?'

He nodded, the wary look never leaving his eyes.

'Is this a confirmed suicide?'

Jones sighed and motioned her to a chair, and Reilly could tell that he was thinking GFU chasing a suicide was the last thing he needed. 'We're waiting for the ME to verify that there was no foul play, but the guy was found hanging from the beams in the dining room of his mansion. Sure, anyone could see it was a suicide.'

This kind of thinking was one of Reilly's pet hates and the reason she rarely took any aspect of an open investigation at face value.

'Was he married?' Jones nodded and looked pointedly at his watch, but Reilly was like a terrier with a cornered rat, pursuing her prey until she got what she wanted. 'So what's the wife's story?'

He waved a dismissive arm. 'Same as ever – the missus is saying otherwise, that there's no way he'd do something like that and that it has to be some kind of accident,' he muttered. 'But then again, she would say that, wouldn't she?'

Reilly raised an eyebrow. 'Any valid reason for her to think that?'

'Nah, just the usual – he was on great form lately, they had a lovely life and were happy as Larry. You know – all pretty standard stuff.'

'OK, so the wife reckons they were happy, but he ...' she

opened her folder, looked at the inventory of evidence, '... he hanged himself with a cotton bed sheet?'

'The old reliable. Although, again, the wife is convinced he couldn't tie a knot to save his life. I don't know – I feel sorry for her and all that but ... well, I think sometimes people just need to face facts. Especially when there's a suicide note.'

At this, Reilly's ears pricked up. 'There was?'

From her point of view, this was good news; it meant there was more likely nothing untoward. But of course, if there was no foul play, the occurrence of the same trace evidence in separate scenes would be even harder to explain. She took a deep breath, reminding herself not to leap to conclusions, to wait and see where the evidence led. Another old training mantra echoed in her brain: *Intuition is a valuable tool – but only when based on evidence.*

'Yep. Laid out right on the dining room table, so you couldn't miss it,' Jones continued. 'It was a strange one though, not the straightforward "Sorry I can't take it anymore" type of thing you usually see.'

'A strange one,' Reilly echoed. 'What did it say?'

He paused, thinking. 'I can't remember it exactly off the top of my head. Hold on there for a minute.' He began to rummage through the stack of files on his desk. 'I've got the report here somewhere.'

Reilly watched as Jones rummaged through the files on his desk, wondering how people could ever expect to operate efficiently in such a mess. She wasn't even terribly interested in the note's contents, more concerned about the fact that one did, in fact, exist.

'OK, here it is.' He held up the paper, and cleared his throat before reading, like a schoolboy reciting for his teacher. '"We are never so defenseless against suffering as when we love, never so forlornly unhappy as when we have lost our love object or its love." That's all it said. Weird, isn't it?'

'It's actually rather sad,' Reilly mused. 'It sounds like a quote of some sort.'

Jones shrugged. 'No idea. The wife says she doesn't know what it is, or what he's trying to say. Obviously, he was saying goodbye.'

'Maybe.' A sudden thought crossed her mind. 'Hey, you couldn't make me a copy of that, could you?'

'Of the note? Why?' Again, Jones sounded defensive. 'Why are you so interested in all this anyway?'

Thinking quickly, Reilly sighed dramatically, as if she too felt that this could all be a complete waste of time. 'Well, the GFU is undergoing a radical transformation at the moment, and they want us double-checking every last thing.' She rolled her eyes. 'You know how it is.'

She didn't want to tell Jones about the trace evidence, not until she'd at least examined things further. Luckily her conspiratorial manner seemed to placate him.

'I get you. All right then, let's do it now while I have it in my hand.'

He stood up and walked over to the copier. Reilly followed.

'By the way, do you know if the Redmonds had any pets?' she queried.

'Couldn't be sure, but I doubt it,' he said. He slipped the note into the machine and pressed the start button. 'They've no kids; apparently he traveled all over the world in his line of work – he was a property developer. Those guys aren't in the country often enough to keep pets. I'll find out though.' He handed her the copy of the note. 'There you go, love,' he added patronizingly and this time it wasn't just the garlic that got right up Reilly's nose. 'Knock yourself out.'

. . .

BACK AT THE LAB, Reilly leaned back in her chair, and studied the words again.

We are never so defenseless against suffering as when we love, never so forlornly unhappy as when we have lost our love object or its love.

It was sad, strangely haunting. Suffering, lost love ...

Yet, according to his wife, Jim Redmond was happily married, so who *was* this lost love? And for a supposedly hard-nosed businessman, Redmond certainly seemed to have the soul of a poet.

She read the note again – both the words, as well as the sentiment behind them; they sounded almost Shakespearean in their simplicity. Could it be a quote from Shakespeare? Not that it mattered all that much in the scheme of things, but curiosity had got the better of her.

Reilly brought up Google on her computer and typed the entire sentence into the search box. Seconds later, a list of results appeared onscreen. *Aha!* she thought, satisfied. So it was a quote – although not one from Shakespeare; nope, this particular quote had been attributed to Sigmund Freud.

Curiouser and curiouser ...

Like most trainees, she'd come across the work of the famous psychoanalyst as part of her studies at the Academy and had a brief knowledge of his works relevant to behaviorism. But this particular phrase wasn't familiar to her.

We are never so defenseless against suffering as when we love, never so forlornly unhappy as when we have lost our love object or its love.

Then again, she thought, perhaps the expression 'love object' should have been a giveaway – wasn't Freud renowned for his insistence that man objectifies everything? Interesting though, that a property developer would have such an interest in Freud, and that he should use the man's sentiments to sign off his life.

Oh well, she thought, putting the photocopy aside and picking up the phone to inform Jones of her findings, perhaps Redmond had studied psychology during his college days or something.

Suddenly, Reilly sat up rigidly in her seat, an icy shiver traveled along her spine. Damn, how could she have missed it, she thought, frantically scrambling around on her desk for a case file.

She was wrong in her thinking that she hadn't come across Freud in a while; she had – very recently. And if she thought about it, way too coincidentally. Reilly scanned rapidly through the crime-scene photos until she found the one she was looking for.

And there it was.

5

T he cop was waiting for her outside Clare Ryan's apartment.

He stood up straight as she approached, as though a tough drill sergeant had just come on deck. 'Bit unusual this, if you don't mind me saying – especially at this time of night.'

Reilly smiled at him. 'Sorry to call you out so late – there's just something I needed to check.'

Carefully selecting the right key, he unlocked the door to the apartment. 'Don't mind at all, to be honest – much more interesting than sitting around waiting to be called out for the next drunken fight.'

Reilly stepped into the apartment, the uniform right behind her. The place was dark, long lines of shadows and light came in from the tall windows and altered the perspective in a disconcerting way. She hesitated slightly, wondering why being here now should feel so different from before, especially as the victims were gone and the initial horror had since dissipated. Of course, the death scene always seemed less threatening by daylight, but Reilly suspected that the disquiet she felt at the moment was rooted in something other than the dark. Now she was aware she'd missed something important the first time round, her senses had automatically gone up a notch and it almost felt as though a third party (the killer ... the victims even?) was there with her urging her forward.

Or taunting her.

The cop flicked the lights on and right away the atmosphere changed. Trying to regain her composure, Reilly headed straight for the bedroom, her companion a respectful couple of paces behind her. She reached inside and, finding the light switch, flicked it on.

In the harsh light the scene looked almost as gruesome as it had when she first saw it. The bodies had gone but the blood splatter on the wall, now dark and dry, looked even more horrific. And the smell – that distinctive scent of blood, brains and death – still hung in the air, a brutal assault on Reilly's sensitive nose.

She stood still for a moment, taking it all in, trying to picture the scene – not as she had before with just Clare and the man, but this time with someone else – perhaps a third party there in the room, and the uneasy knot in her stomach returned.

Concentrate, she told herself.

Putting aside her fears, Reilly took a deep breath and closed her eyes, trying to let her senses take over, trying to imagine it afresh – this time with someone else in the room.

First the killer shoots Clare in the chest, while the boy does what – just lies there, quiescent? She struggled to figure out how he had restrained them. Then, as Clare lay dying, gasping out her last few breaths with a hole in her chest, he turns the gun on the boy and splatters his brains across the wall.

Reilly gradually shook those thoughts from her mind and approached the bedside table – the reason she had come back.

Kneeling down, she carefully scanned the books lined up neatly on the table. She bent closer to examine the pile and still couldn't believe she'd missed it first time round. But now that she was aware, it was screaming at her.

Out of all the books on the bedside table, it was the only one that wasn't covered in blood splatter, which meant that it must have been put there *after* Clare and her boyfriend were killed.

Reilly's heart pounded faster in her chest.

'Find what you were looking for?' the uniform asked. She started quickly; she'd forgotten he was there.

'Sure did,' she replied, trying to hide the tremor in her voice as she stared at the title along the spine.

There, by the side of the victim's bed, and clean as a whistle, was a copy of *The Interpretation of Dreams* by Sigmund S. Freud.

A GRUFF VOICE answered the phone. 'Kennedy here.'

Reilly cursed inwardly. She had been hoping to speak to Chris Delaney. She could only imagine what his cynical partner's reaction would be.

'It's Reilly Steel from the crime lab,' she said. 'I think we've found something relevant to the Ryan case.'

'Go on,' he replied, cagily. As Reilly expected, he made little attempt to hide his suspicion of anything to do with the GFU.

'Well, first of all, we've found material evidence common to yours and another more recent crime scene,' she began.

'OK ...'

'We just processed another case – an apparent suicide

victim, Jim Redmond. Seemed fairly straightforward until we found a sample of paint and animal hair at the Redmond scene that matched samples we found at your Ryan scene.'

Kennedy was immediately skeptical. 'What's a suicide got to do with us? Maybe the common stuff has come from one of you lot – you walked it in or something.'

Reilly was ready for that. 'I'm pretty certain that isn't the case,' she said. 'I've spent the past few months drilling the problems with cross-contamination into my guys and I'd have to say their entry preparation is absolutely meticulous now. You've seen what we wear – nothing can get through those dust suits, and we change them after each crime scene.'

Kennedy remained resistant and Reilly figured the last thing he wanted was complications to his already baffling case. 'Then one of our guys could have walked it in,' he protested. 'There was a bunch of uniforms at the Ryan place – it was like a bloody circus if you ask me.'

'Considered that too,' she countered. 'I've already checked with the attending unit and nobody at the Ryan scene was common to this most recent one – the locations are at different parts of the city.' She cleared her throat. If the paint sample had caused him to bridle, she knew that the Freud connection was sure to push him over the edge. 'But there's something else that links them ...'

It was a moment before he responded. 'Go on.'

'Jim Redmond left a suicide note. I've just discovered it contains a Freud quote.' When Kennedy didn't answer, she went on. 'Sigmund Freud, the father of modern psychology?'

'Yeah, I went to college too,' he growled. 'What about him?'

'Well, here's the other coincidence – there was a copy of Freud's *The Interpretation of Dreams* on Clare Ryan's bedside locker when she died.'

'So? Nothing unusual about that – she was a psychology student.'

'It had no blood splatter on it – so it had to have been added after Clare and the boy died.'

He grunted, unwilling to concede.

Reilly spoke quickly. She could tell she was losing him. 'Don't you think the fibers and the Freud connection are just too much of a coincidence? If there's any chance these two cases could be connected, however remote, it means that someone else must be involved and—'

'Look,' Kennedy sighed, wearily. 'I know that conspiracy theories are all the rage where you come from, but here things are usually more straightforward—'

Reilly was about to reply when on the other end she heard a shuffling noise, and a curse.

'Reilly? Chris Delaney here,' the other detective said, coming onto the line. 'I'm sorry about that. My partner's having a bit of a bad day. What have you got for us?'

She let out a deep, pent-up breath. 'I was just explaining that we have some interesting new evidence on the Clare Ryan murder.'

'What have you found?'

With a feeling of relief, Reilly went on to explain her most recent findings to the one person on the force, it seemed, who was prepared to listen.

6

L ate that same evening, his head heavy and his joints
groaning like a 100-year-old shipwreck, Chris drove
home to his apartment.

He turned the key and stepped in the door, immediately
feeling better. The small, two-bed place on the quays took a
sizeable chunk out of his monthly salary but it was worth it
just for the views down over the Grand Canal and was a
welcome haven for his tired body, and his equally weary
mind.

He dumped his keys and jacket in the hallway and headed
for the living room. The view outside, city lights reflecting on
dark water, instantly relaxed him. He stood still for several
minutes, allowing the magic of the location to work its charm
on him.

Although he was loath to admit it, the combination of
recent events was beginning to take its toll. As well as the Ryan
shooting, he and Kennedy were also working on the headless
torso incident and both investigations were going nowhere.
Despite Reilly Steel's current belief that there was something
unusual about the evidence in the Ryan case, it didn't give

them anything solid, or anything that helped move them forward.

'I'm sorry, Reilly, I don't see how this helps,' he'd said when she'd phoned the incident room earlier.

'Well, surely it tells you that there's more to this thing than meets the eye,' she argued. 'Evidence common to two supposedly unrelated crime scenes – you guys should at least investigate the possibility of a third party.'

But he'd checked with the Ryans as to whether they or Clare had pets (they didn't – she was asthmatic) and also if there was any link with the Redmonds. And as Kennedy pointed out, it was difficult to give the Freud thing too much in the way of serious consideration given that the girl had been a psychology student.

To top it all off, they still had no clue as to who Clare's dead companion might be, and the lack of a solid lead was frustrating, disheartening and unbelievably bloody draining.

Hunger finally getting the better of him, he headed to the kitchen to see what he could rustle up for dinner. He was no gourmet cook, but enjoyed experimenting when he got the time.

He opened the fridge and stared at the empty expanse of white – damnit, he'd been too busy this week to even make it to the supermarket. A half carton of milk and two overripe tomatoes did not sound like the ingredients for any meal Chris could think of.

He checked the freezer in the vain hope that there might be an old lasagne stashed in the back somewhere but no such luck. To hell with it, he'd just order in. There was a great Chinese place down the road that he reckoned he alone had been keeping in business for the past three years.

When he'd ordered his usual and was waiting for the obligatory thirty minutes delivery turnaround, he switched on the television and tried to put work out of his head, at least for the moment. Anything but the news; the media were still banging on about the lack of progress on the Ryan case, and it wasn't as if Chris needed a reminder. A tedious game show was the best he could find, but at least it was something totally mindless, something to take his mind off it all.

But by not focusing on work, Chris couldn't help thinking about his own situation. That spasm the other day at the station and the continuous throbbing in his joints meant that what had a few weeks ago been a barely noticeable ache, was now developing into something much more serious.

He ran through the options in his head, the things he knew of. It couldn't be arthritis, could it? It might explain the aching joints, but would it explain the dead-on-his-feet tiredness?

Of course, the job was tough physically and getting tougher every year, but according to his most recent medical, he was lean, fit and in good overall health. His regular work-outs kept him toned and relatively slim and, Chinese take-aways aside, he ate fairly well.

He exhaled deeply. Arthritis just didn't bear thinking about – not at his age – not in a job like this.

With no home life to speak of, the job was his world. Indeed, it was the only thing in which Chris felt he really excelled. Out on the streets, striving to retain some semblance of justice in a country he loved was the only time he felt truly alive.

Even though these days he was finding it harder to be proud of his country with every violent death file that landed on his desk, any deterioration in his wellbeing, be it arthritis or otherwise, was not good. He ran a hand through his hair and sat back on the sofa, realizing that sooner or later he'd need to do something about it, or at least try to find out for sure what was wrong.

There was no question of his going to the in-house physician – no way. Anything suspicious or out of the ordinary would directly go into his file and be a question mark on his next physical. He might even be dumped into a dead-end desk job. No, he'd have to go an alternative route, go somewhere he wasn't known, or more importantly, where his occupation wasn't known.

He idly remembered reading an article in one of the lifestyle supplements of the *Independent* recently – a feature about a clinic on the Southside that did full-body medicals, like an MOT for people. They tested blood, diet, sight, hearing – the works. It might be worth a shot. At least if the clinic *did* discover something then he, and only he, would know about it. There would be no report or recommendations, no records sent to the force.

The phone rang, startling him out of his reverie and, checking the display, Chris raised a smile.

'Matt, how are things?' he said. Matt Sheridan was his oldest friend and it had been a while since the two had been in touch, what with Chris's heavy workload, and Matt's busy career as a barrister. In addition, he and his wife Emma now had a 6-month-old baby, and to his shame Chris realized he hadn't seen his little goddaughter Rachel since the christening a few weeks before.

'Just checking in to see if you're still alive,' Matt greeted. While Chris couldn't help feeling guilty about his lack of contact, he also knew that this wasn't his friend's intention.

'Sorry to disappoint you, mate, but it'd take a very strong wind to push me over.'

'Don't I know it. Anyway, good to see you're home early for a change. Quiet news day?'

'I wish,' Chris groaned. 'Anyway, never mind me, how's Emma? And Rachel – she must be huge by now.'

'Yep, huge, getting more like her mother by the day actually and ... ouch, Em, that was a compliment!' he gasped. Chris deduced that his wife had given him a sharp dig in the ribs for that last comment. Not that Emma Sheridan had anything to worry about in that regard. With her tiny waist, petite frame and wide-eyed gamine face, Matt's wife was a million miles from huge.

'Tell her I said hello and I'll pop over to see you all soon,' Chris told him.

'That's why I'm calling actually ... wait, hold on, Emma wants to talk to you.' Matt lowered his voice conspiratorially, 'Word of advice buddy, just before she says anything ... if it were me I'd run a mile ...'

Chris smiled, used to this kind of good-natured banter between the couple. Emma came on the line. 'Hi stranger! Are you doing anything this Sunday? We're having some people over for dinner, nothing major just one or two close friends and—'

'Ah, not again,' he groaned, reading between the lines. 'I told you – I don't have time for that kind of thing at the moment.'

'Chris, "that kind of thing" as you call it, isn't something you should have to make time for,' she chided. 'It's called having fun, and Anne Marie, my friend, she's lovely. Really career orientated like yourself. I know you'd have lots in common.'

'Emma, when will you realize that I don't need a matchmaker and I'm perfectly capable of looking after myself?'

'Oh really, and when's the last time you did that? It's over two years since you and Melanie ....' Chris could hear the discomfort in Emma's tone at the mention of his ex and his mouth tightened. No need to remind him.

'HONESTLY, Chris, you need to get out and enjoy yourself more,' she continued quickly. 'It's great that you're so dedicated to work, but one of these days you're going to wake up and realize you're an old man.'

'Thanks, Emma, exactly what I need to hear after a hard day on the job.'

Little did she know that Chris was already feeling like an old man, and he wondered if he should confide in his friends about what was going on. He knew that Emma liked to mother him, particularly after losing both of his parents within a year of each other, but if he told them what was going on she'd be on his case night and day to do something about it. No he wouldn't say anything just yet, but maybe if it got any worse.

'You know what I mean. All work and no play. You need to relax more, take time out for yourself now and again.'

'Well, even if I wanted to, Sunday's no good for me anyway,' he lied. 'I've got something else on.' Just then the doorbell rang and he smiled, grateful for the interruption. 'Sorry, but I really have to go; my dinner's here.'

'More takeaways?' Emma sounded horrified. Glad of the opportunity to avoid another lecture, Chris bade her a quick goodbye and promised to see them all soon.

He knew she was only trying to help, but he genuinely wasn't interested in a relationship these days. Not that he'd have time for one anyway, and as for being a workaholic and a loner, at least he wasn't a demon for the drink like a lot of guys in the force. In fact, alcohol was more of a social thing for him and as Emma had so delicately pointed out, he hadn't done much of that in a while.

Which meant that hard living definitely wasn't the cause of his current problems either, he thought, wincing as he stood up to answer the doorbell. Whatever was causing it, with any luck it would be something that could be dealt with quickly and easily, with no one any the wiser. A few pills, maybe a change in diet, something straightforward that wouldn't distract from the job, or more importantly something he could handle by himself.

But whatever the thing was, Chris thought as he paid the delivery guy for his beef chow mein, it needed to be sorted soon.

7

The narrow hallway was dimly lit, half blocked by a bicycle and a push-chair. Reilly squeezed past and stopped outside number twenty-three. She was reluctant to continue; she felt out of place in the dingy apartment block with her smart two-piece suit, her body language different from the confident persona she projected in her office and in the lab.

Slowly, she pushed on the door. It was unlocked and opened easily into the dark apartment. She stepped cautiously inside.

The hallway was short, just enough room for a small table, a couple of coat hooks and some worn old shoes. It led directly into a small living room.

She moved to the doorway of the living room, still stepping cautiously, taking everything in. She glanced around – the TV was on, the sound turned down low, and even though it was the middle of the day, the curtains were drawn, filling the room with shadows.

Reilly paused in the doorway and her nose picked up the

reek of booze mixed with a pungent stench of stale food – left-over takeout, she guessed.

Finally, she stepped cautiously into the room. A body was on the couch, sprawled out on his back, one arm hanging free and touching the floor, mouth wide open.

Reilly walked around the couch and looked down at him. He was pasty with an unhealthy looking complexion, unshaven, his curly hair thinning.

She reached out and gently tugged at his arm. 'Wake up. It's me.' She looked around, saw the empty whiskey bottle on the floor – no surprise there. 'Dad, wake up.' There was no conscious response. Mike Steel simply grunted, his head rolling helplessly on the grimy couch.

Reilly sighed and shook her head. Even though this was exactly what she'd expected, she always held out a scintilla of faith – a tiny corner of her hoping that one day she would find her father, if not happy, then at least sober and clean-shaven. Something other than this usual passed-out drunk. But she guessed that was too much to expect. Even now, when she'd taken the job in Dublin to be closer to him and to try and help him.

She stepped over to the window and flung the curtains wide open. It was a sunny morning and the light flooded in, hitting Mike Steel full in the face. He grunted, stirred, and then tried to cover his eyes. 'What the hell?'

'Hey Dad,' Reilly checked the nearest armchair for debris and, deciding it was safe enough, sat primly on the edge of it.

Mike slowly hauled himself up, gradually registering her presence. 'How the hell did you get in?'

'You left the door open again. How many times have I got to tell you to be more careful?'

He reached an upright position and peered bleary-eyed at his daughter. 'Did you just come around to nag me again?'

She shook her head. 'I just wanted to see you.'

He finally looked at her for the first time, took in the smart dark blue suit, the black patent kitten heels. 'You not at work?' he grunted.

'Just popped over on the way to the lab.'

'So, have you saved the world yet?' He grinned at his weak joke, looked around on the floor for his whiskey bottle, his face betraying his disappointment when he registered that it was empty. He licked his lips and looked up at Reilly. 'You couldn't lend us a twenty, could you?'

She ignored the question. By now this was an old game. He asked for money, she refused, knowing it would just be used to buy another bottle of booze. How he managed to drink as much as he did on benefits she didn't know, but she certainly wasn't about to facilitate his habit.

'I was thinking of taking a tour of the old Bank of Ireland this weekend,' she replied. 'It's supposed to be fascinating. You want to come with me?'

Her father stared at her. 'Why the hell would I want to go there?'

'Surely this city has more charms than just cheap booze?'

Mike leaned forward and made an abortive attempt to stand before falling back onto the couch, looking dizzy. 'Ah, spare me the moralizing for once, will you.'

'There are other places we could go then,' she offered. 'I just thought it might be nice to go out together, get some fresh air—'

Mike made a second attempt to stand up, and this time he managed to haul himself to his feet. 'I need to take a piss.'

Reilly shook her head as she watched him stagger from the room, his tottering footsteps taking him down the hall and into the tiny bathroom.

He began peeing noisily. 'Now if you wanted to visit the

Guinness Brewery, I might be interested,' he called back
to her.

Reilly stood up, wanting to stay, yet at the same time
hating every minute she was there. She stared at his back as
he hunched over the toilet. 'If you want to come with me, the
offer's open,' she called.

'Right.'

She took a last look around the flat, her face a mixture of
pity and disgust. He was such a different man to the strong,
funny, capable father she and her sister had known growing
up. But a lot had happened since those days, stuff that would
cause the best of men to seek refuge in the bottle. And no
matter how much she tried to help him, how much she'd
hoped that a return to the land of his birth would help him get
over it – help him forget, Reilly knew that the specter of what
had happened to Jess would never escape her father, in the
same way that it never escaped her.

LATER THAT DAY, Reilly was glad to be back in the lab. It
provided a sanctuary, a place where everything was orderly
and made sense.

But not right now.

She looked again at the printout in her hand. It was a
mistake, she was sure of it. It *had* to be a mistake. Otherwise ...

She felt like rubbing her eyes, like a character in one of
those cartoons she used to watch when she was a kid. Maybe
if she rubbed hard enough, when she looked at the results
again, everything would look normal.

But no, the same results were there, written down in black
and white, and seeing as she'd run these samples herself ...

Momentarily worry-stricken, Reilly picked up and
reviewed the evidence chain of custody card. Nope, she hadn't

made a mistake, there they were: Sample A and Sample B – one from the deceased female recently identified as Clare Ryan, the other from the also deceased and still unidentified male.

Although nobody was truly infallible, when it came to evidence she was pretty damn thorough, and she knew in her heart and soul that she hadn't screwed up this sample; she hadn't screwed up a sample in her entire life. There was always way too much at stake.

And again, as her Quantico tutors had taught her, no matter how weird some things looked, no matter how unlikely they seemed, results were results, and the evidence *never* lied.

Particularly when you ran a test twice.

As Reilly looked again at the two samples, she couldn't help but recall how another one of her tutors, Daniel Forrest, had drilled the principles of Ockham's razor into them.

'People,' he would say, addressing a group of trainee investigators. 'Intuition is a valuable tool – but only when it is based on the evidence.'

She recalled the first time he'd introduced the concept to them. Most of the students had never even heard of it, but there was one guy – his name escaped her – who always had an answer for everything.

'Anyone heard of Ockham's razor?' Daniel had queried.

'Yes, sir. It means that the simplest theory is always right,' Clever Clogs had replied.

'Wrong.'

Clever Clogs looked devastated. 'I thought—'

'A lot of people mistakenly think that's what it means,' the profiler explained, the overhead lights twinkling off his glasses. 'But what it actually says is far more subtle than that – and much more helpful to investigators.' He motioned to the evidence they were reviewing – evidence that could lead to two different conclusions. 'What Ockham's razor says is that when faced with two theories, when the available data cannot distinguish between them, we should study in depth the simplest of the theories.'

He watched as light bulbs went on in his students' brains.

'So while it doesn't guarantee that the simplest theory will be correct, it does establish priorities.'

Establishing priorities – that was the perspective Reilly needed right now. Given the results she'd got, there were two possible explanations. One was that all her testing was wrong, her methods flawed, her chain of custody compromised.

And the other ...

Well, quite frankly, the other was no less difficult to comprehend.

Reilly had known there was something wrong with the blood samples when the tox screen had come back. While both samples had been clear of the usual irregular chemicals, upon comparison something that could only be described as unexpected had appeared. So, just to be sure, she'd run the test herself again – this time using separate samples from both corpses. Sure enough, the same results appeared.

Unwilling to jump to conclusions too quickly, Reilly had eventually decided to settle the matter by running a genome scan. And it was those results that she now held in her hand, results that even to Reilly, who had seen a lot of weird things on the job, were pretty damn shocking.

'Ockham's razor,' she muttered to herself as she cast her eye once again over her findings. She picked up the phone and dialed Chris Delaney's cell phone.

When he answered, his voice sounded groggy.

'Detective Delaney, it's Reilly Steel,' she began. When he didn't reply immediately, she felt the need to clarify. 'From GFU?'

'Reilly, hi. What's the matter?'

'How'd you know there's something the matter?' she asked, faintly surprised.

He yawned. 'Because it's 2.15 in the morning.'

'It is?' She peered at her watch, recalling visiting her father that morning and coming into the lab straight afterward. It only felt like a couple of hours ago. Had she really been here that long? 'Oh hell, I'm sorry, Detective, I didn't realize—'

'Call me Chris, will you?' She heard what sounded like him switching on a bedside lamp. 'All this "detective" business is way too formal – especially when you're calling me in the middle of the night.'

'Sure, well – sorry for waking you ... Chris. I honestly didn't think to check the time.'

'That's OK. I'm a bad sleeper anyway. Are you still at the lab?'

'Yes. There was something I wasn't happy about so I kept at it until I could make sense of it and ...' she figured she might as well get straight to the point, 'I've found something else on the Ryan case.' She glanced again at the paper in her hand. 'Something important.'

'What did you find this time?' Now he sounded fully alert.

'Well, you know tox came back negative. But I noticed something else when the bloods came back. Something very unusual.'

'OK.' He sounded guarded now but Reilly suspected that unlike the common trace, he'd take this aspect a little more seriously.

'So I did a couple more tests – different tests.'

'Get to the point. What did you find?'

'Both victims had the same blood type,' she told him, clearing her throat before continuing. 'Now, this isn't unusual in itself until I tell you that they were both AB Negative.'

'And?'

'Well, only 0.6 per cent of the world's entire population is AB Negative – the tiniest proportion imaginable. So, if finding one person of that blood type is unusual, finding two in the same place is damn near impossible.'

'OK, so they're both AB Neg,' he said. 'So it's unusual. Really unusual. But it doesn't really give us anything new, does it?'

You bet it does, Reilly thought. 'That's why I ran a further test, and this time I carried out a genome scan.'

'A *what*?'

'It's a DNA comparison,' she explained.

Chris had gone very quiet. She took a deep breath. 'Clare Ryan and that guy – the other victim? Well, according to their blood samples, they weren't just a couple,' Reilly paused and swallowed hard, 'they were brother and sister.'

8

'W hat the ...?' Kennedy was aghast. 'What kind of sick ...?'

'I don't know – maybe even *they* didn't know. That's what we're here to find out.'

It was the following morning, and the detectives were once again heading to the Ryan household, hoping to get some answers.

Reilly's recent findings were shocking, particularly in light of the pathologist's earlier report confirming the sexual activity. It had never crossed Chris's mind that Clare Ryan's killer could have been a close relative – why would it? Close relatives didn't usually end up naked in bed together. But if the dead pair was in fact, brother and sister – and more importantly *knew* it – well, this case had taken a very odd turn.

'Well, it might be weird, but it brings the case to a fairly simple conclusion, doesn't it?' Kennedy said as they climbed out of the car in front of house.

'What?' Chris had tried to avoid speculating too much about what the implications of the results were but Kennedy was forcing him into it. 'You think that they couldn't live with the shame of incest so they took part in some kind of twisted suicide pact?'

'Maybe.' Kennedy drew hard on his cigarette, his face wreathed in smoke. 'Or maybe he decided to end it and the girl was just a victim. Either way,' he concluded, stubbing his cigarette out beneath his heel and pitching the butt into the carefully manicured flower beds, 'we need to find out what the hell is up with this family.'

They headed up the path to the front door and rang the bell. The chimes rang clear through the huge house.

Clare Ryan's mother opened the door, her eyes wide and hopeful. 'Detectives?'

She urged them into the house and straight through to the living room.

Her husband was sitting ramrod straight on the sofa, his face full of half-hidden hopes and fears. 'Is it Clare?' Bernard Ryan asked as they walked in. 'You have news? Have you found out who ... who killed her?'

The detectives sank into the expensive leather couch and exchanged a brief glance. 'The investigation is still ongoing,' Kennedy said noncommittally, taking out his notebook.

'We just need to ask you both a few more questions,' Chris added.

'Of course, if it helps we'd be happy to—'

'But we've already told you everything we know,' Bernard interjected, irritably. 'If you don't have any news for us, then why are you here? It's been a dreadful time – and we haven't even buried our daughter yet.'

'Why is that, Mr Ryan?' Delaney asked, glad that the man had raised this particular subject. He'd thought of little else since Reilly's phone call. It was now a week since the murders and the Ryans still hadn't buried Clare. They'd said that they were waiting to inform a family member who was difficult to locate. Difficult to locate because he was, in fact, lying on a cold slab in the morgue? 'Who are you waiting for?'

Bernard paused, looked at his wife. 'Our eldest, Justin, Clare's older brother,' he snapped. 'He's abroad somewhere traveling, and as usual we haven't a clue where he is, let alone a means of contacting him.'

Ryan's disapproval of his son was plain to see, but it wasn't the kind of disapproval Delaney was looking for. Apparently the Ryans knew nothing of their children's unusual closeness – or if they did, they were in denial, or doing a damn good job of hiding it.

Kennedy glanced at Chris for a moment before asking his next question. 'Was Clare close to her brother, Mr Ryan?'

The man shrugged. 'Of course they were close – they were brother and sister.' He looked to Gillian for reassurance.

She nodded slowly. 'We've tried everything to locate him, detectives.' She dabbed at her face with a handkerchief. 'He'll be devastated when he finds out.'

'So, Clare and Justin are your only children?'

'Yes,' Bernard replied. 'Justin is five years older than Clare.'

'And when was the last time you spoke to your son?'

Mrs Ryan glanced worriedly at her husband.

'It was a couple of months ago,' Bernard answered, 'before he left for Thailand or Vietnam or whatever godforsaken country took his fancy this time.' He shook his head. 'We had words about it at the time, and we haven't heard from him since.'

Chris caught Kennedy's eye. 'Is there a chance he might have come back, maybe returned home since then without letting either of you know?' he ventured. 'Could he be in the country and you not know it?'

There was a sniff of disapproval from Bernard. 'Anything is possible.' He looked from one detective to the other. 'What I mean is that it wouldn't be unheard of. Justin tends to do what suits him first and foremost.'

Kennedy leaned forward, probing gently. 'It sounds as though you disapprove of your son's travels, Mr Ryan.'

'The boy is twenty-six years old, Detective, and has never worked a day in his life. He's irresponsible and to be perfectly honest, is—' he caught himself, sorrow etched all over his face, '*was* a very bad influence on Clare.'

You can certainly say that again, Chris thought.

'Even so, we can't go ahead and bury his sister without him,' the man continued. 'It just wouldn't be right. He adored Clare and, despite the fact that he was rarely at home, she adored him.'

The detectives exchanged a surreptitious glance.

'Would Justin have ever stayed at Clare's place when he came home from his travels?' Chris asked. 'Maybe without you knowing he was home? After all, her apartment is much closer to the city and the airport than here, isn't it?'

'Yes. No. I don't know.' Torn between anger at his son and grief over his daughter's death, Bernard Ryan's emotions were clearly shot to pieces. 'I suppose he could have – who knows what he might do? He may have preferred that to coming all the way out here. As you can probably tell, my son and I don't always see eye to eye.'

Did that make Bernard Ryan a possible suspect then? Chris wondered. Did he find out that Justin had been corrupting Clare in the most deplorable way and, repulsed and ashamed by his children, decide that he had no choice but to take matters into his own hands?

Reilly had been trying from the start to convince them that something wasn't right about this shooting. She was convinced that a third party was involved in both this, and the Jim Redmond suicide. But he and Kennedy weren't yet in a position to share her view that the unexplained paint and animal fibers common to Clare Ryan's apartment and Jim Redmond's front room meant that these cases were somehow connected.

Still, he decided to try a bit of speculative fishing. 'Mr Ryan, do you know a man called Jim Redmond?' he asked, ignoring Kennedy's surprised glance.

After a beat, Bernard replied. 'You mean Johnny Redmond who plays bridge with us now and then?'

'The person I'm referring to is a businessman from Donnybrook.'

'No. Johnny lives just up the road from us here ...' Ryan looked blank, genuinely blank, and Chris knew instinctively that if there was a connection between Clare Ryan and Redmond's death, it was unlikely it had anything to do with Clare's father. *Their* Redmond clearly meant nothing to him.

'Who is he?' Bernard demanded, glancing in surprise at his wife. 'And what has he got to do with my daughter's murder?'

'Nothing as far as we can tell,' Kennedy interjected, smoothly. 'We're just making further enquiries, that's all. But what we *would* like to do now is help you locate your son Justin. Have you reported him missing?'

'Missing?' Bernard Ryan was dismissive. 'He's not missing – he just hasn't bothered to contact us in a while, which, believe me, is nothing new.'

'Do you have any recent photographs of him? Something that might help us locate him for you?' Chris asked.

Gillian Ryan headed for the sideboard at the other end of the living room, where a small selection of family photographs was displayed. Chris remembered briefly running his eye over these pictures the first time they'd visited, but he hadn't really studied them. He certainly hadn't figured on them helping him identify Clare Ryan's dead companion.

'Here,' Gillian handed them a photo. 'This is probably the most recent one we have of Justin. It was taken at Clare's twenty-first birthday party last year.' Clare looked happy and carefree, sitting on the sofa alongside a young guy playing the guitar. 'That's our son there,' Gillian clarified.

Not that her clarification was necessary. Because almost as soon as he'd laid eyes on the photo, Chris realized that the guy in this picture was the same man they'd found in bed with Clare. He knew this because on his right upper arm, Justin Ryan was sporting the very same oriental-style tattoo as the body they'd found.

But as he continued studying the photograph, something else jumped out at him – something that hit him with all the force of a ten-ton truck. And while the first realization might have brought things to a tidy conclusion, the second sent the entire investigation into absolute disarray.

9

'Y ou were right,' Chris said to Reilly, handing her the photograph they had picked up at the Ryans' house. When he and Kennedy had finished up with the parents, he'd phoned Reilly to ask if she could meet them in the incident room back at the station. If she could confirm what they'd now discovered, they needed to present a whole new set of facts about this case to O'Brien – who would probably go ape.

While the investigation had never exactly been straightforward, there was no question that it had now taken on a much more sinister turn. A murder with incestuous overtones was sufficiently gratuitous to send the media into an even greater frenzy, and if there was one thing their boss despised, it was high-profile cases.

Kennedy had mostly been silent on the drive back to Dublin, as if refusing to admit that they had been going about the investigation all wrong.

'Look, it doesn't prove anything,' he'd protested when they'd left the Ryan household and Chris had filled him in on his discovery.

'It proves that we've been chasing our tails while the GFU was trying to point us in another direction – the *right* direction,' he replied, nodding at the photograph Kennedy held in his hands. 'Reilly was right about them being siblings and now this means she's probably also right that everything isn't as it seems.'

'Come on – we still don't know that for sure.'

'Look at that photograph, Pete. You know as well as I do what it means. Even if he did shoot his sister, the kid couldn't have pulled the trigger on himself – not voluntarily anyway.'

'So what other explanation is there?'

'The one that Reilly's been trying to open our minds to from the beginning,' he reiterated, his mouth tightening into a grim line as he drove. 'There's somebody else involved.'

'But how?' Kennedy couldn't seem to get his head around it. 'There was no break-in, no motive, no nothing other than a few scraps of paint and a bit of dog hair that could have come from anywhere.'

'*Animal* hair,' Chris corrected. 'We already know the Ryans don't have pets. Clare didn't have a pet – and neither, for that matter, did Jim Redmond.'

'You're not telling me that you seriously think this is connected to that guy Redmond's suicide, are you?' Kennedy protested, turning to look at him. 'What the hell has Steel done to you?'

Chris accelerated through an amber light, keen to get back to the station and talk to Reilly. Never again would he make the mistake of discounting her insights so readily, not when she'd been certain there was something off about this case from day one. 'Opened my eyes, that's what.'

. . .

Now, as the three sat together in the incident room, the Ryan file open and the crime-scene photos scattered across Chris's desk, Chris handed Reilly the photograph of Justin Ryan. 'Take a look at that.'

She studied the picture. 'This is the brother? No surprises there, he fits the identity profile, and the tattoo is pretty conclusive—'

'Take a closer look,' he interjected, impatiently, 'a closer look at what he's doing, or more importantly, *how* he's doing it.'

Her interest piqued, Reilly scrutinized the photograph for a few moments more before it finally hit her. 'Whoa,' she said, looking from one detective to the other, her eyes widening in realization. 'The guitar – he's right-handed, isn't he?'

'That's what we thought. Which means—'

'Which means that he couldn't have voluntarily fired the gun.' Reilly tried to keep the exultant tone out of her voice, but her glee was obvious. 'The trajectory went from left to right. I knew it; I *knew* there was somebody else in that room.'

'Yeah well, I hope you don't mind if we save the champagne till later,' Kennedy muttered. 'We've got a case to run.'

'You're welcome, Detective,' she retorted with no small measure of triumph. 'Glad to be of help.'

'Yeah, well,' he shifted in his seat, 'we would have worked it out ... just maybe not as soon.'

'Wow, is that actually a *thank you* I'm hearing?'

'It's the closest you're going to get to it in this place, sweetheart,' he shot back, a hint of a smile on his face.

'Seriously, Reilly,' Chris said, turning to her, 'thanks for the heads-up. If it wasn't for you, we might never have discovered this.'

She shrugged. 'Hey, that's what I'm here for.'

'OK, OK, enough of the you're-great-I'm-great stuff,'

Kennedy growled, sipping on a stale cup of coffee, 'let's get back to business.' He spluttered as the cold coffee hit his tongue. 'Crap, how old is this?'

'It's the one you made this morning – before we visited the Ryans,' Chris replied, sardonically. 'You might want to freshen it up a bit.'

'No shit.' He stood up, hitched his trousers up over his belly. 'Anyone else want one?'

'If you're buying.'

Kennedy waddled over to the coffee machine and busied himself making three cups of coffee. 'How'd you take it, Steel?' he threw back over his shoulder.

'Black, no sugar, thanks.'

'Bloody health freak,' he muttered to himself. Reilly met Chris's amused glance. Clearly Kennedy's bark was worse than his bite and he was likely a big softie behind it all.

The detective returned with three mugs clutched in his big hands and set them down on the desk. 'Firstly, I think we need to get all of this straight before we ruin the boss's year and start giving the tabloids orgasms.' He eased himself back into his chair and sipped his coffee. 'Ah, that's better. Now, it's been a while since I've been involved in ballistics,' he said to Reilly, 'so is there any way of telling whether or not somebody else fired both shots?'

'You mean shot Clare as well as setting up the brother to look like he shot himself?' She shrugged. 'I'll take another look but if you ask me, I think it's likely. I've always thought the gunpowder residue found on the brother was suspect, and there's no reason as yet to believe that he would have shot his own sister.'

'I wonder if this other person might have known that they were brother and sister, that it might have been his – or her – motive?' Chris ruminated. While they'd established that Clare had no jealous exes or current boyfriends that might have taken offense to their relationship, what about Justin? Hell hath no fury like a woman scorned and all that. Surely most women would be utterly repulsed by the discovery that the man in her life was sleeping with his own sister. Hell, who wouldn't be?

'I know what you're thinking,' Reilly said, studying him. 'And I think we now have to assume Clare and Justin's ... close relationship must have been the motivating factor for these murders. Whoever did this discovered them in bed together, or *set* out to discover them in bed together and then ...'

'Which means we can't rule out the parents,' Kennedy mused. 'Although if I found out my kids were up to those sort of shenanigans, I think I'd want to put a bullet in my own head, not theirs.' He shuddered at the very thought.

'So what about the Redmond suicide?'

'I still don't see how it's related to this one,' Chris replied. 'I know about the fibers and the hairs, but still—'

'Well, I'm still willing to bet it's not cross-contamination,' Reilly protested. 'And the Freud connection means something – I'm sure of it.'

Chris started to argue, but hesitated, seeing the conviction in her eyes. 'OK, so say for the moment we go with your belief that these are connected. Where does that lead us?'

She sighed. 'Nowhere, yet.' She toyed with her coffee cup. Chris noted her chewed-down nails and was almost relieved to see a chink in her armor. 'But what it does mean is that we need to formally include the Redmond "suicide" in our case file, and start looking more closely for anything else that might tie the two cases together.'

'Fan-bleedin'-tastic,' Kennedy grumbled. 'Just what we need – an extra case. O'Brien's going to love this.'

She drained her coffee and stood up. 'I'm going to attend

Redmond's autopsy this evening,' she said. 'See if Karen can give me anything else to go on.'

'It's scheduled for later today?' Chris knew the ME's case-load was almost always full and suicide victims often ended up at the bottom of the pile.

'Tonight at eight.'

'We'll come with you,' he said, and out of the corner of his eye spotted Kennedy's surprised look. 'Look, I know it still doesn't feel like one of ours, but if Reilly really believes there might be something—'

'Fine,' his partner growled. 'I said I'll go with the flow on this one but you can count me out for tonight,' He shivered. 'You know I only go to the dungeon if I really have to," he added, referring to the recently built city morgue building. 'It might be all shiny and new but it still gives me the creeps.'

'OK, then *I'll* come with you,' Chris said. 'If there's a chance this might have something to do with the Ryan murder, then it wouldn't kill us to check it out. If it doesn't – great, but if it does, it might just save us a lot of time later.'

'Well, as I said, count me out.'

'Fair enough.' Chris shrugged. 'How about I go to the dungeon – and you can visit the lion's den?'

Kennedy began gathering paperwork and putting photos back into the file. 'Brilliant. By the time I've finished breaking the bad news to O'Brien, we'll be lucky if the two of us don't end up in the bloody dungeon.' He paused and looked again at the photo of Justin, smiling, playing his guitar. 'Families, eh? They can get you into a shitload of trouble.'

10

As they were both going to the city morgue, Chris had suggested to Reilly that they meet for something to eat beforehand. Because the GFU lab was situated on the outskirts of the city and the morgue on the opposite side, they'd agreed to meet halfway, in a small, laid-back bistro off Grafton Street, where the food was good and, more importantly, quick.

Although he was keen to hear what she had to say about the case, he was also intrigued by her. Smart, focused and extremely driven, from what he'd seen so far, she was a terrific asset to the investigative team.

'Kennedy was right, you know,' he said, toying with his spaghetti. 'There *is* something a bit warped about eating before an autopsy.'

'You think so?' Reilly was sitting across from him at the tiny round table, munching her way through a cheeseburger about the same size as her head. Since leaving the lab she had changed into a pair of jeans and a sweatshirt and let her hair hang loose around her face. He'd only ever seen her wear it in a severe ponytail and the transformation was startling. Right then, she looked about eighteen years old. 'Sorry,' she said, swallowing hard. 'I know I shouldn't talk with my mouth full, but I'm absolutely starving.'

He laughed. 'The morgue doesn't affect your appetite then?'

'Not the gruesome stuff if that's what you're referring to,' she replied, wiping a blob of ketchup off the side of her mouth. 'What bothers me is that these guys have died suddenly, and usually violently. I want to know how that happened, who did it, why they did it.'

Chris reached for his water. 'Which I take it, is the reason you went into forensics in the first place?'

She didn't reply immediately. He thought he saw a faint shadow cross her face but the look was gone before he could pinpoint it.

'Pretty much,' was all she said. 'What about you? How'd you make detective so fast?'

'So fast?'

'Sure. What are you – thirty, thirty-three?'

'Thirty-nine, actually,' he corrected.

'Wow. You must work out a lot.'

He shrugged, secretly pleased that she thought that. 'Whenever I get the time. But there hasn't been much of that lately.' He wasn't about to tell her that these days he'd been feeling so worn down he barely had the energy to lift the kettle, let alone a couple of hundred-pound weights. 'So how are you finding life in Ireland?'

'So far so good.' She sipped at her drink. 'My dad grew up here; his family emigrated to the States when he was thirteen.'

'Ah. With a first name like Reilly, I thought there might have been some Irish connection.'

'It was my dad's mom's maiden name so I guess I'm kinda named after her,' she told him.

'Does your dad get back much?'

Her expression closed. 'He actually moved back here a couple of years ago ... but there's no other family left now.'

'I'm sorry to hear that.' Chris could see this was a subject she didn't want to linger on. Yet it certainly explained why she'd left the bright lights of the West Coast to come and work in dreary old Dublin. 'I'd imagine this is a big change from California,' he said, picking up his glass again. 'Whereabouts are you from?'

'Marin County, San Francisco Bay area.'

He gulped his water. 'Never been there. I hear it's a great city though. You must find things very different over here – like the weather for starters.'

'Yeah, that is kind of hard to get used to,' she admitted. 'And I really miss the seafood. The shrimp you serve here is mostly frozen and very pricey. We get some great stuff back home; you can buy it fresh at the harbor, right off the boat.'

A waiter arrived to clear their plates and they were silent for a moment before Reilly spoke again. 'What I really miss most, though, is the waves,' she said, dreamily.

'What? You surf too?'

'All Californians surf,' she replied with a smile. 'You learn before you can walk. This Californian especially.'

'Never tried it.'

'You should, there's no feeling like it.' Her voice softened, and a faraway look came into her eyes. 'Riding the waves, feeling them crash over you ... it's like there's nothing but you and the surf – it's awesome.' Her love was clear in her voice.

'I'm sure it must be.'

'I know there's a place up north somewhere that has some good surf, but I haven't had time to check it out.'

He nodded. 'Maybe when things quieten down a bit here you might get the chance.'

'Do things *ever* quieten down around here? I must admit I expected Dublin to be a sleepy little place, not exactly a hotbed of serious crime.'

'Sign of the times, I suppose,' he replied. 'Though to be truthful, I'm glad we've got someone like you around.'

She cocked an eyebrow. 'You must be the only one.'

'Don't think like that. It's nothing personal. I suppose some people, guys like Kennedy for instance,' he added, 'are just used to doing things the old-fashioned way. Things have changed so much in this country over the last ten years, you wouldn't believe it.'

'Well, I'm glad it's not just me.'

'Definitely not. Give them a bit more time to get used to you.'

'Good, 'cos I've pretty much had it with the dumb blond jokes by now,' she said rolling her eyes good-naturedly.

'I don't blame you, and I'd say you really appreciated that red swimsuit too,' he added, his tone delicate.

'You heard about that?'

'Yep. Sometimes it's like being back in school around here. But you did the right thing by not reacting to it. It's exactly what those lads want.'

She shrugged. 'Well, they got the size just about right so at least I could use it – unlike the cheerleading costume.'

Chris nearly spat out his drink. 'What? When the hell did that happen?'

'Second week on the job.'

'Idiots.' He shook his head. 'I'm sorry, Reilly. I hope you know we're not all like that.'

'No need to apologize.' Her eyes danced with humor. 'The way things were going I thought I'd end up getting a brand new wardrobe for free. Anyway, that's peanuts compared to the stuff we got thrown at us at the Academy,' she added, telling him about the time fellow trainees had planted a cadaver in her dorm room.

They chatted some more about their respective careers, though Chris suspected that Reilly was skimming over the impressive credentials that helped her attain such a position in the force. But when he tried to probe again into her reasons for taking a job in a place that could only be described as a sleepy backwater compared to what she was used to, she again became distinctly closed.

'I just needed a change, that's all,' she said, before deftly changing the subject. 'So how long have you and Kennedy been working together?'

'In Serious Crime? Nearly three years now.' *OK,* he thought. *Obviously certain things are off limits.* And despite this, or perhaps because of it, he found himself become more and more intrigued.

All too soon it was time to leave and Chris signaled for the bill.

'Let me get that,' Reilly insisted, forcibly.

'No, I asked you out ... I mean, I asked you to come and —'*Nice one, Chris,* he remonstrated with himself, completely bewildered as to what the protocol was for this kind of thing. Emma would be proud of him – not.

'Seriously, it's mine,' she said, leaving a couple of twenties. Chris relented, unwilling to embarrass himself any further.

'Well, I'll get the next one then,' he muttered, and was he imagining it, or was there a hint of a smile playing about her lips?

'Do you want to get a taxi?' he asked as they got up and left the table, 'or we can walk? It's not that far.'

'Let's walk then, it's not often I see the outside of the lab – might as well make the most of it.' He held the door of the restaurant open for her. 'I have to tell you though,' she added, referring to the next item on their agenda, 'I'm looking forward to this. It'll be my first time down here on official business – Gorman usually does these.' She laughed lightly. 'He usually prefers to keep me where he can see me.'

And as Chris followed Reilly down Grafton Street, he decided that a woman who actually looked forward to visiting the city morgue was a very rare creature indeed.

'COULD they make this place any more depressing?' he wondered aloud after he and Reilly signed in beneath the dreary fluorescent lights. He looked around at the gray walls, the gray floors, the institutional desks and chairs. Despite being housed in a brand new building, the autopsy suite still felt dank and gloomy.

She chuckled as they headed through the heavy double doors to the observation room. 'What – you think this would be more fun if the walls were painted in delicate pastels and we had some classical music playing? Believe me,' she continued, 'these places are the same the world over.'

When they stepped into the observation room they found that apart from the pathologist and her staff, they seemed to be the only observers that evening, although given that it was an alleged suicide, that wasn't unusual.

Minutes later, they were both suited up and awaiting Karen Thompson's appearance inside the cold and sterile autopsy room.

Chris shivered – although he was used to being around bodies, he always found it damn near impossible *not* to be affected by the smell of the place. And his stomach – which thanks to the bright idea to eat beforehand was still filled with undigested pasta – instinctively began to churn.

He struggled not to retch as the smell washed over him.

The morgue had its own unique odour that clung mercilessly to clothes, hair, skin, everything, and, despite the protective gear they'd been given, the stench of the place was unavoidable.

Karen Thompson, dressed in surgical greens and wearing heavy-duty rubber boots, entered the room and nodded briefly at them before confidently heading toward the utility area at the other end.

'Let's begin, shall we?' she said, moving to the head of the autopsy table and addressing two mortuary attendants. The men, each clad in plastic overalls and using surgical gloves, duly unzipped and removed the polythene body bag before deftly lifting the stiff remains of Jim Redmond back onto the white marble table.

At the head of the table there was a short hose attached to a water tap and at the bottom, a swivel tap fixed to a large sink unit. The autopsy table briefly reminded Chris of a holiday he and his ex Melanie had taken in Cairo a few years back, the large marble slab reminiscent of the ones used by the Ancient Egyptians when preparing bodies for mummification. He still recalled word-for-word the Egyptian tour guide's gruesome description of the process: 'First, they suck out the brains through the nose, then remove the organs and the entrails, before draining the blood away at the end of table ...' Now it was poor Jim Redmond's blood draining away and his organs being handled in a similar manner to those ancients, he thought, solemnly.

Another attendant put up a selection of X-rays, backlit for viewing, and Karen put on a pair of surgical latex gloves before switching on her Dictaphone. Close by, a forensic photographer stood ready to record the proceedings for posterity.

'Case number 1386, post-mortem of James Redmond,' the

doctor began, her tone clipped and efficient as she spoke into the mouthpiece. 'Subject is a well-nourished white male, mid-fifties, with slight receding dark hair, blue eyes and weighing approximately eighty-eight kilos. Height is one hundred and seventy-two centimeters.'

She paused briefly, and moved along the side of the table. 'Time of death was estimated as 9.25 a.m. on Friday, 25th February. Cause of death is due to lack of oxygen.'

She paused, carefully examined Redmond's neck and returned to her Dictaphone. 'Inflammation and V-shaped ligature compression marks on the neck indicate that death occurred by hanging. The characteristics of these marks would seem to confirm that the manner of death – as pronounced by the attending physician at the scene – is in fact suicide.'

Reilly was tight-lipped. She seemed disappointed by Karen's clearly stated verdict.

Chris, on the other hand, was relieved. Maybe her hunch was incorrect – there was nothing on the body to support anything but suicide, nothing to add to the strange coincidences that seemed to link it to the Ryan murders. The idea was a positive one – he and Kennedy really didn't want another casualty to add to their growing list of homicides, whatever intuition Reilly might have.

As they stood watching the ME continue her external examination, Chris gradually began to feel the onset of fatigue. He loosened his shoulders and tried to concentrate on the doctor's movements, his mind struggling to focus.

It had been a long day – a very long day, in fact – and the recent developments in the investigation had taken a lot out of him. So, of course it was natural for him to be dead on his feet at this stage – who wouldn't be tired? This was simply weariness, he reassured himself, good old-fashioned weariness, and nothing to do with the similar bouts of tiredness he'd been experiencing for the last few weeks, nor the persistent throbbing in his joints.

But his fatigue was temporarily forgotten when Reilly suddenly flinched. Something Karen was saying had caught her attention and, bit by bit, he let the doctor's words swim back into focus.

' ... Slight recent trauma to the anus – some bruising, minute lacerations—'

'Excuse me, Doctor?'

'Yes?' Karen looked up from her examination of Redmond's body; if she was annoyed that the other woman had interrupted her flow of observation, she didn't show it.

'The anus shows some form of trauma?' Reilly repeated.

'Consistent with recent sexual activity, yes.' She indicated the body. 'There are also traces of what I suspect may be latex. But nothing major, nothing forcible, if that's what you're thinking.'

'I wasn't suggesting ... sorry for the interruption, please keep going,' Reilly said, giving Chris a sideways glance. He made a mental note to ask her afterward what the hell *that* was all about.

A few minutes later, Karen completed the remaining external visual examination and then, positioning her cloth mask tightly into place, she picked up a scalpel and made a neat Y-incision into Redmond's chest.

As always, he was impressed by the deft, fluid motion of her gloved hands and for a while the room was still as she worked, breaking through the ribcage and skillfully removing and weighing organs, and recording concise observatory remarks for transcription; her soft features all the time fixed in an expression of intense concentration.

Once samples had been taken, the organs returned, and

every incision sutured, the ME finally snapped off her gloves and dropped them in a nearby biohazard container.

'Well?' he asked Reilly when the procedure was complete and they waited in the hallway for the doctor. 'You heard what she said – it was a straightforward suicide.'

'Yes, but what about the anal trauma?' she argued. 'Redmond was a married man; his wife identified his body and was apparently inconsolable. She's the one who is convinced that this was no suicide.'

'Of course she was,' Chris replied. 'Who wouldn't be? Sounds like he might have been a closet homosexual, which makes his suicide even more plausible, doesn't it?'

'I suppose,' Reilly bit her lip, her disappointment palpable. She'd had high hopes that the ME would find something out of kilter. 'I don't know ...' She paused, choosing her words carefully. 'It's just that when you add this to the other strange findings we've had on this case, I think there's something else going on, something we're not seeing.' She looked up at him, her tone of voice almost apologetic. 'You can call it a gut feeling, if you like, but I'd wager a lot that this is no simple suicide.'

'Gut feelings don't count for much in this business,' he pointed out.

'I know, but the trace—'

He cut her off. 'Look, as far as everyone else involved in this thing is concerned, there's nothing suspicious about the guy's death. Now, I know there's evidence common to this and the Ryan crime scene, but as we've said before, there could be a simple explanation for that.' He tried to look sympathetic. 'We've agreed to consider it along with the Ryan case for the moment, because of the fibers mostly, but sooner or later we're going to have to come up with something more substantial than a paint sample and a hunch.'

Reilly had a determined look. 'You may be right – but there's something I want to check with Karen before we go.'

'What?' he asked, exasperated. Did she never give up?

'Remember in there, when she collected penis swabs? I want to take a look at those samples properly, find out what they are.'

'Bloody hell, what do you *think* they are?' he asked disbelievingly. 'We've already clarified that he could be a closet homosexual.'

'There's no harm in checking though, is there?'

'But—' The rest of his sentence was interrupted as Karen, now dressed in civilian clothes, joined them in the hallway.

'Is everything all right?' she said, a penetrating look in her saucer eyes.

'Sure,' Reilly said. 'I just need a favor. Those swabs you took from Redmond earlier? I'd like to take them back to the lab with me tonight for analysis, if that's OK.'

'Tonight?' Karen looked taken aback by the request. 'You can if you want, but we'll be sending everything from today over to GFU in the morning anyway. But, if it's really that urgent, I can sign those samples out for you now.'

'I'd really appreciate that, thanks.'

As Chris and Reilly walked with Karen to her office, she gave them both a searching look. 'It's unusual to have someone from Serious Crime around here for a suicide procedure, let alone a GFU investigator,' she said, her tone wary.

Reilly was noncommittal. 'I'll be honest, Doc, this is a bit of a fishing mission. We have some anomalies in the trace collected at the Redmond crime scene, some things that may connect this with another, on-going murder investigation.'

'The Ryan murders?' Karen was sharp, no doubting that.

'I really can't say at this point.'

'All right.' The ME sat at her desk and pulled out the forms to transfer the samples to Reilly's care. She wrote quickly, signed with a flourish and handed her the paperwork. 'There you go.'

'Thanks.'

As they turned to go, Karen called out to them. 'Ms Steel?' She stopped in the doorway. 'Am I missing something here?'

'I think we're *all* missing something,' Reilly replied, her mouth set in a hard line, 'and I'm determined to find out what.'

11

Gerry Watson's love of the simple things in life belied his young age. When most 26-year-olds would be in their element in a bar or nightclub, he was more content to head for the hills with his tent and camping gear. He always felt most alive in the wilds, an area without a phone signal was not a curse for him and he could happily live without text messages and social networks. No, to him the wide open spaces of nature were the places to be enjoyed most, and the longer he could spend in that environment, the more his worries melted away.

He had acknowledged the place he now laid was one of the best spots he'd set up camp, something that was not easy for a 'local expert' like him to admit, as he had not been the one to discover it. The view from where he lay was awe-inspiring, a 'promised land' view of rivers, waterfalls and sunlit mountainsides. He lay in his tent beside the camping stove and pan; an earlier meal now cold as the afternoon winter sun struggled to emit any real warmth. Gerry didn't care though; he was a million miles from the worries of the world and that was what mattered most.

Of course, nature wasn't all a bed of roses and had its annoyances, even at this time of the year. Though unseasonably mild, it seemed every flying insect within a twenty-mile radius seemed intent on plaguing him, but there was little point in swatting at them.

Also, wilderness such as this had far more nasty inhabitants than a few flies, and when the first rat darted from behind a large boulder, entered the tent and inquisitively sniffed just below Gerry's ear, he didn't notice a thing.

When sharp rodent incisors pierced his flesh, the only resulting movement was his exposed skin twitching, as the larva of swarming flies sought nourishment from inside. The look of terror etched on his face was appropriate, but it was a look Gerry had been wearing since days earlier his life had slowly been taken from him.

REILLY COULD TELL it was nasty even before she got to the campsite – the grim faces of the officers as she approached told her everything she needed to know. It was now eight in the morning and she'd been fast asleep when the call came in around six-thirty.

The uniform standing guard nodded as she approached. 'Might want to put your mask on – it's pretty rank in there.'

She nodded her thanks and pushed through the door of the white forensic marquee that had been erected to enclose an expensive North Face four-man tent.

Given that her sense of smell was one of her best weapons, wearing a mask was actually the last thing Reilly wanted to do –. Still, the wave that hit her as she stepped inside took her aback.

She paused and closed her eyes. At first she found herself fighting back the waves of nausea while she tried to let her olfactory organs filter out the different smells from the chaos and give her some clues, something to work with.

The overpowering odor was the smell of death – the unmistakable stench of rotting flesh. But there were other smells, too, fighting their way through and she tried to relax and let them come to her. Vomit, but that was likely to be fresh, probably from whoever had found the body.

Reilly opened her eyes and saw Karen Thompson moving away from a body which was bathed in the harsh floodlight. Looking around, she could now see that the crime scene was deeply compromised. There were footprints all over the grass where someone had stepped in and out of the entrance to the tent – probably whoever had found the body. There was also a pool of vomit near the tent – again, most likely the first on the scene.

Damn.

The pathologist's dour face brightened a little when she saw Reilly. 'Hey. Sorry to see you again so soon.'

She gave her a small nod in response. 'It's been quite a night, huh?' She looked past her toward the body. 'What have we got?'

'One body, male, single gunshot wound to the chest.' Karen shook her head, a grim look on her face. 'The tent was open so exposure to the elements means time of death isn't immediately obvious; that's pretty much all I can say at this point.' She gave Reilly's arm a brief pat of encouragement as she stepped past her.

Reilly stood and surveyed the scene. She tried to let her eyes scan around before she concentrated on the corpse but it was hard to ignore. *Focus,* she told herself, *look for the details.*

The North Face emblem on the tent caught her eye. She was familiar with the logo from her own love of the outdoors and had often used a similar kind of tent on her many camping trips to Yosemite back home. Reilly let her eyes settle on the victim. Like the Ryans, the guy was young, in his twenties and unremarkable looking, someone you wouldn't look twice at if he passed you in the street.

His position was strange though – he had clearly been posed after death. He was lying inside the open tent with his head propped against his rucksack, one arm loose by his side. The other arm was propped across the open wound on his chest so that his index finger pointed toward the opening of the tent.

Reilly shuddered involuntarily and looked away – the finger seemed to be pointing directly at her. It seemed very personal and made her feel that somehow she was being accused. Trying to ignore these feelings, she turned her attention back to her immediate surroundings.

She closed her eyes, tried to picture it – what had happened? And why? It was bizarre, sinister even – but what did it mean? And the pointing finger – what was it pointing at? The police? Some other unknown person? A clue? It could mean anything. Trying to push these unanswerable questions from her head, Reilly began her examination of the scene.

She pulled her flashlight from her bag and moved in closer to the body, running the beam across it to reveal the little details that could often get lost in the overall picture.

Upon closer inspection of the victim's face she saw that he was actually quite good-looking, with a mop of dark hair, athletic build, and strong white teeth. Teeth weren't normally the first thing she noticed in a situation like this, but this guy's mouth was set in a grimace, gums exposed.

She ran the flashlight over his face; there were no signs of trauma, no marks or injuries here other than the animal bite marks on the neck; just that face, teeth clenched, eyes locked shut in a death mask of horror. A streak of maggot-infested vomit ran down the front of his shirt.

Reilly clicked off her flashlight and sat back on her heels. Who would do something like this? Besides the gunshot wound, the odd posing, twisted grimace and pointed finger seemed to be an attempt to deliver some macabre message. But what?

Could this be drug related? It seemed the mountains were a long-time favorite amongst Dublin drug lords for dumping bodies. But this particular body hadn't just been dumped; it had been painstakingly *exhibited*. Why?

A quiet voice disturbed her reverie. 'Reilly?'

She looked around and saw a bleary-eyed Chris Delaney outside the tent. 'Hey.'

He paused and running his gaze over the body, seemed to shudder. 'The face ... it's beyond weird, isn't it? Wonder what the hell that's all about?'

'I have no idea.'

'Poor bastard; the rats really did a job on his neck.'

She nodded. 'Looks like he's been up here a few days.'

'Kennedy reckons it'll just be another gangland dump but I'm not so sure. Those guys don't waste time setting up tents and camping gear; usually they just toss the body and leave.'

'That's what I thought. It doesn't feel like a dump to me.'

'Well, I've certainly never seen anything like it before. Find anything significant?'

'Not yet. I've not long arrived and the rest of the team are still on their way.'

Chris lurked in the opening. 'Well, we've got the hikers who discovered the scene to interview.' He glanced at his notebook. 'A couple in their thirties. They found the body earlier while out walking the dog.'

And compromised our crime scene, Reilly thought, irritably.

Then she paused, trying not to betray her annoyance. 'Why don't you go talk to them? The crew and I will process this and then we can compare notes later?'

He nodded. 'Sounds good. Anything of interest we'll let you know.'

When he left Reilly's gaze returned to the scene. She was thinking, scanning, looking for anything out of the ordinary. Her eyes fixed on an un-smoked cigar sitting on a camping stool. Well, if this was gangland, somebody involved certainly enjoyed smoking the odd Corona.

Her reverie was interrupted once more by the arrival of the GFU team at the tent, their kit boxes in their hands.

'Bloody hell,' Gary exclaimed.

Lucy said nothing but her face was pale.

'Hey, guys.' Reilly was suddenly struck by how inexperienced they were, how unprepared to deal with this level of decay, and felt a pang for them. She thought fast. 'Gary, you help me with the body. Lucy, you start with the ...' The younger girl's eyes seemed to be fixed on the squirming maggots. 'Lucy?' She finally looked away, her eyes still glazed by the nastiness she had just been confronted with. 'You start processing the camp area.' Reilly indicated the array of expensive camping equipment. 'It seems there was food being prepared at the time as the stove is on but the gas has run out – I'd like to know what was being cooked amidst all of this.'

Lucy finally shook herself back to life. 'Right. I'll get on it.'

Reilly watched her as she crouched beside the stove, set her bag down and snapped on some gloves before pulling out her flashlight. *Good girl,* Reilly thought, *you're learning fast.*

She turned back to Gary. He looked far more composed and was already scanning the area. 'Seems there are two sleeping bags inside. We have some officers sweeping the area in case there's a second victim, but there's also a chance this guy was sleeping with the enemy so to speak, so I want this tent picked through with a fine-toothed comb.'

'No problem.'

'We've got to work quickly,' she told him. 'This guy's been dead a while and you don't need me to point out that our scene is degrading fast.'

MEANWHILE, the couple who'd found the body, Mark and Rebecca Ward, were being looked after by a couple of uniforms. They sat in the back of one of two four-by-four vehicles that were able to negotiate the rocky trail from the forestry road. The Jeeps had now become an assembly point for ferrying people to and from the crime scene. The couple's Yorkshire Terrier, Banjo, sat between them on the back seat. Mark's fingers were looped through his collar, in order to rub his neck and keep hold of him at the same time.

Chris was glad of the opportunity to talk to them so soon after the discovery. Normally by the time reality kicked in and people had time to consider the enormity of what had happened, the less helpful their witness statements were, and the more susceptible to outside influence they became.

'Hey there. Mark and Rebecca, isn't it?' he said, sitting down in the front seat while facing into the back between the headrests. 'I'm Detective Delaney, and this is Detective Kennedy. We'd really like to ask you a few questions if you're up for it.'

They both looked pale and tired as they acknowledged the detectives. Rebecca's entire body was shaking, and Mark raised his eyes with a small nod. Someone had given them blankets and she was trying to pull hers in as tight as she could to stop the shaking, as if it was the temperature and not the shock of seeing and smelling the rotting corpse of Gerry Watson that was making her shiver.

Kennedy stood outside the open passenger door and took out his notebook. 'So, probably best if you just tell us how it happened from beginning to end, or what you can remember, anyway.'

Chris patted Rebecca's arm. 'Talking about it will let it out, help get it off your mind.'

'Yeah, OK.' Mark spoke first. 'We hike this area all the time and often bring Banjo up here at weekends. He loves charging around in the undergrowth and you can't let him off the lead anywhere near our house.'

Banjo looked up, his ears twitching at the mention of words 'walk' and 'lead'. His tongue lolled happily at the side of his mouth as he licked his already moist nose. If it hadn't been for that, Chris thought, the body would probably still lie undiscovered now. 'We always stay on the forestry road, because most of the smaller trails up the hill are muddy this time of year.'

Taking up the story, Rebecca rubbed Banjo on the head. 'We were just on the way back to the picnic area where our car was parked. I couldn't see Banjo anywhere so we called him but there was no sign. Mark started walking back the way we came and shouting louder.'

'He usually comes when he's called,' Mark added. 'I heard him bark and saw some movement amongst the ferns up the hill, so I shouted again. I thought he was probably chasing something or digging in a rat hole, there are so many smells up here he goes crazy.'

Rebecca smiled a little. 'We were just laughing at him as we made our way through the ferns and it was only when we reached the top of the hill where the ground flattens off that we saw the tent.'

She pointed to edge of the clearing two hundred yards from where the Mountain Rescue Jeeps had forced their way through. 'We didn't want to go over at first,' she added.

'Why not?'

'Well, it was so early, I didn't want to go barging over and interrupt anyone's privacy. I called Banjo again, he was sniffing around the side of the tent and then he cocked his leg on it.'

'I was mortified,' Rebecca said, looking less pale as a slight blush crossed her cheeks. 'Little did I know ...'

'Go on,' Chris urged.

She continued speaking. 'I called him again, this time more firmly and walked over with the lead, it was then I—' She stared at the back of the seat and tears pooled in her eyes. 'When I saw the man's legs in the doorway I just thought he was asleep.' She shook her head, and Mark patted her hand for reassurance.

'When I reached Becky's side and saw Banjo sniffing the guy's shoes I thought it was sort of funny. That was before she started to scream.' He paused and looked away, reliving the memory. 'I ran over and saw rats at the guy's neck ... maggots moving ... and then the smell.' Mark rubbed the side of his face as if trying to remove any lingering traces of the deathly air he'd breathed. 'Then I threw up,' he added, somewhat ashamed.

Always the blokes, Chris thought, wryly.

Reliving the scene was obviously taking its toll on Rebecca and she was sobbing gently. 'What do you think happened to him? I mean, that look on his face ... and the way his arm was pointing ...'

'It's too early to make any assumptions at this stage,' Chris soothed, cringing slightly as he knew he sounded like a press officer throwing out sound bites to dodge the question. But the truth was there *was* no room for speculation.

Kennedy studied his notes. 'Can I just clarify a point before we go any further? You said, when you first saw the tent – quote: "I didn't want to go barging over and interrupt anyone's privacy." So you thought there was more than one person, correct?'

'Well, yes,' Mark confirmed. 'When I said that I just meant that I naturally assumed it would be more than one, what with the size of the tent and the amount of gear lying around.'

'Did you see anybody else in or around the campsite, or pass by anyone going to or from the scene?' he queried.

'No, there was nobody else around; we didn't meet another soul on the walk. Sometimes you might, but it was so early, not to mention it's a pretty unknown area round here, most people are drawn to the more popular walks like Glendalough.'

'How did you alert the authorities?' Chris continued.

'I had my phone but there's no signal up here so we went back to the car as quick as we could and drove until we got one.'

Rebecca spoke while looking in the direction of the white illuminated forensic tent, which looked so out of place in the surroundings. 'After we called in the report and gave directions, we traveled back up to the car park to wait for the first officers to arrive like the lady on the phone told us. Then, when they arrived it was dark and Mark showed them the way.'

He nodded. 'I actually wasn't sure if I'd find the trail again so I brought Banjo hoping he'd lead the way back in.'

'Looks like we have a police dog in the makings,' Kennedy quipped, reaching in to pet the terrier's head, but Banjo quickly flashed a sideways snap at his hand.

'Feck me!' he cried, massaging his hand, even though no contact had been made.

'Banjo! Oh, I'm so sorry.' Rebecca said, coloring.

'Don't worry, Detective Kennedy often has that effect on people too,' Chris said wryly, hoping to relieve the tension. 'Thanks for that; I think we have all we need for now. You've been most helpful and here's my card just in case anything else springs to mind.' The couple looked relieved and he and Kennedy shook their hands, all the while trying to keep out of range of the little terrier. 'I'll get one of the Mountain Rescue guys to drop you back to your car.'

He knew that there was in reality very little light these people could shed on what had unfolded here; once again, there would be no quick and easy solution.

And until they could find one, this misfortunate camper was simply another addition to the city's burgeoning crime statistics.

12

D arkness had fallen and Mike Steel was just about to settle down to a well-earned cold beer when he heard the scream.

'Goddamnit!' He got up from the sofa and headed down the hallway toward the source. 'What's going on?' he grunted, switching on the overhead light.

'Monstaw – in the closet,' Jessica announced, the 3-year-old's fluffy blond head barely visible above the bedclothes. Her blue eyes were wide with fear as she pointed to one corner of the small room.

Sighing, Mike shook his head from side to side. 'Jess, honey, we talked about this before, didn't we?' He went to the closet and opened the doors. 'There are no monsters in there – look, it's just your clothes and your toys, nothing else.'

The toddler shook her head in defiance. 'See shaw him too!' she insisted, pointing her stubby finger accusingly at her sister in the bed opposite.

'Did she now?' Mike raised an eyebrow at her. 'Reilly? What's going on?'

'Look, I'm sorry, OK?' Reilly shrugged guiltily, her eyes

downcast. 'I was trying to get to sleep, and she was driving me nuts, yacking on and on ... So, I told her that if she didn't shut up, the monsters would come out and get her.'

Mike's jaw tightened. 'Christ, I don't need this shit ...'

He sat at the side of Jessica's bed and gathered her into his arms before softly stroking her downy curls.

'Want Mommy,' the little girl moaned into his chest.

Me too, Reilly thought, sadly.

'Don't want the monstaw to get me, Daddy.'

'Hey, nobody's going to get you, OK? Whose gonna get past a big, strong guy like me?' At this, a faint smile appeared on Jessica's face. 'Anyway, remember what I said before, OK? There are no monsters in that closet. Your sister was just playing tricks on you. And your mom should be back soon.'

'I was only joking,' Reilly said. 'Sorry, Jess.'

'OK,' Apparently satisfied, Jessica nodded before yawning widely.

'Now, try and get some sleep, honey. Your sister has to be up early for school in the morning and she needs to rest too.'

'Will you stay with me, Daddy?' Jessica's eyes were huge as she stared mournfully up at him.

'Of course I will,' Mike held her close and continued to rub her back, hoping to soothe her into slumber. 'I'll stay as long as you like.'

For a short while, there was silence in the small bedroom as they waited for Jess to go to sleep.

'Look, try not to scare your little sister like that, OK?' Mike whispered when the toddler eventually drifted off. 'The last monster in the closet was there almost six months before he left and I can't be dealing with a new one right now. I've got too much going on, honey.'

Duly chastened, Reilly hung her head. 'I know, I'm sorry.'

She *was* sorry too but Jess was really starting to get on her nerves with her stupid singing and dancing and endless jabbering about nothing. Reilly wished she could have a room of her own, but their house was just too small for that, and although she wasn't supposed to know it, anyone could tell that money was tight.

'Dad?' she asked. 'You said Mom will be home soon – is that true?'

Mike sighed and Reilly's face fell, realizing that he'd only said this to make Jess feel better. Cassie, their mom, sometimes went away for a little while before reappearing again. When this happened, nobody ever seemed to know where she'd gone or when she'd be coming back. But, according to Mike, Cassie just got sad sometimes and needed to be by herself. 'I certainly hope so, sweetheart.'

There was silence in the room for a moment.

'Hey, I know Jess can be an almighty pain in the ass sometimes, but don't forget she's only three and she doesn't mean any harm.' Carefully lifting the now-sleeping Jessica out of his arms, he lay her back down and gently covered her with the blankets.

'I know.'

Mike then moved to sit on the edge of Reilly's bed. 'So, from now on, promise you'll help me convince your little sister that there are no monsters and she's got nothing to worry about, OK?'

'OK.'

A few minutes later, when her dad had left the room, Reilly was just about to nod off when she heard an all-too-familiar voice. 'Wiley?' her little sister called out in a tentative whisper. 'Wiley? Are you awake?'

'What now?' she groaned, turning her back to her. She couldn't believe that Jess was awake again. Two minutes ago, when her dad had left the room she looked to be dead to the world.

'Are there really no monstaws? No monstaws in the whole wide world?'

In the darkness, Reilly rolled her eyes, wishing her little sister would just shut the hell up. Then remembering that her dad had asked for her help, she spoke softly. 'Yeah, Jess, Dad was right. Just go back to sleep, OK?' She pulled the bedclothes tightly around her and closed her eyes. 'There really are no monsters – none in the whole wide world.'

13

T *here are no monsters ...*
At the sound of her alarm, Reilly's head shot up off the pillow, her brain still fuzzy. Almost instinctively, her gaze rested on the closet at the foot of the bed. But it was OK. She was no longer ten years old and sleeping in the room she shared with Jess back home in Marin County. Instead she was an adult, sleeping in her own bed, or at least, trying to sleep in this excuse for an apartment she was leasing for crazy money.

And there were no monsters. Not in the closet anyway.

The dream – the one of her and Jess as kids – she hadn't had that one in a while. Afterward, it was the scene that kept coming back to her, the one she kept replaying over and over in her head and in her sleep – the one in which she'd promised her sister that there were no monsters, no bad guys, and that no one could harm her.

She bit her lip. If only they knew.

Reilly got up out of bed, unsettled that the dreams were starting to come back with increasing frequency. Maybe she should think about taking the advice Dr Kyle had given before she left California about seeing someone here. But she was fine, wasn't she? Anyway, she really didn't need – or want – to try and explain it all to some strange Dublin shrink who knew nothing about her or her family, and probably wouldn't be able to understand her fears anyhow. As it was, Reilly could barely understand them herself.

She went into the kitchen and set about grinding some coffee beans, unwilling to let thoughts of her past get her down. Measuring out exactly a tablespoon, she took a deep breath, and allowed the rich aroma of freshly ground beans to fill her senses. Some people liked to grind them the night before as a timesaver, but Reilly knew that once the beans were ground there was a lot more surface area exposed to the air and this was how much of the flavor escaped, so what was the point?

No, Reilly was firmly of the belief that good coffee shouldn't be rushed and having poured in enough water for a single cup, she loaded the percolator and waited patiently for the grounds to pass through.

The reason she took it black wasn't (as Kennedy thought) because she was a health freak but simply because this was a sure-fire way of ruining good coffee. People who added sugar or anything else were just trying to mask stuff that was badly made.

She took a sip and almost immediately felt re-energized and ready for the day ahead. Last night had been another late one at the lab, but this morning she wanted to get there early to review the inventory and post-mortem report the ME's office would be sending over from the camper murder. Not that she could expect to find much – thanks to those dumbass hikers who'd trooped all over the place.

She had only been at the lab for a couple of minutes and

was casting an eye over some recent paperwork when she got a call from Karen Thompson.

'Hey, good hearing from you,' Reilly said in greeting. 'Unless you're calling about a delay, that is.' Her voice was light and she knew the woman wouldn't take offense.

'Actually, I hate to bother you with this,' the pathologist replied, tentatively, 'and normally I wouldn't ask but ...'

'What's up, Karen?' From her tone, Reilly immediately knew that something wasn't right. Damn, she really hoped it wasn't a delay.

'Well, it's from the post-mortem I did on that camper ...'

'Sure. Good timing, actually – it seems we've just got a positive ID on him: Gerry Watson, twenty-six years old, from the Dundrum area,' Reilly told her, reading from the file. 'No criminal links that we know of but Delaney and Kennedy are still checking that out. I'll fax through the details for your records as soon as I can. What have you got?'

'Well, there's a particular sample here I want you to take a closer look at. I have a sneaking suspicion as to what it is, but I'd like to make sure before I finalize my report.' Reilly raised an eyebrow. Karen's usually assured tone sounded very off and she wondered what was up. 'Now, I know you're very busy, but if you could fast-track this one for me, I'd appreciate it.'

'Of course. So did you find something interesting?'

'You could say that,' the doctor's voice was grave. 'Official cause of death was from the gunshot wound of course,' Karen reiterated, then paused again before continuing. 'It's what I found in the vomit and stomach contents that I'd like your opinion on. It's undigested and ... well, I think it might be better if I just let you take a look for yourself.'

'OK, I was expecting something from the lab today on this anyway, but do you want to send your sample over this morning and we can compare? We inventoried a frying pan from there that had been recently used – our guys are looking into what had been cooked. I'll get them to take a look at yours too, and between us we should be able to find out what they were eating.'

Karen gulped. 'To be honest, Reilly, I think I already have a pretty good idea.'

'No WAY. No bloody *way*. That's sick!' Kennedy paced around the incident room, his face purple with disgust. In his hand was the report the GFU had just faxed over to them. 'It's sick, that's what it is.'

Chris sat at his desk just as stunned, telephone receiver still in hand.

'Reilly, are you absolutely sure?' he asked, knowing that the question was pointless, never mind redundant. He'd known her just long enough to realize that when it came to forensic analysis Reilly Steel was not the type to make mistakes. Still, he'd phoned her office in the vain hope that this *was* a mistake, or that there had been some explicable mix-up.

'I'm absolutely sure,' she told him. 'And Karen is too. She had her suspicions, that's why she had us double-check the sample this morning. It is what it is, Chris. The evidence doesn't lie.'

Chris pictured Gerry Watson's body at the campsite, pictured the used frying pan on the stove. 'But how?' he asked, hoping that she at least might be able to make sense of it. 'And why?'

'I guess we'd have to ask the killer that question,' she replied, grimly. 'Karen's still putting the finishing touches to the post-mortem report – she just needed clarification from us on this first – so you should know more soon. We're running further tests on the sample so we can find out exactly what was on the menu.'

Considering the discovery, Chris was astonished at the dearth of emotion in her voice. Reilly was discussing this like it was just another piece of evidence, something ordinary but curious, like that unidentified paint and hair sample she'd found before. A stark contrast to him and Kennedy, who upon reading the report had been so shocked and repulsed it was a few minutes before either of them could speak.

'Reilly,' he had to ask. 'Have you ever found ... I mean would you have come across something ...' his throat dry, he swallowed hard, '... something like this before?'

He could almost sense her shrug on the other end of the line. 'A couple of times at Quantico and once back home. The FBI did a lot of work with the German Government a couple of years back on that guy Armin Meiwes. Ever heard of him?'

The name didn't immediately ring a bell with Chris.

'He put an ad out on the Internet for a willing victim, some guy responded – wholeheartedly, apparently. Either he genuinely liked the idea, or maybe he didn't think Meiwes was being serious. It took the courts ages to get a conviction on Meiwes, and from what I heard, the investigation was so disturbing some of the German cops needed lifelong counseling after it.'

Delaney swallowed. *Now* he remembered. 'Christ. Let's hope we don't have something like that on our hands,' he finally responded. He didn't want to even contemplate the media hysteria, or the general public's reaction to this one.

'Cannibalism is not as uncommon as you think, Detective,' Reilly continued. 'And in this line of work, you eventually come across all sorts.'

14

T he lecture hall was full but not a soul moved. Their eyes were all fixed on the man at the front of the room. Daniel Forrest cut a slight figure; his thick, dark hair was turning gray at the sides, but behind his glasses his eyes burned with a fierce intensity. He moved restlessly around the stage as he talked.

'Serial killers are among *the* most reckless of murderers. Their need to keep killing far outweighs their need to be cunning or discreet. In fact, what allows most serial killers to keep killing is that their carelessness is dwarfed by police and investigative incompetence.' Forrest looked up as a low ripple of laughter filled the lecture hall. 'Don't believe me?' he said, cocking an eyebrow at his audience. 'Let me tell you the story of Henry Louis Wallace, and see if it's something you recruits can learn from.'

As he spoke, he flicked through a series of pictures on the projector.

'When he was arrested on 4 February 1994, in Charlotte, North Carolina, Henry Louis Wallace had already raped and strangled to death five young black women. Each of his victims worked in the fast-food industry and, more significantly, each knew Wallace and was a friend of his girlfriend. In fact, his name appeared in the address books of several of the deceased.' He paused and gazed out at the sea of rapt faces.

'In addition, at the time of his arrest, Wallace had a burglary record and a prior charge of raping a woman at gunpoint. Add to that a connection to all five murder victims. Pretty compelling, you'd think?' He looked around the room and waited for the nods from the eager students.

'Unfortunately for Wallace's next four murder victims, all this meant nothing to the Charlotte-Mecklenburg police and the prosecutor's office – they released Wallace from custody that same day. Wallace had not, after all, been arrested for murder. He had been arrested for allegedly shoplifting at a mall.'

Another low murmur ran through the room.

'How could this happen, you may ask? Because at the time of Wallace's arrest on the shoplifting charge, the police didn't consider the string of murders of the young black women related,' Forrest continued. 'They had no significant leads on any of them. Emboldened by his release, Wallace killed again just sixteen days later, and would continue to kill until he was finally arrested a full two *years* later, at which point he confessed to eleven murders in all.'

Forrest returned to the podium and rested his hands lightly on it. He had no need to refer to his notes. 'On 29 January 1997, Henry Lewis Wallace was given nine death sentences and is currently on death row in Raleigh, North Carolina. One of the reasons the police department gave for its inability to catch him was its inexperience with investigating serial murders.'

He paused and looked up. 'Now here's the interesting bit.

Early in 1994, when the rate of murders in the area was at an all-time high, the department sought the help of the FBI, who erroneously declared that the rash of murders in the area was not the work of a serial killer. Why? Because Wallace didn't fit the profile: He was black, whereas most serial murderers are white. Also, serial killers are expected to kill strangers, whereas Wallace killed friends and co-workers.' Daniel smiled at his audience. 'Needless to say, I was not working on behalf of the Bureau at the time,' he added, and again, the students laughed.

'So, what's the point I'm trying to make?' He paused and waited for a response.

Finally a hand shot up. 'Don't make assumptions?'

Forrest's face lit up. 'Exactly. When it comes to serial murders, there are no hard and fast rules or answers. In fact, don't presume to know *anything* when It comes to these people. Of course, to a certain degree we need to work from an existing framework – that's why they call us profilers – and sometimes the profile fits just fine.'

He moved out from behind the podium to the front of the stage to get his final point across. 'Most of the time, serial killers are reckless, haphazard individuals who just enjoy killing. On the other hand, some of them are extremely cunning, have a set plan, a point to make. Who can tell which you might be dealing with? But what you have to remember, what links them all, is that ultimately they make mistakes. What we need to do, people, is spot those mistakes when we see them.' He pointed up at the screen behind him, upon which was displayed a blown-up mug shot of Wallace. 'Don't make the same error the Charlotte-Mecklenburg police did when dealing with Henry Lewis Wallace. Recognize those mistakes, those tiny seemingly insignificant mistakes, the things that, in the end, will help us find our killer.'

Daniel switched off the projector and shuffled his notes. 'That's it for today, guys. See you next week.'

As the students headed toward the exits, chatting excitedly to each other, Forrest made his escape through a side door.

One of the secretaries waylaid him in the hallway as he returned to his office. 'Eight messages for you, Agent Forrest, all of them urgent,' she said, thrusting the slips of paper at him.

'Is there any other kind?' he replied with a sigh, taking another sip of coffee from the paper cup in his hand.

She gave a polite smile and hurried off down the hall.

Forrest pushed open the door to his office, pitched his empty coffee cup into a nearby bin, and sat down behind his large oak desk. The office was immaculate, shelves lined with books and case files, a couple of specimen jars, one small shelf of family photos.

He ran a hand through his hair and flicked through the messages. Most got just a cursory glance, but when he got to the fourth piece of paper, Daniel paused, and a look of surprised pleasure crossed his face. Checking his watch, he picked up the phone and, peering at the paper for reference, dialed a number.

'GFU, Reilly Steel speaking.'

'Good afternoon, Reilly,' Daniel said warmly. 'How are you? I just got your message. Is Dublin treating you well?'

'Daniel, hey, thanks for getting back to me so soon.'

'You're welcome. What can I do for you?'

'Well, I wanted to talk to you about a case if you have a moment ...'

Daniel's door opened and his assistant stuck her head around it. 'Agent Forrest? Dr Williams is here to see you—' He held up five fingers – a plea for five minutes. The woman nodded and withdrew.

'Of course, Reilly. What's up?'

'What would you say if I told you there was an apparently coincidental Freudian connection between two different crime scenes and that we'd found a cigar at a third?'

Daniel sat forward, intrigued. 'Sometimes a cigar is just a cigar,' he said, quietly.

'That's what I thought. Not so coincidental anymore, is it?'

He said nothing for a moment, and wondered if the Irish authorities had any real idea how lucky they were to have Reilly Steel working alongside them. She'd always been unbelievably smart, and had made sense of what was in reality a completely obscure connection. And so typical of Reilly to use a psychological challenge to get him interested.

'It's clever, that's what it is – clever and very subtle,' he said eventually. Although perhaps not so subtle to someone like him.

Sometimes a cigar is just a cigar. One of Sigmund Freud's most famous quotations, and one that served to poke fun at his own self-confessed obsession with all things phallic. While Daniel was extremely familiar with the works of the famous psychologist (in his line of work he couldn't *but* be familiar) he was decidedly impressed at how Reilly had so easily grasped the cigar's significance. But of course, the girl had always had excellent instincts, hadn't she?

'How did you know?' he asked her.

'We found identical trace evidence at two otherwise unconnected scenes – that provided our first connection. In addition, one of them had a copy of Freud's *Interpretation of Dreams* on the bedside, while the other – a supposed suicide – left a quote from Freud as a farewell note.'

'Coincidental?' Daniel threw it out to her as a challenge, despite knowing that Reilly was too clever to fall for something that simple.

'You sound like the detectives here,' she said, and he could hear the smile in her voice. 'A couple of days ago we again picked up similar trace matter at the third scene, and I knew without question that all three had to be linked. But I still needed to know for sure, so I took another look at the inventory for the most recent site, this time actively looking for something Freud-related. The cigar stood out.'

'I didn't know you were that familiar with Freud—'

'I'm not,' she responded quickly, 'but the cigar is a classic phallic symbol now, isn't it? You know, thanks to Bill and Monica ...'

Daniel had to smile, he'd been forgetting how influential popular culture could sometimes be.

Reilly continued, 'When I researched it further, I came across Freud's cigar quote, and figured that we'd found the killer's calling card – the Freudian connection. *Sometimes a cigar is just a cigar.* Not this time.'

'Good work,' he said, admiringly.

'Maybe, but that's about as far as we've got,' Reilly said, her tone growing anxious. 'We've got a solid investigative team here, and I know we can find this guy, but without specialist help, I'm not sure we can do it before he kills again.'

'What's your pattern, your timeline?'

'Three – possibly four – killings, one a double homicide, all within the last ten days. One body took a while to discover so it's difficult to pin down a definitive timeline, but that's a lot for this town and it's got the authorities spooked. The media are circling, and while they haven't got hold of any connection just yet ...' Forrest rocked back in his chair, nodding as he listened. 'You know how these things go, Daniel. If he's using a calling card, then it's likely he's toying with us, testing us. It's also likely he'll start to escalate soon, and when he does ...'

The remainder of her sentence trailed off. 'Look, the

reason I'm calling is because we need outside help – fast. As I said, people are getting nervous around here; the force have limited experience with this kind of thing, and while they usually work with behaviorists from the UK, I've convinced them that you're the best man for the job – probably the *only* man for the job.' She paused. 'Would you consult with us on this? There's no one here remotely experienced or qualified enough – actually, I don't think there's anyone other than you who *could* provide insight into something this complex.'

'Well, you're right, of course,' Daniel joked, but then his tone grew serious. 'But I don't know, Reilly. I've got a lot going on at the moment. Anyway, I'm not even sure if there's a precedent for my coming in on something like this—'

'It would only be on a consultancy basis, we don't expect you to travel here or anything.' She spoke quickly. 'I know it sounds presumptuous, but I've already spoken with the relevant people here and they're going through the motions as we speak. The top brass want this guy found and stopped as soon as possible, particularly before the public get wind of it.' At this, there was a note of resignation in her tone. 'But still, there's no point in us trying to arrange it unless you're interested in helping. Frankly, Daniel, we don't have any time to waste.'

Still in two minds, Daniel sat forward in his chair, his face thoughtful. 'How about you send me what you've got so far then maybe we can decide whether having me on board would be of any help?'

'Believe me, it would.'

His curiosity had already got the better of him. OK, so he was busy with a multitude of government agency stuff at the moment, and he had his weekly lectures here at the Academy, but this case excited him more than he cared to admit. Not to mention that he owed it to Reilly, didn't he? After all she'd been through, he owed the poor kid something at least.

He sat up straight, his voice suddenly decisive. 'All right then, I'll see what I can manage,' he told her. 'Do whatever you have to do to get the paperwork sorted at your end and I'll do what I can from here.'

'I appreciate this, Daniel – *we* really appreciate it,' she replied, the relief in her voice palpable. 'I'll get the relevant people here to iron out all the technicalities.'

His door opened again and an overweight man in a long blue overcoat poked his head around the door. Daniel waved his visitor to a chair in front of his desk. 'Send me what you've got, Reilly, I'll have a look over it, and then we can talk.'

But based on what little information she'd already given him, Daniel was already hooked. A killer using Freud as his calling card? What self-respecting profiler *wouldn't* be interested?

15

'Shhe's done what?' Kennedy was so outraged that he put his coffee down.

'That's what O'Brien said. Apparently, he's some profiler from the FBI training program in Quantico – the boss says he's considered one of the top guys in America.' Chris didn't seem bothered by it, but Kennedy was already up on his soapbox.

'Why don't they bring the whole shaggin' FBI over here and just pension us off? Or the CIA and Special Forces too while they're at it.'

Chris shook his head. 'I think you're overreacting.'

'Do you now?' Kennedy was boiling, ready for a fight.

But for once, Chris wasn't in the mood to roll over. He closed the file he was trying to read and spun his chair around to face his partner directly. 'Yeah, I do actually. I sure as hell have never worked a case like this before, and I'm willing to bet my life savings you haven't either.' He looked challengingly at Kennedy. 'Any recent experience with Freud or cannibalism you might like to share with me?'

Kennedy looked disgruntled. 'That's not the point.'

'Then what is?'

'The point *is* ...' he replied, adding emphasis with his stubby nicotine-stained finger, '... the point is we don't need a load of Yankee know-it-alls coming over here and telling us how to do our jobs!'

Chris couldn't help but smile at the outrage his partner managed to muster about anything that didn't fit into his narrow view of the world. 'So would it make you feel any better if I told you he *isn't* coming over here?' He's just going to be acting as a consultant and helping out with the profiling. According to the boss, Reilly's the one who'll be dealing with him.'

'Oh. Right.' Kennedy snorted, his annoyance somewhat assuaged. 'Well ... of course *you* would think this is a good idea; you already think the sun shines out of Steel's backside.'

Chris didn't rise to the bait. Instead, he turned back around and busied himself in his work. As usual, Kennedy was overstating things. He was more receptive to Reilly's avant-garde way of thinking, that was all. Still, there was no doubt that the recent brief glimpses of her personality he had grasped intrigued him and there was a guardedness about her that made him wonder what else was going on in that sharp mind.

Not that they all had enough to be thinking about at the moment. This investigation was much bigger than any of them could ever have imagined. A serial killer was a deeply unsettling prospect at any time, and he could completely understand why O'Brien would want this nipped in the bud as soon as possible.

There was even some mutterings about trying to get Jack Gorman to come back early from his anniversary cruise; something that Chris was sure wouldn't go down at all well with the older forensic investigator. Personally, he saw no need; as far as he was concerned Reilly and her team were doing a fine job and if it weren't for her, they might not even have made the link between the killings. And getting this FBI guy on board had to be a coup, despite what Kennedy might think.

In the background, his partner was still muttering away to himself about 'bloody interference' but Chris knew it was mostly bluster. At the end of the day Kennedy, like himself, couldn't deny that this was way beyond their limited experience. They needed all the help they could get.

REILLY WAS busy working in her lab, oblivious to the commotion her request for external help had caused. In truth, she'd been somewhat taken aback by Inspector O'Brien's ready agreement to her suggestion about bringing a profiler on board – particularly one that the force hadn't already worked with.

Still, she knew she'd scored some brownie points by connecting all three cases in the first place, and having already got Chris Delaney and Karen Thompson on side, Reilly suspected the top brass would have little choice but to bow to her demands. The authorities just didn't know what they were dealing with, and in the meantime these grotesque murders would undoubtedly continue. O'Brien was first and foremost a political animal, and Reilly suspected the guy wanted such a situation dealt with as soon as possible – and definitely before the press began baying for blood (and subsequently the head of the Minister for Justice).

With Daniel on the case, surely they would be able to make some kind of breakthrough, and something would emerge that would allow them to get ahead of the killer – find that one mistake, and use it against him.

That morning, she had her team assembled for a briefing, the files from all three cases spread out on the table. It was time to expand their horizons and maybe even find something she herself might have missed.

'So, who did their homework?' she asked.

Almost inevitably, Gary was the first to reply. He pushed his glasses up on his nose and stepped forward. 'Sigmund Freud, the father of psychoanalysis, was born on the 6th May 1856, in a small town called—'

Reilly cut him off. 'The biog is great and, yes, it is important for you guys to know a little about his background, but how is he relevant to our case?'

Gary looked disappointed and fell silent.

'Because you told us there was a link?' Lucy said, tentatively.

'Actually you're right, Lucy – that's the problem.' As they all gazed at her, Reilly explained further. 'We know there is a Freudian link – the book, the quote, the cigar – but we don't know what it means. *That's* the problem.'

'You mean the killer is trying to tell us something, but we don't know what it is?' Lucy suggested.

'Yes.'

'So it's sort of like a game of cat and mouse and he wants us to catch him,' Rory wondered.

'I read that somewhere, too,' Lucy added, nodding at him.

Reilly pursed her lips. 'Not necessarily. Serial killers can be highly organized, though they clearly have a disturbance in the way their personality functions. So while they typically have an antisocial personality disorder, they aren't actually mentally ill,' she explained.

'So they're weird but they're not crazy?'

'That's one way of putting it, Lucy.'

Rory wore his usual serious expression. 'So if he doesn't

want to be caught, why the clues? Why not just be as careful as possible and leave us nothing?'

'It usually comes from a psychopathic need to share. They are tremendously excited by what they do, but they can hardly go down to the pub and tell people about it. So, by leaving us little clues – just enough to attract our attention, but not enough to give themselves away – they can reassure themselves that someone is thinking about them.'

Gary peered at the crime-scene photos and moved them around on the table top, studying hard.

'What are you thinking?' she asked him.

'Well, I'd imagine you'd have a lot more experience with this kind of thing than we do but I read that serial killers usually have a *modus operandi*, and that it will give you clues as to how they are thinking.'

'True.' Reilly couldn't deny that he was right; she did know a lot more about this particular subject than she cared to admit.

'So what's this guy's MO?'

'Good question. Anybody got any ideas?'

'I thought Freud was all about sex,' Lucy said, eventually. 'Yet the Clare Ryan murder was the only one in which sex was directly involved.'

There was a long silence while they all absorbed what she had said.

'That wasn't about the sex itself though.' They all turned to look at Gary. 'It was about getting someone to do something they didn't want to do.' He rearranged the photos in a line. 'Look, the brother and sister – seems like the killer forced them into some kind of intercourse – then Justin was forced to shoot his sister.' He grabbed a photo of Gerry Watson and slid it across the desk. 'Then he made this guy – he made Gerry eat human flesh ...' Finally, he picked up the photo of Jim

Redmond. 'We thought this was a suicide, but didn't you say there was a homosexual angle?'

'We're waiting for the results, but it seems likely that Jim Redmond had anal intercourse not long before his death,' Reilly replied

'So what if that too was coerced? And then he was forced to commit suicide?'

She nodded; he had made a good point. 'Whether the sex was coerced or not we still don't know.'

The room fell silent for a moment, before finally Julius spoke. 'So what does all of that tell us? What is he going to do next? That's the point here, isn't it?'

'Exactly,' Reilly agreed. 'So we can help the investigation go from being reactive to proactive.' But based on what little they had, where did that take them? What would the killer do next?

16

I t was another dreary Dublin winter's day; the gunshot metal clouds hanging low, the air still and damp, a light drizzle coating the pavements and cars in a fine film of water.

As he climbed wearily from his car, Chris was wondering much the same thing as Reilly – where was this going? O'Brien was giving him and Kennedy hell over the slow rate of progress, and now the press, who up until then had been largely co-operative, were getting antsy, bemoaning their lack of a suspect on either the Clare Ryan killings or the Gerry Watson death. And Chris had a feeling that this afternoon might be when they started to turn up the heat.

He closed the car door, straightened his tie in the wing mirror, and buttoned his jacket. He always felt uncomfortable in a suit but this was no place to dress down.

Satisfied that he looked suitably grave, he began to walk slowly across the sodden grass of the cemetery, the drizzle forming a fine haze across the solemn location as he approached the mourners.

He hated being here by himself but Kennedy had cried off

citing a mountain of paperwork as an excuse. He could have asked Reilly of course, but somehow he couldn't bring himself to suggest it. Chances were she wouldn't be interested anyway; something like this was unlikely to give her anything that would help with the investigation. Although perhaps that was unfair; it wasn't as if she was cold or unsympathetic, more that she was totally focused on finding the answers that would help bring this thing to a conclusion.

He stopped twenty meters from the service, content to remain at a distance.

Bernard and Gillian Ryan stood closest to the graveside, the rest of the family behind them. Two open graves lay in front of them, and alongside them, two coffins waiting to be lowered in.

Chris was off to one side, half-hidden behind a tree, simply there to observe and provide a dignified police presence. As he watched Clare and Justin's parents, he was glad he had not been the one to deliver the news that their son was the other victim at the crime scene. He could only imagine what it must have been like for Bernard to have to identify his son, half of his head missing. Upon O'Brien's advice they'd decided to spare the family's anguish by not informing them of the sexual nature of the crime. Chris privately suspected this had less to do with compassion and much more with controlling the predictable media reaction to such a detail. And given the undeniably horrifying nature of that and the Watson case, he was greatly relieved.

The priest, head lowered, finished the prayers and said a quiet blessing over the coffins, before stepping back.

The mourners shuffled their feet, solemn beneath their black canopy of umbrellas, as the coffins were slowly lowered in, side by side.

Gillian Ryan was crying, her whole body shaking as she

was racked by violent sobs. Bernard had his arm around her and held her close, his face a stoic mask, but nothing anyone could do or say would be able to assuage the grief of a mother burying her two children. Chris looked at their mute figures and wondered how anyone found the mental strength to carry on at a time like this.

He shifted slightly, uncomfortable no matter what he did. His legs ached constantly now, whether he was exhausted at the end of a long shift or just out of bed in the morning.

The fact that he didn't get much sleep the night before didn't help either. Chris swallowed, the message he'd found at home on his answering machine after work still repeating in his head.

'It's me, Melanie,' his former girlfriend said, as if he wouldn't recognize her voice. Still it had been such a long time since he'd heard it, and caught off guard, he'd found himself rooted to the spot. 'I just... I'm not sure why I'm telling you this but I thought you should know,' she continued hesitantly. 'Peter's asked me to marry him and I've said yes. And ... well, I'm pregnant.' There was a brief pause, while Chris tried to figure out his reaction to the call, let alone the explanation for it. 'That's not the reason we're getting married though, it's just one of those things that happened....'

Chris walked over to the window and stared out, seeing nothing.

'Well, I just thought you should know,' she continued and the discomfort in her tone was almost palpable. 'It's silly really, but I suppose I just didn't want you to hear it somewhere else. Anyway.... I'd better go. Hope you're well.'

He'd stayed standing at the window for a long time afterwards, before going to the machine and resolutely deleting the message.

Now, trying to put the whole thing out of his mind, (what

did it matter?) he looked around and immediately saw them. Moving in like a troop of hyenas scenting a fresh carcass.

The press had arrived.

He stepped away, and hurried across the soft grass to intercept them.

'Detective Chris Delaney,' he said, holding up his badge. 'Can we give the family a little peace and privacy, please?'

A flurry of questions came at him all at once:

'Did they kill each other?'

'Was it a suicide pact?'

'Was anyone else involved?'

They were so loud and insistent that several of the mourners turned around to look at the commotion. Chris pushed through the reporters, trying to lead them away from the service. 'If you'll step over here, I'll be happy to answer any questions you might have.'

Reluctantly, almost like kids not wanting to stop playing a favorite game, the reporters followed him.

Once they were at a respectful distance, he turned back to face them. 'OK, one question at a time.'

'Is it true that Justin killed Clare then turned the gun on himself?' It was Morag Doyle, a well-connected crime reporter from the *Irish News*.

'The investigation is still on-going, but that is a strong possibility.'

A face he didn't know thrust to the front of the group – a young guy with thick curly hair and an eager expression. 'Isn't it true that there may be someone else involved? A third party who killed them both?' Chris groaned inwardly. He really hoped they'd managed to keep a lid on that one.

'We have no evidence of any third party, but we are still very much open to all possibilities.'

'Is there any link between this and the recent campsite killing?'

What the hell? Where were they getting this stuff? Chris wondered. There was no way anyone could have made a link between those two cases, unless ... He cursed whatever idiot in the department had been shooting his mouth off. There was always at least one uniform who after a few drinks in the pub on a Saturday night would forget himself and was happy to gossip to all and sundry. 'There are absolutely no similarities between the two crimes.' The lie tripped off his tongue surprisingly easily.

'What's it like working with the new GFU? She's quite a looker, isn't she?'

Chris finally smiled. It was the young guy again. 'Exactly to whom are you referring?' he shot back.

'Reilly Steel. I've heard her methods can be unpredictable to say the least.'

'And who might you be?'

'Ronan Cassidy, *Clarion*.'

'Well, Mr Cassidy, I'd have to say that the appearance of Ms Steel is neither here nor there, but her observations and her impressive record in the US are both hugely welcome on a case of this type.' But before Chris had even finished his sentence he'd lost his audience. The burial had, in the meantime, finished up, and the press hurried off to intercept the family before they left.

Morag Doyle patted Chris's arm as she walked by. 'Nice try, Delaney, but you'll have to offer a lot more than platitudes if you want to keep the attention of this lot.'

17

The waves were perfect, breaking left to right about thirty yards offshore, sweeping across the bay. Reilly lay on her board, waiting for the next set, rocking gently with the swell of the ocean. Here it comes ... She began to paddle hard, feeling the swell rise beneath her as she picked up speed and prepared to climb to her feet.

But something was wrong. No matter how hard she paddled she made no progress – the wave was growing and growing, looming over her, and she was stuck to her board, unable to climb to her feet, unable to ride with it.

She kicked harder, but still she made no progress. She looked up. A great wall of water, deep, dark green, was rising above her, the white curl of the breaker already starting to form as it bore down on her.

With a crash, the wave engulfed her, ripped her from her board, grabbed her and tumbled her over and over again, spinning and turning, desperate for air, choked and blinded by a roaring mountain of salt water and sand.

Reilly sat up in bed with a gasp, startled and disorientated. She stared around her apartment, unrecognizable in the darkness. The shrill ring of her phone broke through her nightmare. She grabbed it from the bedside table.

'Reilly Steel.'

'Reilly? Did I wake you?' Chris Delaney's calm tones brought her back to reality.

'Chris. What time is it?'

'Just after three. Sorry to wake you.'

She sat up and brushed her hair back out of her eyes, trying to push the images out of her mind, and focus on what he was saying. Another disturbing dream. This wasn't good.

'It's OK, I owe you one,' she said, trying to keep the tremor out of her voice. 'Did you get something on one of the cases?'

'Yes and no.' He paused and she could hear the weariness in his tone. 'We have another murder – and while I hate to jump the gun, this one looks weird enough to be our guy again.'

18

R eilly drove through the dark streets, her mind spinning, disorientated not only by the unfamiliarity of the wrong side of the road but also by the peculiarities of this case. She thought about everything they had on the murders so far. What was the thread, what was the killer thinking, trying to tell them? Or was there any point at all?

With the Freudian connection it seemed hard to imagine that there was not some other hidden message; the murders were all just too bizarre. But if the killer had struck again – and so soon – it meant they were still chasing, still simply reacting to the twisted whims of a madman.

It was easy to find the house. Four or five police cars lit up the night with their flashing blue lights, illuminating a small crowd of onlookers who, even at that time of night, had been drawn to the scene, hoping to catch a glimpse of something gruesome. No doubt the press wouldn't be far behind.

Reilly parked behind the barrier of police cars, grabbed her bag from the back of her car, and then stopped to look around.

The house was small, at the end of a quiet residential street. This was an older area of the city, probably inhabited by a lot of retired people – there were gardens full of rose bushes, neat lawns and old-fashioned floral curtains. Number forty-seven stood alone at the end of the cul-de-sac, a redbrick cottage with a well-tended garden, a black wrought-iron gate, and a narrow concrete path leading between the flower beds to the open front door.

The uniforms parted like waves to let her through. Chris was waiting at the door. 'Hey there,' he said in greeting. 'You were fast.'

She looked up at him and frowned. 'You look tired.'

'And why wouldn't I be? It's after four in the bloody morning.'

She followed him into the hallway, which was cool and quiet, almost serene after the melee outside. He pushed the door closed behind them, immediately shutting out the noise and the flashing blue lights. Two uniforms stood guard in front of a doorway.

'We caught a break on this one,' Chris began. 'Unlike the last, the scene is almost completely undisturbed.'

Reilly smelled the air. 'They've been dead a while though.'

He nodded. 'Uniform came round to follow up a lead on a missing person, peered through the letterbox, caught a whiff of that stench and called it in.' He led her toward the doorway. 'Once they got inside they took one look and figured it was one of ours.' Chris stopped at the door and nodded to the uniforms. They both reached up and covered their mouths with their hands, then one of them slowly pushed the door open.

The smell, already strong in the house, flowed out of the room like a wave. Fighting back the nausea, Reilly stepped forward slowly. A garish red light bathed the scene.

It was another bizarre tableau. The room was lit only by an electric fire, which produced stifling heat and had obviously contributed to the decomposition of the bodies. And decomposed they were, both bloated and sickly colored.

Reilly stood in the doorway, struggling not to gag from the stench. There were two people sitting at a table and despite the advanced state of decomposition, she could immediately see that one was elderly – a thin, frail, old woman with wispy silver hair. The other was also female, dressed in a white uniform, well built, and from first impressions looked to be in her mid-forties though at this point it was hard to tell.

Chris stood in the doorway, a troubled look on his face. 'According to the neighbors the victims are—'

Reilly put up a hand to cut him off. 'Give me a minute – let me just take a look without knowing anything, before the rest of them get here.'

He nodded. 'OK. Should I ...?' He indicated the door.

'If you wouldn't mind.'

He closed the door behind him, leaving Reilly alone with the bodies. She slowly circled the scene, the red light of the fire making her own shadow dance on the opposite wall, her senses wide open, just taking everything in.

There were no signs of trauma on the older woman, no stabs or gunshot wounds, no weapons, nothing to suggest cause of death. She didn't even look distressed. In fact, she had an almost peaceful expression, as though her death was a relief to her. Clad in her flower-print dress and white cardigan, she looked like a hundred other little old ladies that you'd see tottering around Dublin every day.

The younger woman was slumped over, leaning on the table, arms limp by her side, her dark hair draped across her face. The white clothes Reilly had noticed earlier looked on closer inspection to be a nurse's uniform, and she wore sensible rubber-soled shoes and no jewelry.

Despite the decomposition, Reilly could see that this woman had been killed by a gunshot to the head, at close range – just like Justin Ryan. But this time there seemed to be another gunshot wound, on her foot. What was that all about?

She stepped back a little, looked around and sighed. Once again it seemed that these victims were no criminals, no drug-dealing lowlifes whose illegal activities helped bring about their own demise. Instead, they looked to be just normal people living normal lives who'd been deliberately sought out to play a part in this unspeakable horror. Chris was right; the mere ordinariness of the victims suggested that this was likely their killer again.

Keeping this in mind, she scanned the room, searching for anything that would tie it to the other scenes. Anything obviously Freudian, or loosely related to Freud, anything at all.

After a few minutes more, her gaze fell on a nearby couch that was littered with photos. Reilly moved closer. They looked to be very old; black and white family scenes from a long time ago. A father and a little girl walking along the street, another of the same people dressed up formally for a family portrait. Peering closer, Reilly noticed that several of the photos were damaged, torn, mutilated even. Had something or some*one* been removed from the photos – excised from the old lady's life?

Leaving them for the moment, she glanced back at the older woman, then around the room. It was clearly the old lady's house – everything from the lace curtains to the traditional dark wood furniture, fine china teapot and doilies on the table screamed old lady.

Reilly stepped over to the fireplace. A small collection of framed black-and-white photos were laid out on the mantelpiece – several were of the same family featured in the photos spread so artfully on the couch. So they had be related to the older woman, perhaps pictures of her family, her childhood.

'Chris,' Reilly called out and waited a moment before he re-entered. 'I think I've found something.'

He stepped into the room and followed her gaze to the photos on the couch. 'You mean these photos? What about them?'

'Take a look, but remember not to touch.'

'Of course.' Raising an eyebrow, he walked over to the couch and ran his gaze across the array of photographs. 'What am I supposed to be looking at?'

'Well, what do you see?'

He shrugged. 'Mostly old family shots – some of them seem very old, a couple are torn.'

'Torn through age, or on purpose?'

He looked closer. 'Now that you say it, I'd wager on purpose. You think they're the old woman's?' he said, moving away. She knew he was finding it almost impossible to resist picking them up.

'Looks like they could be of her childhood.'

'Any idea why they've been torn like that?'

Reilly moved over to the mantelpiece and pointed to a family portrait. 'Look – this is the complete family, but in all of these,' she indicated the ones on the couch, 'someone's been removed.'

'The mother,' she and Chris said in unison, and Reilly looked at him as he continued. 'The mother has been ripped out of the photos.'

'Exactly. It's Freud again,' she said. One of the pillars of Freud's psychodynamic theory was that childhood had a profound effect on the things we do, the way we behaved as adults.'

'Are you sure that isn't too much of a leap? I mean, are we trying to make a Freud connection now? All this could very well be coincidence.'

'I know.' She sighed, having thought the very same thing. Perhaps she was just clutching at straws at this stage. Goodness knows, Daniel had cautioned her against that kind of thing, against trying to make the crime fit the circumstances rather than approaching it all with an open mind. It was a rookie mistake and she really should know better.

A troubled expression crossed Chris's face. 'Look, we'll take this thing with the photos on board, but I wouldn't automatically assume we're dealing with the same guy just yet.'

She shook her head. 'You're right. It's just ... well, all this has really gotten under my skin and I don't like being played.'

'It's getting to me too – and I don't think I need to tell you what it's doing to Kennedy.'

She gave a crooked smile. 'Where is the miserable old bastard tonight anyway?'

'Next door, interviewing some of the neighbors. I might as well warn you, he isn't exactly over the moon about having this profiler guy treading on our toes—'

'It's not like that,' Reilly told him. 'Daniel won't be stepping on *anyone's* toes. And despite what Kennedy – or anyone else might think,' she added pointedly, 'we've got a much better chance of catching this guy with him on board.'

'Well, you know Kennedy, always suspicious of the touchy-feely stuff,' Chris joked, and Reilly was heartened to think that he himself wasn't nearly as dubious. Which was important given that they all needed to work together on this.

He looked again at the photos. 'And speaking of touchy-feely, let's just assume for a moment that this thing with the missing mother *is* Freud related? Where does it get us?'

'Absolutely nowhere,' Reilly replied, feeling more disheart-
ened by the minute.

A WHILE later she and Chris stepped out into the cool night
air, both relieved to be out of the stifling heat of the house.
Karen Thompson was just arriving.

'Good luck with that one,' Chris said. The ME gave him a
quizzical look and he nodded to the house 'The fire was left
on, turned up full – it's like a sauna in there. It'll really mess
up your time of death.'

Karen shrugged. 'Every case has its difficulties – that's
what makes the job so much fun, isn't it?' she added drily,
shouldering her bag as she headed on in.

'God help her husband is all I'll say,' Chris said under his
breath.

Reilly looked at him. 'Whose?'

'Well, I know if I woke in the middle of the night to see
Karen Thompson's face beside me, I'd be more than a little
worried about having my organs weighed, if you know what I
mean.'

'You should be so lucky,' Reilly said with a grin. 'So what
else do we know about the victims?' she asked, wondering if
Chris's findings would concur with her first impressions.

He sat on the bonnet of his car and took out his notebook.
'The old lady was Vera Miles, eighty-seven years old. She owns
the house.' He flipped a page. 'The younger woman was her
niece, Sarah Miles, forty-five.' He jammed the notebook into
the pocket of his jacket. 'Sarah's a nurse, she was reported
missing about a week ago, didn't show up for work at the
hospital one day apparently.'

'Husband, boyfriend?'

'Single, no kids, lived alone. As a missing person investigation it was a real dead end. Then last night someone reported her car had been parked here,' he indicated back over his shoulder, 'for over a week, so the uniforms came around to check it out.'

Reilly looked up and down the street. It was quiet, residential, the kind of street she imagined where everyone kept to themselves. 'Any of the neighbors see anything suspicious?'

'Nobody knows nothing,' Kennedy growled, walking up behind them. He propped himself on the car beside Chris and the suspension instantly groaned. 'Mrs O'Shaughnessy across the road says the car has been there for days. Says she thought nothing of it, because Sarah had parked it there a few times before when she was away on holiday. It's a quiet street and close to the airport, so that wouldn't be out of the ordinary. In fact, I got all the usual guff about how these things didn't happen around here, and you couldn't meet a nicer more generous family who gave money to charity and everybody loved them, blah, blah, blah. It's funny how these things only come out when somebody snuffs it.'

'When did Sarah disappear?' Reilly asked.

'She was reported missing five days ago by a colleague,' Kennedy told her.

'So chances are whatever happened here was before then,' she mused. 'Maybe a week or so ago ... that would certainly explain the decomp.'

Kennedy looked at her. 'Did you find anything useful inside?'

'Team's not here yet, so hard to know, but just out of interest ...' she glanced at Chris, who nodded, 'I'm thinking there might be a clue, something related to the others.'

'You're joking.' Kennedy stared from Reilly to Chris and back again. 'You seriously think this is another one?'

'Realistically, we can't rule anything out,' Chris said, quietly and Kennedy shook his head.

'Look, Steel, call me old-fashioned, but from my experience physical evidence always trumps everything else.' He squared his shoulders, and looked straight into her eyes, the doubt on his face accentuated by the orange glow of the sodium streetlights.

'Actually, Detective—' Reilly tried to interject, before he cut her off.

'Look, all I'm saying is I worry there's a danger of this investigation becoming too narrow. Where are we on those paint and hair traces you found before? Are we any closer to identifying those?'

'I can assure you that my team is leaving no stone unturned,' she replied. 'We're still processing trace evidence from the campsite, which was more difficult because it was out in the open. Of course, we have yet to run *this* scene for physical evidence, so all we have at the moment is what I've been able to establish from my initial run-through.' While she took Kennedy's point, deep down she had a very strong suspicion that this was another related murder.

'All right, all right,' he sighed, reluctantly playing along. 'What was it this time?'

She explained about the photographs and their potential significance. 'Yes, I know it's tenuous and I don't blame you for being skeptical. Just let my team give the place a good going over and see what they find. Then maybe we can call it one way or another.' She put her hands in her pockets. 'But connection or not, we're still collecting way too many dead bodies around here.'

. . .

WHEN THE BREAKTHROUGH FINALLY CAME, it was again courtesy of the ME's office a few days later.

There was a brief tap on the door of Reilly's office and she looked up to see Karen poking her head round the door. 'Would you have a couple of minutes?' she asked.

'Of course. Come on in.'

Karen stepped into the room, somber as always in a dark gray suit. Her serious expression matched her choice of clothes. 'I just wanted to tell you in person that we got the tox screens back on Vera Miles and it looks our cause of death is from barbiturate overdose.'

Reilly frowned. 'The old lady died of a drug overdose?'

'Yes.' Karen paused briefly before continuing. 'But what's interesting is that this particular drug was something that, in retrospect, was also present in the Ryan, Redmond *and* Watson results.'

'What?' Reilly was almost afraid to breathe.

'To be honest, I'm really very cross that we missed it before, but there were only very small traces in the other cases and it's really not the kind of thing you'd expect to find—'

Reilly leaned forward, her head buzzing. 'What is it, Karen?'

'Barbiturates are common enough in sleeping pills, antide-pressants and the comparatively minuscule amounts in the screens for the others weren't exactly a red flag. But since we've had some overlap, I've been directing the lab to auto-matically crosscheck anything new with all most recent reports. Hence the result.'

Reilly couldn't get her head around it. 'You mean the drug that killed Vera Miles was also present in the others? What was it?'

Karen opened the folder and slid it toward Reilly. She pointed at a specific section of the report. 'Pentobarbital.'

Reilly stared up at her, her mind racing. 'Enough to kill Miles, but nowhere near as much for the others. I'm not sure if you're familiar with it, but it would certainly explain how the killer subdued them enough to—'

But Reilly didn't need to read through the report to know that Karen was right. Pentobarbital was the perfect choice.

19

'What the hell is pento—?' Kennedy asked, frowning at the file.

'Pentobarbital,' Reilly explained carefully, 'is a barbiturate. It's occasionally used as a recreational drug – apparently you can get high off it in smaller doses – but it's most often used by vets to put animals to sleep.'

Chris rocked back in his chair and looked across at Reilly, 'Does it help us in tracing our perp? I mean, is it something that's restricted to the veterinary profession?'

'Not particularly. They sometimes use it in general hospitals as an anesthetic, but I would guess anyone who really wanted to get hold of it would just have to break into their local vet's and they'd find it there.'

'So how do you administer it?' Kennedy wondered.

'Injection. Karen's checking each autopsy report for anything that might indicate needle marks. If she finds some, and she thinks it likely, then combined with the pentobarbital in the tox screens, we've now got a solid commonality in all four murders.'

Once these results were confirmed, Reilly made a mental

note to call Daniel and give him this new information to help with the initial profile he was currently compiling. She figured the 'control' aspect, albeit of a chemical nature, would be of significant interest to him.

'So this drug ... it was the reason he was able to convince Clare and Justin Ryan to ...?' Chris didn't need to finish the sentence. 'Do you think they knew what they were doing?'

'I would say so. Coercion seems to be a big part of the killer's MO. It certainly was in that case and with Watson, and perhaps in the Redmond so-called suicide too.'

'And what about the Mileses?' Kennedy asked. 'Why the need for the drug there? There was nothing that I could see there that suggested coercion of any kind.'

Reilly sipped at her coffee. 'I know, I was wondering the same thing.' She looked around the room suddenly. 'Do you guys have an empty room, a quiet meeting room or something – somewhere we wouldn't be disturbed?'

Chris looked at her, intrigued. 'There's an interview room down the corridor, it should be empty at this time of day. What did you have in mind?'

'If we're going to have any hope of figuring exactly how this whole thing works, I think we need to do a re-enactment.'

'You're kidding me,' Kennedy spluttered.

Chris looked at him. 'What – you have such a clear picture that you can describe exactly how all the murders were carried out?'

'Well, you know, there's—'

But Chris cut him off. 'Go on then, tell me. Even with this drug, how does a person subdue a big strong guy like Gerry Watson, and get him to eat human flesh? How does he get Jim Redmond to hang himself? Or Clare and Justin Ryan to—'

'Enough. Enough. You've made your point.' He turned to Reilly, sullen. 'So what is it you want us to do?'

A couple of minutes later, the detectives sat at one end of a long table and Reilly stood in front of them.

'So let's say you're Gerry Watson—'

'I don't have to eat anything, do I?' Kennedy joked and she flashed him her best schoolteacher look. He held his hands up. 'OK, OK. Right, I'm Gerry Watson.'

She opened her handbag and pulled out her mobile phone. 'Now, let's assume this is a gun—'

'Bloody Americans, always have to use a gun.'

She paused and looked at the two men. 'I would think it was a given – how else would the killer get into the flat?'

'Hey, I'd let you into my flat any time and you wouldn't need a gun,' Kennedy joked. Chris joined in laughing but almost immediately they stopped, catching sight of Reilly's sudden serious look.

'What?' Chris asked.

'That's a thought, isn't it?' she mumbled, almost to herself. 'Hell, why didn't I think of that?

'What?' They repeated in unison, unsure what she was getting at.

'We're assuming that the killer is by himself, but perhaps he has an accomplice – or a partner? Someone who helps him with the victims, choosing them, picking them up, whatever. If they're using pentobarbital to subdue people, then neither would need to be particularly strong.'

The silence filled the room. Chris and Kennedy stared at each other as the implication of what Reilly had said slowly began to sink in.

'And if this partner happened to be female, it would certainly make it easier to find victims,' Chris ventured, thoughtfully. 'In Watson's case at least. Can you mix this drug in a drink?'

Reilly nodded, realizing where he was going with that.

'You think it might have been some kind of pick-up situation and the drug was slipped in a drink?'

He shrugged. 'It's a theory.'

They were all quiet with their own thoughts for a moment.

Kennedy coughed. 'How about the other two, the Miles's and Ryan, how would being a girl helped there?'

'Women are automatically more trusted than men. It would certainly help her to get her foot in the door – and once she's in ...'

'Then the partner, the one who does the heavy stuff, turns up,' Chris finished.

'That would be my thinking.' She sighed. 'Although I still think she, or at least one of them, has a gun too.'

'Intimidation?'

'It's the best method of crowd control I know of.'

'And most likely the only way to get Clare and Justin to do what they did,' Chris added, softly. '

'It would explain the second gunshot wound to Sarah Miles's foot, too.' Reilly tapped her own foot, thinking harder. 'Maybe she baulked at whatever he wanted her to do?'

'What *do* you think he did want her to do?' Kennedy asked. 'If you think he forced the Ryans to do the nasty, Redmond to take his own life and Watson to eat ... that, then what's the torture method for the women?'

Reilly had wondered this too and, while she had her own suspicions, she'd decided to wait and see if today's conversation led them anywhere different.

'Pentobarbital,' Chris said eventually, breaking the silence. 'You mentioned vets use it to put animals to sleep?'

She looked at him, impressed that they seemed to be on the same wavelength. 'That's right.'

'Does it have the same effect on humans?'

'In high doses, yes.'

'So let's assume they tried to force Sarah to inject the older woman with the stuff. A nurse would surely know what kind of effect it would have.'

'"First do no harm,"' Reilly stated, locking eyes with the detective. 'Of course. Our killer tried to get Sarah to put the old lady to sleep.'

20

I f Reilly was excited by the progress they had made, she wasn't showing it to her team. Following the revelation that the drug must have been used to kill Vera Miles, she'd asked Rory to educate the others on pentobarbital. Now he stood in front of them, solid and steady in a dark sweater, his big hands looking uncomfortable as he clutched his notes.

'In veterinary medicine, sodium pentobarbital is used as an anaesthetic, while for veterinary euthanasia it is either used alone, or in combination with complementary agents such as phenytoin, as an injectable solution. You can find it sold under trade names include Euthasol, Euthatal, Euthanal—'

Lucy cut him off. 'So they use it to put animals down?'

'Yes. And also for human euthanasia in permitted countries or American states.' He peered at his notes. 'It's also sometimes used in China by the state for lethal injection, though in—'

'That's what the Miles killings were all about,' Julius said, suddenly. He so rarely offered spontaneous comments that the others all looked at him in surprise.

'How's that?' Lucy asked.

'Euthanasia.' He pulled the case file across the desk, flipped it open. 'Sarah Miles was a nurse, and it says here that Vera had a variety of health problems ...' He scanned the notes, 'Hypertension, angina, emphysema ...'

'So the killer had her niece – a nurse – kill her?'

'The Hippocratic Oath,' Reilly said, pleased that they'd figured it out so quickly. '"First, do no harm."'

'Once again – like the Ryans and the others – getting someone to do something they really don't want to do,' Gary said.

'You're right,' Reilly replied, 'but there's another level, even deeper than that – and that's where Freud comes in.'

'TABOOS,' Daniel said.

Reilly shook her head, a grin on her face. 'Why did you have to tell me what I'd just figured out for myself?'

The profiler's rich baritone laugh rumbled down the phone. 'I didn't get it at first. A homicide/suicide with incest and a strange firearm trajectory, a forced suicide of a possible closet homosexual ... and then the guy – what was his name?'

'Gerry Watson,' Reilly supplied.

'Right. The poor guy forced into doing a Hannibal Lecter.' He sighed. 'It's all so obscure, I think you've done an amazing job getting it this far. A lot of people would have dismissed it as pure coincidence.'

'Thanks.' Reilly smiled, despite herself. Even now, getting a compliment from her former tutor made her feel like an eager-to-please student all over again. 'And he's already struck again.'

She could almost hear him sitting up and paying attention.

'Already? Four separate incidents in two weeks? This one is wasting no time.'

'It's another double murder this time,' she told him. 'A nurse was forced into killing her own aunt.'

There was a brief silence as he pondered this for a moment. 'Let me guess, the aunt was old, ill?'

'Correct.'

'So this time the taboo in question would be euthanasia.'

'That's what we're thinking.'

He breathed deeply. 'I think perhaps we could both do with a little bedtime reading. Ever heard of *Totem and Taboo*?'

'Sure.' Reilly knew that *Totem and Taboo* was one of Freud's most famous works. Published in 1913, it was an application of psychoanalysis to the fields of archaeology, anthropology, and the study of religion. In it, he examined the occurrences of cultural taboos in different parts of the world, questioning their relevance and importance to both individuals and society.

Taboo ... The word continued to echo through Reilly's mind.

'I was going to e-mail through my initial thoughts on a profile today, but based on this additional evidence and information, I think we can safely say the same person's involved in all these murders,' Daniel mused. Reilly was relieved to have her suspicions verified.

'If it is they've got a pretty sick MO,' she said. 'Think about it, if it wasn't enough to just kill these people, he tortures them by forcing them to commit something completely unacceptable, something utterly repulsive to general society.'

'How *does* he get them to do it?' Daniel wondered. 'We're talking lines that many people won't cross even under extreme duress.'

'I'm sure the barbiturates help.' Reilly stifled a yawn. She knew her tiredness and frustration was coming out in her voice. 'And maybe he tells them that if they do whatever weird thing he asks, he'll let them live, or let them go.'

'Most people will do just about anything if they think it will keep them alive,' Daniel said, softly. 'Poor bastards.'

'But still he kills them anyway,'

'Yes. So he's already used incest, suicide, cannibalism, and euthanasia,' Daniel pondered. 'What in hell's name is he going to try next?'

'That's what we need to find out – and fast,' Reilly said grimly. 'And it's why we need your help so badly.'

The profiler was silent for a moment, lost in his own thoughts. 'Society's deepest, darkest taboos ...' he began aloud. 'Looks like I've got a long night of reading ahead.'

AFTER DANIEL'S CALL, Reilly flitted around the lab, her mind unsettled.

She tried to pass the time half-heartedly working on other cases, but her mind kept returning again and again to the taboo killings. *The taboo killings* – she was finally giving them a name. The team had avoided doing so up until now, as if afraid that it would somehow encourage the murderer, make it all seem more real somehow, but it was so obviously real at this point that there was little use in pretending otherwise.

Reilly stood up, gathered her charcoal leather satchel and keys, and was just slipping into her coat when the phone rang. She dumped the bag on the desk, and let her coat fall back onto her chair.

'GFU, Reilly Steel speaking.'

'Reilly – it's Chris.'

'Hey, Chris.'

'So did you get to speak to Forrest?'

'Yes, sorry I was going to call. Daniel isn't quite ready to send through the initial profile. He's in broad agreement with what we've figured out so far, though.'

'The taboo thing? He reckons it's feasible?'

'Yes.' Reilly knew that both Chris and Kennedy were almost hoping that her theory on the murders was an overstatement of the situation, as it suggested that they were dealing with something much bigger – an actual serial killer. And she knew they didn't get too many of those in Dublin, and certainly not with such a distinctly macabre MO.

'Right.' She heard him exhale deeply. 'Listen, I was just wondering are you doing anything this evening?'

She raised an eyebrow. He sounded nervous, unsure of himself. 'I was just about to leave the office actually, why?'

'Well, I just wondered ... I'm about to head home myself and I thought maybe you might like to get a bite to eat or something. Just to talk things over.'

'Sure. Where did you have in mind?'

'Um ... how about the Chinese place across the road from the station?' he suggested, sounding as though he hadn't really thought it through.

'You mean the one with the dubious health cert that's full of every uniform we've ever worked with?'

'Good point. OK, maybe—'

'I'll tell you what, there's a good Thai place I know not far from here. It's called The Orchid or something like that.'

It had been a while, years in fact, since she'd been asked out to dinner, Reilly mused. Not that this was 'dinner' per se, and given that she was the one picking the restaurant, it felt doubly offhand and casual. Back home, she'd gone out now and again for beer and pizzas with the surfing gang but it had been years since she'd been out for a meal with someone other than a work colleague. The bonus this time was that

Chris was good company. Although he was undoubtedly great at his job, she liked the way he always seemed slightly unsure of himself too; possessing little of the cockiness and bluster of some detectives.

'I know it,' Chris replied.

'Great, see you there in about twenty minutes?' Reilly said, looking forward to it more than she'd anticipated.

21

W hen he reached the restaurant, Chris found Reilly waiting just inside the door. He brushed the raindrops from his shoulders.

'Great weather, huh?' she commented.

'You think *this* is wet? Wait till summer.'

The waiter led them to their table. The restaurant was pleasantly crowded, a mix of locals and tourists; oriental music played softly in the background and the room was lavishly decorated with golden Buddha statues.

Reilly picked up the menu and immediately chose rice noodles with tofu, but Chris was lost. 'I'm more used to Chinese,' he admitted. 'I order in from my local takeaway far too often but I'm not sure about Thai.'

She scanned the menu. 'You like beef?'

'Of course.'

She turned to the waiter. 'My friend will have the beef in black bean sauce, house fried rice, and some mixed vegetables on the side, please.'

The waiter scribbled a note and hurried away. She looked up to find Chris staring at her smiling.

'What?'

'You are *so* American.'

'Is that a compliment or an insult?'

'A compliment, I think,' he laughed. 'It just seems that Americans are much more comfortable and confident in any situation. Nothing seems to faze you.'

She smiled. *If only you knew.* 'You should see me trying to set the alarm on my cell – I can never remember how to do it.'

The waiter brought their drinks – a beer for Chris and fruit juice for Reilly. He nodded at her drink. 'Even that's very American. No self-respecting Irishman or woman for that matter would go out for dinner and drink *fruit juice*. I'm not a big drinker at the best of times and even I wouldn't go for that.'

'What – I should be drinking beer?'

'After the week we've just had, damn right you should.' He raised his bottle. 'Cheers.'

He started to take a sip but Reilly stopped him. 'Hold on.' She flagged down a passing waiter who hustled over. 'Could you get me one of those – what's it called?'

'Chang,' Chris informed her.

'A Chang beer, please?'

'Yes, ma'am,' the waiter replied and headed toward the bar.

'That's more like it,' Chris said. 'Now we can have a *real* Irish toast.'

'With Thai beer?'

'Ah, it's the thought that counts.'

The waiter was soon back with Reilly's beer, and she held it up for a toast. '*Slainte*, isn't that what you guys say? So, what are we drinking to?'

Chris clinked his bottle against hers. 'Here's to catching the bad guys.'

Reilly nodded slowly, clinked her bottle and brought it to her lips. 'To catching bad guys.'

Their food arrived and they set to it with gusto, all the while discussing their thoughts on the case so far. The beer bottles quickly piled up on the table, Reilly easily keeping up with Chris, and gradually their tongues loosened, and the conversation became more relaxed.

Finally, Chris pushed away his empty plate. 'If you'll excuse me, I need to visit the loo – all that beer.' He slid his chair back and pushed himself to his feet, then let out an involuntary groan as the pain shot up through his knees and hips.

Upon his return, he was pleasantly surprised to see a coffee waiting for him. 'How did you know I wanted coffee?' he asked her.

She grinned. 'You're a cop.'

'Touché,' he smiled, then took a sip. 'You got it spot on too – white, no sugar. How did you know that?'

Reilly shrugged. 'I've seen you drinking white coffee before, and you obviously look after yourself, so I figured no sugar.'

He shook his head. 'A regular Sherlock Holmes in our midst. I'll have to be careful what I say and do around you.'

'It's already way too late for that.'

He looked at her, expecting to see a grin on her face, but instead realized that her expression was serious. 'What do you mean?'

'I already know everything I need to know about you.' She gave an enigmatic smile as she sipped at her coffee.

He sat back and crossed his arms across his chest. 'You do, do you? Go on then, let me have it.'

Reilly peered at him over the top of her cup for a moment, her smile half taunting. 'Are you sure?'

'I'm a big boy, I can take it,' he insisted, lightly. 'But go easy on me ...' he added, a little more seriously.

Reilly set her coffee down and settled back in her chair. OK, let's start with family. It's something that was always very important to you, but I'm guessing your parents aren't around anymore.'

She was right on the money, but Chris wasn't going to let her know that. 'Hardly a headline grabber. You just got lucky.' His dad had died last year, his mother just under a year before. Although the official diagnosis was a heart attack, Chris very much succumbed to the belief that Tom Delaney had died of a broken heart. A fanciful and impractical notion, but given how close his parents had been he reckoned it was completely feasible.
'

Ignoring his comment, she continued. 'You're a bachelor – not because you don't like the idea of marriage, but because you've been burned in the past – big-time burnt and you still haven't got over it.' She took another sip of her coffee. 'Am I right?' Chris was trying to hide his surprise by burying his face in his own cup. This time, she was only partly right but he wasn't going to tell her that. 'Interesting theory,' he replied, cautiously. 'Go on.'

'The job is the most important thing in your life, you take it very seriously, and are dedicated and quite ambitious but not ruthlessly so.' Then she drained the cup and set it down in the saucer with a clink. 'And you have a medical condition that you don't want anyone to know about.'

The final comment hit home the hardest, and for a moment he stared at her, pale-faced. Then he shifted in his seat. 'Wow, you were doing so well there and then you blew it at the end.'

Reilly narrowed her eyes. 'You're trying to tell me that

you're not in pain, something like that?' Her tone was challenging.

'The odd ache and pain,' he said, 'but nothing out of the ordinary.'

'I may have had ...' she paused, counting on her fingers, '... well, three or four beers, but I'm not drunk.' She fixed him with a fierce gaze. 'For a supposedly fit guy who works out a lot, you move pretty gingerly at times.'

Chris looked at her for a moment before replying. Music tinkled quietly in the background. 'You seem very sure of everything.'

'Most of it was an educated guess,' she admitted. 'But the pain thing? That's the one I'd put good money on.'

He nodded slowly. 'I don't know what to say ...' He worked his jaw hard. 'Does everyone on the force know I've got a problem?'

Reilly shook her head. 'I doubt it. Kennedy, maybe. Has he ever said anything?'

'No. As you know he's pretty out of shape himself – probably considers groaning to be a normal part of getting up out of a chair.'

'So what is it?'

'I wish I knew,' he admitted, shrugging. 'It's been coming on for the past six months or so. I have no idea what it could be.'

She looked at him in amazement. 'And you've done nothing about it?'

'It's not that simple. If I go to the force's doctor and there's a problem, it's on my record. They'd put me behind a desk quicker than you can say surfboard.'

She nodded and he knew she understood that for someone like him, that would be a virtual prison sentence. 'What are the symptoms?'

'A lot of joint pain – knees and hips mostly. And the tired-ness – it's just overwhelming,' he admitted. 'There are times when I can barely make it out of bed in the morning. Then other days it's not that bad.'

Reilly looked thoughtful. 'It could be any number of things, really.' She was clearly thinking something through. 'Tell you what, why don't you come by the lab tomorrow and I can run a blood test, try to at least get some idea of what the problem might be? We can do it on the quiet, nobody needs to know.'

He hesitated before finally speaking. 'You'd do that for me?' It was a big deal, not to mention a punishable offence, and he was slightly taken aback by her concern. Then he figured that the dogged investigator in her probably just wanted to get to the bottom of it. Either way, he wasn't going to refuse.

She nodded. 'On one condition.'

'Which is?'

'Whatever it is, you promise to get it dealt with.'

He thought for a moment. 'Fair enough.'

Just then the waiter arrived with the bill and Chris grabbed at it before Reilly could get her hands on it.

'Not this time; you got the last one.'

'Well, then we'll split it.'

'No. And if you're willing to do the blood test for me, the least I can do is pick up the tab for this.'

Reilly relented. 'OK.'

Chris peeled three twenties from his wallet, and handed them to the waiter.

'Why don't you call over to the lab about ten o'clock tomorrow – it's usually quiet around that time,' she suggested.

'Ten o'clock,' he repeated, wishing he could feel more

excited about it. 'It's a date.' Immediately, he cursed his choice of words.

She smiled a little. 'Whatever you say.'

22

T he following morning, Reilly arrived at the lab early as usual, looking to take advantage of a few minutes of peace and quiet before everyone else arrived.

Last night at dinner Chris had given her the heads-up that, given the seriousness of the situation, Jack Gorman might be called back from vacation early and she wanted to be sure she had a complete overview of the investigation so the older guy wouldn't be able to call her out on anything.

And truth be told, she wanted to make sure she was far enough into it that Gorman couldn't elbow her out of the way. He was so determinedly old school that she guessed he'd go crazy at the idea of relatively inexperienced forensics like Gary and Lucy being allowed to process a crime scene. And although Reilly knew it wasn't a problem and their work was meticulous, she wanted to satisfy herself that no one else would be able to find fault with her methods.

The call of the security guard halted her as she approached the lift.

'Ms Steel?'

She turned to see him walking toward her. He was in his

early sixties, a bit overweight, with trim gray hair brushed neatly back to cover the growing bald patch. Smithson ... Simpson ... something like that. Reilly had noticed him before, mostly because he was always friendly. She had him figured for a retired cop.

He hurried over to her, his limp noticeable, and handed her a large manila envelope. 'A courier brought this by for you this morning.'

'Thanks a lot, Mr ...' she peered at his name badge, 'Simpson.' He gave her a small nod in return and she continued on to the lift, lost in her thoughts.

'You're welcome.' Simpson turned and limped back to his desk.

Reilly felt the package. It was heavy, and felt like there was a folder or a thick file in there. The lift arrived, and she stepped inside and pushed the button for the fourth floor.

As the lift jerked into motion she opened the envelope and slid the contents out. It was a book, and catching sight of the title her heart skipped a beat. *An Introduction to Freud.* She quickly looked inside the envelope – there was no note, no compliment slip, nothing.

Half intrigued, half scared, Reilly rapidly flicked through the pages. Sure enough, there was a bookmark and a section of text had been highlighted. She read the heading: 'Little Hans.' It meant nothing to her.

The elevator stopped at the fourth floor. Clasping the book tight, Reilly hurried into her office. She flicked on the coffee machine, slung her coat and her bag down on an empty chair, then settled herself down and began to read.

. . .

'LITTLE HANS' *was a young boy who was the subject of an early but extensive study of castration anxiety and the Oedipus Complex by Freud.*

Hans developed a strong fear of horses, to the extent that he was afraid to go outside. He said that he was afraid that if he did a horse would bite his penis off.

Freud interpreted this as a fear of his father, as a result of what he called the Oedipus Complex. The Oedipus Complex describes a process by which boys acquire their gender identity, their sense of being male.

Freud believed that during the phallic stage (between around three and six years old), boys develop an intense sexual love for their mother. As a result of this, they see their father as a rival who wants to get rid of them.

However, because the father is far bigger and more powerful, the young boy develops a fear that his father will see him as a rival and castrate him.

The only way to resolve this castration-threat anxiety is to adopt a defense mechanism – in this case what Freud called 'identification with the aggressor'.

The boy, therefore, begins to stress and magnify all the ways that he is similar to his father. He does this by adopting his father's attitudes, mannerisms and actions. He thus develops a sense of being male, his gender identity.

A similar process in girls is called the Electra Complex.

REILLY SAT BACK in her chair, puzzled. What did it all mean? And, more importantly, who had sent it to her?

Then the thought struck her; Daniel, it had to be.

She looked at her watch, then picked up the phone and dialed his number. Clearly, Daniel had figured they should do some synchronized reading on Freud, irrespective of time zones. It was the very early hours on the East Coast but knowing Daniel he would have been up all night, researching and familiarizing himself with all things taboo.

The phone rang for several seconds. 'Reilly?' He sounded surprisingly groggy. 'What's going on? Did something else happen?'

'No, I ...' she said, suddenly wrong-footed. 'Sorry to wake you, but I thought ... well I just got the book you sent me and—'

'I'm sorry – what book?' he asked.

By the tone of his voice Reilly immediately knew she was mistaken. Daniel hadn't sent her this book with its carefully underlined passage. And if he hadn't, then who had?

'You didn't send me a book on Freud?'

'No. You've got enough going there and I figured it's my job to get the lowdown on such matters. Why?' Now he sounded distinctly more alert.

'I got a delivery this morning, a book on Freud with a high-lighted passage. I presumed it was from you.'

'Absolutely not,' he confirmed. Reilly felt a shiver run up her spine. 'What was the passage?' he asked. 'The one that was highlighted, what was it about?'

She tried to fill him in quickly; eager to talk to the front desk and find out how this book had ended up here. 'It was about some child, I think. Little Hans?'

There was a brief pause before he spoke again. 'OK, leave it with me and I'll call you later. And, Reilly ... tread carefully on this one, won't you?'

Assuring Daniel that she'd speak to him later, Reilly hung up the phone and immediately called the front desk.

'Simpson here.'

'Mr Simpson, it's Reilly Steel.'

'Oh hello again, Ms Steel.'

'That book you gave me just now – do you know who brought it in?'

'Couldn't say for sure; it was some courier – he had a motorbike helmet on with one of those blasted visors.' He sighed. 'There's a sign up saying they're supposed to take them off when they come in, but they're in such a hurry that most of them just ignore it. I remember when—'

'Can you give me any description at all?' she interrupted. 'Any company name? Logo? Anything distinctive?'

'Sorry, I really didn't take any notice,' he admitted, sheepishly.

Reilly sighed. 'Thanks anyway.' She was just about to hang up when she heard his voice again.

'Wait a minute, thinking about it now – there was one thing that was a little unusual.'

'Yes?' Reilly's voice was sharp, hopeful.

'Well if you don't mind me saying ...' he sounded apologetic, almost unsure of himself, '... well, I'd have to say that it was the probably the most shapely courier I've ever seen.'

Reilly tried to keep the surprise out of her voice. 'You mean it was a woman? The courier who delivered the package was female?'

'Yes, miss,' Simpson replied. 'Most unusual really, even in this day and age.'

Reilly hurried down to the lab. Julius was already in and working alone, mixing and analyzing samples. He looked up when she entered.

'Good morning, Reilly.'

She got straight to the point. 'I need you to run this for fingerprints – right now.' She held the book and the envelope out to him. 'You'll need to use mine for a match, they'll be all over it.' She thought for a moment. 'Oh, and also Simpson, the security guard from the front desk.' She set the book and envelope down on the counter. 'If you find any other prints let me know straightaway.'

WHEN CHRIS STOPPED by the lab just after ten, Reilly welcomed the interruption. She was tired of turning things over in her head; she didn't want to interrupt Daniel's sleep again and anyway she knew he'd call her later. The chance to talk to the only other person who was sympathetic to her theories was exactly what she needed.

As soon as he walked in she noticed how tired Chris looked. He moved wearily, had dark circles under his eyes, and his face looked drawn and haggard, but she said nothing.

Granted, they'd had a few beers last night, but nothing that should make him look like that. If he looked that bad, she figured that he probably felt lousy too and she hoped more than ever that she could help him shed some light on this – and soon.

Reilly led him to the privacy of her office where she had a syringe and a couple of blood vials ready and waiting on her desk.

She directed him to sit down.

Chris looked anxiously at the syringe. 'The moment of truth. You will be gentle with me, won't you?' he joked as he rolled up his sleeve and she could only imagine what was running through his mind.

Reilly picked up the syringe, and pointed it at him. 'Sit still and don't be a baby,' she admonished. She rubbed his arm to bring out the vein, before skillfully inserting the needle. As his blood filled the vial, she updated him on the morning's developments to distract him.

'I got some interesting mail today,' she began.

He looked at her. 'Cheap double glazing? That's all I seem to get in the post these days.'

'This was from a courier actually. A book about Freud – sent anonymously.'

He raised an eyebrow. 'Anonymously?'

'Exactly.'

'You think the killer sent you the book?'

She switched out the vials. 'Who knows? I thought it was Daniel at first but he said it wasn't him; I can't think who else it could have been. Julius is running it for fingerprints right now.'

Chris watched her face as she spoke. 'You don't really expect to find anything, do you?'

Reilly removed the second vial and slid the syringe out. 'No, I don't. So far we've only been permitted to find what he wants us to find. If this is him, I don't have any reason to expect this to change with something so blatant.' Reilly placed a small gauze pad on his arm, secured it with tape.

'Still, it's quite a risk sending you something directly like that,' Chris said, as he rolled his sleeve down and buttoned the cuff. 'And very personal, too, I would have thought.'

Reilly nodded. She'd thought the very same thing. Did the killer know that she was overseeing the evidence in this case and was one of the leading investigators? If so, then it was likely he was outwardly challenging her, daring her to catch him.

'While some of the scumbags we've put away get their lackeys on the outside to mess with our heads now and again, it's rare enough for the ones who haven't been caught to try anything,' Chris pointed out. 'They're too busy making money to bother with anything like that.'

'You mean the drug dealers and gang bosses?'

'Yeah. There's always a bit of posturing going on – usually

harmless, but nothing like this. This is a bit too close for comfort for my liking. Do you think this guy *wants* to get caught?'

Reilly sat down behind her desk and leaned forward, her chin resting in her hand. 'Not particularly,' she explained. 'If we're talking serial – and I think there's little doubt about that – the one thing we do know is that murder excites our guy. The reason he – or, if there's an accomplice, *they* – keeps killing is because it's the only way he can feel the same excitement. The problem is, each time he kills, the excitement wears off sooner, so one way to recreate the same kind of thrill is to start taking greater risks—'

'Like taunting the people who are trying to catch him?'

Reilly nodded. 'Yes. By increasing the risk, they also increase the chance of getting caught, thus the higher level of excitement.'

Chris slipped his jacket back on. 'You said the book was about Freud?'

'Yes,' she said, explaining about the highlighted passage. 'Whatever else this guy does, subtle isn't part of it.'

'What's the significance, then?'

'I'm not entirely sure yet,' admitted Reilly, wondering what Daniel would make of it. 'But at least we now have someone on our side that can help us make sense of it.'

23

Daniel Forrest had been spending a lot of time thinking about the taboo murders. When he called Reilly back later that day he had both questions and observations for her. But the new information dominated the early part of their conversation.

'The highlighted section on Little Hans – what do you think it means?' he queried.

Reilly sighed. 'Daniel, I recognize that tone of voice. I'm not one of your students anymore so don't play games with me. I already feel like the killer is treating us like morons – having to point things out to us. I don't need you to as well.'

His voice grew serious. 'This is significant, Reilly – all too significant I'm afraid.'

'You're familiar with Little Hans, then?' she asked. He could hear the weariness in her voice and hoped she wasn't overdoing it and burning herself out with the investigation. That was Reilly all over, and Daniel couldn't believe that she'd traveled all the way across to Atlantic only to stumble into yet another nightmare. When he'd first heard about the move, he'd figured it would be a good thing, maybe a quieter pace of life, and more time outside of work for her to develop a life of her own. An opportunity to reconnect with her father and help put the past behind her, rather than always pushing herself to the limit, as if trying to prove something.

'Yes, it's a well-known story,' he replied, 'to psychologists at least – so it's significant for the killer, and for us.' He paused, choosing his words carefully.

He felt he was getting on dangerous ground with Reilly here, moving into areas that in truth, he would far rather leave undisturbed. 'Reilly, the story of Little Hans is all about gender identity and how the things our parents do affect us for the rest of our lives.'

Reilly's silence spoke volumes. Like a small pebble thrown into a deep, still pool, he knew the ripples of his comment were spreading out across her mind, disturbing areas she tried to keep hidden.

Daniel leaned forward, speaking quietly into the phone, wishing he could have this conversation in person, not through an impersonal piece of plastic with thousands of miles between them. 'The killer is letting us know that what he is doing here is profoundly motivated by an incident – or incidents – from his childhood. It's a huge and rather telling insight into his MO, his thinking, everything about the case.'

'An incident from his childhood? Why would we care about that?'

Daniel sighed. 'Well, as you know these people aren't exactly rational, to say nothing of sane. We already know the killer enjoys a symbolic style of killing, hence the gratuitous use of taboos. So with the book he's pushing the symbolism a step further and making it much more personal. He's reaching out to his pursuers, the people he considers his enemies – namely you.'

'But why me?'

'Clearly, and I don't mean any disrespect to the investigating team by this, but he's identified you as the brains behind the operation. You're the forensic investigator, the one who found the relevant clues and put them together, perhaps a lot faster than he'd anticipated.'

'But how on earth would he know that?'

'Actually that's another thing I wanted to talk to you about. I'm e-mailing my initial thoughts over to you this morning, so you can read through them in detail at your leisure, but in all honesty, I have my doubts as to whether or not the perp is your typical white male working alone.'

She sat up. 'You think he might be working with an accomplice? I thought so too – and I'm thinking now it could very well be a female.'

'Well, it's still too early to make too many assumptions, but again, I'm thinking you're wasted in that backwater,' Daniel said, proudly.

'It wasn't that difficult,' she said. 'The level of organization seems particularly high and there also seems to be two distinct parts to the operation – first the coercion and then the murders.'

'Good point. But let's not start jumping to too many conclusions just yet,' he commanded, his tone decisive and business-like. 'We need to keep an open mind – stay alert to all the possibilities until we have something more conclusive.'

Reilly exhaled deeply, torn somewhere between relief and disappointment. 'Of course,' she agreed. 'It's just that—'

'I know, time is of the essence – it always is – but we need to be patient.' The tone of his voice suddenly changed, softened. 'Anyway, when I tell you what else I've come up with you'll realize I was really kind of cheating on the Little Hans thing.'

'What? You mean there's more?'

He smiled. 'You're gonna love this one.'

Although she had admonished him earlier for his tendency to lapse into teacher mode, he knew part of the reason she wanted him on board was because of his instructive style. 'I feel another lesson coming on,' she groaned good-naturedly.

'A lesson?' he laughed. 'Not really – more of a chance to celebrate my genius.'

'Sometimes I have a hard time telling one from the other.'

'OK, have you got your case files there?'

He heard the rustle of paper as she spread them out on her desk. 'Of course. Which one are we looking at?'

'Ryan. Get the photos out.'

'OK, done.'

He looked down at his own copies of the relevant crime-scene photos and found the one he wanted. 'Great. Now, I want you to focus on the bedside table.'

'Where I found the other Freud book?'

'Exactly. Now, have you got a magnifying glass handy?'

'Daniel, where is this heading?' He could tell by her tone that she was getting more and more intrigued and could sense something interesting coming up. He didn't reply. 'Give me a second, there's one in the drawer.' He waited patiently for her to find the magnifying glass. 'OK, got it.'

'Now. I want you to look closely at the books on the bedside table.'

'I'm looking at them.'

'What do you see?'

He tried to tone down the self-satisfied tone he sometimes used when pointing out a discovery. He could just picture Reilly scanning the photo, trying to notice the little details.

'Well, nothing really, apart from the brain spatter and—'

'Make sure you're not missing the woods for the trees,' he urged.

There was a brief silence and then a gasp. He smiled, knowing immediately that she'd spotted it. 'Oh, crap. Why didn't I see that before?'

'Tell me what you see,' he asked, carefully.

'The books are all the same size,' she said. 'It's more like a careful arrangement than a random bunch of books on a bedside table.'

'Right,' he confirmed. 'So that means ...?'

'Either that Clare was anally neat and organized – which the rest of the apartment gave no evidence of – or else that the Freud book wasn't the only one that was planted there?'

'Right. So now you've seen the woods, look more closely at the trees ...'

'I'm still not getting it,' she admitted.

'OK,' Daniel said, teasing it out. 'The Freud book is on the end. What's the title of that one?'

'*The Interpretation of Dreams*,' she replied.

'Right. So the title of that one begins with a T. Now do the same for all the books – write the titles down in order, from left to right.'

As he waited for her to write the titles down as directed, he looked at his own notes.

Yellow Moon
One Life
Unusual Times Long Forgotten
Russian for Beginners
For People and their Pets
All Our Loves Are Not Lost
Under The Bridge
Last to Know
The Interpretation of Dreams

'OK, I've done that,' Reilly said. 'And I'm still not seeing anything.'

'It's an acronym,' he said, unable to wait any longer. 'Read what it says.'

'Shit, I see it!' Reilly exclaimed. 'Your fault ... it reads "Your fault"! Goddamnit, Daniel.'

'INTERESTING, YES?'

'Interesting?' Reilly was practically shouting at him now. 'What the hell does it mean?

His tone was somewhere between an admonishment and a reminder. 'My theory is our killer is trying to suggest that his motive is driven by something other than simple bloodlust.'

'He's punishing his victims for something they've done in the past? Maybe he sees himself as some kind of vigilante,' Reilly interjected, excitedly. 'In which case we need to take a closer look at the victims' pasts, maybe there's something common there that might be relevant, something we can use, something to help us find a link between these people ...'

This time Daniel stayed silent, unwilling to share for the moment his thoughts on a third possibility, one that he felt was just as feasible – but far more worrying.

24

C hris knew it would take a while for Reilly to run his blood tests and tried to reassure himself that it was unlikely she'd find anything; it was probably more a case of his working too hard. Even so, he found he was doing everything he could do to keep busy and stop himself thinking about it.

He was at the station, reading through a witness report from another on-going investigation, when the phone rang. 'Detective Delaney,' he answered.

'Delaney? It's Jones from Donnybrook. I got a call earlier from the wife of that suicide guy from before.'

'Jim Redmond's wife? What did she have to say?'

'I wasn't here when she called – just picked up a message to call her back. And seeing as you lot are looking after all that now ...'

'No problem, give me the number and I'll phone her back.'

'Great.' Jones rattled off the number, more than happy to shift the burden of a grieving relative onto someone else.

Chris hung up and immediately dialed Debbie Redmond's number.

'Mrs Redmond? I understand you phoned the Donny-brook station earlier. I'm Detective Chris Delaney and my office is currently handling your husband's case. What can I do for you?'

'You are? But I thought ... Well, OK.' She seemed surprised, but didn't comment further.

'So, what can we do for you, Mrs Redmond?' Chris repeated, gently.

'Well, I'm sorry to bother you but ...' The voice was hesitant, nervous, and he could hear her voice crack as she spoke, the pain of her husband's death still raw. 'It's just ... there's been something nagging at my mind ... about Jim,' she continued. 'It's probably nothing but I wondered if I could talk to someone about it?'

'Of course. I could pop over this afternoon if you'd like?' he offered. A chance to get out of the office – *exactly* what he needed.

'Would you really? I'd be so grateful.'

THE REDMOND HOUSE was in an upscale area of the city, just off Haddington Road, and Chris relaxed as he drove down the tree-lined avenue. He parked outside the Redmond house and climbed from the car, trying not to groan as he stood – the pain seemed to have become worse over the last couple of days and, Christ, he was starting to sound like Kennedy every time he moved.

Debbie Redmond was waiting on the doorstep looking very prim in a tweed skirt and black blouse as he labored up the driveway. He wondered what it was she wanted to talk about. Having a gay husband with a secret life would probably have never entered the poor woman's mind, he thought.

Inside, Debbie took her time – she had to observe the

proprieties of getting Chris a cup of coffee before she would even start talking. Finally, she began trying to explain what was bothering her.

'I know you'll probably think I'm being silly, Detective ...' Chris sipped at his coffee and said nothing, preferring to let her get whatever it was out in her own good time. 'It's just that I can't get the events of that day out of my mind. I keep replaying it, seeing again what I found when I came home.' Her voice cracked and she stopped and dabbed at her face with a handkerchief. 'I walked in, expecting Jim to be in the living room, watching the golf – he's always watching golf.' She paused and then gave a bitter smile. '*Was* always watching golf ...'

Another dab with the hankie, while Chris waited patiently. 'He was just hanging there – it was so ... shocking. I just ... it took me a minute to even realize what I was looking at.'

'I can only imagine ...'

Again she paused, drawing on her reserves of strength to get through. 'It's so hard to understand why something like this would happen. Jim wouldn't hurt a fly. He was unbelievably generous, donating to charity, always willing to help people out and do a good deed for anyone who asked, so I can't understand how anyone would want to hurt him.'

'Back to that day,' Chris directed, gently. 'What exactly was it that you wanted to talk about?'

She looked pained. 'The thing is, Detective, what I didn't realize at the time – and I know you're going to think I'm crazy, but the sheet, the sheet that Jim used to ...' She took a deep breath, steeling herself. 'Well, I'm almost certain it wasn't one of ours. I wasn't thinking straight at the time of course, but as I said, I keep going over and over the scene in my head, and then one night late last week, I realized.'

Chris looked at her, not sure what to think. 'I don't understand. Are you saying that the sheet Jim used didn't belong to you?'

'No. I've never seen it before. As I said, at the time I didn't notice the details, but since then I've been picturing it in my mind and I know that we didn't have anything like it. For one thing it was plain white and all our bed linen here is colored or patterned.'

'Are you certain? It wasn't some old sheet you used as a dust sheet for decorating?' Chris probed. 'Something from the back of the linen cupboard?'

'No. I'm absolutely certain,' Debbie Redmond assured him. 'That sheet definitely didn't come from this house.'

REILLY BENT OVER THE MICROSCOPE, peering at a blood sample. She'd expected to find something simple, anaemia maybe, but this was beyond her normal range. She checked the slide again, before referring to the medical textbook lying on the desk alongside her.

Julius was working nearby and Reilly called out to him. 'Julius, could you come here a minute?'

He looked up and dutifully hurried over. 'No problem.'

'You used to work in a hospital lab, right?'

His face fell. 'Don't remind me,' he said with a roll of his eyes. 'Running the same bloody tests all day long – if you'll pardon the pun.'

Reilly smiled. It was rare for the ultra-serious Julius to attempt a joke, never mind such a lame one. 'Well, with that in mind, take a look at this for me, would you?'

Julius bent over the slide, made a minor adjustment, and studied the sample for a moment. 'That's unusual. Whose blood is it?'

There was a brief pause. 'That's classified for the moment.'

'Oh.' He straightened up, looked at Reilly for a second and then nodded. 'I get you.'

'So what do you see?'

'It's a transferrin saturation test, yes?'

Reilly nodded. 'What do you reckon?'

'Well, it's a very high transferring ratio, possibly too high, actually.'

'That's what I thought.' Reilly pondered over this for a moment. 'So at the hospital, if you had a sample with such a ratio, what kind of check would you order next?'

He chuckled. 'I never thought my days at Queen's would come in so useful. Well because the transferrin isn't completely reliable, I'd likely order a serum ferritin test next – might be more conclusive.' He looked at Reilly for a moment. 'You want me to run one for you? I could fit it in this afternoon.'

She nodded. 'I'd appreciate that. Thanks, Julius.'

'No problem.'

She handed him the vials of blood. 'Oh, and one other thing—'

'Yeah, keep it quiet,' he said, gently. 'I get it.'

Reilly smiled as he headed back to his workstation, and said a prayer of thanks for competent, discrete staff.

She was just heading back to her office when the phone rang. She looked at the display. Speak of the devil ...

'What's up, Chris?'

'Well, I don't want to rush you but I was just wondering—'

She didn't want to admit that the results so far were frustratingly inconclusive. 'Nothing definitive yet, but I would think you're likely to survive the next twenty-four hours at least.'

'Ha, you're a great source of comfort,' he quipped. Then he

paused. 'Well, thanks anyway, but it's not the only reason I'm phoning. I've got a strange one for you.'

'Go on.' Reilly walked along the hallway in the direction of her office.

'I've just left the Redmond house – Debbie Redmond says that she's been playing the scene of her husband's death over and over in her mind.'

'Well, that's perfectly normal.'

'Of course. But she reckons she's come up with something.'

'OK.' She paused, her interest piqued.

'She says that the sheet, the one Jim supposedly hung himself with, isn't theirs – says she's never seen it before in her life.'

Reilly had reached her office and closed the door before perching on the edge of her desk. 'Seeing as we know it wasn't a suicide, I suppose we probably shouldn't be surprised at anything that emerges.'

'Can you check into it? You've got the sheet there, haven't you?'

'Yes. To be honest, I only studied the inventory, not the sheet itself, but I can go and get it from the evidence room – we can take another look at it, see if there's any additional trace on it we might have missed.'

'You don't think the killer would be stupid enough to use his own sheets, do you?' Chris asked.

'We should be so lucky. But even if he did, we'd have to already have a comparative sample for it to mean anything.'

'Of course.'

'Still, it's worth checking,' she concluded. 'I'll do it myself now.'

.　.　.

Lucy followed Reilly into the evidence room, and scanned her clipboard for the right case number. 'This way.'

They headed down the long rows of dusty metal shelves, the dim fluorescent lights giving the entire room a dreary pallor.

'So why exactly are we doing this?' Lucy asked.

'Because Mrs Redmond reckons that the sheet that her husband hanged himself with wasn't hers,' said Reilly. 'So we have to follow up.'

'That's hardly a revelation though. His boyfriend probably brought some sheets over whenever they ... you know.'

She nodded. 'You're probably right.'

Lucy stopped at the end of a row. 'It's down here.'

Reilly followed her down the row until she found the right box. Lucy lifted the box from the shelf and carried it to the end of the row before setting it down on the table.

She pulled a small knife from her pocket, and sliced through the security tape that sealed the box, nattering away as she opened it. 'Even if the sheet isn't theirs, it's not likely to tell us much, is it? It certainly didn't before.'

'Probably not,' Reilly said, lifting the lid. She rummaged through the box and quickly located the bed sheet. Pulling it out to take a better look, she frowned.

'What?' Lucy asked, spotting her baffled look.

Reilly said nothing, just stared at the sheet she was holding in her hands, her mind racing.

'Reilly? What is it?'

'Weird ...' she mumbled, almost to herself. 'I think I recognize this.'

Chris took a deep breath, carefully choosing his next words. 'You're absolutely sure?'

'Yes.'

At Reilly's request, he'd come immediately to the crime lab to try to figure out what this latest discovery meant.

'I mean, I couldn't tell the difference between one white sheet and another,' he admitted.

'But I'm a linens snob, Chris,' she explained. 'And this is six-hundred-count Italian linen. Hell, I buy this type myself exclusively from Scheuer Linens in San Francisco.' Which meant that, rather than a random, generic piece of evidence, the sheet could now be considered specific, classified evidence, and in theory should be easier to narrow down.

'And can you get hold of them in Ireland?' he asked.

'I'm not sure. Lucy's calling Brown Thomas and some of the more specialist haberdashery stores around the country, but make no mistake, if these aren't Jim Redmond's sheets, then the killer's given us a crucial piece of evidence.'

'Give me a minute and I'll talk to Debbie Redmond again, see if any of this rings a bell.'

He went outside the room to make the call and spoke briefly to the victim's wife before coming back inside.

'Says she knows nothing about thread-count and whatnot, and buys most of her household stuff from Debenhams or House of Fraser and mostly only based on what it looks like.'

Just then Lucy came back into the room. 'Brown Thomas is faxing over a list of their linens inventory and said we should have it later this afternoon. It'll take longer to track down suppliers elsewhere though.'

'Still, it's something to go on,' Reilly said, pleased they'd finally caught some kind of a break. If the killer had used this sheet to kill Redmond and wasn't aware that the type was uncommon, then it could tell them something useful about the killer, perhaps where he might be hiding out.

'What about hotels?' Chris asked, obviously on the same

track. 'Could the killer have picked the sheet up from some-where else?'

'The Four Seasons would be a good bet,' Lucy mused. 'Seeing as it's only around the corner from the Redmonds' house.'

'Great. Then we'll try that as well as some of the other more upmarket hotels in the city,' Chris said. 'If one of them happens to use those exact sheets, then we can work on getting a guest list and see if anything jumps out.'

Lucy headed for the doorway. 'I'll get going on it.'

'The lab is running DNA testing on it right now too, but I'd be amazed if we found anything other than Jim Redmond's profile,' Reilly said.

Chris nodded at her. 'Good work spotting that,' he said. 'It could be the break we need.'

'Don't thank me,' Reilly replied, grimly. 'Thank the wife of the poor guy who got stuck in the middle of all this.'

25

The wooden framed house was dark, quiet. It sat on the corner of the block in a San Francisco suburb, just one of thousands of similar family houses.

Reilly sat on the couch, her legs tucked up underneath her, homework scattered around her, half studying, half watching TV.

A figure flitted silently across the darkness of the back yard, pressed up against the side of the house.

Reilly paused in the middle of a sentence then muted the TV and listened intently. Nothing.

She turned the volume back on and resumed her studies.

The figure slid along the wall and tiptoed onto the porch, moving soundlessly to the back door. A hand reached out and gently tried the door handle – it turned and the door swung silently outwards. The figure slipped quietly into the kitchen, passing through a band of light from upstairs.

Reilly was engrossed in her books, oblivious to the intruder. He peered round the door into the living room, spied her sitting on the couch.

Closer and closer he crept, tiptoeing up behind her.

'You're going to have to be a lot quieter than that,' she said, suddenly turning around.

'Damn, your hearing is awesome!' The teenage boy vaulted the couch and landed beside Reilly, scattering her books.

'Tommy, mind my homework,' she admonished.

'Homework, schomework!' Then he grinned. 'I've got a different kind of homework for *you* ...'

They wrapped their arms around each other, lips locked together, oblivious to the passing of time. Finally, they came up for air.

'When's your dad back?'

Reilly shrugged. 'Who knows? Probably when people stop buying him drinks or when they throw him out.'

'Great,' said Tommy, going straight back in for more.

Their mouths locked again and he began peeling off Reilly's sweater. She responded passionately and soon they were both half-naked, hands exploring frantically.

A sudden noise made Reilly break away. She sat up, listening hard, her gaze moving anxiously around.

'What is it?' Tommy was not in the mood to stop.

'I thought I heard something – Jess sleeps very lightly.'

'Who's Jess?'

'My little sister.'

Tommy nibbled at Reilly's neck. 'So? Who cares?'

She shivered as he kissed her. 'But she might see us ...'

'So what? She might learn something.' He reached for Reilly's jeans and started to unbutton them.

She tried to stop him. 'We shouldn't – not here – not now.'

Tommy persisted. 'Come on, baby. `You know I love you.' He laughed. 'We're seventeen – this is what we're *supposed* to do.'

Reilly still looked uncertain but Tommy, knowing her

weak spot, resumed the offensive on her neck. 'I love you,' he crooned, slowly sliding her jeans down over her hips.

She couldn't resist any longer. 'I love you too,' she whispered, lying back and letting Tommy finish undressing her.

'What are you doing?' a voice called out quietly from nearby.

Tommy looked up, startled. 'What the—'

Reilly looked round and saw Jess staring at them, her fluffy blond hair pulled up in a ponytail, a peculiar look on her face.

'Jess, it's OK,' she said, reassuringly.

'What's he doing, Reilly? Is he hurting you?'

Tommy was smiling now, regarding Jess with interest. 'Well, well ... what do we have here? You never told me you had such a cutie for a sister, Reilly.'

Reilly stared at him, feeling uneasy. What was it about Jess that made every guy – young or old – go weak at the knees?

'Reilly?' Jessica was staring at her in disbelief. 'You were doing it – with him?'

Damn. 'No, Jess. You don't understand – we were just—'

'We were just fooling around,' Tommy interjected, sitting up and buttoning his shirt.

Jess continued to stare at Reilly as if she'd let her down. And oddly enough, she felt like she had. Jess looked up to her, saw her as a mother figure and Reilly felt like she had to protect her.

'Yeah,' she pulled her jeans up and scrambled to her feet. 'It was nothing, Jess.'

'You *were* doing it with him!' her sister accused, her expression darkening. 'You're just like her! You're a whore and I hate you!'

Tommy looked bemused. 'What the hell?'

'Jess,' Reilly spoke softly but simmered with rage inside.

'You have no right to talk to me like that. Now go to your room.'

'I'm telling Dad,' Jess remained defiant. 'I'm telling Dad that you were doing it with some guy in our living room when you're supposed to be taking care of *me*. You're just like her, aren't you, Reilly? And just like her you'll end up leaving us too.'

REILLY SAT UP IN BED, disoriented. This time the dream was so real it was almost as though Jess were really there.

She shivered and stared into the darkness – every shadow suddenly seemed to contain a threat, lurking in wait, ready to spring out on her.

She glanced around the room for a moment, at the small wardrobe in the corner, the window with its lace curtains, letting in the yellow glow of the streetlamps, before finally settling back down on her pillow. She tried to close her eyes and relax, let sleep overtake her.

'Goddamnit,' she muttered, sitting up again. There was no point; she was wide awake now, sleep had completely deserted her. She climbed out of bed and wrapped herself in a toweling robe, before heading into the living room.

Reilly flicked on the overhead light and the glare immediately chased away the shadows and the ghosts that had haunted her sleep. This case was obviously getting to her more than she'd care to admit, subconsciously unearthing memories and emotions she thought she'd long left behind.

She stood in the doorway of the living room, trying to decide what to do now she was so alert. Unable to think of anything else, she sat down on the couch in front of the coffee table and fired up her laptop. Might as well do something useful.

While the computer flickered to life, Reilly sat and gazed around the apartment. While it was clean, there was no denying it was pitifully small, and try as she had to give it some kind of personal touch over the last few months, it still didn't feel like hers.

She thought dreamily of her old place back in California just minutes from the beach, with its huge wood-framed windows which let in the warm light and cool ocean breezes. Then she suddenly froze as her gaze rested briefly on her bookshelf.

Something didn't look right.

She stood up and walked over to take a closer look. No matter how hard she stared, she couldn't figure out what was bothering her. Was something missing, something out of place, but what?

She shook her head, putting it down to edginess about her most recent dream. That was all it was; it had to be. Still, Dr Kyle's admonishment before she left California echoed in her mind. *'If you're feeling fragile, don't be afraid to seek help. Being vulnerable isn't the same thing as being weak.'*

Was the return of the dreams making her feel vulnerable? No, they were just dreams; they couldn't hurt her and they certainly couldn't make her weak. In any case, everyone had their own worries, their own fragilities that they tried to keep hidden from the rest of the world. She thought about Chris and his stubborn refusal to admit to what was his own weakness. Yes, everyone had their own demons, Reilly assured herself and she was no different.

She returned to the couch and picked up her laptop. Resting it on top of her thighs, she opened up Google and typed in the word 'taboo'.

.   .   .

HOURS LATER, Reilly woke slowly, her neck and back sore. Something was beeping at her. She was still on the couch and she felt groggy. She looked down – it was her laptop beeping to tell her the battery was about to run out. She snapped it closed, then sat up and ran her fingers through her hair.

In the gray morning light everything looked so normal, so unthreatening, that it was hard to believe she was trying to get inside the mind of someone so sick they used society's most forbidden as a means of terrorizing people. As if threatening and then eventually taking their lives wasn't enough, he had to put them through psychological torture too.

Reilly looked at her watch – shit, it was 7.15! She needed to be in the office early today to prepare for that afternoon's interdepartmental meeting and knew she'd need to be on her game for the inevitable questions from O'Brien later.

She climbed groggily to her feet and headed to the bathroom, shedding her robe on the way. Turning the shower temperature down, she stepped inside, letting the tepid water wake her up.

Afterward, she dressed quickly and brushed her hair back in a simple ponytail. Breakfast would have to wait; she could always get something from the staff canteen. She grabbed her handbag, mobile phone and keys from the small table by the door, then stopped in frustration. Where was her GFU staff ID? She always left it on the table when she came in. She tried to picture coming in last night. Had she done anything different? Or did she even have it with her last night? It was hard to know, one day tended to blend in with all the rest. Figuring she must have left it pinned to her lab coat yesterday, she headed out the door.

. . .

'WHERE DID YOU POP UP FROM?' Simpson was on duty again that morning and he gave Reilly an amused glance as she hurried in to the lobby of the GFU building.

She paused, surprised. 'I'm just running a bit late this morning.' She headed for the lifts but his voice stopped her in her tracks.

'What do you mean you're running late?' Simpson said, somewhat bemused. 'You beat me in this morning.'

Reilly spun around. 'What? What are you talking about?'

Simpson gave her an odd look then held the large blue logbook out for her to look at. 'See, I have you signed in right here.'

Reilly hurried over back to him and stared at the logbook. She was indeed registered as having arrived at seven. She gave him a sharp look. 'Well, I don't know who you have signed in but it certainly isn't me.'

Simpson removed his peaked cap and scratched his thinning hair. 'Maybe you just popped out for a coffee or something then?' His voice was uncertain and more than a little confused.

Reilly shook her head. 'No. I've only just got here.'

'Then who came in earlier?'

Her stomach twisted as suddenly she remembered the misplaced ID. 'Do you remember anything about the person who checked in?' she asked him hurriedly, trying to keep the concern out of her voice. 'The one you thought was me.'

'Like I said, I wasn't actually here at the time – I just came on shift half an hour ago so it would have been the night guy Murray that registered you.' He looked worried, like this was the kind of thing that was going to get him into a whole lot of trouble. 'Ah, I'm sure it's just a mistake. I wouldn't worry about it.'

But Reilly didn't need to hear any more – she was already

racing toward the lifts.

'There's an intruder and it could be a murder suspect,' she called back at him. 'Call it in.' She stabbed the button on the elevator repeatedly, waiting impatiently for it to come. After what seemed an eternity the bell announced its arrival and Reilly stepped inside. 'And if you see anything suspicious,' she threw back at Simpson, 'do not attempt to stop this person by yourself.'

Inside the lift, she cursed the fact that she wasn't in the States – she had no gun. Even though it was unlikely the intruder was still inside, there was an undeniable reassurance that came just from having a firearm . Not only that, but it was what most of her training had focused on. Instead, she would have to do what Daniel always encouraged his recruits to do – use her instincts.

Stepping out of the lift, she quickly looked right and left – there was no movement, just the cold flicker of the fluorescent lights. The corridor was deathly silent at this time of day – the other staff didn't usually arrive until between eight thirty and nine. Which to check first, her office or the lab?

Reilly took a deep breath and opted for the office – it was a more personal space, and therefore a more likely target for the killer – if that was indeed who it was. She slipped her shoes off and headed quietly down the corridor.

She was working hard to control her breathing and stay calm. She'd been trained to deal with circumstances like this. She looked down at the black, low-cut shoes that she clutched in her left hand. Her instructors at Quantico wouldn't know whether to laugh or cry if they saw her right now, looking to potentially apprehend a dangerous suspect, armed only with a pair of Italian leather mules.

She slowed her pace as she approached her office, and paused outside it, listening for any sound, anything that might indicate an intruder was in her office. The building groaned quietly, the central heating gurgling and grumbling, but there was no noise from her office, nothing that suggested anyone was there. One shoe raised as a weapon, Reilly turned the corner into her office.

As soon as she looked at her desk, she knew that someone had been there. Last night, when she'd been checking the bookshelf at her apartment, she'd known something was missing but she couldn't pin down what it was. *Now* she knew.

Sitting upright in the middle of her desk was a photo album – her photo album. Oh Christ, had the killer somehow got inside her apartment? How ... and more importantly why? Recalling last night's edginess and the gut feeling she'd so easily discounted, her heart began to thunder inside her chest. What was going on here?

The album was turned away from her, the cover facing forward so that Reilly had to walk into the office and around to the other side of her desk to see which page it was opened at.

It was a family photograph, at least fifteen years old, from a different time, a different life. The Steel clan were still innocent, still happy. Their mom had left for good this time – the seeds of the future were already sown – but the three of them were happy, Mike and his two girls.

It was Halloween. Reilly had a protective arm around Jess who was staring up in admiration at her. But it was the costumes that made the picture so pointed, so revealing. Reilly had never been comfortable with the whole Halloween thing, the witches and devils and vampires the other kids liked to dress up as. So, as usual, she was wearing an outfit she had put together herself – some kind of angel/fairy outfit with a pair of diaphanous wings. *Any therapist would have had a field day with that one*, she mused.

Jess, on the other hand, had always loved the whole dress-ing-up thing. She was looking positively radiant, dressed all in pink –her favorite color – and clutching a pretty bunch of flowers.

But perhaps most disconcerting of all was the Post-it note affixed to the photo. It simply read, *'Happy families.'*

Reilly stared at it for a moment, temporarily forgetting that there could be a crazed criminal loose in the building. Suddenly, she longed for those long-ago halcyon days when she and Jess adored each other, their dad was sober and Reil-ly's biggest worries were getting her homework done on time, or whether she'd still have a blackhead on her face when she went out on her Saturday night date.

Reluctantly, she dragged her gaze away from the photo and brought her mind back to the grim reality of the present day. What was all this about? Was the killer taunting her? Did he know about Jess and what had happened to her? But how could *he* know? No one knew, no one except Reilly and her dad, and of course the people involved ...

Reilly shook her head to clear her thoughts, trying to work this out. The killer had been in her apartment and in her office, of that there was no doubt – but where was he now?

She looked around office for a more appropriate weapon – the shoes just weren't going to cut it. Her eyes glanced over books, magazines then finally settled on a bottle of wine sitting on her shelf – it was a gift from the Christmas party and she'd forgotten to take it home.

Reilly dumped the shoes by her desk and grabbed the bottle. Holding it around the neck she gave a couple of swings – that felt better, something with a bit of weight to it. She listened once more, then headed out of her office toward the lab.

The dreary corridors had never looked remotely threatening before, but now every door she passed was a potential hazard. Reilly pressed herself against the wall and slid along, checking each door she passed. Every time she eased open a door her heart was in her mouth, nervous in case the door creaked, fearing that someone would suddenly leap out – and do what?

As Reilly paused in the doorway of a deserted office she realized that she didn't even know why the killer would be here. The photo album showed that he had been in her apartment – which was a scary enough thought – but he could just as easily have left the album on display there. The effect would have been just as dramatic, and without the same risk.

With sudden comprehension, Reilly realized *that* was the key. The killer was showing off. He was showing the police that there was nowhere they could go, nothing they could do that he didn't know about – which also meant that he could have access to the case files, the evidence ...

Reilly slid the door closed, eased down the corridor, hoping that Simpson had obeyed her instructions and called the nearest unit for backup.

Finally, she reached the lab. She paused, took a deep breath and tried to picture the layout in her mind – where there was good cover, where an intruder might be hiding, what he might be looking at.

It was a large room with plenty of places to hide – there were benches, desks, filing cabinets, equipment. Shit, she thought, you could hide a whole SWAT team in there. Reilly listened one last time, then slipped into the room.

The lights were off but there was a dim glow coming in from the corridor outside. She looked right and left and saw no movement. She listened intently for any sound, any movement, but still it was silent. Breathing quietly, she bent low and crept along a wooden bench that ran toward the back of the room, in and out of the odd-shaped shadows cast by the testing equipment.

As Reilly neared the end of the bench she could see straightaway that the intruder had been there – several of the large gray filing cabinets were open and the Taboo murder case files were scattered over the desk.

Feeling certain that the intruder was no longer there, Reilly stood up slowly and set the wine bottle – her only weapon – on the counter. She scanned the room one more time then looked at the file. It was spread out across the desk, the photos lined up, the papers out of order. *Had the killer been looking for something, or was he trying to communicate something? What had he thought of it?* she wondered. *Had he taken or changed anything?*

Trying to clear her head of her doubts and fears, Reilly ran her gaze across the desk.

Her thoughts were interrupted by a faint sound from behind her, by the door. She spun around just in time to see a figure glide from the room and turn into the corridor.

Damn! He had been there the whole time, watching her. How could she have been so stupid as to relax and start looking at the file when she hadn't cleared the room?

Fueled by adrenaline and anger, Reilly sprinted after the intruder, her stockinged feet sliding on the slick floor. She scrambled to the door, just in time to see someone disappear into the stairwell. Reilly careened after him, her feet slipping and sliding, cursing the lack of a walkie-talkie, a gun, backup – all the things she would have taken for granted back home. And as that thought crossed her mind, she realized that the killer would be all too aware of just how patchy her resources were.

Reaching the door to the stairwell, Reilly threw it open – and ran straight into the barrel of a .38.

26

C hris pushed open the double doors to the GFU unit and stepped inside to be met by a worried-looking Simpson. 'That's it?' the guard asked him, accusingly.

He was confused. 'That's what?'

'You're the backup?'

'Backup?' Chris looked at the security guard like he was crazy. 'I'm just here to see Reilly Steel.'

'She's the one who told me to get backup,' Simpson hurriedly informed him. 'She said that there was an intruder in the building.'

'And she told you to call it in?'

'Said the person was dangerous,' the man went on, 'and told me not to try and stop him myself.'

His heart started to race and he was immediately concerned. 'So where is she?'

'Ms Steel? She went on upstairs.'

Chris was puzzled; none of this was making sense. He made a snap decision. 'I'm going to go up and check on her,' he informed the guard. He stepped toward the lift, then paused, turned back to Simpson. 'You did call it in, I hope?'

'Of course. They said they'd send a patrol over as soon as they could.'

Whatever that meant, Chris thought, worriedly. Chances were neither Simpson nor the nearby patrol had a clue of the urgency of the situation. The GFU building was new enough as it was and few on the force would expect to have to fight off a potentially dangerous suspect there. Still, if Reilly's suspicions were correct, he hoped the cavalry arrived sooner rather than later – for both their sakes.

'When they arrive, tell them everything you've told me, OK?' The lift arrived and he stepped inside. 'And make no mistake, this guy could be *very* dangerous.'

Reaching the fourth floor, he emerged slowly from the lift and looked left and right. Silence. Unholstering his gun, he edged along the corridor. If this was indeed the killer then they knew that he would be armed, and more than willing to kill.

Chris headed toward Reilly's office, pausing briefly to glance through the small window of the door to the stairwell. What he saw froze him to the spot – there was a woman crouched on the stairs. She wasn't moving.

Taking a deep breath, he shouldered the door open.

'Put your hands where I can see them!' he instructed.

The woman lay very still, face down, her blond hair covering her face.

'I won't ask you again!'

Still no response.

Certain now that this was no feint, Chris bent down and gave the woman a nudge. She groaned and slid further down onto the steps. He bent down and brushed her hair back from her face.

'Christ.' There was no mistaking Reilly. He turned her over but she just flopped against him, her face deathly pale, not showing any sign of life. He pressed his fingers to her throat, feeling for a pulse and leaned over her mouth, trying to catch any sign of breathing. Then, very faintly, he felt a tiny, weak pulse against his fingers.

'Reilly. Reilly, are you OK?' he called out, trying to rouse her. But she made no response. Then, despite the groaning ache in his limbs, Chris wrapped his arms around her and slowly climbed to his feet. What the hell had happened?

REILLY WAS DROWNING. The waters were rising fast and she was trapped, her foot caught, held fast beneath the murky waters. She struggled, pulled with all her might, but her foot wouldn't break free.

The waters were swirling around her face. She held her chin high, trying to keep her face above the tide as long as possible, but the progress was inexorable. The water lapped at her neck, her chin, her ears, reached her lips.

Reilly had never feared the water – she had always been comfortable in and around it, seeking it out as a playful companion, but this was different. This water was cold, murky, eddying around her as the level rose, chilling her to her very core.

She clamped her mouth shut, aware for the first time in her life how truly precious air was. Breathing only through her nose she looked up at the gloomy sky, dark clouds raining down on her upturned face.

The clouds veiled the whole sky, a dark cloak over her life, her dreams. But for a moment, just before the waters closed over her nose and eyes she thought she saw a chink in the clouds, a tiny point of sunlight trying to break through the utter and endless darkness.

Then the waters swirled over her and she gave in, allowed the calm, cool darkness to overwhelm her and carry her away.

It was peaceful. She opened her eyes, could see nothing in the murky water. She closed them again, feeling the pressure building slowly in her lungs as the carbon dioxide level rose, as her body's instinct to breathe grew stronger.

But she didn't answer the call. She fought down the urge, forced herself to relax. The water was fluid, soothing, swirling around her, supporting her, relaxing her. There was no more fighting now, just blessed peace ...

'Reilly? Reilly. Open your eyes, come on.'

The darkness was welcoming. If she could just sleep ... no more work, no more worries, no more ...

'Reilly.'

The light shone again, brighter this time, intruding on her tranquillity, pulling her back from a long, peaceful sleep.

'Reilly, open your eyes, love.'

Like a leaf tugged along by the wind, Reilly felt the two different forces pulling at her. The calm, quiet, dark peace of the water, and the loud insistent voice, the bright light.

Her eyes opened with a start. She looked around, bewildered, trying to find something familiar, something that made sense. There was a sharp stabbing pain in her arm. She tried to pull at it, wrench the source of the pain out, but a strong hand stopped her.

Slowly, fighting hard to control her muscles, to focus her eyes, she looked over and saw a paramedic firmly holding an IV in place.

'What ...?' She couldn't form a question. Her mouth didn't want to obey her commands, her eyes were rolling around in her head as the ambulance rattled over the city streets.

It was all too much effort. It had been so much nicer in the water. She closed her eyes again, wanting desperately to return to the sleep, the cool, calm depths of the water.

'Reilly, come on – stay with us.'

Something familiar in the voice made her open her eyes – and there, leaning in to look at her was another face. This one she recognized but couldn't place.

Names spun through her mind, like memories rising up from a deep, faraway place – Jess ... Mike ...Tommy – none of those sounded right. Who *were* those people? Then suddenly her eyes blazed in recognition. 'Chris ...' She reached a hand out to him.

A smile creased his face. 'Good girl.'

Her eyes tried to roll back, but Chris was in her face, keeping her alert and conscious. 'Focus on me, Reilly,' he ordered.

She let out a deep sigh, finally back in the present, and fought to bring her senses back under her control. She tried to raise her head a little and looked around. She was in an ambulance, though she couldn't figure out why. 'Where am I?'

'I found you in the stairwell of your building,' Chris volunteered gently. 'Simpson said you'd reported an intruder.'

As soon as he said it, everything came flooding back. The killer. The killer was there, in the building. Like a scan of a movie at high speed, a series of images flashed across her consciousness: the photo album in her office, her and Jess in their Halloween costumes, the files spread out on the counter in the lab, and then finally the stairwell. She remembered seeing a gun, that cold, unwavering flash of metal, and then something had ... what? Maddeningly, her memory failed her.

'What happened?' she asked, her mouth dry.

'You were out cold when I found you,' Chris replied, a

concerned look on his face. 'I guess they'll have to run some tests to see if—'

Suddenly the final image locked into place in Reilly's brain. A hypodermic. 'Pentobarbital,' she gasped.

Chris looked at her in amazement.

Reilly licked her lips. Speech was still hard work. 'He was there, Chris. He was there. I think he was trying to get a look at the files – and then I interrupted him and he injected me with pentobarbital.'

Chris looked puzzled. 'How the hell did he gain access to the lab?'

'He must have broken in to my apartment and stolen my ID. I couldn't find it this morning and then Simpson said—'

Then something struck her. 'Actually no,' she told Chris, the realization striking her. 'It couldn't have been him who attacked me just now. We were right before – there has to be somebody else involved.'

27

Later, Reilly lay quietly in the hospital bed while a plump young nurse fussed around her. When she leaned over she smelled pleasantly of white jasmine, and maybe mint. Jo Malone, Reilly pinpointed, it was a popular brand in this part of the world.

She had slept on and off throughout the day but was feeling better now. The nurse changed her IV bag, plumped her pillows, then tucked the crisp white sheets up under her arms. Finally, she stood back and regarded her.

'You feeling all right now, honey?' She had a delightfully distinctive North Dublin accent, the kind that made Reilly want to smile just listening to it.

'I'm fine, thanks. What time is it?'

The nurse checked her watch, clipped to the front of her uniform. 'Almost four o'clock,' she informed her.

'Four? I've slept for most of the day.' She managed a tired smile. 'Wow, after that much sleep I think I feel better than most mornings.'

The nurse looked at her for a moment then nodded.

'There's been a fella waiting outside for a while; are you up to a visit?'

'Sure. I could do with a distraction.'

'I'll send him in.' She glanced over toward the door and gave Reilly a surreptitious wink. 'Good-looking fella he is too ...'

She bustled out, and moments later Chris hurried in, a small bouquet of tiger lilies in his hand. He held them out like a trophy, as if unsure what the correct protocol was.

'How's it going? These are for you.'

Reilly smiled. 'They're great, thanks – you can put them over there.' She nodded to the bedside cabinet. 'I'll have the nurse put them in water later.'

Chris duly lay the bouquet down on the bedside table, then turned and dragged a chair over to sit beside the bed.

He settled himself on the chair and then looked around at the other patients in the ward. There was a mixture of young and old, some sleeping, others propped up in bed watching TV. 'So how are you feeling?' he asked, finally. 'You gave us all a hell of a scare.'

'Yeah, I'll bet Kennedy was *really* worried,' she said, chuckling.

'He sends his regards,' Chris informed her. 'In fact, he was the one who warned me not to turn up without flowers.' Despite his jovial tone, there was concern written all over his face. He was watching her carefully, as if searching for anything untoward in her eyes.

She felt oddly touched by his concern. 'I'm tired, but OK,' she said. Then she paused. 'I gather from the nurse that I have you to thank for getting me here so quickly?'

'Yeah, well when I found you on the stairs I was in two minds whether or not to leave you there. All that surfing and swimming, I thought you'd probably weigh a tonne with those muscles ...'

Reilly looked down at her short-sleeved hospital gown and playfully flexed a muscle. 'Yep, a real heavyweight, that's me.'

'But, somehow, I managed to get you down to the lobby.'

She rewarded him with a warm smile. 'Thanks. I really mean that.' It couldn't have been an easy task in his weakened condition.

'Once the paramedics took over I went back up to your office to see if there was any sign of him – or her.' He paused a little. 'I noticed something on your desk.'

'The photo album?' she said, having almost forgotten about that.

Chris nodded.

'It was taken from my apartment. I think it's supposed to be some kind of message.'

'What kind of message? I saw the photo – it looked like a standard family shot.'

'I wish I knew.' The appearance of such a personal item had shaken her badly. Besides breaking into her apartment and invading her home, what was the killer playing at with that photo?

'It's a bit of a mindblower, Reilly,' Chris admitted. He gave a deep sigh. 'This is serious shit. Someone broke into your apartment, stole your ID, could have bloody killed you and now they're leaving you cryptic messages?'

'I know.'

'Fancy a cup of tea, love?'

They both looked around in surprise at the tea lady making her rounds. She looked over at Reilly, inquiringly.

'No, I'm fine, thanks.'

She was warm and motherly in her apron, clearly determined that everyone should have the comfort of a warm cup of tea at least three times a day. But unlike the nurse, her scent was unrecognizable to Reilly. Some kind of floral concoction, and not a fragrance, but perhaps a body lotion or face cream. 'And what about your husband?' she asked, turning to Chris. 'How about you, love?'

'I'm not – I mean, I'm ...' Chris looked back at Reilly and saw her trying hard not to laugh. 'A cup of tea would be lovely, thanks,' he finally replied.

They sat in silence while she poured his tea, only to dissolve in a fit of laughter when the woman finally moved on to the next patient.

'Christ, do I look that settled?' he protested.

'If only she knew,' Reilly added, wryly.

He sipped at his tea. 'Still, a cup of brew is fairly welcome right now.'

'Enjoy it,' said Reilly. 'You know, in the States they don't have little old ladies coming round offering you free cups of tea when you're in hospital.'

'Yeah, I've heard they charge you for everything over there – even aspirin.'

Reilly slipped back into silence. She knew the small talk was simply their way of delaying the disturbing reality that still loomed large over them. Chris sipped his tea and waited for her to tell him more about the photo album.

She sat up and pulled the covers up around her. 'The picture ... it's of me and my dad and my baby sister, Jess. My mom left when we were young – Jess was only a toddler – so I pretty much raised her.'

'What's the age gap?'

'Five years.'

'That's pretty young to become a surrogate mum.'

'Dad was always at work, there *was* no one else.'

He nodded. 'Still, it must have been tough.'

Reilly looked at him and while she couldn't be absolutely sure, she was still almost certain Chris knew more about her family situation than he was letting on. *Damn ...*

'So it was up to you to take care of your little sister?'

'Yes. My dad – well as I said, he worked a lot and then ... later he drank a lot too.'

'You mentioned he lives here in Dublin now.'

She nodded.

'What about your sister? Are you two still in touch?'

Reilly glanced up quickly, certain that he was testing her but no, his expression was as clear and open as it always was.

'No,' she replied, softly.

'So what's all this about?' Chris asked. 'Why's this guy so interested in you and your family? What's it got to do with the murders?'

Reilly looked down at the IV drip in her arm. 'I'm not sure yet,' she replied. Looking up, she spotted a nurse across the ward. She tried to catch her eye. 'Excuse me?' she waved. The nurse saw her and signaled at her to wait a moment.

'What are you doing?' Chris asked, surprised at her sudden change in mood.

'You're right, we need to know what's going on and we've already wasted too much time today,' she said, starting to climb out of the bed.

'Reilly, what are you doing?' Chris protested, reaching out and trying to restrain her. 'You've been injected with a potentially lethal anaesthetic. You've got to give your body time to get over that. You need to rest.'

'Yeah, well I think I got enough rest today to last me for a lifetime.' Reilly ripped the IV from her arm. 'Right now, I need to talk to Daniel.'

IN THE EVENT, Reilly had to wait. Forrest was out of his office
when she called, so the best she could do was leave a message.
But she knew that the voicemail she left would guarantee that
he called her as soon as he picked it up: 'We think the perp
broke into the lab and attacked me. We need to talk.'

She hung up the phone. 'If that doesn't get him to call,
nothing will,' she informed Chris.

When it became clear that she was going to leave the
hospital no matter what anyone said, Chris insisted on accom-
panying her back to the lab – reluctant to leave her alone. He
still hadn't quite got over the sight of her fading away in the
stairwell, or the moment in the ambulance ride to the hospital
when he'd thought she was gone.

As soon as word got out that Reilly was back, her staff
hurried in to check on her and ask questions.

The last to appear was Julius. After saying all the right
things, he was straight back to business, dropping off the most
recent report from the lab on the evidence collected at the
Miles scene.

'You'll be happy to know that there's some decent trace
here, something that also appeared at the Ryan and Watson
scenes but in more minuscule amounts.'

Reilly picked up the report and began reading. 'Anything
interesting?'

He nodded. 'Could be. Check out the fifth item down.'

'Calcium sulphate,' she read out for Chris's benefit.
'Gypsum.'

'What's that?' he asked, eager to hear about anything that
might help break this – especially when this guy seemed to be
not only escalating, but getting bolder too. You didn't need to
be a big-shot profiler to know that breaking into Reilly's place
and attacking her at the lab was a clear statement of intent, or
even worse – an assertion of control.

'Technically, it's a naturally occurring mineral, but has a number of applications in everyday life – blackboard chalk, plaster board, plaster of Paris—'

Julius cut in. 'I was thinking that the plaster of Paris, coupled with the pentobarbital and animal hair samples adds even more weight to the veterinary angle.'

'You think our guy might work in a vet's?' Chris asked and Julius looked at Reilly for affirmation.

'It's certainly a possibility – and a useful find. But it could just as easily be chalk dust from a teacher or lecturer or even a lab worker ...' He watched her turn the list of possibilities over in her head. 'Thanks, Julius. It gives us something to think about.'

'No problem. Erm ...' He lingered a little, looking somewhat uncomfortably at Chris.

Reilly picked up on it. 'Anything else?'

'Well, I also got back those blood test results you wanted ... for that other case,' he said, cryptically, a second sheaf of paper in his hands. 'I thought you might want to take a look at them, but I can bring them back later if you like.'

Reilly held out her hand. 'Great. Right now is fine, thank you.'

'Yes, well ... again, we're all glad you're OK.' He nodded, then turned and left.

Chris looked carefully at her. 'Blood tests? Would those happen to be ...?'

'Why don't you close the door?' she suggested, quietly.

He did as he was bid, then sat down and faced her expectantly – he was unsure if he wanted them to have found something or not. While it would be a relief to know what was wrong with him, to have it out in the open and to try to deal with it, another side of him was hoping that there was nothing at all wrong, maybe just old-fashioned fatigue or something he'd get over in time. He fixed his gaze on Reilly, trying to read her face as she read through the report sheet. She looked thoughtful.

'What is it?' he urged, unable to contain his impatience any longer. 'Do I have cancer or something?'

Her eyes gave nothing away. 'Chris, to be honest, I still don't know. There was something out of kilter in my initial screen, so I ordered another, but ...'

'Out of kilter?'

'Some of the numbers were above normal parameters, but the second test seems to have come out fine.' She exhaled deeply. 'Look, I'm no doctor, and there's a limit to what we can do at the lab here – you need to see a specialist, someone who can look at the overall symptoms. A blood test is really nothing more than a shot in the dark.'

He nodded, trying not to betray his disappointment, and he could tell by Reilly's frustrated expression that she felt the same way. 'Thanks for trying anyway, I appreciate that.'

'I'm only sorry I couldn't put your mind at ease. But Chris, you need to get this looked at; you can't ignore it indefinitely.'

'You're right,' he conceded. 'Although coming from someone who's just skipped out of hospital against doctor's orders ...'

She gave a weak smile. 'That's different, we've got a lot to do. And speaking of which,' she stood up, 'thanks for babysitting me this morning, but you need to go away now and let me get some work done. I need to read through this latest batch of results and see if I can—'

'Can't do that, I'm afraid.' Chris folded the papers and slipped them in his pocket.

She looked at him sharply. 'What?'

'Reilly, it might have been water off a duck's back to you,

but a major crime was committed here today,' he explained. 'And we need to debrief you.'

'We?'

As if on cue, there was a knock at the door.

Kennedy poked his head round the door and grinned sheepishly. 'We ready? I'm looking forward to this.'

ALTHOUGH REILLY WASN'T in the mood to talk about her recent experience, she understood the necessity of it. In fact, it was only when she sat down with the two detectives that she realized how shaken up she actually was.

It was now late evening, and while she had been sleeping at the hospital, her team had already processed the crime scenes – the lab and her own office.

And despite the personal aspect, she knew her assessment of the evidence they'd collected had to be as cold and ruthless as it would with any other.

Kennedy was in an unusually conciliatory mood. Although he had been dismissive of some of her methods in the past, he seemed to understand that this was no time to press his agenda. He carefully walked her through the whole scenario as it had unfolded, from the moment that Reilly had walked in the door of the building that morning until the point where she had blacked out.

'But you don't remember actually seeing the perp?'

She sighed heavily, frustrated at herself. 'No. I was hit over the head as soon as I entered the stairwell, so I didn't have time to register anything but the gun and then the hypodermic. I'd still wager that the person was female though. How else would they have got through security with my pass?'

'We'll have to keep an open mind on that one for the

moment,' Chris said. 'Seeing as there's no CCTV in operation in this building.'

'Yeah, what brainbox decided that?' Kennedy growled.

'I raised it when I took the job but was told it wasn't considered a priority. I thought it was cute at the time,' Reilly replied, kneading her forehead in frustration. 'Little did I know.'

Kennedy closed his notebook with a snap and settled back in the chair. 'So what have we learned from all of this?'

'We know how brazen our killer is for starters,' Chris offered. 'Getting up close and personal like that ...'

'But where is this all going, Reilly?' Kennedy asked. 'You're the expert here.'

She rocked back in her chair, suddenly feeling drawn and tired. She ran a hand through her hair. 'That's the sixty-four thousand dollar question, isn't it?'

'OK,' said Kennedy. 'Let's start with an easier one. Irrespective of whether or not it was our guy or some accomplice, why did the perp come here today? Why expose himself, why take that risk?'

'Because he's enjoying himself and he wants us to know it,' Chris suggested.

'Right,' she concurred. 'He wants us to know it's him, to think about him. It makes him feel special, important, to know that he's constantly on our minds.'

'Looking for attention, you mean? Sounds like a school kid,' Kennedy said, gruffly.

Chris looked puzzled. 'How's that?'

'You don't have kids, you wouldn't understand.' He turned to Reilly. 'You'll get it though – seeing as you're into all this psychological claptrap.'

'Go on.'

'Well, when our kids started school, the teachers told us

that one of the things that helps them adjust – and not be
scared about going to school and all that nonsense – was for
us parents to let them know that we're thinking about them.'
He looked uncomfortable, admitting something so personal.
'So we did. Every morning when I dropped the girls off at
school, I reminded them of the family photograph I carry
around in my wallet. And it worked.'

'So they felt like a part of them was always with you,'
Reilly added, thoughtfully.

'Yeah.'

She looked at him, lips pursed in concern. 'We really need
to talk to Daniel.'

28

R eilly woke from a deep sleep. She looked around afraid, half imagining someone hovering over her, hypodermic in hand. The sharp trill of her bedside phone brought her back to reality.

She glanced at the clock – 2.25 a.m. – and snatched up the handset.

'Hey, Daniel.'

'Reilly? Did I wake you?'

Just hearing his warm baritone with its soft Virginia burr calmed her. 'Yeah, but it's OK.'

'I was out earlier – I just got back and picked up your message.' He let out a deep breath. 'That's been quite some day you've had. Are you OK?'

She sat up, pulled the covers up tight around her, and swept her hair back out of her eyes. She was wide awake now. 'It's fine, I'm OK.'

He cleared his throat. 'The tone of your follow-up e-mail was informative but rather dry.'

Reilly chuckled humorlessly. 'What – did you expect to see evidence that I'd been crying on my keyboard as I typed?'

'How are you – honestly?'

She considered a moment. Earlier she'd been too busy to really think about how all this had affected her – she'd just been trying to deal with it. 'I'm ...' She paused. 'I guess I'm still trying to understand what it means.'

Daniel laughed softly. 'A classic Reilly answer.'

'What do you mean?'

'I ask you how you are – that's a question on an emotional level. You tell me you're trying to understand it – that's an answer on an intellectual level.'

Reilly gazed out the window at the cloudy night sky as she spoke. 'It really wasn't meant to be evasive, Daniel,' she replied. 'I mean, yes I'm struggling to understand what all of this means. The photograph, that one in particular and the note – what's going on here? It's like the killer knows me, knows about Jess too, but how? I'm worried now that there's a lot more to this than meets the eye.'

And just then, the shell cracked, the cold, professional demeanour that Reilly always presented to the world finally broke, and the tears began to flow freely.

Daniel, three thousand miles away, heard her soft sobs and knew what it meant. He felt three thousand light years away for all the comfort he could offer. All he could do was sit and listen, knowing it was what she needed, knowing that she just had to cry herself out. 'It's OK, Reilly, it's OK,' he murmured, softly.

She clutched the phone tightly, comforted simply by his presence on the other end of the line, images of Jess and her childhood flashing through her mind. He knew probably better than anyone how much it had affected her back then, how hard she'd tried to move away from it, put the horror of it all behind her. But now, to have it come back to haunt her, and here of all places ...

Finally, the tears began to lessen. Reilly grabbed a tissue from the box on her bedside, dabbed her cheeks and blew her nose. 'That was embarrassing,' she sniffed, finally.

'Not at all,' Daniel said, gently. 'I was just concerned that your phone might get too soggy and we'd lose the connection.'

She laughed quietly, and realized as she did so that she was already feeling better. 'Thanks. Honestly. You're the only one I can talk to about this. The guys I'm working with here don't know, at least I don't think they do.' She thought again about Chris's gentle questioning at the hospital earlier.

'Well, that's neither here nor there. The question is what does our killer know and is he using the information to try and undermine you? That would be my first guess. After all, these days it's easy enough to do a basic background search on a person using search engines and whatnot.'

Reilly nodded. Of course, it would be easy enough for anyone who wanted to know more about her to have stumbled across the old newspaper articles and reports from back then. And if you were searching for a weak spot ...

'Exactly,' Daniel concurred when Reilly suggested that this might be the killer's intention. 'We already know that psychological games are a huge part of his MO. He's getting a huge buzz from pitting his wits against one of the FBI's finest. Middle-aged, red-nosed Irish cops don't have quite the same appeal, do they?'

She smiled, realizing he was echoing her earlier description of Kennedy back to her.

'So assuming he *has* locked onto me as an opponent, and figured Jess as my weak spot. How do I deal with it?'

'Deal with it as you would any other. Disregard the personal – so as not to give him that leverage – and don't afford him any special treatment.' But there was something in his voice that made Reilly wonder if he had another, alternative theory to the one they were discussing.

'You really think it's that simple?' she asked. 'That he's trying to gain an edge over the investigation by undermining me personally?'

'It's certainly the most likely option, yes.'

Ockham's razor ...

'And the other? Because I've known you long enough to tell that there's something else on your mind, Daniel. Something you're not telling me.'

Daniel's voice was measured. 'Whatever makes you say that? Clearly the killer has singled you out, dug up some information on your past and is using it to try and unsettle you. End of story.'

OK, so he wasn't going to share his thoughts just yet, Reilly realized, at least not until he was sure of them. But there was something else Daniel was considering, she was certain of it. And whatever it was, she really hoped it wasn't something that would necessitate digging up that troubled past and facing the pain of it afresh.

TWO DAYS LATER, Reilly was chomping at the bit to return to work. At the insistence of her lab boss, she'd taken a day off to recover from the attack and while she'd been adamant this wasn't necessary, there was no arguing with him.

She hated having to cool her heels at home when there was a killer on the loose and had used much of the time researching Freud and taboos online. This morning she was itching to get back to the lab to find out what evidence the team had uncovered from the break-in but had been summoned to the incident room for an early meeting with Inspector O'Brien. She could hardly refuse given what had happened at the lab and it was vital that communications and relationships between all strands of the investigative team were solid.

However, it was no secret that O'Brien was good friends with Jack Gorman, the senior forensic investigator, and was likely to find Reilly's methods about as appealing as he did. Reilly just hoped Chris and Kennedy would be there to stick up for her.

Armed with a strong coffee and a stack of case files, she made her way to the main conference room at the station. She gave a sniff of disgust as she entered the room – even though a smoking ban had been in effect for a couple of years, decades of tobacco usage had permeated the carpet and the furniture and stained the ceiling yellow. The room stank of it.

As was her habit, Reilly was the first to arrive. She was a good ten minutes early, which gave her time to choose a seat on the far side of the room and get her files organized.

It was a little after eight thirty when O'Brien rolled in, with Chris and Pete Kennedy right behind him. Reilly studied the older man as he made himself comfortable. She'd put him in his early fifties, thick salt and pepper hair, worn a little too long for his age. He'd probably had the same hairstyle since the Seventies, she mused. He had a round face, a country boy's charm, but Reilly could tell that under the bluff exterior he was sharp – you didn't get this far in the job without being something of a player. It took thick skin and good political skills to rise to the top.

He gave Reilly a charming smile. 'Heard you had quite a week, Ms Steel. You feeling all right now?'

'I'm fine, thanks.'

He turned straight to the detectives. 'You boys turned up anything useful on the break-in?'

Kennedy shook his head. 'Nope, the guy just disappeared like a ghost.'

'No CCTV at street level?'

'We've picked up about twenty seconds from the cameras in the street,' Chris said. 'The intruder left the lab and headed straight into the café across the road. No one matching that appearance reappeared.'

'He would have been prepared,' interjected Reilly.

O'Brien spun around on her. 'Would he now? How do you figure that?'

'Assuming he is our suspect, our perp is a meticulous planner – the murders tell us that.' She leaned forward to make her point. 'That little visit would have been planned for days – I would imagine there was a change of clothes stashed somewhere in that café, or a back door out of there, something along those lines.'

Chris nodded. 'We checked out the café – it does have a back door, out past the loos. It was busy with breakfast trade at that time, anyone could have slipped out the back unnoticed.'

'Where does the back door lead?' O'Brien asked.

'Back alleyway – again, no CCTV. From there, a person could have gone just about anywhere.'

O'Brien snorted in disgust. 'I can't believe we had a suspect right under our noses – in our own shaggin' building – and we let him get away!'

'Bloody hell Chief,' Kennedy replied, defensively. 'This person was armed, knew the territory, had the element of surprise in his favor—'

The rest of his sentence was cut off by a loud thump as O'Brien dropped a pile of newspapers on the table. Judging by the screaming headlines on the ones Reilly could see, the media had well and truly begun running with the serial killer angle.

'Look at this shit!' O'Brien thundered. 'Taboo Killer! They even have a name for this gobshite now! And I'll tell you one thing, if it gets out that there was a break-in at the lab, we're in even deeper shit because they've the public thinking he's running rings around us as it is.'

'Sir—'

'And what about the victims?' he interjected, pointing at the front-page photographs of Gerry Watson and Clare Ryan. It could only have helped that these two victims in particular were younger and more attractive than poor old Sarah Miles and her aunt. There seemed to be no mention of Jim Redmond though, which meant that either they hadn't realized his death was a part of this, or the manner of his death was simply not gratuitous enough for them. 'What's the connection?' O'Brien thundered. 'How is he finding them?'

Reilly looked at Chris. 'We still don't know that yet, sir,' she replied. 'Although based on what trace evidence we have, we're thinking he might work in a vet's practice, or maybe a lab somewhere – the lab identified traces of calcium sulphate at—'

'Chalk dust?' the older man sneered. 'The state paid out millions for the fancy equipment the GFU have over there, and all you can come up with is feckin' chalk dust?'

'With respect, Chief,' Kennedy began. 'If it wasn't for Steel we might not have made a link between the first two victims at all.'

Reilly looked at him, amazed at this concession. Meeting her eye, he gave her the briefest of winks.

'Well that makes ye a shower of even worse imbeciles then, doesn't it?' He threw his pen down on top of the pile of newspapers. 'Tell me,' he demanded, his tone suddenly harsher, 'if we know so much about this psycho how come we haven't caught him yet?' His gaze traveled the room, finally coming to rest on Reilly again. It was what she had been expecting.

'We do seem to know a lot about the perpetrator—' she began, but he cut her off.

'*Seem* to! We're paying this profiler guy you wanted a *fortune*, for Christ's sake! How much more bloody information do we need!'

She stayed calm. 'We should have Daniel's profile by the end of the working day.' At least, she hoped they would. 'But what I was about to say was that we seem to know a lot about him for a reason,' she went on. 'What we know is exactly what he wants us to know – no more, no less. He's made no mistakes, no slip-ups. The trace evidence is the best chance we have of finding out more about him, where he works, the places he frequents, or where he might be hiding out, that kind of thing. Everything else we know is based either on clues he has deliberately left us. Like I said, we'll have an official profile to work with soon, but in the meantime, please be advised that my team and I are working literally around the clock on this.'

O'Brien continued looking at her for a moment, then finally relaxed his gaze before turning to look at the two detectives. 'So, if the lab doesn't have anything useful to contribute, where are you two these days?'

Kennedy gave a resigned shrug. 'We're following a couple of leads, especially in relation to the victims' families, but other than that—'

'So we're really no nearer solving this than we were when those Ryan kids showed up dead?' he concluded.

'I'm still not sure that's a fair summary, Chief—' Chris began.

'Oh you're not, aren't you?' O'Brien glared at him. 'So tell me, Detective Delaney,' he spat his name out with almost a sneer, 'Who is this guy? And where is he going to strike next? Can you answer me that?'

The room fell silent. O'Brien slurped noisily on his coffee, stared from one to the other. 'Let me tell you lot something, with a high-profile case like this, results are *everything*. I don't care how fecking clever you all think you're being, or what your lab results and profiles tell you – until the moment you have that fecker banged up with a pair of handcuffs on him, you're all just pissing in the dark. And right now I'm the one who's getting wet!'

There was a soft knock at the door. He stood up and glared around the room at them all. 'You'd better come up with something positive soon because I don't like the way this investigation is being run – and it's not about to get any better in my opinion.'

He walked to the door and stepped outside. The others looked at each other, all deducing that this wasn't just a standard briefing – something else was going on.

'Not about to get any better? What does he mean by that?' Chris asked.

'I have a feeling that guff we've just heard was only for the cameras,' Kennedy said.

They could hear O'Brien in a whispered conversation outside the door. He still sounded worked-up but was trying to keep his voice down.

Finally, the door opened again and the Inspector walked back in, followed by two other men. His deferential manner toward them made it quite clear that these were his superiors.

He waited for them to sit down and fussed around fetching them coffee. Reilly recognized one of them – Chief Superintendent Armstrong who'd been involved in her recruitment from the States. He was a big man, huge hands, a strong jaw.

In his sober dark suit you could see his muscular build. He had short cropped gray hair, and could have been anywhere between fifty and sixty years old.

The other man was older. He was small, dapper, in an immaculate gray suit with a matching tie and pocket handkerchief, an expensive haircut, an air of calm superiority on his face as he surveyed the room.

Armstrong nodded to the two detectives as O'Brien finally sat down. 'These are Detectives Kennedy and Delaney, and the current acting head of GFU, Reilly Steel,' he introduced them one by one to the other man. 'This is Commissioner Patrick Moloney.'

Moloney nodded to each of them in turn, letting his gaze settle on Reilly a little too long. 'Ms Steel – I've heard some good things about you.'

Reilly wasn't sure how to reply. She finally managed an embarrassed, 'Thank you, sir.'

Moloney took a delicate sip of his coffee, and looked at everyone in turn. He spoke quietly, calmly, each word carefully chosen. 'This unfortunate affair took a rather ... unexpected turn recently, didn't it?' No one responded. 'A dangerous intruder assaults one of our own people, in our laboratory.' He sipped again at his coffee. 'Which means that this matter has rather slipped the coop, so to speak.' He sighed, as though this was all rather bothersome. 'When something of that nature happens it ceases to be simply a local matter.'

Kennedy was right, Reilly realized, they were bringing in the big guns now, and judging by the look on O'Brien's face, not with his blessing.

'We're dealing with this fine,' O'Brien growled. 'In fact, one of our senior investigators is returning early from annual leave to row in on this.'

At this Reilly's head snapped up. Jack Gorman would indeed be back in the mix sooner than she'd thought. Damn.

Moloney smiled with all the charm of a Nile crocodile about to consume its prey. 'I'm sure you are, Inspector. However,' he glanced around, making sure he had everyone's full attention, 'as already explained, this investigation has become top national priority.'

'It's already top priority,' Kennedy said shortly and O'Brien glared at him too.

'We have a murderer running around Dublin dispatching our citizens at a frightening rate,' Moloney went on. 'This is naturally of huge concern to the public, the Minister and the Irish Government as a whole.' He looked toward Reilly. 'And without wanting to devalue the expertise of our own, we felt we could do with more specialized on-the-ground help in a matter of this magnitude.'

He now had everyone's attention. Reilly glanced around, wondering where this was leading. O'Brien definitely wasn't happy about it – he looked like he'd just bitten into a lemon.

'I believe you've recently begun working with Mr Daniel Forrest from the FBI?' Moloney continued, turning to Reilly. She nodded, an unsettling knot suddenly appearing in the depths of her stomach. 'Well, it appears that his superiors in Quantico feel that in order to assist us in apprehending this murderer in the fastest possible time, it might be more beneficial to have him on the ground here.'

'Here – in Dublin?' she echoed.

'Yes. Needless to say the Minister and I are all for anything that might assist in our bringing this ... situation to a timely and satisfactory conclusion.'

In other words, Reilly thought, *the public are baying for blood and the pressure is on.*

She swallowed hard. There was no way Daniel would

allow himself to be uprooted from Quantico on the whim of a
government official, no matter how pressing the circumstances might be. Far more likely he'd instigated this himself,
most likely because of the break-in and perhaps also because
of her mini breakdown on the phone the last time they'd
spoken. Reilly cursed herself for letting her guard down and
allowing her emotions rise to the fore.

Yes, Daniel was behind this, she was sure of it. But what
she couldn't be sure of was whether he was coming to assist
her, or protect her.

29

The meeting over, Reilly headed straight to the GFU building. She went directly to the lab to see what her team had discovered from their survey of the evidence from the break-in.

'Hey there. How are you feeling?' Lucy asked. Reilly looked around at their faces, touched by their obvious concern. She allowed a small smile to crease the corners of her mouth but was anxious to get back to business. 'I'm fine, guys, thanks for asking. So tell me, what do we have from yesterday?'

Gary spoke first. 'We processed as much of this floor as we could. Lucy took your office, Rory covered the lab, and I took the stairwell.'

'Good job.' She was proud of them. Even without her supervision they had covered all bases.

Lucy held some papers out to her. 'The main thing in your office was the photo album. We figured you would know the significance of the photo.'

Reilly could still see the attached note in her mind. '*Happy Families.*'

'Not exactly, but I think it's safe to assume that whatever message he's trying to get across it's personal.'

Lucy looked troubled. 'I also analyzed the notepaper, but it's just a generic yellow post-it pad, could have been bought in a million different places or even taken from your own desk drawer, so no lead there.'

Reilly nodded, expecting as much. 'What else do we have?'

'I processed the lab.' Rory said. 'Whoever was in there was looking at the case files – they were spread out on a table at the back of the room, as you probably saw.'

She recalled that all too clearly. 'Yeah, they distracted me while he slipped out behind me.'

He pulled a large eight by ten photo out of a file. 'When we looked at what he'd done with the files, how he'd put them almost in order, we started wondering if there might have been a pattern.'

'A pattern to the killings, you mean?'

'Yes.'

Reilly studied the photo. One lab report from each crime scene had been neatly laid out in a row, in chronological order, from the Ryans to Redmond to Watson, with the Sarah and Vera Miles killings following on. But there was also a gap, a space left between the Miles killings and the Watson photo. Reilly looked up at Rory and Gary. 'What do you think?'

Gary spoke, careful and considered as always. 'The first killing – the Ryans – was blatant, eye-catching, guaranteed to get people's attention.' He paused, looked around at the others who were watching him intently. 'He could have killed them in just about any way he wanted, but he chose the gun – loud, attention grabbing. It guaranteed that that first crime scene was found almost immediately.'

'Good point,' Reilly agreed. 'What else?'

'Well, Jim Redmond was pretty much the same – we know

that our killer tracks his victims very closely, so he would have known his wife's movements, would have known that she would soon discover the body.'

'So again, no time delays,' Lucy mused.

'Right. And once his calling card – the whole Freud thing - is discovered,' he pointed to another file, 'we come to the Miles and the Watson killings. Both were designed and executed in such a way that they would take that bit longer to find. Watson out in the open in a deserted area and the Mileses a quiet family who kept to themselves.'

Rory spoke up again. 'So when we saw a gap in the layout of the photographs that he left us, we wondered if it meant something.'

'That we've missed one,' Reilly concluded, her heart racing.

'Right.' Rory cleared his throat again. 'We know when the Miles women were killed,' he checked his notes 'on the 28th, so we thought maybe the police should check missing person reports for anyone who went missing in the weeks leading up to that date.'

Reilly stared at the photos of the crime scenes. 'Good thinking,' she said, making a mental note to share this line of thinking with Chris and Kennedy.

'You said you swept the stairwell?' She turned to Gary again, whose serious expression never seemed to change, whether he was discussing a sub-standard sandwich from the canteen or a gruesome murder. It was a trait she appreciated – he was going to make a great investigator.

'Yes.'

'What did you find?'

'The perp didn't leave much. No sign of the weapon and there was very little of note in the line of trace – except for this.' He held up a clear evidence bag.

'Well, I'll be damned.' Reilly reached for the bag and slowly turned it over in her hand. Inside was a single strand of blond hair – long and straight. 'Real or imitation?' she asked Gary, wondering if the intruder had worn a wig and disguised himself as a female in order to get past security.

'Definitely real,' he replied. 'It was one of the first things I checked.'

Reilly stared at the hair. Given the intruder's interest in the case files, there was little doubt that it was someone connected to the killings. So was this yet another piece of staged evidence designed to throw them off the scent, or was there a possibility that the person they were looking for was actually a woman?

LATER THAT EVENING, Reilly left the lab and headed toward the city centre. It was time to pay her father a much overdue visit.

In truth, she was dreading seeing him again. After their last conversation she had called him a couple of times but he hadn't answered his phone. That was pretty normal – Mike spent a lot of time drunk or passed out and rarely bothered with social niceties like communicating with his daughter. But given the current situation, she couldn't simply assume that he was OK.

Reilly looked out at the gloomy streets. Although spring was making its first tentative appearances in the city's parks – she had already seen daffodils in the Phoenix Park – here in the grimy run-down inner city, there was nothing but gray, damp concrete beneath her feet, and gray damp sky above.

She rang Mike's doorbell, listening for sounds of life inside. Nothing, as usual. She slid the spare key into the lock and pushed the door open.

'Dad? It's me,' she called as she stepped inside.

Silence.

She stood in the hallway, her senses fully attuned. The flat was completely still but there was a strong, overpowering odour. Reilly scrunched up her nose in disgust and headed to the living room.

She wasn't surprised by what she found. Mike was asleep – or passed out – on the floor. He was lying in a pool of his own vomit and surrounded by empties.

Reilly counted at least nine empty beer cans, plus several drained spirit bottles. It was clear that last night he had settled down for a long, hard session and had only stopped when his body had finally reached its limit.

She stepped over his inert body and opened the curtains. The dim light from the street lights made little difference, but once she got a couple of windows open, the fug gradually began to clear.

Reilly was fit and strong but it still took all she had just to roll Mike across the floor and prop him against one of the armchairs. How on earth was she going to move him into the bathroom and get him cleaned up?

She stood up and looked down at her comatose father. He was a big man, muscular in his prime, and even now he carried a lot of meat on his frame. He was at least fifteen stone, and fifteen stone of dead weight took a lot of moving.

Reilly suddenly reached a decision. She pulled her phone from her coat pocket, and snapping it open, punched in a number.

'Chris – hi, it's me,' she said when he picked up. 'Are you still at the station?'

'Unfortunately yes,' he replied. 'Why, what's up?'

She paused. 'Well, look, I know you're tied up at the moment, but I need to ask you a favor.'

'Of course, what do you need?'

She looked again at her father, snoring loudly. 'You've

shared a secret of yours with me – I think it's time to let you in on one of mine ...'

CHRIS WAS EXACTLY the sort of guy you needed when you were in a bind, Reilly thought. He was at Mike's dingy flat in less than half an hour.

Now, he surveyed the room, his gaze resting on the empties from Mike's drinking binge. 'He likes his gargle, doesn't he?'

Reilly arched an eyebrow. 'Bit of an understatement.'

'I suppose.' He looked at the older man's snoring carcass. 'What do you want to do with him?'

'I figured if we can get him into the bathroom we can dump him in the shower,' she explained. 'The water will wake him up and clean him up at the same time.'

'Sounds like a plan.'

Grabbing an arm each they hauled him across the living room floor, down the hall, and into the tiny bathroom. It took some maneuvering, but finally they had him propped up against the edge of the bath. Reilly slumped down on the toilet seat. Chris seemed pretty tired too.

'Sorry to drag you into all this, particularly in your state,' she said.

'It's not a problem, honestly.'

'Have you made an appointment to see someone yet?'

He shook his head. 'I haven't really had the chance. Maybe when all of this is over ...'

She gave him a doubtful look. 'Doesn't seem like you should wait that long.' But there was little point in forcing him; she'd done her part and it was up to Chris to follow through on the rest. She couldn't get too personally involved.

She turned on the shower. 'Let's get him situated.'

They both grabbed Mike's arms, lifted him up and unceremoniously dumped him in the shower. As the cold water rained down he gave a violent shudder, coughed, then sat up, with a shake of his head.

'What the hell?' he cried, looking around wildly. Then his gaze settled on Reilly. 'I might have bloody known.'

She shook her head in dismay. 'You're welcome,'

He suddenly noticed Chris. 'And who the hell are you? Some new fancy man or something?'

'He's a colleague,' Reilly said, testily, 'and he helped me move your stinking carcass.'

Mike was still slumped against the back wall of the shower cubicle, his feet sticking out. He looked up at Reilly reproachfully. 'Guy can't even drink himself to death without some busybody coming round and trying to save him.' He reached up and batted feebly at the water. 'Can you turn that goddamn water off? I'm awake, all right?'

Reilly looked at him for a moment longer, then slowly turned off the shower. 'I'll get you some dry clothes and a towel.' She turned and left the bathroom.

Mike's voice followed her out of the room. 'And put the damn kettle on. Now you've woken me up it's the least you can do.'

A few minutes later, Chris and Reilly perched on the two armchairs, sipping coffee. She had cleaned the place up a little – the vomit was gone, the empties were out with the rubbish, and she'd rearranged the furniture.

Her father was standing in his bedroom doorway – he looked pale and shaky and his hair was still wet, but at least he was upright and dressed.

'Your coffee's here,' Reilly said, pointing at the table.

'I see it,' replied Mike. He began to make his way toward them, still obviously unsteady on his legs.

Chris stood up. 'You need a hand, Mr Steel?'

'I'm not a shagging invalid, man,' he snapped. He reached the armchair and lowered himself into it.

Chris looked embarrassed. 'Maybe I should go ...'

'Good idea,' Mike grunted.

'Dad, don't be so rude.'

Mike reached carefully for his coffee and, managing to wrap both hands around it, brought it slowly up to his mouth. He paused before taking a first sip. 'He offered to leave – I was just being obliging. Wouldn't want him to feel uncomfortable or anything.'

'Honestly, I should go,' Chris insisted.

'Wait a few minutes and I'll come with you – I'm not staying either.' Then she turned back to her father. 'Dad, the reason I came here today is to warn you. Something weird is—'

'Warn me?' Mike spluttered over his coffee. 'Warn me about what? That booze is bad for my health?' He laughed bitterly.

'I think it's a bit too late for that, don't you? But no, this is serious. There's this case I'm working on at the moment with Detective Delaney, and I'm worried this guy might be a threat.'

'What would any of that have to do with me?'

'This particular criminal has made some threats against Reilly, Mr Steel – threats of a personal nature. As a result, it might be a good idea for you to be on your guard.'

Mike raised his eyes to Chris. 'Sonny boy, I've faced down more than a few scumbags in my time, and no two-bit skanky Irish drug dealer would have a hope of getting one over on me.' Derision dripped from his every word.

'This guy is different, Dad. He's not your typical scumbag. And he seems to know a lot about me – about us ... and our family.' She gave Chris a sideways glance, deciding that there was no harm in revealing that much in front of him. With luck her father would cotton on to what she meant, and she knew for certain that he wouldn't mention anything about Jess in front of Chris. Mike hadn't been able to contemplate thinking about – let alone talking about – what had happened to his youngest daughter for a very long time.

This time her father paid attention. 'What do you mean? What the hell has that got to do with anything?'

'I don't know yet,' Reilly said, now almost sorry she'd started the conversation. 'As I said, just keep an eye out for anyone watching you while you're out and about or maybe in the pub. This guy is dangerous, Dad and I don't want anything bad happening to you.'

Mike snorted. 'A bit late for that now, don't you think?' he drawled and she winced. Chris had moved to the window, evidently sensing the tension and trying to give them some privacy.

'Ah feck it,' Mike said then, waving an arm in the air. 'If you say so. I'll do my best to watch my back.' Then his gaze rose to meet Reilly's and it was as clear and focused as she'd seen in years. 'Just make sure you do the same. I already lost one of my girls and I don't think I could handle it if it happened again.'

30

F or Reilly it was an almost surreal experience. Within barely forty-eight hours of news of his arrival, Daniel Forrest was standing in the boardroom addressing the investigative team. The profiler had initially been reluctant to do so – concerned he might be treading on toes – but she had convinced him that diving right in was the only way.

She scanned the other's faces as Daniel spoke, his warm southern tones, softly modulated, drawing the detectives in. That was another trick she'd learned from him – if you lectured to people, they tuned you out, but if you lowered your voice, they needed to pay attention in order to hear you.

Chris and Kennedy were certainly paying attention – despite their initial misgivings about having a stranger on the ground, they understood that the profiler was visiting royalty in the world of criminal investigation, and a chance to gain insight from the very best. Kennedy was wearing his usual dour expression, but was taking notes as Daniel spoke. Inspector O'Brien sat quietly but wasn't missing a word. Chris looked the most relaxed – he was listening intently but clearly thinking too and Reilly figured he was the most likely to have questions.

'By definition, the nature of this case changed when this person tricked his or her way into the lab,' Daniel explained. 'Up until that point you had yourself a suspect with a Freud fixation, but you were still very much fishing in the dark.' He cleared his throat. 'Once direct contact was made – and by that I mean targeting Reilly directly and signaling a missing crime scene – now it looks like we have a wild goose chase on our hands.' Daniel stopped and let the significance of his last remark sink in, waiting for someone to rise to the bait.

Kennedy was first to respond. predictably. 'That sounds very negative,' he said. 'Almost like you're giving up already.'

Daniel gave a wry smile. 'Detective Kennedy, I presume?'

He nodded.

'Of course you've got a good point – we should always expect to catch such a killer. But why won't a standard manhunt work?' He scanned the faces and saw that Chris was nodding thoughtfully. 'What's on your mind? You look like you agree.'

'Because this guy's not ready to be caught?'

Daniel exchanged a brief glance with Reilly. 'Correct.'

'Everything we have so far, he's given us,' Chris added and again Daniel agreed.

'But surely Reilly walking in on him was a mistake, maybe we're giving this person too much credit?' O'Brien suggested, looking almost apoplectic that the supposedly great Daniel Forrest hadn't already produced their suspect on a plate.

'Perhaps, but it was obviously a chance he was willing to take,' Daniel replied. 'After all, it wasn't as if he had to run a gauntlet of high-tech security and armed guards. What we know about criminals as deeply organized as the taboo killer suggests that he'll be extremely difficult to find. As I'm sure you know, guys like this don't operate by the same rules as you and I. Generally speaking, serial killers have disorders in their social make-up – they are antisocial. According to the DSM – the Diagnostic and Statistical Manual of Mental Disorders – that means they consistently display the following criteria.' He ticked each point off on his fingers. 'Firstly, they don't conform to social norms – for example by repeatedly performing acts that are grounds for arrest. Secondly, they are deceitful; they repeatedly lie, use aliases, and con others for personal profit or pleasure.' He paused. 'Starting to sound like anyone we know?'

The team nodded solemnly.

'They are also likely to have a reckless disregard for the safety of themselves or others and lack remorse – in particular they are able to rationalize having hurt or mistreated other people.'

Kennedy looked thoughtful. 'So what you're saying is that the guy will do anything to get what he wants – to achieve his goal.'

'Exactly,' Daniel replied. 'But based on the recent escalation of not only the killings but the personal contact, he isn't finished yet. And until he is, anything is fair game,' he concluded somberly.

Reilly shivered involuntarily. 'That's a scary thought.'

'It is, yes.' He looked serious. 'Which brings us to where we stand now. We have two goals at this point,' he continued. 'Firstly, we need to try and figure out what he's going to do next.' He turned to Reilly. 'And from what you've told me about the arrangement of the files, it looks like there's also a missing crime scene to find.'

O'Brien stood up. 'Better get moving then. Delaney and

Kennedy – keep going on the missing person's reports and see if anything turns up there. Seems like a needle in a haystack to me but if that's all we've got to go on at the moment—'

'Actually there is something else,' Chris said and the others looked at him with interest. 'The hotline took a call this morning from someone who thinks they recognize Clare Ryan and Gerry Watson from the newspaper reports.'

Reilly raised an eyebrow. 'Both of them?'

'Yes.'

Her heart pounded. If the tip worked out, it could ascertain what had up to now been an elusive link between any of the victims.

'Well, what are you doing sitting here then?' O'Brien moaned. 'Follow it up.'

'We were just about to, before we were summoned to meet Agent Forrest here,' Kennedy said sardonically, getting up out of his chair. 'So if that's all—'

'Just put a lid on it and get a move on,' the Inspector barked before turning to Reilly. 'Steel, you review everything on the existing crime scenes and bring your friend up to speed on what we have so far. See if we've missed anything that might help us get ahead of this guy.'

'What about the accomplice angle?' Reilly asked. She'd told them about the blond hair and her belief that the killer might not be working alone.

'That sort of speculation is Agent Forrest's department, I believe,' the Inspector told her, his tone brusque. 'For now, we can only work with what we've already got.'

'Thank you for having me,' Daniel told the other men, solicitously. 'I promise I'll do my utmost to help bring this to a satisfactory conclusion.'

Reilly gathered her things. While she was relieved to have

Daniel on board she couldn't help but wonder how, with so many people already dead, that this situation could ever be concluded satisfactorily.

31

C hris and Kennedy weren't quite sure what to make of Mick Kavanagh, the 50-odd-year-old alcoholic, who from his miserable surroundings in the St Vincent de Paul shelter, told them how he knew Gerry Watson and Clare Ryan.

'They were nice to you,' Kennedy repeated with no small measure of frustration.

'Yeah, not everyone is you know,' Kavanagh said, eyeing the detectives suspiciously. In truth, Chris was amazed that the tip had come in at all; the homeless community were for the most part hugely distrustful of the law, and it was rare for them to offer a response to the most basic of questions, let alone offer help on something that didn't concern them. But this case was big news. 'I normally wouldn't get involved in stuff like this, but the things that are going on, and to ordinary people ... well, it's terrible.'

'We know,' Kennedy agreed. 'Tell us about Clare Ryan.'

'The blond one? She was a bit of bleeding heart ... you know the type, trying to get me to reconnect with my family and give up the gargle that kind of thing,' he said. 'Poor kid doesn't know much about the real world, although I s'pose she does now,' he added, shaking his head morosely. 'She was a nice kid though and I liked talking to her; she reminded me of my own one when she was that age.'

'What about Gerry Watson?' Chris asked, pointing to a photograph of the young camper. 'Now that fella never said much, but if he passed me on O'Connell Street in the mornings, he used to come back with cup of coffee,' the older man replied. Chris recalled that Watson was a student at the Dublin Institute of Technology just off the city's main thoroughfare. 'Never gave me any money, though.'

'So Clare Ryan tried to rescue you, and Watson gave you coffee?' Kennedy clarified flatly, his tone of voice leaving Chris in no doubt that he thought this was an almighty waste of time.

'Yep. I'd prefer a few bob of course, but you take what you can get. And you tend to remember – not so much the people who are nice to you, but who actually *look* at you, you know? Some people might throw you a few coins but only 'cos they feel guilty, and then others pretend you're not there and rush off in case you might infect them or something.'

'I can imagine.' Chris produced photos of Jim Redmond and the Miles women. 'Do you happen to recognize any of these?' he asked.

Kavanagh seemed to take a good long hard look at the photos but Chris could tell by his expression that nothing was registering. 'Don't think so,' the man said, eventually.

'You're sure?' Kennedy pressed.

He shrugged. 'Well, unless they're some of the ones I talked about who just threw me a few coins here and there, but the faces don't ring any bells, you know what I mean?'

Chris did, and while it might be helpful to know that Gerry Watson and Clare Ryan had both been kind-hearted enough to help someone less fortunate than themselves, it didn't do much toward establishing a conclusive link between them and the other murder victims.

Thanking Kavanagh, they left the shelter.

'What do you reckon?' Kennedy asked, lighting up a cigarette on the street. 'We could ask around some more in there, show those pictures to some of the others and see if our victims showed the same sort of charity to anyone else.

Chris looked at him. *Charity* ...

Hadn't Jim Redmond's wife mentioned something about her husband going out of his way to do a good deed? His mind raced. And given Sarah Miles' occupation as a nurse it was likely that she too could be involved in charitable causes in some shape or form. Actually, now that he thought of it, didn't Kennedy himself bemoan their neighbor's trite comments about the Miles women being generous and kind-hearted?

Granted, it was a tenuous theory, but up to now had been the only one they had that might just link these victims.

'I suppose it's worth considering,' Kennedy said when Chris outlined his thinking, 'but even if our victims were all bleeding hearts, I still don't know how it helps us catch this psycho.' He dragged hard on his cigarette. 'Unless these days being *nice* to people is some kind of taboo.'

Chris followed him back inside the shelter, his legs dragging behind him. Damn. Reilly was right; he'd have to see someone about this thing soon – otherwise it would start to get out of control. If things were quiet tomorrow, he'd try and slip in an appointment with a doctor in the morning, give a fake name and address and see how things went. He shook his head, not at all comfortable with this kind of underhanded thinking, but he figured it was necessary for the sake of keeping his job. And without that, without the one thing that gave his whole life meaning, Chris was afraid of ending up a charity case himself.

DANIEL FORREST PORED over the crime-scene photos with his magnifying glass. He moved slowly, methodically, taking his time to look at each detail of every picture.

Reilly watched him, admiring his thoroughness, his patience and his relentless attention to detail. She knew she was a decent investigator and for the most part thorough, but compared to Daniel she was an impatient novice. Fortunately, what she lacked in patience she made up for in instinct and ability to see patterns where others just saw a muddle.

He looked up and caught her watching him. He grinned. 'This always did drive you crazy, didn't it?'

'I don't know how you maintain such focus for so long,' she admitted.

He shoved a picture toward her. It was from the Jim Redmond hanging. 'You have to find ways to make the evidence come alive for you each and every time you look at it,' he said. 'Here, try this.' He spun the photograph around so that it was upside down. 'Does it look any different now?'

She leaned in to train her magnifying glass on it, and scanned the photograph, trying to see it through fresh eyes. 'Any particular reason you gave me this one?' she wondered.

'This is the one that intrigues me the most,' he admitted.

She looked up from the photograph and carefully put the magnifying glass down. 'It seems the most straightforward to me,' she observed.

'Exactly.'

'Ah.' Reilly sighed. 'So perhaps we were guilty of taking it for granted?'

Daniel shrugged. 'I'm not sure if you did that,' he replied.

'But it does stand out – mostly because of what's *not* there.' He nodded toward the photograph, Jim Redmond suspended from the beam of his expensive home, the Italian cotton sheet round his neck. 'The killer has shown more than once that he can handle two people at a time, so why not get Jim and his boyfriend together, make it a double suicide, a lovers' pact?'

Reilly looked back at the photo, and considered this. 'Maybe the killer didn't know?'

Daniel looked at her dubiously. 'About the lover?'

'Yeah. Maybe it was just a coincidence that he was in such a relationship, something we turned up that the killer didn't know about.' She knew that Chris and Kennedy had conducted a deep trawl of Redmond's contacts and tried long and hard to establish a lover but to no avail. Of course, it was just as likely that the man frequented gay bars and had no one steady companion, but again a recent search of the city's watering holes had turned up nothing. Yet the killer's knowledge of Redmond's secret life would have been a suitably powerful form of persuasion to coerce him into taking his own life.

Daniel looked at the photograph again. 'It's a lonely looking scene,' he said, 'and in the largest room too, as if the killer wanted to emphasize something ... loneliness,' he finished, eventually. 'The loneliness of suicide.'

Reilly said nothing for a moment, letting him draw whatever conclusions he needed to establish a clear profile. 'What do you make of the accomplice possibility?' she asked, anxious to see if her own theory fit.

Daniel turned to look at her, his face expressionless. 'Personally I feel it's nothing more than that – a possibility. As for the hair, well ... have you even considered that it might be yours?'

She stared at him, feeling like a scolded schoolchild.

'Damn.' She'd been so focused on the evidence taken from the scene that she had actually forgotten she'd been there, had in fact been part of it. Now she felt like an idiot for not thinking of this sooner. 'I don't think so, but I'll get the lab to run it against my file controls,' she mumbled, referring to the control blood and DNA samples all GFU staff were required to supply.

'That might be a good idea,' he said. Was she imagining it or did his casual tone sound forced?

She flicked through a pile of papers on her desk, afraid now that her little slip had somehow disappointed him.

'So tell me, how is life in Dublin?' he asked, deftly moving the conversation away from professional matters. Reilly knew for sure that she had disappointed him, or at least dropped the ball in some way.

'It's fine, busier than I expected, certainly.' She tried to make her tone sound carefree. 'I think I might have rattled a few cages at the beginning—'

'Detective Kennedy, I take it?' he interjected.

She smiled. 'Yeah, but he's actually OK behind it all.'

'What about the younger one, Detective Delaney? He seems pretty sharp.'

'He is.' Reilly wondered now if Chris would keep his word and see someone about his blood condition. 'Actually, you might be just the person to ask about—'

A soft knock on the door of her office cut off her question.

'Reilly? Sorry to bother you both,' Julius gave a courteous nod toward Daniel, 'but there's something on those hair samples from the taboo killings I'd like you to see.'

'The animal ones? Sure.' She followed Julius down the hallway to the lab, Daniel at her heels.

Inside, he led her to the microscope.

Leaning over it she peered at the slide. 'What am I looking at?'

'*Sus scrofa*,' he informed her. 'It's our mystery animal.'

She looked up, puzzled. 'It's been a while since I took Latin ...'

'It's boar hair,' he informed her. 'It took me a while to identify it, mostly because it's not in its natural state.'

'Boar hair?' While she knew at first glance the hair wasn't from a cat or a dog, she had certainly been expecting it to be from some form of domestic animal, perhaps a gerbil or guinea pig. 'How would our suspect be coming into contact with *boar* hair?'

She looked around for Daniel, wanting him to hear this, and saw him at the farther end of the room talking to Lucy, who was gazing at him with a degree of respect that bordered on adoration. Reilly had seen that look before – hell, she was pretty sure she'd once looked at him that way herself. For a young investigator, the chance to work with someone so talented and insightful was something akin to a religious experience.

She turned back to Julius. 'I'm sorry, you said something about it not being in its natural state?'

'Yes, which is why it took me so long to identify it. Classification was bothering me, so I kept at it, and upon closer inspection I realized it was indeed animal hair but it had been refined in some way, most likely through the manufacturing process.' He put his glasses on, and slid them into position with one finger.

'Manufacturing process for what?'

'Boar hair is used in some paintbrushes,' he told her. 'Particularly those used for applying oil-based paint, like varnish or gloss.'

Reilly's mind raced. 'You're saying the samples we found are actually paintbrush bristles?'

'I believe so, yes. And coupled with the paint specks collected at the same time which are indeed from oil-based materials that you could pick up at any DIY store—'

'It would suggest that either our killer has been doing his own spot of decorating or frequents a place where renovations have been taking place.'

'That's what I thought, but I wanted to consult with you first.'

She thought then about the calcium sulphate, what O'Brien had derisively referred to as 'chalk dust'. But thinking about it now, perhaps it wasn't chalk dust at all, but actually a form of gypsum used in plaster rendering, which would add weight to the renovations angle?

Reminding herself of Ockham's razor, she glanced again over at Daniel, who was still talking to Lucy. 'Good work, Julius – this kind of thing could be very well be the key to finding this guy's workplace, or maybe even his hiding spot.'

'No problem.'

She noticed Daniel signaling her over.

'What's up?' she asked, approaching Lucy's workstation.

'Well, it appears one of your very clever team may have found something else of interest.'

Lucy colored a little, thrilled by such esteemed praise.

'What is it, Lucy?' Reilly said, somewhat testily. She was much more interested in what the younger girl might have uncovered than this flattery.

'Sorry, yes – well, as I was just explaining to Agent Forrest, in relation to the erm ... food sample taken from the Watson scene, I hope you don't mind, but I took the liberty of contacting Dr Thompson's office.'

'You mean the cooked human flesh?'

'Yes. At first I wondered if the killer might have fed the victim some of his flesh but then I figured that this would be too risky – he wouldn't leave anything of his that might track him down through blood or DNA etcetera. So I got to thinking, if this particular piece of flesh wasn't from the killer, where did he get it?'

'Good point.'

'So I analyzed it further, and looking at it more closely, recognized what looked to me like some latent crystalline fibers ...'

'Crystalline fibers?'

'Yes. Which later turned out, as I suspected, to be water crystals, which suggested that the sample wasn't necessarily fresh and had at some point been frozen.'

Daniel was unrestrained in his praise. 'An excellent spot in my opinion.'

Reilly nodded, thinking the same thing. And what she liked most about this was that Lucy had done all of this on her own steam without needing to consult with her superiors beforehand. This boded well for the role of the GFU.

'So I asked the ME's office to take a look at the Ryan and Redmond autopsy reports, in case he may have taken it from one of those victims and frozen it until he was ready to use it.' Her eyes shone with exhilaration. 'You know the way you're always telling us never to rule out a hunch, however crazy it might seem?'

Daniel was smiling. 'Sounds like good advice.'

'It's good thinking, Lucy, that's what is. So was the ME's office any help?' Reilly urged. 'Did the sample come from one of those victims?'

'Well, yes, it seems it did. But oddly, not from the ones I'd considered. Dr Thompson called me herself this morning. I was going to tell you, but first I wanted to lay it all out properly in my report ...'

'What do you mean "not from the ones you'd considered"?'

Lucy looked mightily pleased with herself. 'Well, I'd mentioned the sample's crystalline elements in the request, and when Dr Thompson called to ask me about that, I told her what I was looking for.'

'And?'

'This morning, she told me that she'd asked her office to widen the search and they'd matched the sample to a victim from another on-going investigation – an identified floater from a couple of weeks back. I believe Detectives Delaney and Kennedy have been working on it.'

Reilly was dumbstruck, but in a good way. 'That's a fantastic find, Lucy. I'm sure they'll be hugely grateful.'

The younger girl smiled. 'Thanks, although I guess it also means we have yet another victim to add to the taboo killer's list, doesn't it?' she added, her tone suddenly grave.

'Even so, that was excellent work, young lady,' Daniel pointed out.

'Absolutely,' Reilly agreed. 'I'm going to call the detectives and advise them of this right away. In the meantime, keep up the good work.' Reaching the doorway she turned back to Daniel, who was looking thoughtful. 'Aren't you coming?'

'You go ahead,' he said, distractedly. 'I'm going to talk some more to your staff, see if there's anything else that might be helpful for my profile.'

Reilly shrugged. 'Sure.'

Leaving the lab, she returned to her office, looking forward to giving Chris and Kennedy the heads-up on this latest piece of information. Although the lab's discoveries weren't exactly going to break the case wide open, this new information was yet another glimpse, a brief insight into the world of the deranged killer they were tracking.

O'Brien was wrong; they were learning more and more about this guy by the hour and Reilly was determined that by the time they were finished, there would be no safe place for the taboo killer to hide.

32

I t was the following morning before Chris returned Reilly's numerous calls. 'Reilly, sorry I was late getting home last night and just got your messages now.'

He sounded tired, she noted, and wondered what he might have been doing. Maybe blowing off steam with Kennedy in a bar or something, although she remembered him mentioning before that he didn't drink much. A first for a homicide detective, and an Irish one at that, she thought wryly, then she berated herself for the lazy stereotyping

'Well, firstly I have some new information on your unidentified floater *and* I think we might have found out more about this guy's whereabouts—'

'Actually, I was just about to call you,' Chris interjected. 'It looks like we've found the missing crime scene.'

Reilly was stunned. 'What – where?'

'A couple of uniforms reported something out by the airport earlier this morning. Kennedy's on his way there now, but I've got erm ... something else to do before I can get down there.' By the halting tone of his voice, she understood that he'd evidently decided to see someone about his condition, but understandably he couldn't confide this in earshot of everyone at the station.

'I understand. Good luck with that.' Out of the corner of her eye, she noticed Daniel come into the room. 'I'll rustle up a crew here in the meantime and see you down there later?'

'Yes, I was going to cancel but the witness I'm seeing could only see me this morning.' Chris was clearly trying to justify his absence to someone in close proximity.

'Well, you do what you have to do; I'm sure Kennedy can hold the fort until you get there. Can you give me some idea of what to expect – from the crime scene, I mean?' she said and she saw Daniel raise an interested eyebrow.

'Pair of teenage boys,' he confirmed. 'They've been missing for just under a week, everyone had assumed they had run away to London or somewhere.'

'Sounds like they should have.'

'Yep. Look, I'd better go. I'm sure I'll see you down there, but if not we'll catch up later.'

'Hold on a sec,' she interrupted, seeing Daniel gesturing in the background. 'Daniel's here and I think he wants to talk to you.'

'OK, put him on.'

'Detective Delaney?' the profiler said, smoothly. 'I'm just putting the finishing touches to my official profile and I'd like to discuss a couple of things with you before I do. I realize this is a very busy time but if you could spare me a moment I'd appreciate it.'

'Right. Well, why don't you pop over now? I have to leave for a meeting at eleven, but I could fit in a few minutes before then.'

'If you don't mind, Detective – it's just there's just something specific about the investigation that I'd like your opinion on,' he said, and Reilly looked at him, realizing that by engineering a one-to-one with Chris, Daniel was expertly making sure that the rest of the investigation team didn't feel side-lined by his appearance. While it was customary for him to speak to investigators in detail before signing off on a profile, Reilly knew that she was providing him with all the informa-tion he needed on the killer, and this was more of a shrewd co-operative move on his part. But more to the point, she knew that Chris would appreciate it and rather than feel threatened by Daniel, would instead be much more open to his partic-ipation.

'OK, fine. Talk to you soon.'

'Thanks, Detective. I look forward to speaking with you,' he said, before hanging up the phone.

'Nice move, Forrest,' Reilly quipped, letting him know in no uncertain terms that she realized exactly what he was up to.

'I don't know what you're talking about,' he replied, smil-ing. 'Just doing my job and making sure everybody's on the same page.'

THE CRIME SCENE was as unappealing as any other. The two boys were found in an old battered blue Ford Transit owned by one of them. They had been dead for a while, and even in a chilly Dublin spring the decomposition was advanced enough to make the inside of the van a very unpleasant place.

Karen Thompson was in discussion with Kennedy when Reilly arrived. 'Looks like this one's more than a few days old,' she told Reilly.

'Were you able to ascertain time of death?'

'Not yet, decomp is too far advanced for that. And as for cause ... nothing obvious but there are indeed needle marks, which could well be from our pentobarbital-happy friend. I'll be able to rule that in or out once I've run the tox screen.'

'Cheers,' Kennedy mumbled, miserably.

Karen picked up her bag. 'I'll put a rush on it and let you know as soon as I have something.'

'Appreciate it,' replied Reilly. She turned to Kennedy. 'Shall we?'

The van had somehow survived thirty-odd years of hard work and neglect. Between the rust and the dents and the half-hearted re-sprays it was a sorry sight – the perfect vehicle for a pair of teenage boys to use and abuse.

Rather than head straight inside it, Kennedy walked slowly round the outside of the van, Reilly beside him.

'Think it's our guy?' he asked, quietly.

She shrugged. 'The Doc seems to think it might be.'

They paused, staring at the front of the van, its cracked windscreen, a dirty pair of black and white fuzzy dice hanging from the rear-view mirror.

'Kids ... businessmen ... old folks ... what's the connection?' Kennedy asked, having filled her in on what little they'd learned from the homeless man. 'Does he know these guys beforehand or what?'

'I'm not sure there is a relationship of any kind,' Reilly said, making a note to talk to Daniel about the charity angle. 'I think he simply tracks down someone who meets his criteria. Daniel thinks he's a watcher,' she added, thinking about their conversation earlier.

'Great, If that's the case, the asshole could be around here now watching us, couldn't he?'

In the windscreen of the van Reilly looked at the reflection of the surrounding buildings. It was a rundown industrial area full of abandoned warehouses, their broken windows looking back at them like toothless homeless people.

'I certainly hope not.' She put a gloved hand on the door handle. 'Let's check this out.'

The GFU team were nearby – they had waited patiently, already knowing better than to disturb Reilly when she was talking to the police.

'Lucy, you take the outside of the van. Gary, check the area around here – this is a pretty deserted spot.' She glanced involuntarily up at the windows around them again then back at him. 'Take a uniform with you – check if any of these buildings are unlocked.'

'What am I looking for?'

'Anywhere accessible that overlooks this site – if you find somewhere, look for any sign that someone has been there.'

'Got it.'

Gary headed off and began explaining what he needed to one of the attending officers at the scene. Reilly watched him and couldn't help but smile – he'd picked the biggest uniform he could find. Lucy meanwhile, had her kit open and was already taking photos of the outside of the van.

'You've done a good job with them,' Kennedy observed, quietly.

She turned, surprised by the unexpected praise. 'They're a good group.'

'They still needed training though.'

Reilly shrugged. 'Just needed someone to awaken their instincts.'

They peered in the van. The two boys were naked, stacked one on top of the other. If it was the work of their killer, this time it was pretty obvious what he'd had them do.

'Christ, how does he get people to do these things?' Kennedy said, sucking air through his teeth. 'I've met some persuasive types, but this one really takes the biscuit ...'

'The threat of death can be very persuasive,' Reilly replied.

She climbed up and squatted in the van, Kennedy right behind her.

'Want me to wait out here while you have a sniff around?' he said.

She couldn't help but smile. 'You know, you really should think about trying some touchy-feely stuff yourself sometime; you might surprise yourself.'

'That's what the wife keeps telling me,' he replied with a grin and Reilly shook her head indulgently.

She closed her eyes, trying to picture the scene.

The killer was in the back of the van with the two boys, there was an old mattress, a couple of grubby blankets, speakers from the van's stereo fixed to the ceiling. They were ... they were ...

'Anything coming to you?' he asked, this time without cynicism.

She opened her eyes. 'Could be the female accomplice we wondered about. Maybe she let the boys pick her up, knowing they had the van.' She gestured to the mattress, the blankets, the speakers. 'This was their little love nest, a place they brought girls.'

'And our guy knew about it.'

'Right. He needed two guys who weren't homosexual to fit the taboo – there would be no fun if it wasn't abhorrent them to.'

'Good point. What else?'

Reilly tried to picture it in her mind. 'Maybe she would pick them up, tempt them with an offer of a threesome, something like that. Then, when they got started – I think she'd let them have some fun for a while, knowing all the time that she was in control. Then he'd show up—'

'And turn the tables?'

'Exactly. It feeds directly into that need for risk, excitement, control ... and in the end the taboo act itself – ultimate control.'

Kennedy looked around inside the van. 'Didn't leave us much this time, did he?'

'No, and that's worrying me a little.'

'Why? He knows that by now we'd identify it as his work, so why bother leaving anything extra?'

'Because he has done so far.'

He looked at her. 'You think there's something we're missing?'

'Either missing or haven't found yet.' She looked around. 'Remember, based on the clue left at the lab, this one is supposed to have happened before the Miles women, and that one had a very clear Freudian message.'

Kennedy shone a torch around the gloomy interior of the van. 'Not much space in here to hide something though.'

'There are plenty of ways to hide something if you want to make it hard to find.'

Their conversation was suddenly disturbed by Reilly's phone. She glanced at the display and saw that it was Gary. She stepped out of the van and looked up at the surrounding buildings, wondering where he was. 'What's up?'

'I'm in the warehouse - there's something up here you need to see,' he said, sounding breathless.

'Give me a second; I'll be right there.'

Kennedy looked at her, expectantly. 'He found something?'

She nodded. 'Don't tell me you're surprised.'

'I'll keep going here – you go and see what it is.'

Minutes later, Reilly pushed open the broken door of an abandoned warehouse – it was just a few meters up the road from the van and would have a perfect view of the grounds. A set of dusty stairs took her up to the third floor, where the uniform waited at the top of the stairs to meet her.

'In here,' he said, somewhat unnecessarily, pointing at the only open door.

Reilly stepped into a huge dusty storage room. Abandoned boxes of files and papers littered the floor, and a rat quickly scuttled away into the shadows as she walked over toward the window where Gary stood.

'What have you got?'

He pointed out the window. 'Look.'

Reilly stood beside him and peered out through a broken window at the van, two stories below them. Her blood ran cold as she read the words, painted carefully onto the roof:

'To lose one parent is unfortunate. To lose both is carelessness.'

Oh Christ ....

Reilly snatched her phone from her pocket and quickly punched in her father's number. It rang, cold and harsh in her ear, once ... twice ... three times ... and then on and on without an answer.

'Shit!' She darted from the room, her heart hammering, and charged down the old wooden stairs, her footsteps echoing through the building as her feet threw up clouds of dust. She stormed out of the building, eager to get back to Kennedy, and ran into the one person in the world she least wanted to see.

Jack Gorman stood blocking her path. And the head of the forensic unit clearly wasn't at all happy about being summoned home early from his anniversary cruise.

'What the bloody hell is going on here?' he demanded. He was a small man with a sharp face and the bluster such men often wore to cover up for their insecurities.

'Gorman?' Reilly gasped, both amazed and horrified to see

him standing in front of her. 'I didn't realize you were coming back so soon—'

'Didn't have much of a choice, did I?' he snorted. 'What with the shenanigans that have been going on in my absence.' He pointed accusingly at the GFU van. 'And what do I find? Young Lucy processing a crime scene and Gary running around like he's in an episode of *Miami*-bloody-*Vice!*' His face was almost puce – he looked in danger of exploding. 'It's like the whole place has gone mad since I left. This isn't how we do things, Steel.'

As Gorman ranted, heads popped out from all over – Lucy from the front of the van, Gary from the building behind, Kennedy from inside the van. Reilly cursed inwardly; this was the last thing she needed right now.

'Let's talk about that later, but first I need to—'

'Let me assure you that I've not let myself be dragged halfway round the world for nothing. I want to be brought up to speed with where we're at *right now*,' he ordered, his Caribbean tan masking the blood rushing to his head. It was difficult to tell what was upsetting him most, the fact that they were facing potentially the biggest serial murder case the country had ever seen, or that his trip of a lifetime had been cut short. 'Lucy, I don't even know what you're doing here – get back to the lab.'

Lucy stayed rooted to the spot, seemingly unsure what to do, and Reilly faced Gorman, refusing to be intimidated by him. 'She's here at my request,' she explained, patiently.

'Lucy, are you deaf? I told you to—'

'Excuse me – you have no right to speak to a member of—'

'It's OK, Reilly.' Lucy interjected. She eyed Gorman. 'I'm going, Dad.'

Shocked, Reilly whirled around and stared at her protégée. *Dad? What the hell ...?*

For the life of her she couldn't remember hearing or being told anything on arrival at the GFU about Lucy being related to Gorman. No wonder he was always so dismissive toward her and she in turn so understandably eager for Reilly's approval. Christ, as if she didn't have enough to get her head around just now.

'Good. Let the rest of them finish things off. In the meantime, Steel, I want you back at headquarters and in my office – we need to get to the bottom of this investigation.' Clearly he was determined to show everyone who was boss.

Reilly stared at his angry face for a moment, then pushed past him. 'I'm sorry but I really don't have time for this just now,' she replied. Gorman would have to wait; making sure her own father was safe was her biggest priority.

'Excuse me?' He seemed shocked that she didn't immediately bow to his demands.

'I'm sorry but there's something I need to do—'

'May I remind you that I am head of this unit,' he continued, puffing out his chest. 'Which makes me your superior.'

Reilly gave a resigned nod, then hurried toward Kennedy, who was watching the exchange with interest. 'I need a favor,' she said, breathlessly.

He put his hands up. 'Hey, don't get me involved in this.'

'No, it's not about Gorman ... it's something else entirely. I think ... I think my dad could be in danger,' she said, quickly explaining about the message Gary had found.

'Bloody hell ...' Kennedy's gaze moved to Gorman who was approaching fast.

'How dare you ignore me, Steel!' the older man shouted. 'I refuse to be treated like this.'

'Please,' Reilly implored. 'I need to check on him, make sure he's OK.'

'Do you think there's a real chance that—'

'Yes.'

'Steel. Are you listening to me?' Gorman continued.

'Gorman, maybe this isn't the time—' Kennedy began.

'All right then. The two of you, back in my office – right now!'

Kennedy seemed to make a snap decision. He pulled out his mobile phone. 'I'll send a unit over there straightaway. Where did you say he lived?'

'In the Liberties,' Reilly said quickly. Then she thought of something. 'Wait a second, Chris knows the house; do you think he would—'

'Of course he would,' Kennedy said, making the call.

33

I don't understand,' Chris said. He was facing Daniel Forrest who sat at the opposite side of his desk. 'You don't buy Reilly's accomplice theory?'

'No.' Daniel's expression was neutral.

'But what about the coercion, or the blond hair?'

'Just bear with me for a moment,' the profiler sat forward, about to explain. But their conversation was interrupted by Chris's mobile.

'Just one second,' he said, holding up a finger. 'Kennedy, what's up?' He listened for a moment then frowned. 'Is she sure? Yeah, I know exactly where it is – of course, I'll go straight away.' Hanging up, he looked at Forrest. 'Reilly found something at the latest scene that makes her think her father's a target. She can't contact him on the phone and can't get away to check on him, so asked if I would.'

From the sound of Kennedy's voice, he guessed that Reilly was frantic. If so, his eleven-thirty doctor's appointment would have to wait.

The other man picked up his coat. 'I'll come with you.'

'I don't know if that's a—'

'Detective, if Reilly thinks her father might actually be in danger because of this, then I think it's important we both check it out, don't you?'

Chris didn't have time to waste arguing. If the guy wanted to tag along, let him.

'You don't really think the killer would target her father, do you?' he asked Daniel as he negotiated his way skillfully through the busy morning traffic. It was really more for something to say, as the American had been uncomfortably silent since they'd left the station. He'd tried Reilly's mobile to see what the problem was but it went straight to voicemail.

'Did your partner tell you why she thinks that?' he asked in his usual calm, measured way. His manner actually creeped Chris out.

'No, he just told me to get over there fast. Reilly wanted to go herself but she's too far away and apparently time is of the essence. And besides the crime scene, she's caught up with another work issue.'

Kennedy had mentioned something about Gorman's appearance and given the circumstances of his return, Chris could only imagine the stink the man had raised. He felt for Reilly and could imagine how panicked she was feeling. While he himself wasn't sure if there was anything to worry about, he was happy to help set her mind at ease. Would the killer really go after Mike? Or was it just an empty threat, another psychological power play designed to throw Reilly off her game?

Daniel nodded thoughtfully. 'She must have found something ... something relevant,' he said, as if talking to himself.

Chris said nothing. Truthfully, all he expected to find was Mike Steel passed out on his living room sofa.

The flat was silent when they arrived. After knocking and calling out a couple of times, Chris sought out the spare key that (upon Reilly's instructions) Kennedy had told him about. Slowing entering the hallway, the two men moved from room to room continuing to call out.

'Mr Steel? Mr Steel, are you there?'

The lights in the living room were on and the curtains were drawn.

Daniel stood quietly in the living room doorway, as Chris allowed himself time to form an impression. For some reason, the hairs on the back of his neck stood up. The flat was tidy, the cushions arranged neatly on the couch, the carpet vacuumed, the shoes in the hallway lined up in a straight row.

He turned to Daniel and frowned. 'A little bit different to the last time I visited.'

'How so?'

'Place was like a bomb had hit it – even after Reilly did a clean-up job on it. This ... it's too tidy.'

Daniel nodded. 'I figured that as soon as I walked in – it smells clean.' He sniffed the air. 'Pine cleaner, something like that.'

'Whereas it should be smelling of booze, leftover food and stale cigarettes.' Chris paced the room and ran his finger lightly across the mantelpiece – no dust.

'Before we jump to any conclusions, maybe we should take a better look around,' Daniel suggested, calmly. 'Why don't I take the bedroom and you try the kitchen.'

Chris nodded. He watched Daniel as he stepped into the bedroom – his flashlight was in his hands, he was alert, on his toes, all senses attuned. While Chris would have preferred working with someone he knew better, someone he trusted, he understood that there wasn't much of a choice. Let Forrest look around and see if he could make head or tail of this. It couldn't hurt, could it?

Chris entered the kitchen, thinking about how he often

complained about the boxy kitchen in his own apartment, but compared to this one, it was positively spacious. More like the galley on a boat, it was a narrow passageway with high cupboards and a tiny electric cooker on one side, a counter top on the other – but then you didn't need much space in the kitchen when your diet mostly consisted of booze.

Like the rest of the flat, the kitchen had been transformed. He thought about the last time he'd set foot in it a couple of days ago with Reilly he had almost been afraid to touch anything. But now it positively sparkled, all the surfaces cleaned, the cupboards wiped down, even the chrome on the taps polished.

It did seem odd, but then again there could be a perfectly reasonable explanation for it. He took out his phone and was about to call Reilly when a noise from behind startled him.

'Who the hell are you?' A female voice called out and he turned to see a middle-aged lady standing there. A neighbor, he figured, judging by the set of keys she held in her hand.

'I'm a friend of Mr Steel's,' he replied, thinking quickly. 'Well, of his daughter's actually and I was just—'

'His daughter?' The woman's face softened somewhat. 'Oh. I thought you might be a burglar,' she added. Chris wondered if she made a habit of sneaking up on burglars and putting her life in danger instead of just calling the police. In this case, he was glad she hadn't as he would have quite a bit of explaining to do.

Chris put on his most reassuring smile. 'Not at all,' he said. 'Tell me, do you have any idea when Mike will be back? I'm assuming he asked you to keep an eye on the place.'

Again, the woman's face shuttered. 'If you're his daughter's friend then you should know that, shouldn't you?'

'Actually—' But before he could say anything more, Daniel appeared in the doorway.

'Hello there, I'm Daniel Forrest, an old friend of Mike's from California. Nice to meet you, Mrs ...?'

'Kelly,' the woman replied, reluctantly taking his hand. Chris immediately understood that Forrest was trying to put her suspicions at ease by mentioning a shared history.

'Mrs Kelly, I take it Mike has you to thank for his lovely clean home,' he continued, laying on the charm.

The woman blushed a little. 'I thought I'd take the opportunity to give it a bit of a brush-up – have it nice for him when he comes home.'

'Very nice of you – and a great job too. I must get you to look over my place sometime,' Daniel joked. Mrs Kelly blushed and Chris began to suspect that Mike Steel had a fan in his helpful neighbor. Judging by her coquettish reaction to the attractive profiler, she wasn't immune to other men's charms either.

'Yes, well, I'm sure he won't even notice,' she trilled. 'You know what men can be like. But it'll be nice for him when he gets back, although he didn't actually say when she'd be bringing him back.'

'She?' Chris repeated.

'Well, yes.' Her expression changed to one of downright disapproval. 'Now I know she's a friend of yours, but really, I think that daughter of his could be doing a lot more than just swanning in when it suits her and deciding to take him away for a few days. What about all the other days when he needs someone to keep an eye on him?'

Chris and Daniel exchanged glances.

'How do you know this, Mrs Kelly?' Chris asked. 'That he's gone away for a few days?'

'Seems his daughter arranged some sort of break for the two of them, so I told him I'd keep an eye on the flat. I don't think he realized that she'd arranged that too, with yourselves I mean.'

'And did you happen to meet Mike's daughter?' Daniel asked, fishing for a possible description.

'Well, I didn't *meet* her as such,' the woman replied. Reading between the lines, Chris knew that luckily for them, Mrs Kelly had been keeping a very close eye on Mike Steel. 'I just caught of glimpse of her in the car before they left. It was the first time I'd seen sight or sound of this one actually, and was surprised because I didn't think she looked a bit like him, very little resemblance really. Not like the other one.'

Chris looked up quickly. 'The other one?'

'Yes, the older daughter – the one who works for the cops. Now she's the spit of him whereas the younger one—'

'Mrs Kelly, did Mike Steel tell you specifically that he was going away with his daughter?'

Picking up on Chris's urgency, she looked hesitant. 'Well, no but ... I thought you said ...'

'Thank you, you've been a great help,' Daniel interjected, smoothly before guiding her toward the doorway. 'I'm sure Mike will want to thank you too when he gets back.'

As she left, Chris ran a hand through his hair, not knowing what to think.

According to the neighbor, Steel had simply gone away for a few days with a relative, or at least someone he knew, which meant that there was nothing for Reilly to worry about. Yet, what was all this about a daughter?

'What do you make of that?' he asked Daniel, who'd come back into the room. 'Sounds like he's just taken off for a few days and Reilly's got nothing to worry about.'

The profiler looked thoughtful. 'On the contrary, actually,' he said, his tone grave.

'What do you mean? You heard what she said: Steel took off with someone he knew, and not some deranged killer.'

Forrest looked at him. 'Someone he knew, yes. But if this person is who I suspect it is, then Reilly's got a lot more to worry about than you or I can even imagine.'

34

B ack at GFU headquarters, as Jack Gorman's complaints about her activities in his absence (as well as the surprising revelation about Lucy) shifted in and out of focus, Reilly prayed that Chris would be able to locate Mike.

That message – she knew in her bones that it referred to her and by association, her father. Daniel was right; the taboo killer was now openly targeting her and her family. But how did he know so much about her?

To lose one parent is unfortunate ...

Her mind drifted back to that awful day, a day that at first had seemed little different to any other but would turn out to be one that would haunt their lives forever.

BY THEN, Reilly's mother had been absent from their lives for many years; she and Jess had no idea where Cassie was or why she had gone. When they were little, they'd grown used to their mom's erratic moods and sudden disappearances, but when one day Cassie left and didn't return, it was as though everyone sensed that this time was different. Mike was saying nothing and in the intervening years the family seemed to have drawn a veil over the entire business.

But as the sisters grew older, questions eventually began to rise in their minds – particularly Jess's – and although Reilly never wanted to come out and actually ask their dad, she got the impression that their perpetually restless mother had gone off with another man.

Ghosts – to say nothing of monsters – were hard to keep in closets and that year in particular her curious sister had become more and more inquisitive, and more demanding about why Cassie had come to abandon her family.

'Let it go, Jess.' Reilly had admonished, but she knew she was wasting her breath. When she got something into her head, Jess could be like a dog with a bone.

One day, Reilly had been out driving her car – Mike had bought it for her eighteenth birthday and knowing how hard he'd worked to scrape the money together made it all the more special. It was just a little two door Mazda – a rice burner her dad called it – bright cherry red, but it was hers and she loved it.

It was lunchtime, there wasn't much traffic, and Reilly had slowed for a red light when she got a call from Jess.

'Reilly? It's me,' her sister cried, her voice somewhat manic. 'I'm at Mom's house.'

'Mom's house? What?' Reilly was stunned. 'Jess, have you gone crazy? How did you ... I mean, what ... where...?' Her thoughts were going a mile a minute. Jess had located their mother? How and, more importantly, where?

'I need you, Reilly. I need you to come here.' There was something desperate in her voice, a sound Reilly hadn't heard since she was a pre-schooler. 'What? Come where? I don't understand, Jess. Where are you?'

'Reilly, I need you to come here right now.' Jess's voice had suddenly fallen flat, which somehow sounded even scarier than the frantic way she had started the conversation. Something was wrong. Of course, their mother had never been predictable; never your typical apple pie housewife, and Reilly suspected that the much-longed for reunion with Cassie had not gone as planned.

'OK, honey, just calm down and tell me where you are. How do I get there?'

She listened wide-eyed as Jess quickly rattled off directions to a place only about a mile away. Had Cassie remained living in the Bay area all this time? For some reason, Reilly had always assumed that she'd taken off somewhere back east, where she was from. So to think that for all these years she'd been nearby and yet never once made an effort to contact either of them ... Yet, knowing Cassie, was it really that much of a surprise?

She swung the car up the ramp and on to the freeway. How Jess had located her, Reilly had no idea – but as she well knew, when Jess set her mind on something, there was absolutely no way anyone could stop her.

She sped down the freeway, her heart beating fast, unable to imagine what awaited her and more importantly what could have got Jess so upset. Clearly Cassie had no interest in reuniting with her daughters, or playing happy families.

A little later, she navigated her way through some narrow suburban streets, finally pulling up outside the address Jess had given her. It was a pink stuccoed house, mission style, on a quiet residential street of similar properties.

She paused in the car for a minute, trying to remain calm. Her mother – the woman who'd given birth to her, yet whom she hadn't seen since she was eight – lived here? It looked so suburban, so normal, that she couldn't quite get her head around it. Then again, what else did she expect?

She jumped from the car, hurriedly locked it, then approached the porch, keeping an eye out for Jess. There was no sign of anyone outside, but the front door of the house was open.

Reilly approached cautiously, something telling her that all was not right.

She slowly climbed the wide steps to the porch. Like the other houses on the block it had a faded wooden swing seat, which moved very slightly in the gentle breeze. A small white side table sat beside it, two drinks on it. Both were half empty, the ice melted, a film of condensation running down the glasses to pool on the table.

Reilly stepped slowly across it, the boards creaking beneath her feet. For some reason, the street seemed deathly quiet – no cars passed, no birds sang, no children called out. She reached the front door and paused. There was no doorbell.

Reaching out to knock on the door, she realized that it was not fully closed and she gently touched it, swinging it open to reveal a pretty room with polished wooden floors and several brightly colored ethnic rugs. A large couch filled the centre of the room.

And oh God, there it was. Her mother's unique scent, so recognizable and achingly familiar, it almost made Reilly feel weak. Despite her best efforts, and having rummaged through her mother's stuff many times over the years, she'd never been able to figure out what the fragrance was exactly; it wasn't perfume and definitely not body cream. Floral and yet faintly spicy, to Reilly, it represented carefree summer days at the beach, and lazy family evenings in the garden – the peace of mind and happiness she'd always craved.

She gingerly stepped inside and called out. 'Hello? Anyone home?'

There was no answer, no movement. From where Reilly stood it might have been deserted, abandoned. 'Jess ... Jess it's me, Reilly.'

The late afternoon light was forcing it way through the pale wooden blinds, casting long beams of yellow light across the room. As Reilly's eyes gradually adjusted to the light, she saw, on the far side of the room, a dark trail of something smeared across the floor. There was a strong smell in the air, one that in the future she would come to know only too well.

She stepped through the room, heart beating faster. All her senses were on edge, raw and open, though she didn't understand why. A deep, almost primal instinct again screamed that something was very wrong. Wanting desperately to turn and flee, she moved slowly across the floor, her footsteps the only sound in the quiet house.

Only worry for her sister, and the desperate pleading in Jess's voice when she'd called, kept her moving forward.

As Reilly reached the far side of the room, she saw with horror that the dark trail she was looking at was blood – a long, wide smear of it trailing across the room, leading her toward the kitchen. With rising horror, she realized that someone had dragged themselves, bleeding, across the floor.

She paused, her heart in her mouth, not wanting to go further, yet knowing that she had to. Every fiber of her being screamed at her to turn around and run, call the cops and let them deal with whatever was in there. But she knew she couldn't.

Not while she thought that Jess was in there. Jess, her little sister, whom Reilly had spent most of her life looking after. She couldn't quit now, even if she wanted to.

The blood trail led into the kitchen and, heart pounding,

Reilly slowly turned the corner, knowing deep down that what happened next would change her forever.

There was a man lying face down on the floor, surrounded by a pool of his own blood. He looked to have been stabbed – two or three times – and had dragged himself into the kitchen to try ...

Reilly put her hand up over her mouth, fighting back a horrified gasp and the same time an unbelievable urge to gag.

On the far side of the kitchen lay their mother – still so recognizable even after all these years. She had the same soft face that haunted Reilly's dreams, the same light blond hair framed her face.

In those dreams she was always smiling down at Reilly, yet, today there was no smile. Instead, her mother's face was twisted into a grotesque expression of horror, and a large kitchen knife was embedded in her stomach. She had bled profusely, her hands covered in blood where she'd held her stomach, trying to staunch the flow of life seeping out.

She put a hand over her mouth, torn between shock and terror.

Oh my God ...

'I knew you'd come.'

Reilly jumped at Jess's voice and then Jess herself gradually swam into focus. She was holding their mother's head in her lap, gently stroking her hair. She looked up slowly, seeing Reilly standing in the doorway.

'Christ, Jess, what's happened?' Her throat seemed to close over as she tried to find the right words, something, *anything* to say.

Jess fixed her gaze on Reilly for a moment, before looking down again at their mother. 'She's at peace now,' she said, finally. 'She was so upset, so ashamed about what she had done.' She continued stroking her mother's hair, leaving a bloody streak across her forehead. Yet rather than seeming stunned or sad, the gesture struck Reilly as being eerie more than anything else.

'Jess, I think we need to call the police—'

'She was a whore, Reilly!' Suddenly her sister's face changed, her peaceful expression replaced by a snarl of almost animal-like ferocity. 'Always leaving us, always abandoning us. She was a miserable, stinking whore – it was what she deserved!'

'What?'

It was as if all the walls had suddenly begun closing in on them. She stared in horror as Jess defiantly met her gaze as if daring her to contradict her. Jess ... was she involved in this ... somehow responsible for this? Reilly swallowed hard, as her brain struggled to take in what she was witnessing, unable to deal with the dark and dangerous animal her sister had suddenly become.

Her first instinct was to try and calm things down, take control, be the big sister she'd always been. She took a fearful step closer, looking down at the blood on Jess's hands. 'Honey, what happened here today?' she asked softly. 'Are you OK?'

Jess looked up at Reilly with a soft, almost beatific smile. 'I'm fine – now,' she replied, finally. She looked around the room and her gaze settled on the man. Almost like a switch being clicked her mood changed again and her face shuttered. 'He got what he deserved,' she snarled. Reilly stayed rooted to the spot, tears welling up in her eyes as she struggled to understand what on earth had taken place.

Jess looked down again at their mother. 'As did Mommy,' she went on, continuing to smear blood across her forehead. She glanced up at Reilly, as if suddenly remembering something. 'We won't see her in heaven either; there's no place up there for lying whores.' Then she leaned down and kissed their mother's bloody forehead. 'You should say goodbye to her too now, Reilly, seeing as it's the last time you'll see her.'

Reilly stood there, her shoulders heaving, huge tears rolling down her cheeks. 'Oh my God,' she whispered. 'Jess, what have you done?'

Jess gently set her mother down on the cold wooden floor and climbed to her feet. She examined the body as though looking for defects, before finally reaching down and gently crossing Cassie's hands across the gash in her stomach.

Then, she padded lightly across the kitchen floor, and wrapped her blood-soaked arms around her sobbing sister. 'It's OK, Reilly,' she murmured into Reilly's ear. 'I fixed it – now everything is OK.'

35

Having endured a thorough chewing-out from Gorman, most of which she didn't hear, Reilly finally escaped from his office and immediately checked her cell messages.

Nothing from Chris other than a missed call from earlier that morning.

Damn, why hadn't he called since? Even if the news wasn't good, surely he'd have the decency to keep her updated.

She quickly dialed his number but frustratingly it went straight to voicemail. Next she called Kennedy, who'd apparently heard nothing in the meantime either.

'Don't worry, I'm sure he and Forrest have got everything under control,' the detective assured her.

'Daniel? Daniel went with him?' For some reason this seemed to panic her even more.

'That's what the guys at the station said. They left here about an hour and a half ago. Look, try not to worry, I'm sure everything's fine – if it wasn't, Chris would've been in touch.'

She wanted to believe him, she really did, but if the killer's message had indeed been meant for her, Reilly knew she couldn't take anything for granted. How could he have known about Cassie – or about Jess? Her sister had been underage at the time, and so she hadn't been named in the newspapers.

If the killer did know, she could see why he'd have a field day with it. Daniel was right; to think that one of those trying to catch him had a personal insight on his preferred *modus operandi* and knew all about taboos ...

Had Daniel suspected this all along? Had he realized that the killer had gained an advantage by tapping into Reilly's murky past, exposing her shameful family secrets? And if he had, what was he intending to do about it?

There was nothing Reilly could do to change things, in the same way that back then, there was nothing she could do but turn over her badly damaged 14-year-old sister to the cops. Jess, having discovered their absent mother's whereabouts, had sought Cassie out and subsequently learned that she had indeed left Mike for another man.

As was often the case with Jess, the encounter had evidently been fraught and angry, and when mother and daughter were interrupted by Cassie's partner, the highly emotional teenager grabbed a kitchen knife and lashed out in the most unimaginable way.

Even now, Reilly could hear Jess pleading with her not to call the police.

'I didn't mean it, Reilly, I swear I didn't. He just crept up behind me. I was protecting myself, I swear.'

'But you killed him ... you killed him and Mom.'

'I didn't mean to, I swear I didn't. She was screaming at me, even after I told her how much I missed her, how much *we* missed her, Dad too. You know what she's like, Reilly – it wasn't my fault.' She grabbed at Reilly's arm, a wild look in her eyes. 'Come on, let's get out of here – nobody saw us, they'll never know.'

'Jess, we can't just walk out of here. You killed two people.'
Reilly could barely move. 'We should call Dad, maybe he'll
know what to—'

'No, you can't tell him, you can't tell anyone! Reilly, you're
my sister, you promised to look after me, to protect me. Now I
need you to help me.'

There was something eerily matter-of-fact in her voice, as
if she'd decided all along that Reilly had no choice but to go
along with all this or, worse, had no choice but to help her get
away with it.

'This is different, Jess. This is serious. Big-time serious.'
She moved toward the phone at the end of the kitchen
counter and Jess grabbed her arm, a feral look on her face.
'Don't you dare,' she said in a tone that made Reilly stop in her
tracks. Quick as a flash, the vulnerable, teenage demeanour
disappeared and was replaced by a calm control that was
deeply unsettling. 'Don't be the bad guy or you might be
catching up with Mommy dearest sooner than you think.'

This, and the cold, terrifyingly threatening way she said it,
made Reilly wonder if the preceding event had played out as
accidentally as Jess painted it. And in that brief, horrifying
moment, she remembered seeing the same look the day her
little sister teased and assaulted Randy Reynolds and her
matter-of-fact pronouncement that 'bad guys had to be
punished'.

But, luckily for Reilly, the decision was taken out of her
hands. Soon after, the cops arrived. Someone – a neighbor
probably – had heard a commotion in the house earlier and
called 911.

Recalling the look on Jess's face as each girl was led sepa-
rately away, she knew her sister would never forgive her for
failing to protect her like she'd sworn to do.

It was a look that remained that day in court, when Jess

was sentenced to fifteen years in the Central California Women's Facility. Reilly had sat in the courthouse alongside a shocked and broken Mike who, it turned out, had inadvertently revealed Cassie's whereabouts to Jess. Reilly felt utterly torn and betrayed, having always hoped their mother would return someday. Instead, she would be forever haunted by that last memory of Cassie as a grotesque, lifeless corpse.

Now, Reilly sat at her desk and put her head in her hands. That was the last time she'd seen her sister, the last time Jess had allowed any of her family to see her. Despite Reilly's pleas, she continuously refused to appear for any of her and Mike's visits to the CCWF.

As the years went by, Mike dealt with the tragedy by turning more and more to the bottle while Reilly, unable to get a handle on her sister's actions, had found herself drawn into forensic psychology. But, unlike Daniel Forrest, she'd eventually found the study of dark and troubled minds far too difficult and unsettling, preferring instead more hands-on crime scene investigation.

Then, when a few years earlier Mike, in a sudden attempt to rouse himself out of the booze-filled existence he'd been living, decided to return to the country of his birth after retirement, Reilly agreed, hoping that it would be the start of a new life for him, the perfect opportunity to start over. But very quickly it became apparent that the vastly changed Ireland did little to calm his spirit and all too soon he was back in the same self-destructive cycle.

While Reilly had hoped that taking the job in Dublin and being nearby might help, now it seemed that her actions had indirectly put her father right in the path of danger.

'Reilly?'

Her head snapped up as she heard the soft knock on the door and saw Lucy standing in the doorway looking hesitant.

'Lucy, hi, sorry – I was miles away.'

'Um ... hope I'm not interrupting but I just wanted to say that I hope I didn't get you into trouble earlier – with my dad, I mean.'

Reilly looked at her. 'You must have known I had no idea.'

The younger girl wouldn't meet her gaze. 'I wasn't sure to be honest. Everyone else knows and it's mentioned in my personnel file, but I try not to draw to much attention to it at work.'

'Lucy, if I was ever disrespectful—'

'Are you mad? I don't know how you managed to stay so nice. My dad ... I know better than anyone how he can be sometimes.'

'Even so.'

'This doesn't change anything though, does it? You still want me on your team?' Her voice was so small and uncertain that Reilly's heart went out to her.

'Of course I do – you're the fastest learner I know.'

Lucy exhaled. 'Thanks, Reilly. I've learned so much from you since you came here and I love working with you. We all do.'

She couldn't help but feel touched by this. 'Feeling's mutual. And don't worry about your dad. We've sort of come to an understanding.'

'You're sure? He was pretty mad.'

'You can say that again.' The man's rant still echoed in her head, but it was faint amongst the cacophony of everything else on her mind just then.

'Well, anyway,' Lucy hovered a little in the doorway, 'a couple of things have just come through from the lab, stuff from the break-in actually.' She dropped a sheaf of papers on Reilly's desk. 'Dead ends mostly. For example, that hair you found in the stairwell? We ran the DNA like you asked and it looks like it's your own.' When Reilly frowned, she looked apologetic. 'I know, I suppose we should have thought of that but—'

'You're sure?' She snatched up the papers and looked for the relevant report.

'Well, yes – the genetic profile came back a high percentile match against your registered sample.' It was standard procedure for all law enforcement personnel, but most importantly for GFU staff to provide DNA samples – essential to rule out any form of evidence contamination.

Yet, Reilly was still hopeful that the hair she'd found was her attacker's and it had been this that had sent her down the female accomplice route. She kneaded her forehead. Clearly, Daniel had a point and she'd been wrong. She flicked through the bundle for the relevant report and quickly scanned through the profile for the hair. It seemed there was a high percentile comparison but what caught her attention was the short scribbled note in the lab comments.

'Hold on, this isn't right ...' She stood up. 'Who ran the sample?' she asked, heading for the door.

Lucy followed closely at her heels. 'Julius, I think. Why?'

Reilly didn't answer, instead she went directly to Julius. He was bent over, studying something under a microscope when she arrived.

'What kind of anomalies?' she asked, without preamble.

'Sorry?'

'The hair sample – in your notes you said that notwithstanding allelial anomalies, there's a high probability it's my DNA.'

'Correct.' He turned to give her his full attention, and for the first time since she'd known him, he looked somewhat uncertain. 'I ran the test twice.'

'And?'

'Well, let me clarify.' He stepped forward and pointed to the printout. 'On first glance it's a solid comparative to your file DNA, enough to suggest the hair is yours. However, if you drill down and compare the alleles ...'

She looked again at the attached printout; a more detailed comparison of both samples, which told a slightly different story. The DNA alleles were a close match certainly, but not a complete one. Reilly's brain felt foggy, as she tried to get her brain around what she was looking at.

'What's going on?' Lucy asked. 'I thought it was a straight-forward match.'

Julius cleared his throat. 'Not quite. It's a genetic match certainly, but ... well it's one you might expect to see between—'

'Siblings,' Daniel Forrest finished the sentence as he came into the room, closely followed by a strained-looking Chris. 'Reilly, why don't we head back to your office? We need to talk.'

36

'Jess? You think Jess is here – in Dublin?' Reilly gasped, unable to grasp what Daniel and Chris were hypothesizing.

Back in the privacy of her office, they'd told her exactly what had happened at Mike's place and the neighbor's belief that he'd gone off somewhere with his daughter. While she was relieved that this had to mean Mike wasn't in any immediate danger, she couldn't understand how this was possible. 'But how? I mean ... she's not due for parole until ...' Then, remembering Chris's presence, she flushed, realizing her shameful family history was unlikely to remain a secret for much longer. 'I'm not sure if Daniel's told you, but my sister—'

He cut her off. 'You don't have to explain. I know what happened.'

'I thought it wise to fill him on most of it,' Daniel added, quietly.

'I haven't seen her in years, Chris. After she ...' Even now Reilly couldn't say the words. She covered her face with her hands and tried to compose herself.

'She got out of CCWF early – was released late last year, but skipped parole within a couple of weeks,' Daniel said. Reilly looked at him and he met her accusing gaze with a level stare. 'I made a few calls.'

'What?' All at once she was flabbergasted by the knowledge that her sister was not only out of detention, but by all accounts had made her way here. But how and, more importantly, why?

'I spoke to her parole officer who said she went completely off the radar, hasn't been seen in months. He tried to contact you, and had no idea you'd moved here.

'And now you think she followed me?'

Daniel sat directly across from her. 'To be frank, I've had my suspicions for some time.'

'But why would you think that? And if she did come here, what difference would that – oh my God,' she whispered, as realization gradually dawned. 'Jess ... you think *Jess* could be responsible for this ... is behind all this craziness?' She stared from Daniel to Chris, willing them to dispute it, but their faces remained impassive. Jess a suspect? No, that was impossible.

'Reilly, we can't discount the possibility,' Daniel was saying, but the words couldn't penetrate through the myriad emotions she was feeling just then. The implications were almost too much to take yet, deep down, she knew she couldn't discount the idea either. The break-in at her apartment, the family photograph, the incident at the lab, and then of course the blond hair ...

OK, so those things could potentially have been Jess, but none of them pointed at any involvement in the murders, did it? Unless ...

'You knew, didn't you?' she said, rounding on Daniel suddenly. 'You figured she might be involved in this – it's why you're here, why you were so insistent about offering help on the ground.' She stood up, her face red with anger. 'How could you not tell me, Daniel? How could you knowingly put all these people in danger, my *father* in danger?'

Chris put a hand on her arm. 'Reilly, calm down ...'

'I never thought for a second that Mike would be in danger,' Daniel replied, patiently. 'It was *you* I was worried about. After all, you're the one she's always been angry with. And you're right – of course I wouldn't have knowingly put others in danger, but Reilly it was only a hunch, I didn't know for sure. And I didn't want to lay such a thing on you over the phone. So I thought if I came here and got a better idea of what was going on, I would be better able to help.'

'He's right, Reilly,' Chris interjected. 'Nobody could have anticipated this, and in any case, all of the murders were committed before Daniel arrived. He couldn't have prevented anything. As it is, it's only we now have a suspect because of him.'

Jess. Was it really possible? Could her little sister actually be the person they were looking for, the taboo killer? It was a thought so devastating that Reilly couldn't get a grip on it. Then she thought again about the acronym arranged on Clare Ryan's books.

Your fault ...

'I need to get out of here,' she said, suddenly bolting toward the door. She needed to figure this out, to try to get her head straight so she could work it out, because at the moment it was all too overwhelming to comprehend.

And her dad, what about him? Was he truly in danger? Was it another part of Jess's grand plan for revenge or whatever the hell this was?

'Reilly wait, where are you going?' She heard Daniel call after her but she ignored him. She couldn't deal with him right now. To think that he'd known all this time that Jess had got out early and never said a word ...

'Hold on.' Chris was following her down the hallway. 'Reilly, please, we need to talk about this – for more reasons than one,' he added, pointedly and right away she knew what he was getting at.

Personal feelings aside, this was an on-going case in which she was heavily involved; now it seemed that one member of her family was a suspect, another a potential victim. So to say that she was in the middle of one hell of shit storm was a huge understatement.

'I know.' She ran both hands through her hair. 'I just ... I had to get out of there. Daniel should have said something.'

'In fairness to the guy, he didn't know for sure, not until we talked to the neighbor at any rate. After telling me about Jess, we started putting things together, about how he worried right from the start that the symbolism of the murders was far too personal, and seemed to be increasingly targeted toward you. He was worried about you, that's all there was to it. And then back in the lab when we heard you guys talking about the DNA thing, he figured there was little doubt. Your sister's involved somewhere along the line, Reilly; how much we don't know yet. Maybe she's carrying out the murders herself or she has an accomplice, we can't say. Either way, we really need to figure it out.'

She shook her head. 'It's just ... so much to take in.'

'I can only imagine, but perhaps now more than ever, I need you to think straight, for the sake of your dad if nothing else.'

She bit her lip, nodding. 'I know.'

He put a gentle hand on her arm. 'For what it's worth, Daniel doesn't believe Jess intends to harm Mike – instead he reckons she plans to use him as bait somehow, some way of getting your attention.'

Her resolve softened a little. 'He's probably right. After all, I'm the one she hates, the one who let her down.' Her mouth was dry and her lips felt as though they were glued shut, but suddenly the tears were flowing, rolling down her cheeks in a steady stream to her chin, before dripping on to her blouse. 'I ...' She tried to speak again but could get no further. Her shoulders began to heave and a wild animal sob broke free. Then her legs grew weak and she began to stumble.

Chris crossed the space in three huge strides and wrapped a strong arm around her shoulder before steering her into the vacant office nearby.

She collapsed on a chair, grateful for his silent understanding, his strength. Leaning forward she put her head in her hands, unable to staunch the flow of tears now they had finally broken through. A series of images flowed through her mind: Jess as a baby, her fluffy blond curls pulled up on top of her head like a fountain, a huge grin splitting her enormous cheeks ... their mother, smiling and vibrant, playing tag with the girls in the back yard, while Mike sat drinking beer and watching them ... then her beloved mum shut away for days in her room, refusing to speak to anyone ... and finally Cassie lying in a pool of her own blood.

She sat up suddenly and scrubbed at her face to dry the tears. Chris sat back and released his arm from around her shoulders, but said nothing.

She sniffed, pulled a tissue from her pocket and wiped her face. 'God, that was really embarrassing ...'

'It's perfectly understandable.'

She looked out the window at the quiet streets below. A woman hurried across the road, her coat pulled tight around her as two young guys walked the other way. Everyday scenes from everyday lives, a million miles removed from what Reilly was facing – from what she was about to face.

She dabbed at her face again with the tissue, then wadded it up and crammed it in her pocket. Now the tears were gone, now she had released all the emotions that had built up inside her for so many months – or was it years?

Chris spoke tentatively, suspecting he was moving onto thin ice. 'Why the hatred of you, Reilly? Why is she targeting you?'

'Because she blames me. I was supposed to take care of her, I promised her I'd take of her. And, like Mom, I let her down.'

'How? Because you refused to help cover up what she did? Why would you do that?'

'I don't know, I don't really understand any of this. But – and of course I didn't understand this as a child, but my mom ... she had some mental health issues. And then Jess ... well, her mind never really worked like anyone else's. Daniel and I went over it so many times ... him and Dr Kyle, my shrink back home, reckoned that she had all the hallmarks of a classic sociopath. I guess until now I never wanted to admit that. I made myself believe that what happened with my mom was just an accident, a rush of blood to the head but now, thinking about what she could have done to all these innocent people ...'

'What was she like afterward – when they put her away? Did she show any remorse or explain why she'd done it?'

Reilly stiffened. 'I don't know. She never let me see her. I was enemy number one after that.' She thought back to all the times she'd tried to visit, tried to talk to Jess and let her know that no matter what, she was still there for her. But every time, Jess refused to come out and meet her.

'I thought I could outlast her,' she admitted to Chris. 'But

there was never really any chance of that with Jess. She was –
is – the most stubborn person I've ever met.' She sighed. 'I
went to CCWF almost every week at first, determined to be
there when she changed her mind, but she never did. Then a
couple of years later, I went away to college, and after that I
guess I just gave up.'

'This whole taboo fixation,' Chris ventured. 'That would
be tied in with Jess killing her own mother?'

'Yes, remember Daniel told us that patricide, or in this case
matricide was the ultimate taboo – the highest form of
depravity.' Her expression tightened. 'Looking back, all her life
Jess was a little like Mom – always prone to sudden emotion,
often liked to test limits and break rules.' Still, to think she
could be responsible for such violent acts, and so many gruesome deaths ...

Chris stood up. 'Reilly, you and I both know the top brass
are going to want you off this now. With your sister a suspect,
and your father a potential victim, there's a massive conflict of
interest—'

She bit her lip. 'I know, but how can I just sit back especially when my dad is in danger? Not to mention that I need to
find Jess, to try to get her to stop all this.' She looked at him. 'I
know her better than anyone, Chris and, more to the point, it
looks like she's doing this *because* of me.'

'I understand that, I do. But you have to think about the
consequences, think about the families of the victims. You
can't work this anymore.'

'But—'

'Reilly, if Jess is doing this, when we catch her – and we
will – we can't risk compromising the prosecution. Every
piece of evidence has a lawyer's name on it, you know that,
and if you continue with this, knowing what we know now,
everything we've already worked for will be shot to hell.

Christ, you'd never be able to work for the department again.'

'I know.' Reilly wanted to put a fist through the wall. Of course he was right but it was so damned frustrating. This was her family they were talking about! To think that she'd no choice but to sit on her hands and let someone else try and sort out the mess ...

'I'll talk to O'Brien,' she conceded, grudgingly and Chris seemed relieved, as if he'd been expecting more of a fight. But Reilly wasn't an idiot and, maddening as it was, she knew the score. 'But first, I need to go check out my dad's place – there might be something, some clue as to where they've gone, or where she's taken—'

'I'm sorry, but I can't allow that either.'

'What? But it's my father's house—'

'Which is also now part of a criminal investigation,' Chris finished, solemnly.

'You cannot be serious ...' But again, she knew he was right and his hands were tied. She wanted to scream.

'I've already ordered a team over there to sweep the place – see if there's anything usable, or more to the point, anything our friendly neighbor left untouched. Useless as evidence but maybe we can unearth something that'll help point us in the right direction.'

Or establish whether or not Jess coerced Mike into leaving, Reilly finished, silently.

She looked at Chris. 'Please don't tell me Gorman is handling this,' she asked as the realization struck her.

'There was little other choice,' he conceded, then put a reassuring hand on her arm again. 'Reilly, no matter what you might think of the guy personally, he's a good investigator, and anyway, he won't be doing this alone,' he added, referring to the team she herself had spent so much precious time training.

She looked away, feeling more helpless than she'd ever been. Possibly the biggest, most important crime scene of her life and she couldn't run it. Instead she had to sit on her hands and rely on people for whom there was nothing at all at stake.

'They're a good group, Reilly, you should know that better than anyone.'

She gave a grudging nod.

'Now you need to trust them and, more to the point, trust *us* to get the rest of the job done.'

'I know,' she conceded, hoarsely. But it was so hard to have to just stand back and do nothing. 'As I said, I'll talk to O'Brien – but on one condition,' she added, firmly. He looked at her. 'Just give me a little more time to go through the files, see what I can find—'

'Reilly—'

'Chris, please, just give me this much, not as a cop, but as a friend. All I'm asking is a couple more hours at the most. I know I'm off this; we don't have any other choice. But I'm only off it once Jess is officially a suspect and right now we're only working on conjecture. Just give me the rest of the afternoon, tops.'

'Reilly, you know I can't—'

'You and I both know that occasionally things need to stay off the radar,' she said, staring purposely at his left arm and leaving him under no illusions that she was referring to his illness. It was a cheap shot and they both knew it but Reilly was desperate.

For a long moment he stared at her, then he sighed and she knew she had him. 'For what it's worth, I think this a really bad idea.'

'It isn't and you know it. Let me look over the evidence one last time, see if I can give us anything that'll help you find her. What you guys uncover yourselves after today has nothing to do with me.'

There was a long silence as she watched him mentally weigh things up.

'Please, Chris, you owe me this much.'

'We could both get fired over this.'

'Not if we keep things quiet. Daniel won't talk until you do and nobody other than the three of us know what's going on – right?'

'Well, I was just about to call Kennedy—'

'A couple of hours, Chris, that's all I'm asking, then I'm off it, I swear.'

He nodded almost imperceptibly and she breathed an internal sigh of relief.

'You have until the team briefing at eight tomorrow morning; we can all talk to O'Brien then.' He reached for the door. 'In the meantime, this conversation never happened.'

'Of course. But you'll keep me in the loop, won't you? I can still help – unofficially of course and—'

'Reilly, as far as this thing goes, I think I've given you more than enough,' Chris said, his tone steely. 'Right now, I need you to let me do my job, so I can get out there and stop anyone else from getting hurt.'

37

Y ou're right, I should have told you,' Daniel admitted. It was much later that evening and he and Reilly were at her apartment sifting through what they had so far on the killings, searching for anything that might help them locate Jess and, by extension, Mike.

'But I didn't want to upset you, or indeed prejudice your handling of the case – not until I knew more. As far as I was concerned I needed to treat this as just another profile and leave my personal suspicions out of it.'

'Which was why you so readily offered to help on the ground.'

'Yes.'

While she could perhaps understand Daniel's professional reluctance to say anything, personally she still felt hurt and somewhat betrayed by his actions. At the very least, he should have told her that Jess was out of CCWF.

As her tutor, he had been aware of her personal history, and having gradually drawn Reilly out and earned her trust, they'd discussed the situation throughout her time at Quantico. For her part, she'd been desperate to try and understand how her little sister could have committed such a killing, and the profiler in return had been fascinated by his protégé's history and how it had shaped and perhaps even driven her professional life.

Not only that but, given her mother's mental health issues, Reilly always worried if she too might be genetically predisposed to some kind of psychological fragility in the way that Jess was. It was something that had haunted her every day since that horrific incident at Cassie's house, despite Dr Kyle and Daniel's assurances that this wasn't a given.

What if some day, like Jess, some deep-seated malaise was triggered in her?

Reilly had always clung to the notion that her sister was not at heart an evil person, that her personality had instead been shaped by her experience, and the trauma of losing her mother at such a young age. But as Daniel had repeatedly told her, sociopathic or psychopathic personalities are innate and almost always rise to the fore, irrespective of family circumstances or outside influences. Still, it was a disturbing and unsettling thought.

She stood up and stretched her limbs, unwilling to dwell on that aspect just now. 'I don't know what Jess is trying to achieve with all this.'

He looked at her, his expression dubious. 'Come on, Reilly, stop deluding yourself; you really have no idea what this is all about? The power play, the personal challenge, the family connection ...'

'I guess the obvious answer is that she blames me. She blames me, on some crazy level, for what happened with Mom, and what she did. And she wants me to be punished.'

Your fault...

She slumped back down on the sofa. Despite the disconcerting thought that Jess was somewhere out there, watching her, stalking her even, it seemed unlikely that she would actually attack or kill her – if she had wanted to do that, she could have easily done it before now. Instead, the murders, the throwing down of a challenge to Reilly's professional abilities … Jess was clearly trying to punish her in a very different way.

'You yourself were the one who admitted Jess always had a simple sense of right and wrong. An eye for an eye …'

Reilly nodded. 'And now she has Dad and she wants me to find them.'

He was silent for a moment before asking the next question. 'And when you do?'

'I really have no idea.'

'The taboo fixation …' Daniel ventured. 'Professionally speaking, my belief is that this aspect of the killings is especially significant, given her history,' he added.

'I know. Even as a kid, she was always pushing limits, daring others to break the rules. It was like she got a kick out of it. Of course, there was no way I could have anticipated …' Reilly's eyes shone.

'Of course you couldn't. Who could? But tell me more about her relationship with your parents, as much as you can remember.'

Reilly sat forward. 'As a young child, she always observed people, saw things and picked up on things that others didn't see.' She looked away into the distance, thinking back to their childhood. 'She adored my dad though, that's why I find it hard to believe she would hurt him now. They had a special relationship, different to the one he had with me after Mom left I guess, because she was the baby, the one we both needed to look after. It was why I was so sure it was only because of him that she hurt my mother – and her boyfriend – in the first place. She was trying to protect him.'

That had always been the thread of hope Reilly had clung

to when trying to make sense of it all. Jess had only committed that horrible act out of love and loyalty to her father, who she knew had been devastated and betrayed by his wife's desertion. But, deep down, she and Mike both knew this wasn't the case; there was much more to it.

'So why has she taken him now?' Daniel asked. 'Why bring him into this?'

She looked at him, noticing the change in his tone. He was trying to lead her somewhere. 'You think she's using him as part of this game, as a pawn of some kind?'

'Think about everything she's done so far. The killings were all about forcing people to do what is most abhorrent to them. Think about it, Reilly. What would be most abhorrent to Mike, or to you even?'

She couldn't reply, couldn't even comprehend an answer to that question. It was utterly beyond her realm of thinking – as was everything Jess had done.

She took a deep breath. 'I don't know, but either way it's a disconcerting thought.'

'Of course,' he replied. 'But she *thrives* on your discomfort. That's a big part of what she's doing.'

'Challenging me? Being noticed?'

'Yes. Chances are she knows that you've made the connection by now and that you're trying to figure out what's coming next. She loves that.'

The events of the past few days raced through Reilly's mind like a DVD on fast-forward, images piling one on top of the other. 'My apartment, the lab, my dad's place – she's been watching me for weeks, hasn't she?'

'I would think so, yes.'

Despite Daniel's belief that Mike wasn't in immediate danger, everything pointed toward another violent death – but whose? Jess had already shown that she could get to Reilly whenever she wanted to – at home, at work, seemingly anywhere. So if she had simply wanted to kill her she'd had ample opportunity.

No, there was more to it than that. The theatrical nature of the killings, the way she'd left the victims, all suggested that in her own sick way Jess saw herself as an artist, painting a grim tableau that told her own very particular story, in her own unique way. But what would it be? Even with this new information, coupled with the mass of evidence they'd accumulated, they were still no nearer to knowing what Jess might do next. She was still fully, totally, in control.

Reilly stood up and headed for the coffee maker. 'I need a break.' She suddenly felt exhausted. After all that had happened over the past few hours – days even – finding the right way to channel these powerful emotions and relive things that had happened so long ago was almost impossible.

But for her father's sake, and the sake of anyone else Jess might have her sights on as a target, Reilly tried to tell herself that this was just another case, and she needed to treat it as such.

'What are you thinking?' Daniel asked, accepting the mug of coffee that Reilly had just made.

She sat across from him, and looked away into the distance. 'If this really is Jess and she's doing all this to challenge me, to punish me, why bring so many innocent victims into this? All those people, some of them just kids ...'

'Because that's what you do, Reilly, that's your strength. Your job as an investigator is to find as many pieces of a puzzle as you can, and help the authorities make the rest of them fit. For someone like Jess, it's purely that – a game, and the morality of it doesn't come into it. As to why she chose those particular people, well, I have a theory about that.'

'You do?'

He nodded. 'Detective Delaney told me earlier about the witness they'd spoken to, that homeless man who recognized the young college girl and the camper.'

'Yes, Kennedy did mention they were looking at a possible charity angle – something that might help tie the victims together.'

'Well, if you think about it, upon entering the country someone like Jess would have had to live under the radar, at least for a while, until she found somewhere to base herself. It's very common for criminals entering new territory to align themselves with the homeless population. They have access to food, shelter and, for the most part, afford complete invisibility.'

Reilly nodded; it made sense. She'd been wondering where Jess had been basing herself, particularly when planning all of this.

'Now if it's established that those victims routinely went out of their way to help such people, then there's a very good chance Jess may have come into contact with them, even briefly,' Daniel continued. 'Think about it, an attractive blond in her twenties begging on the streets? Certainly the type to attract more attention or pity than the usual junkie and alcoholic types.'

'So you're thinking Jess picked these people because they tried to *help* her?' The suggestion was more cruel and even more horrendous than believing they were chosen at random.

'Well, for a lot of people, helping others, particularly those in dire straits, is a form of taboo in itself. The majority of people don't like to cross that particular social divide, mostly because they're afraid to. Deep down they don't want to be confronted with the reality that such a break from society can happen to any one of us. People like the young college student or perhaps that well-to-do businessman – who not only acknowledge down-and-outs but go one step further by engaging and actually trying to help them – are actually breaking a social taboo, albeit a very positive one.'

'And Jess may have picked up on that. After all she has spent the last decade with people trying to help her, rehabilitate her.'

'Yes, and given her history, I would think this aspect of their personalities would have intrigued her. If nothing else, it would certainly throw a degree of light as to why such a disparate group of people, who have no known connection to one another, ended up dead at the hands of a murderer. Chances are Jess may have learned a great deal about them and their lives through one or perhaps repeated conversations. We both know that she's very skilled at eliciting information in order to get what she wants.'

Reilly thought about it. To think that these people had gone out of their way to talk to her, maybe tried to help her, and she repaid them by using them in her sick, murderous game.

'I know what you're thinking and there's little point. There is no morality involved; for people like Jess, there never is.'

Reilly nodded. The fact remained that all these people were dead; their only sin possibly being that they'd been too kind-hearted for their own good.

She set her empty coffee cup on the table. 'Do you think she's still living in that environment? Could she have taken my dad to a homeless shelter?'

Daniel shook his head defiantly. 'No. The shelters would have been a two or three week thing at the most, simply a stopgap before she found somewhere more permanent, somewhere private for her to hole up, preferably unnoticed.'

But where might that be? Reilly asked, silently, looking again at the evidence files. There had to be something amongst the trace that might lead them to where she was holding Mike now.

Daniel followed her gaze. 'I'm not sure the answer is in there just now. Knowing Jess, she'll throw a few additional crumbs your way somehow – it's what she's been doing all along.'

But Reilly's biggest frustration was that she was now no longer in a position to find those crumbs, whatever they might be. 'She's planned this carefully. And no doubt, she'll keep doing so until you catch her,' he concluded. 'Which is why we'd better get back to this and try to help your friend Delaney and his crew do just that.'

Reilly looked at her watch. It was now past 2 a.m., and the team briefing with O'Brien was scheduled for eight. Time was running out.

'I'll keep going on this stuff all night if I have to, but really, you should be getting back to your hotel. Where are you staying again?'

'The Merrion, but actually, I have no problem making this an all-nighter – or at least catching a couple of hours on your couch before we head in for the meeting.'

'There's no need Daniel, honestly.'

'Yes, there is. So far, I'm sorry to say I've been more of a hindrance than a help, but now that everything's out in the open ...'

'OK, if you insist.' Reilly got up and moved to the cupboard where she kept a spare set of bed linen. 'Might as well get you organized then.'

In truth, with all that was going on, she was almost relieved she wouldn't have to stay here alone tonight. If Jess was watching and planning something, who knew what? But upon opening the cupboard door, the rest of her thoughts trailed away.

'Now, don't go to any fuss on my behalf. Believe me, I've spent many nights with my head on nothing more than a cold wooden desk and—' Daniel paused, noticing her stillness. 'What is it?'

Reilly's face had gone deathly white. 'Oh my God.'

38

The interdepartmental briefing began at 8 a.m. sharp, but by 8.15, Reilly was still nowhere to be seen. Chris was worried – despite her reluctant agreement to let him handle things, had she in the meantime turned renegade and decided to pursue this her way?

That was the last thing he needed and already he regretted allowing her continued access to the evidence; it was a stupid spur-of-the-moment, completely unprofessional decision, but her concern for her father, and her sneaky aside about him walking a thin line of his own, had got to him.

Now, he just wished she'd show her face so that she could defend some of the accusations or at the very least, deflect some of the heat that O'Brien was currently throwing at him and Kennedy.

'Bloody hell! The press are having a bloody field day with this taboo thing and now you're telling me one of our *own* is directly involved!'

'Not quite one of our own,' Jack Gorman put in smugly and Chris knew the older man was dancing an inward jig at the new revelation Chris had just outlined. 'I worried from the start that Steel wasn't to be trusted. For one thing her methods are—'

'Shut it, Gorman,' Kennedy interjected and Chris looked up, surprised. While his partner seemed to have developed a grudging respect for Reilly over time, he'd been incandescent upon hearing that her sister had become a suspect, which Chris was sure meant all bets were off when it came to co-operating with her any longer. 'Her insights have got us a lot further in this thing than yours would have.'

'And how do we know these so-called insights aren't merely figments of her imagination designed to throw us off the scent?' the older man argued. 'How do we know Steel herself isn't knee deep in all of this and helping cover it up?'

'For Christ sake, Gorman, her family background is on her personnel file, there for all to see,' Chris retorted. 'And if the top brass were confident that this wasn't an issue, then we should be too. Right, sir?'

O'Brien met his gaze. 'Well, this morning, I must admit my first instinct was to think like Jack but yes, I myself knew about Steel's family situation before she was brought in to the GFU. Difference is, we were told the sister had been locked away.'

'She was – up until six months ago,' Daniel Forrest, who'd so far remained silent, clarified and Chris wondered if Reilly had yet forgiven him for keeping her in the dark about that.

'So what about it then, Forrest?' the Inspector asked. 'You're supposed to be the expert; could the sister seriously be in the mix for this?'

'I'm afraid so. Jessica Steel is a classic sociopath. From what I know of her psychological background, she's perfectly capable of such violent acts and, in my opinion, is very likely the person behind these murders.'

'But why?' he thundered. 'And never mind how –how she

gained access to the country in the first place is one for your own boys in the States.'

Gorman was shaking his head. 'I don't know why we're even entertaining this. I've looked at the case files and there's nothing, not a single shred of evidence supporting Mr Forrest's claims that Steel's sister is connected to these killings. If anything, this is little more than a personal spat between two family members, and is confusing the real issue, namely how do we catch our real perpetrator?'

Chris stayed silent, conceding that Gorman did have a point. He was right; in isolation the so called evidence – the break-ins at the lab and at Reilly's apartment and the blond hair – didn't actually point to any wrongdoing on Jessica Steel's part, and could indeed be viewed as just some family incident separate to the task in hand. Except for Daniel Forrest's assertion that she was the one responsible.

Forrest spoke again. 'I take Mr Gorman's point, but we do, in fact, have some cryptic clues—'

O'Brien rolled his eyes. 'Cryptic clues? If you ask me, this whole case has been one long cryptic clue!' He sat back and looked around the table. 'Do we have any real evidence – I mean actual, solid police evidence, to prove that this girl is involved in this?' His look was challenging. 'Anything? Anyone? And where the hell is Steel, anyway?' *Good question,* Chris thought, staring at the door. 'She should be here for this, considering the accusations that are flying around, and not least because this is partly her doing.'

Daniel sat forward. 'Are you doubting Reilly's loyalties?' he challenged.

'Agent Forrest,' O'Brien said, patiently and Chris knew the chief was frustrated as hell but trying his utmost to tread lightly, given Daniel's high level contacts. 'I know you're a big supporter of Ms Steel – you trained her, yes?'

'Correct.'

'But surely even you would admit that what's been outlined here is pretty thin evidence on which to launch a nationwide manhunt? At best, Mike Steel is drunk in some bar somewhere. At worst he's with his own daughter.'

'Who has killed nine people,' Daniel reminded him.

'Exactly,' Gorman nodded. 'In fact, it's all pretty incestuous, isn't it? I mean we supposedly have a murderer who is the sister of a senior member of our own GFU,' he spat, all the bitterness over Reilly's appointment coming through. 'And now she is alleging – on flimsy evidence – that the sister has kidnapped her father and intends to kill him.'

Daniel climbed slowly to his feet and Chris gave him a look.

'Are you leaving us so soon, Agent Forrest?' O'Brien asked. 'We'll miss you, I'm sure.'

Daniel leaned forward, his hands on the table. 'Reilly Steel is one of the finest investigators I've ever worked with. You should be proud to have her on your team – she's an incredible asset to this department and, don't forget, the only reason you've made this much progress.'

'Well, if your assertions are correct, she's the only reason we're even in this mess!' Gorman thundered. 'If she'd stayed back where she belongs, all these innocent people would still be alive today.'

Chris looked at him. 'You're blaming Reilly for that? So you *do* think her sister could be involved ...'

Gorman shrugged, realizing that he was contradicting himself.

O'Brien nodded. 'I agree. If nothing else, it's true that Ms Steel's presence here that has drawn her nutcase sister to Dublin. As if we hadn't enough of our own to deal with—'

'And what about my father?' a female voice said. Chris

turned with relief to see that Reilly had crept silently into the meeting. Her expression was strained. 'Are we to get any help in finding him before she does something else?'

'What? You need half the department's help to find your father?' Gorman scoffed. 'From what I hear, you might want to start with some of the bars off Capel Street.'

'Jack is right.' O'Brien conceded. 'I'm sorry, Steel, but we just can't spare the manpower for what looks to be nothing more than a family issue.' He looked at Kennedy and Delaney. 'From what I can see, we're getting nowhere on this taboo killer thing, and until something concrete turns up, there's also the small issue of the other hundred or so open cases in this department—'

'Something has turned up,' Reilly blurted. Chris stared, wondering what was coming. 'I know I'm late and I'm sorry, but I needed to check something with the lab before I could say for sure.'

'Say what for sure? Get on with it,' O'Brien urged, impatiently.

Reilly met Chris's eye. 'We do have evidence linking my sister to the killings, sir. That bed sheet that was used to kill Jim Redmond? It's mine.'

39

The meeting finished shortly afterward and, as anticipated, Reilly was removed from the case and placed on temporary leave.

She was in her office collecting some personal belongings to take home with her when Daniel walked in, a serious expression on his face. He closed the door behind him.

'Well, I suppose that went as well as could be expected,' he said, drolly.

'At least they're taking us seriously and Jess is now a prime suspect.'

Unfortunately, this didn't mean they were any further along in the search for her father, but if nothing else it was a step in the right direction. Chris and Kennedy had gone to re-interview Mike's neighbor and canvass anyone else in the immediate area that might have seen anything. In the meantime, Jack Gorman and the GFU team had been charged with going through the evidence, hoping to find some indication of where Jess was and what she might be planning next.

It was frustrating no longer being in the thick of it but Reilly was counting down the hours until her father's flat was released from the investigation and she could get down there herself and take a proper look around.

Daniel dropped a sheaf of papers on her desk. 'A copy of my official profile,' he said, meeting her gaze. 'There's also a report from the CCWF which makes for interesting reading – I've highlighted the parts I think may be useful, namely the list of psychology books Jess hired from the library, as well as the psych reports.' He indicated some sections with yellow post-its of his handwritten notes. 'Although most of this may not be that helpful now. After all, who knows Jess's mind better than you?'

'I only wish that were true.'

A gentle smile crossed Daniel's face. 'Actually, you don't need me anymore either,' he added. She went to say something but he waved her protests away. 'You never really needed me in the first place, Reilly,' he replied. 'I only came here to make some observations and to—'

'Push me in the right direction?' She smiled and he grinned in return.

'You would have figured this out for yourself – the problem was you were too close to see it. Same as before.'

She bit her lip, knowing he was referring to the day of her mother's death. 'I know now I couldn't have done anything to stop her but maybe this time I can.'

'She was never your responsibility, Reilly; I've tried to tell you that time and time again. And despite what you might think, you and Jess are opposite sides of the same coin.'

Reilly shook her head. That was easy for him to say.

'But now she's waiting for you, and using your dad to draw you out,' he continued. 'So while you might be off the case, that doesn't mean you can't still figure this out.'

'But I feel so damned helpless, Daniel.' She looked around the room 'Where do I even start?'

'I know you can do it, but you need to have your wits about you.'

She made a face. 'I'd feel a hell of lot happier if I could carry a gun.'

Daniel laughed softly. 'Yes, that does take some getting used to,' he admitted, patting his ribs. 'I feel almost naked without it.'

There was a brief silence and Reilly looked at him, understanding all of a sudden. 'You're going back to the States, aren't you?'

Daniel nodded.

'Why?' She couldn't keep the disappointment out of her voice. He couldn't leave now, not at such a crucial point.

'I don't really have much of a choice, there's been something of a breakthrough on a case I've been working on back home and they need me back. Anyway, this was only ever going to be a few days, just so I could make sure you were OK. And now I know you are.'

'You think so?' Reilly gave a hard laugh.

'I know so.' He leaned forward and placed a gentle kiss on her cheek.

While Daniel's leaving saddened her, she realized that he was right. His presence had been reassuring and some of his insights illuminating, but ultimately it was her, Chris and the team who had carried the case forward.

'They've got a car coming to collect me from the hotel later. I'd like to say goodbye to your team this afternoon before I go – you've got a really good group together there, Reilly. They're a testament to your skills.'

'Just make sure Lucy keeps her hands off you,' she joked, weakly.

He gave an expression of mock perplexity. 'Now which one's Lucy?'

'Like you didn't notice the cute blond with the puppy dog eyes?' she grinned.

The two embraced, a long, warm hug of mutual respect and friendship.

'Be careful,' Daniel said, finally. 'She has all your smarts but none of your morals. And we both know there are no limits to what she's prepared to do ...'

40

The following day, Reilly and Chris stood in the doorway of Mike's flat. The residence had since been swept for evidence and released from the investigation, and she was at liberty to take a look around.

On the case or not, she was on a personal mission to find her father and, as locating Mike meant potentially locating their now prime suspect, Chris was willing to go along with it.

'Well, for a start it's not usually like this,' she said, sniffing the air.

'I know – that neighbor of his really gave it a good scrub.'

'Silly cow,' Reilly said through gritted teeth. Despite her best intentions, that woman Kelly may well have obliterated the trail to her father. Jess liked leaving clues and Reilly hoped against hope that there was something here that she, unlike the forensic team who had no personal stake in this, could identify as significant.

Earlier, Reilly had herself spoken to Mrs Kelly in the hope of finding out more about her dad's supposed trip away.

'Did he seem OK to you? Physically, I mean,' she asked, hurriedly, unable to hide the desperation in her tone. She couldn't help but notice that Mrs Kelly smelt badly of stale tobacco.

'No different than normal.' Kelly replied, eyeing her with interest. 'Why?

'Would he have had a drink or two, I wonder?' Chris asked, casually and Reilly knew he was trying to figure out if Jess had given him a shot of pentobarbital, or if he'd just been his usual tanked self.

'I wouldn't think so,' Kelly replied, surprised by the notion. 'Although, now that you say it, he did seem a bit ... under the weather.'

'In what way?'

'Well, he's normally not very talkative, you know? Difficult to get a word out of him the best of times, but this time he started going on about how his daughter was visiting from America and hoping to find her roots, that kind of thing.' Then she looked at Reilly. 'Why are the police asking me all these questions about your father anyway? Is there something wrong?'

'Did he mention anything specific about where they were going?' Reilly went on, purposely ignoring the question.

'No, nothing really. To be honest, I wouldn't have known anything about it all only I bumped into him on the way out.' Her lips narrowed slightly. 'Your father, he's a lovely man but well, he isn't really the chatty type, you know?'

Reilly nodded.

'So, I mentioned something about keeping an eye on the place for him while he was gone and he said that would be great, then off they went in the car.'

'You're sure you can't describe that car for us, Mrs Kelly?' Chris asked.

She bit her lip. 'Like I told you before, I really couldn't say for sure. It was black I think, and quite big, one of those people carrier things, but I didn't really pay much attention.'

People rarely did, Reilly thought, feeling more frustrated by the second. Kelly's account had given them nothing else to go on, although she supposed she should feel grateful that the woman had given them the heads-up about Jess in the first place.

She and Chris stepped into Mike's living room. 'So, what are we looking for?' he asked.

'I wish I knew, but based on what we've found previously I'm thinking anything that looks out of place. Papers, photographs, scraps of paper, anything that might give us some idea of where she's taken him.' She recalled what Daniel had said about Jess laying down crumbs. 'She enjoys leaving clues, however vague or insignificant they might appear.'

Reilly tried to picture her sister there, what she had said, what she had done.

What had Mike thought when she'd appeared? Her dad, like herself, had no clue Jess had been let out on parole, and she was probably the last person he expected to see. Was he happy – or scared? What did Jess say, if anything? Had she drugged him to get him away or was he compliant? What had she said to convince him to leave and where had they gone?

Leaving Chris to comb the living room, she went through to her father's bedroom.

The room was pretty bare – spartan almost, and contained only a narrow bed with a cheap headboard, alongside a small bedside table, and a chipboard wardrobe. There was no character in the room, no decoration, nothing that showed any touches of personal care apart from a cheap, generic *Home Sweet Home* sign above the bed. Reilly stared at it for a moment, thinking it was almost ironic.

Home Sweet Home? Hardly. So much for Mike's big dream of returning to the land of his birth ...

All at once, Reilly felt guilty for not seeing enough of her father, for not taking better care of him. Now, if Jess had her way, she might never get the opportunity to do so again. What did she want? Had she only taken him to get at Reilly, use him as some kind of pawn in this sick mind game she was playing?

She took a deep breath and sat down on the side of the bed, hoping that wherever Mike was, he was holding up OK. Then, almost without realizing it, she lay down and rested her head on the pillow. She could still smell her dad's distinctive scent on it and it instantly took her back to childhood – a place that made her feel warm, safe and secure.

She could still remember how her father used to hold her, and put his strong arms around her. Whenever Cassie left during one of her 'episodes', Reilly suffered nightmares, and would wake in the night in fear, an empty darkness haunting her dreams, a vast black pit of despair waiting to swallow her up. But Mike was always there, a shoulder for her to bury her face in until the darkness receded.

'Are you OK?' Chris asked from the doorway.

She sat up, quickly wiping away the tears. 'It's just ...' She indicated the sparsely decorated room. 'This whole place is just so impersonal, so ... soulless. He had so much invested in coming back to Ireland, you know. When we were kids, he always talked about it so wistfully, the vibrant green of the fields, the sea – gunmetal gray he used to call it.'

Chris raised an eyebrow. 'Then how did he end up here in crappy inner city Dublin?'

'Honestly, I'm not sure – all he could afford, I guess. And of course, Ireland's changed so much in the meantime that the reality failed to live up to the fantasy.'

He nodded. 'Happens a lot. Sounds like your father was quite the romantic back in the day.'

'He was, before ... everything,' she said sadly. 'But little by little life and the bottle sucked it all out of him.'

'His love of the ocean came out in you, though, ' Chris said, gently.

'Maybe.' She gave a weak smile and began straightening the bedclothes. 'Anyway, there's nothing helpful here.'

'Well, I found something in the living room you might want to see. It was sitting on the coffee table and I don't remember seeing it the last time I was here.'

Her head snapped up. 'What have you got?'

She followed him through to the living room, where he sat on the sofa and picked up a slim leather volume. 'Looks like the family photo album,' he said.

Reilly sat beside him and he slid the album over so they could both look at it.

He had it open about halfway through and pointed at an old photo – two girls sitting side by side on the swings in some long-forgotten park. Jess, about seven years old, smiling sweetly, her blond hair forming an almost angelic frame around her face.

And beside her, Reilly, her hair pulled back into a ponytail. It was the only style her dad could manage for them until she'd learned to take care of herself. She had an altogether more serious expression on her face and was staring intently at the camera. Not sad, but not happy either.

Reilly reached out, gently touched the photograph with her thumb. 'I remember that dress,' she sighed.

Chris looked at the photograph, then back up her. 'You haven't changed much,' he commented. 'Still that same serious expression.'

'I had to grow up fast.'

'What age would you have been there? About twelve?'

She nodded. 'I was eight years old when Mom left for the last time – that was really the end of my childhood. With her gone I had to take on so much and I remember that feeling, the realization that there really was nobody else to do those things – look after Jess, cook for my dad, clean the house.' Even now, the memory of her lost childhood haunted her. Reilly gazed at the cheap curtains, the outside lamppost visible through them. 'I had to be Jess's mom – and she was still missing the old one.'

'So she resented you?'

'She wanted a sister to play with and a mom to do all the things moms do. What she got was a sister bossing her around and struggling to cope. So yeah, I guess she resented me. I could never replace mom, but she'd kind of lost her sister too.'

Her thoughts were far away, replaying the dark days of her childhood that had somehow led to the present day nightmare.

'Here, these are the ones I thought you might want to see,' Chris said, turning back to the first few pages.

Reilly dragged her thoughts back to what he was showing her. These were much older photographs, black and white – old people she didn't recognize, standing very formally for photographs, dressed in their Sunday best.

'Mike's folks,' she said. 'I never met them, but those are his parents and the ones the back must be his grandparents.'

'They're a happy looking bunch, aren't they?'

It was true. Despite the Sunday best clothes and formal pose, there was a certain gaiety in the faces, a love of life that shone through. It was an expression Reilly remembered from her father when she was young, before Cassie left.

Chris turned the page again and Reilly couldn't help but smile. 'That's Dad, as a baby.' A round-faced infant gazed from the pages, piercing blue eyes seeming to see right through the camera. 'He always had those amazing eyes ...'

'Is that him too?' Chris asked, a sudden excitement in his voice. He was pointing at another black and white photograph of a young boy, about seven years old standing on a quayside holding up a large fish, a triumphant expression on his face.

'Yep, that's my dad,' she confirmed. 'He used to love fishing, said he and his father used to go almost every chance they had.'

'You said the family were originally from a fishing village?'

'Yes, why?'

'I know where that is,' Chris said. 'My father used to take me fishing there in the summer holidays.' He peered intently at the picture. 'No doubt about it – that's Greystones. I still go down there from time to time – it's only a twenty-minute drive south. It's hardly a village anymore, more of a big commuter town now, but there's an area of older houses down by the harbor, and I'd swear that's where most of these pictures were taken.'

'Greystones,' Reilly repeated, letting the name roll off her tongue. 'It does sound familiar.'

Chris sat forward. 'This might be a bit of a long shot,' he began tentatively, 'but didn't Mike mention something to the neighbor about his daughter wanting to go—'

'Back to her roots.' Reilly closed the photograph album with a loud thud. What did that mean? Was it a kind of tip-off from Mike, who knew Jess's appearance meant trouble, and hoped that Reilly would notice his absence and start asking questions? If so, the fact that he had the presence of mind to do such a thing could only mean that Jess had coerced him, couldn't it?

Then suddenly she thought of something else. 'The sign

...' She jumped up from the sofa and headed back into Mike's bedroom.

'What is it?' Chris asked, following her.

She pointed to the *Home Sweet Home* sign on the wall. 'That's new, I don't remember seeing it before today.' Earlier she'd thought it ironic, but now she realized it might very well be significant. A crumb of sorts.

She looked at Chris. 'Let's go for a drive. I think now might be a good time for a spot of fishing.'

41

They drove south through the early afternoon traffic, Chris at the wheel. The N11 was lightly trafficked at that time of day and Reilly almost relaxed, looking around at the green countryside rushing past the window. She had been so busy since her arrival that she had never left the city, barely finding the time to squeeze in a little sightseeing around the centre.

She thought about where they were going and what they might find. Yesterday she had joked with Daniel about how naked she felt going into situations without a gun, and for him it would have been almost unimaginable – after thirty years in the FBI, old habits die hard.

Use your instincts, he had told her – one of his mantras to all trainee investigators. Still, Reilly thought wryly, she would be much happier using her instincts and a .38.

'Penny for them.'

She jumped a little at Chris's voice. She had been so wrapped up in her own thoughts that she'd almost forgotten that he was there. 'I was just thinking about what Daniel said before he left,' she told him.

'I bet you wish he was along for the ride instead of me,' he said.

'Actually, no.'

Surprise showed in his face.

'Don't get me wrong,' Reilly continued. 'He's an incredible investigator – the best – and it has been great having him around. But ultimately,' she paused. 'Ultimately, I guess, this is our show, Chris. We've come this far, and now we need to finish it – one way or the other.' She bit her lip at the thought of what they might find. Despite her fears about her father, she didn't think she was ready to come face to face with Jess.

His face grew serious, as if he knew what she was thinking. 'If we find something, we can call for backup.'

'Right.' Reilly gave a short bark of laughter. 'And the Greystones SWAT Unit will be on the scene in seconds, I suppose?'

He chuckled. 'Not quite, but there's actually a decent-sized station based not far from there – in Bray. Either way, Kennedy knows where we're going and I promised to keep him updated. So if we find her, and things get out of hand—'

'Somehow I don't think that it's going to pan out like that,' she told him.

'What do you mean?'

'Think about it, Chris,' she began. 'Without trying to sound negative, Jess has been in control of this from the very start. Everything we've got that has moved us forward has come from her – and she's still in control.'

He sighed. 'So she's expecting us, and whenever we do find her—'

'Everything will be played out according to her rules.'

Chris accelerated to pass a large articulated lorry. 'So what does that mean – in reality, on the ground?'

'Exactly what Daniel said to me before he left,' Reilly said grimly, 'We need to have our wits about us.'

. . .

A LITTLE WHILE LATER, Chris turned off the motorway and onto the secondary road leading to Greystones village.

'You must know this place pretty well to recognize it from those old photos,' Reilly said

'I used to love coming down here with my dad,' he admitted. 'He grew up in Enniskerry, down the road and inland a bit – and he used to bring me out here most weekends when the weather was good.'

'So you're into fishing. All that talk of me surfing and you never once mentioned that you were into fishing.'

'Actually, I'm not,' he replied. 'But my old man loved it and I loved being with him.'

'Sounds like you guys haven't been here for a while,' she ventured.

'It's been a few years,' he said, quietly. 'The last time I came here with father he was already seriously ill - he had heart disease - so we just came and sat on a bench down there at the harbor, enjoying the views. He died a few weeks later.'

'I'm sorry.'

He glanced sideways at her. 'No, it's OK – it's a good memory actually.'

'So what's Greystones like?'

'It's changed a lot. Lots of new houses built for commuters.'

'Same story the world over, I suppose.'

'Right. Big draw for tourists too as it still has that traditional Irish seaside town thing going on – a pretty harbor, fishing boats, the sea. There's a new marina under development at the moment too'

'It sounds pretty idyllic.'

'It is,' Chris confirmed. 'Quite a few city dwellers have moved down this direction for the "good life".'

'So amidst all the blow-ins, one more out-of-towner like Jess really wouldn't stand out much,' Reilly pointed out.

Chris shrugged. 'You'd be surprised. You've got the genealogical info on your family that I asked you to get?'

Reilly patted her bag. 'Right here.'

He nodded. 'Good. There are still a few old haunts where the locals hang out and some families here go back hundreds of years, know everyone and everything that's happened since the Vikings arrived. I'll just turn on my local charm and they'll tell me everything we want to know.'

Reilly looked dubious. 'It could very well be like trying to find a needle in a haystack.'

'Maybe yes, maybe no,' admitted Chris. 'But keep in mind that at the back of it all this, Jess *wants* us to find her.'

AS THEY ROLLED into the village, despite her nervousness, Reilly was impressed by her first glimpse of the pretty Victorian houses on the way toward the seafront. Gray clouds swirled overhead, tugged along by the wind. The harbor was full, small blue, red and white pleasure cruisers jostled on the moving water alongside rusty orange fishing boats. They all rocked gently back and forth to the rhythm of the waves and wind.

'You weren't joking,' she said. 'It is beautiful. Look at those houses, they must be at least a hundred years old.'

He watched her face. 'Of course, I was forgetting,' he teased, lightly. 'You come from a country where anything that pre-dates Ronald Reagan is considered historic.'

Pulling into the harbor, they found a small car park and pulled into an empty space.

As soon as they stopped, Reilly climbed out of the car, glad to stretch her legs. The fresh air hit her, a strong spring breeze coming in off the sea. She ran her fingers through her hair and breathed deeply.

'Nothing like it,' Chris said, watching her carefully. He led her along the edge of the harbor. The boats were bobbing gently on the waves, the lines slapping frantically against the masts in the breeze, setting up an insistent, repetitive beat. Seagulls wheeled overhead looking for scraps.

'I can see why you liked coming here with your dad,' she commented.

And now she could also see why Mike had been pining for a return to the place. Was there a possibility that she'd got this all wrong, and that her sister had brought him here, not out of malice but of love? No, that wasn't Jess's style; she had never been sentimental, never had any time for Mike's old tales of yore. If she had taken him here it was for her sake, her own reasons, not his.

Reilly closed her eyes and let the wind blow directly into her face. She longed for this to be over, longed for the time and the peace of mind to come somewhere like this and truly relax – not for thirty seconds, but for a day, a week ...

Then a sudden shiver ran through her. It was beautiful, but also bitterly cold, and who knew what awaited them here? She looked over at Chris – he had his jacket wrapped tight around him.

'So, where do we start?' she asked.

'There.' He nodded to a building up ahead of them, a large pub with pale yellow walls and a slate roof.

'What's that?'

'The Beach House – it used to be the centre of things around here but it's changed a bit since I was last here. It looks to be pretty upmarket these days.'

'So what do we do?' she wondered.

He glanced sideways at her. 'We? *We* do nothing.'

'What do you mean?'

'What I mean is that you are not the person to be talking to the folks around here.'

Reilly looked affronted. 'Why not?'

'Because you're too damned American.' He gave her a small wink as he pushed open the door. 'You'll scare the life out of the locals.' Inside, he took off his windbreaker and carefully placed it across the back of a chair, then loosened his tie and undid his top button. 'Whereas plain old Chris Delaney, who used to come fishing here with his dad, will blend in so easily that he'll open them up like a fresh clam.'

Reilly raised an eyebrow. She supposed she couldn't argue with that. 'OK, plain old Chris Delaney,' she said, taking a seat at a nearby table, 'go and work your magic ...'

He gave a wry grin. 'I'll do my best,' he said, turning slowly. 'Wish me luck ...'

42

Chris strolled into the bar and looked around. It was virtually a maritime museum, the walls of the pub were decorated with a huge range of maritime artifacts, many of them recovered from local wrecks by the pub owner and his diving mates.

Ignoring the displayed items, Chris focused on the patrons. There were several noisy Dubliners at the bar, drinking cocktails and telling jokes in loud voices, a quiet couple sitting solemnly at a small table with cappuccinos, and over in the farthest corner, three old guys hunkered down over pint glasses.

Chris moved to the bar, ordered himself a pint, and quietly watched them from a distance. They were deep in conversation, talking and laughing with the easy familiarity of old friends. All looked to be in their late sixties or early seventies and might have known the Steel family, and maybe even Mike himself as a kid.

He sipped at his pint for a couple of minutes, waiting for just the right moment – preferably when their glasses were almost empty. When the time had come, he made his way over to their end of the bar.

'How's it going, lads?'

The three looked up, eyes showing different degrees of suspicion. There was a grunt and a couple of idle nods in response.

Chris kicked straight into his story. 'When I was a boy my dad used to bring me down here fishing a lot. We had some family here we used to visit and I was trying to track down their house, for old times' sake – I was wondering if you gentlemen might be able to help me out?'

The men looked from one to another, trying to decide how to respond. Chris acted quickly. 'It looks like you're all running low there – can I get you another one?'

'Why not?' The oldest of the three – at least he looked that way, with his wispy white hair and missing teeth – thrust his glass out toward Chris. 'Same again, if you don't mind.'

'Well if you're buying ...'

Chris waved to get the barman's attention. So far so good. 'Same again, all round,' he told him.

REILLY FIDGETED as she waited at the table. She wasn't good at waiting at the best of times, but now was even worse. She tried to get into the mind of her sister, tried to figure out where Jess was going with this. Attempting to guess her next move was virtually impossible – they hadn't managed it once yet in the investigation.

Clearly, she'd taken Mike to get Reilly's attention, and brought him somewhere (here?) that was significant – namely their dad's ancestral roots. *Home Sweet Home*.

But then a second thought, even more disquieting, crossed Reilly's mind. What if they were wrong and they didn't find her here? What would Jess do then? Would she harm Mike and then seek Reilly out to finish it? Or would she just vanish, leaving no trace, nothing but a trail of bodies?

No, that wasn't an option. They were here for a reason and Jess wanted them to find Mike – to find her.

But where would she be keeping him? Was it somewhere she herself had been hiding out? This place was a very short drive from the city, so if Jess had found somewhere around here to hole up, it would have been all too easy for her to stay out of sight, just close enough so she could keep an eye on her handiwork and Reilly's reaction to it. But even if their hunch was right and she had taken Mike or based herself here, how on earth were they supposed to find her?

'Can I get you anything?' A member of staff appeared by Reilly's table as she was daydreaming.

'Oh, a coffee please,' she replied, automatically.

'No problem.'

He hurried off with her order and she gazed around the pub once more. Well, if nothing else, it would be interesting to see if Chris could come up with any local info on her family history.

Come on, Chris, she thought, glancing toward the four men at the bar, *use that Irish charm.*

THE BARMAN RETURNED and distributed fresh pints to the men. All three took a slow, solemn first sip, as if sealing the deal, and then turned back to Chris.

'So how can we help you?' the oldest guy asked. He had wrinkled skin, deeply tanned, and more hair on his nose and ears than on his head.

'Chris Delaney, good to meet you.' He held out his hand and all three men solemnly exchanged handshakes.

'Patrick Riordan,'

'James Murphy.'

'Peter O'Callahan.'

'What family are you looking for?' wondered Riordan, his blue eyes sparkling in his wrinkled face.

'Steel is the name,' Chris told him, recollecting what little family history he'd gleaned from Reilly. 'Michael Patrick Steel, father and son – the father was a carpenter and so was his father before him, Connor Michael Steel.'

The three looked at each other. 'There was a Steel family,' Murphy said. He was younger than the others, still had his own teeth, and was dressed in a dark blue cabled sweater.

'Bunch of them around here,' O'Callahan confirmed. Chris stared at his hands. They were huge, gnarled – he'd been some kind of mechanic, Chris would bet good money on it.

Riordan stayed silent and sipped at his beer, deep in thought.

'Any idea where they lived? They moved to America when I was quite young as I recall.''

A light went on in O'Callahan's eyes. He leaned forward, revealing worn holes in the elbows of his faded wool jacket. 'You're right – there was a local family that moved out to America – Steel the carpenter, that was him, I'm sure.'

Chris felt faintly excited, sure he was getting somewhere. 'Do you know where they lived?'

O'Callahan scratched at his stubbled chin. 'Can't say as I do ...' He thought a moment more. 'I think he had a workshop out on the old Bray Road,' he added.

Sullivan nodded. 'I remember him now, hell of a footballer, wasn't he?'

'Goalkeeper, wasn't it?'

'He could stop the ball like no other I've ever seen.'

'It was a sad day for that team when he left,' O'Callahan concluded.

'A sad day.'

All this time Riordan had sat silent. Then he suddenly sat forward. 'Lived out near those new builds on the Cliff Road, I think.'

'New builds?' Chris frowned. There were lots of new estates in Greystones, mostly occupied by commuting Dubliners.

The man smiled. 'Well, they were new back then compared to the rest of the stuff here – a few bungalows, built in the Fifties, I think.'

Chris's heart began to race. This was something. 'And you think the Steels lived in one of those?'

'Now, I couldn't tell you that. All I know is they were from out that direction somewhere.'

'And what direction is that?'

'Windgates, up the hill there, about a quarter of a mile out the Bray Road,' he said, pointing vaguely to the location.

Having got what he came for, Chris finished his pint and held his hand out. 'Gentlemen, you've been very helpful, thank you.'

One by one they shook his hand. As he turned to leave, Riordan called out to him. 'Mr Delaney?'

Chris turned back around, wondering what other crucial titbit one of them might have remembered.

The older man had a sparkle in his eye. 'Which branch of the guards do you work for then?'

43

'B ungalows?' Reilly queried as Chris slipped on his jacket.

'Yes, not far outside the town, the way we came in actually. They reckon your father's family lived out that direction.'

The wind hit Reilly with a blast as she stepped outside. What had been a pleasant fresh breeze when they arrived had now turned into a strong wind, laden with Irish drizzle, blowing hard in her face. She pulled her coat tight around her and stepped outside.

Chris was right behind her. He looked up at the darkened sky, clouds racing past overhead and they both quickened their step as they made their way to the car.

Although the area in question was according to locals only supposed to be a quarter of a mile up the hill, it seemed to take forever for Reilly and Chris to locate it.

Inside the car, she glanced at her hands, realizing her knuckles were white. Unclenching them, she tried to relax and slow her heart rate. But it was just too difficult. Now, they were no longer operating on a hunch; her father had indeed grown up around this area – this place was his roots.

Alongside her, Chris was keeping a close eye out for the Fifties bungalows or anything that might indicate they were in the right place. But Reilly thought it was almost impossible to differentiate any of the residences from the ones they were looking for, as it seemed there were countless older one-off houses, interspersed between the newer, more modern ones.

When the housing gradually thinned out a little and they emerged in a sparser, less populated part, he slapped the steering wheel. 'Damn it. Cliff Road my arse! We're almost into Bray now and I can't pinpoint anything like the area those guys talked about. Can you?'

Reilly said nothing, just shook her head in silent frustration.

'I'll drive down a little further and find somewhere to turn. Maybe we'll spot something on the way back.'

'Good idea.' Reilly thought her mind would explode if they didn't make more progress soon.

Some three hundred meters down, they spotted a man with a walking stick along the side of the road. He looked to be older than the three men Chris had been talking to in the bar and pulling the car up alongside him, Chris rolled down the window and called out to him. 'Excuse me, sir?'

Reilly studied the man as he approached the window. She would guess he was in his mid-eighties, maybe even ninety. Like many old men he had shrunken with age, though it looked like he'd never been huge to start with. He was probably no more than five foot one or two, bent over, and looking worn and tired. He wore a worn tweed jacket and a dark gray flat cap pulled down over his eyes.

'I'm sorry, we're a bit lost and I wondered if you might be able to help us.'

It was a moment before the man looked up, but when he did his eyes were clear and bright, an almost startling shade of blue.

'We're looking for a row of bungalows out this road,' Chris continued, pleasantly. 'I believe the area is called Windgates?'

'How was your drive down?' the man asked, suddenly

Reilly saw that Chris was momentarily put off stride. 'Drive down?'

'You're from Dublin, right?'

'Well, I am yes, is it that obvious?'

'You've got big city written all over you,' the man commented. 'The smart clothes, the accent, the impatience.'

'Well, sorry if I seem a bit rushed, but it's quite important.'

'Important, you say?' the man repeated. Reilly leaned across Chris hoping she'd have better luck getting what they needed out of this old-timer.

'My family is from round here and we're trying to track down my grandparents' place.'

The man looked at her with interest and she could tell he thought she was just another Yank trying to trace her Irish roots.

'That's nice,' he said slowly, and Reilly felt like shaking him. Was this guy going to help them or not?

'My father was Michael Steel – so was his father,' she continued, quickly. 'He was a carpenter, moved to California in the early Sixties ...'

'I remember Steel the carpenter,' he replied, softly and Reilly's heart sped up. 'He was a good craftsman, as I recall.'

'That's the one,' Chris said, quickly. 'Do you know where they lived?'

The man never took his eyes from Reilly. 'Aye, I remember.' He took a step back and leaned on his walking stick. 'Do you know what they call me around here?' he said. Reilly wanted to scream with frustration. They didn't have time for a chat, goddamnit!

Chris's tone was measured. 'No idea.'

'The walker, that's what they call me.' He looked back and forth at the two of them. 'Ever since I was a lad I've loved to walk – all over town, out of town – when I was a lad I used to walk all the way as far as Wicklow sometimes. It's been a good few years since I did that,' he said with a chuckle, 'but I still walk, downtown, up and down these roads.'

Reilly felt the hairs on the back of her neck stand up as suddenly she realized this guy wasn't as she'd first thought a doddery old fool, but was in fact, sharp as a tack.

'What have you seen, sir?' she asked, quietly.

'The Cliff Road,' he continued, as if she hadn't spoken. 'I remember when that whole area was just fields ...' He scratched his chin. 'It's still a quiet place to walk though, mostly young families, so there's often kids playing around outside.'

'That's where the Steels lived?'

He nodded. 'It's just a little way off the main road here once you get to Windgates, a cul-de-sac. I used to go down to the end and stare out at the harbor, watch the seagulls swooping in on stormy days to peck at the crops.' He sighed. 'Last house on the left was the Steels'. Of course, for the last thirty years old Mrs McGovern lived there. Kept herself to herself, while the house gradually became more and more run down around her.'

'And then?'

Reilly could feel Chris squirming with impatience beside her. She stayed quiet, gave the guy the time he needed to tell his story.

'A good while back, Mrs McGovern moved out, to one of

them nursing homes – don't fancy it much myself, but I guess it suited her.'

'And now the house is empty?' Reilly prompted, almost afraid to take a breath. That had to be it, it *had* to be where Jess was hiding out.

'No, next I heard, some Dublin family had bought it.'

'Oh.' Reilly's face fell.

'But the place a few doors down, that's empty,' he said, his blue eyes watchful. 'It's being done up and far as I know nobody's moved in yet. You know the way people these days need everything perfect before they'll set foot in a place. Hasn't been touched in a while though so whoever owns it must have ran out of money. Nothing new these days.'

Being done up. Reilly froze, all at once recalling the paint flecks they'd found at the early crime scenes, the gypsum plaster, paintbrush bristles ...

That had to be it; the renovated house had to be Jess's hiding place.

'Thank you so much for your help, sir,' she said, quickly, eyeing Chris. 'You said it's just off the main road?'

'Yes. If you head about a quarter of a mile down the direction you came from and take a turn to the left, just after the vet's.'

'The *vet's*?' Reilly wanted to cry out with joy. That must be where Jess had been getting the pentobarbital. Suddenly all the pieces were fitting into place.

'You're been a great help, thanks,' Chris told the older man, and without waiting for a response, maneuvered the car into a three-point turn. 'He said the house has been vacant for a while. That's where she's been hiding, Chris, I'm sure of it.' Reilly's mouth set in a thin line. 'And chances are, it's where she's taken my dad.'

.   .   .

'THERE IT IS,' she said, quietly. They had turned off the Cliff Road and soon came upon a row of small, nondescript bungalows a little way down. One of them had various building materials scattered outside and was very obviously undergoing renovations

But instead of turning into the cul-de-sac, Chris pulled the car over to the side of the road. Reilly gave him a quizzical look.

'I just want to talk this through,' he explained. 'At this point, we should probably call for backup.'

Reilly inhaled deeply. 'Do what you like, but I'm going in now.'

'Reilly. We—'

'We what?' She cut him off. 'Chris, surely you knew I didn't come all the way down here to just sit and wait in the car?'

'Well, if we aren't waiting for backup, what are we doing?'

Reilly stared out the window at the surrounding area, such a mundane setting for what could be the conclusion to a tortuous week. A man hurried past in the rain, coat up tight around his neck, a small dog dragging on a lead behind him. 'I think I need to do this myself. She's my sister and she's made it very clear this is all about me.'

Chris looked at her in amazement. 'You're joking. Reilly, she's a unstable killer, responsible for the deaths of at least nine people—'

'I know, but my father is in there. We can't just go in all guns blazing and risk messing this up. Well, if we had any damned guns, that is.'

He looked at her. 'Well you might not, but I do. And before you ask, no, I'm not giving it you; that's more than my job's worth.'

The truth was, she still had no idea how to approach this, but the one thing she did know was that if Jess was in there, she wanted to face her alone. Chris was right; she had been responsible for untold damage, but now that it had come to this, Reilly could only look at it as a family matter. She might be able to talk to Jess, make her see sense, or at the very least, prevent her from hurting Mike.

When she explained this to Chris, he was dubious. 'Not a good idea, you can't go in there alone, not when you have no idea what to—'

'Then I'll just make it look like I'm alone,' she interjected, her tone urgent. 'Damn it Chris, we don't have time to wait around! It's my dad in there, who knows what Jess could be doing? I need to go in *now*.' She put her hand on the door handle. 'Call in the others and, in the meantime, see if you can find another way in, around the back maybe so you can keep an eye on what's happening.. Then if something goes awry we can both work it from there.'

Chris shook his head grimly. 'As plans go, I've heard better—'

'Hop out,' she ordered, unwilling to wait around any longer. 'You're on foot from here.'

Chris reached for the door handle, then paused. 'Reilly, can I just say—'

She hushed him into silence. 'Don't say anything – it's bad luck. I'll see you in a little while, OK?'

He gave her a steady, appraising glance. 'Just be careful. And don't do anything stupid.' He threw open the door, letting a blast of cold air into the car, before disappearing between the nearby bushes.

REILLY EASED herself across into the driver's seat. The pedals were too far away for her to reach so she slid the seat forward. She was about to put the car in gear when she paused. The confidence she had displayed when convincing Chris that they should face this without delay seemed to seep out of her now that she was alone.

Suddenly, she felt like a small vulnerable child again, a million miles from a highly trained FBI investigator. Everything she was doing was wrong; Daniel would have kittens if he knew. She was going in blind to a suspect's house, no reconnaissance, no weapon, almost no backup, intending to just accept whatever she found and deal with it on the fly. Was she crazy?

But another voice, a more calming one, rose up in her mind. She was doing something that her old tutor had also drummed into her – using her instincts. Her instincts, he used to tell her, came from deep inside the subconscious mind. And the subconscious mind – ten times larger than the conscious mind – had access to a range of information that the conscious mind could only dream of. Listen to your instincts, he would say, they'll usually guide you in the right direction.

And what Reilly's instincts were telling her was that this was the only way to do it. That Jess was waiting for her, had taken her dad captive, and that if they went in with force her sister would simply kill Mike and make her escape for another day.

Reilly slipped the car into gear and moved closer to the renovated house. At this point, the best way to handle this was face to face.

It was a small, three-bedroom house near the end of the cul-de-sac, easily identifiable by the skip, loose plasterboard and other DIY materials strewn around it.

Without thinking, Reilly turned the car around at the end of the row and parked it facing up the road, ready for a quick getaway. Conscious of the rapid beating of her heart, she took several deep breaths before turning off the engine.

In the sudden silence she could hear the blood rushing in her ears, the wind whipping up the rain past the window. She wondered where Chris was. Well, wherever he was, he was undoubtedly getting wet.

She stowed the keys up behind the visor – again, out of habit – then kicked the door open. The rain had turned heavy, blasting in her face as she stepped from the car and forcing her to hurry up the path toward the house. With the moist drops in her eyes it was hard to see clearly and as she neared the house Reilly peered at the door, trying to find the doorbell – but there was no need.

The front door opened wide as she approached. A woman was half hidden behind it, a gentle smile on her face. 'Terrible night, isn't it?' her little sister said, casually. 'Come on in and get dry.'

44

Reilly stepped inside, brushing the rain from her hair. Jess closed the door behind them and slid the chain into place. She was holding the .38 loosely, not pointing it at Reilly, but it was there just the same, a quiet threat, a gentle reminder of who held all the cards.

Reilly looked around her. There was a smell of fresh paint in the air. The hallway led straight down toward the kitchen, a door on the left leading to the living room, another to the right.

'Where's Dad?' she asked.

'He's fine – you'll see him soon.' Jess nudged Reilly toward the living room with the gun. 'Go on through.'

She stepped into the room. It was small, newly decorated with a neutral carpet but almost devoid of furniture. A small battered sofa sat in the middle of the room and over by the window was a workman's bench on which stood a laptop.

The back wall had been opened out into an archway and led through to a dining room. In the darkened room Reilly could see a small dining table and four chairs.

'Sit down,' Jess commanded.

Reilly did as she was told and looked properly at her sister.

It had been such a long time since they'd seen each other, the last time had been back in the courtroom when Jess was being led away in handcuffs. Of course she looked older, but the same fine bone structure was there – she'd not put on any weight and her high cheekbones still dominated her delicate face.

What had changed was her expression. Jess had always had a searching look – she was the most demanding kid Reilly had ever met – but she had always tempered it with an underlying sweetness. Now, as her cold blue eyes gazed down at Reilly, that sweetness was entirely absent. In its place was a calculating look, a chilling gaze that seemed to be constantly assessing and calculating, looking for weaknesses, points of advantage.

'You look tired,' she observed.

Reilly gave a bitter laugh. 'Hardly a surprise. I've been kind of busy lately.'

'Really? Anything interesting?'

She met her gaze. 'Just some warped individual who seems intent on wiping out innocent people for kicks.'

Jess raised an eyebrow. 'That does sound interesting – you making any progress?'

'Of course. We know who it is; but personally I'm at a loss to understand why anyone would do such things.'

Jess gave a little smile. 'It's always so hard to understand other people's motives, isn't it? How can we ever truly understand what someone else feels, what they've experienced?'

Tired of the games, Reilly suddenly moved straight to the heart of it. 'Why, Jess? Why this mayhem, all these innocent people? And why here?'

Jess shrugged. 'Twelve years is a long time, Reilly. A long time to be locked up with a bunch of crazy psychotic people.

When you first go in you look at them, and think, I'm here by mistake, I'm not like them, I'll never be like them. But then, little by little you stop seeing the differences and actually start to notice how similar you are ...'

Just keep her talking, Reilly thought. *Keep her talking while Chris finds another way into the house.* 'But you weren't like them,' she argued. 'You were just a kid, a kid who was pushed too far.'

'Maybe I was when I first went in,' Jess looked sad for a moment, almost melancholic for the person she used to be. 'But if you're smart, you learn to adapt, learn to do what you can to survive.' She stared back at Reilly. 'I adapted, I survived, and mostly I learned about people – parents – and what they can do to you, how they can mess you up.'

'But you're out now, Jess. You survived. So why carry on? Why not stop all this right now?'

Jess's look was challenging. 'And do what?'

'I'm not saying I can let you go free,' Reilly continued, aware that she was babbling, but she was trying hard to hold Jess's attention, 'you've gone way beyond that – but they have no death penalty here ...'

Twelve years of accumulated bitterness rose up in her sister's voice. 'Oh. So I should go back to prison then – for the rest of my life?'

'Dad and I are both here – we would be able to visit you—'

A bitter laugh. 'One big happy family, right?' Jess shook her head. 'The messed-up mother, the freak daughter behind bars, and then the caring father and sister coming to visit every Sunday with their newspapers and fruit cakes and the scent of the outside world hanging on them? I don't think so.' She stepped back toward the computer and glanced at the screen.

'Then what?' Reilly asked. 'What is the point of all this? How does it end?'

Sitting there on the couch, wondering what was going to happen next was driving Reilly crazy. Where was her father? And where was Chris?

She leaned forward, trying to get a glimpse of what Jess was doing with the PC. 'What are you looking at?' she asked.

'Wonderful things, computers,' Jess answered, nonchalantly. 'Did you know that you can track someone's movements, twenty-four hours a day, seven days a week, just from their cell phone? It's great to be able to finally use some of the skills from all those courses on the inside.'

As her words sank in, realization hit. 'So that's how you tracked me ...'

Jess suddenly moved the screen round so that Reilly could see what she was looking at. 'That's not all you can do with them,' she observed, dryly.

Reilly stood up to peer at the screen. It was split into four: four images from four CCTV cameras covering the outside of the house. Damn, Reilly had been so focused on what she might find inside the house, she'd neglected to spot that. Three were still, showing nothing – but the fourth was trained on the back door of the house and clearly showed Chris, trying to pry the back door open with some kind of gardening tool.

'Ah, I was wondering where your boyfriend was,' Jess said, grimly.

'He's not my boyfriend.' Reilly began to inch closer, willing Jess to drop her guard, or perhaps give her an opportunity to get the gun away from her.

'He's almost in – time to say hello.' Jess spun around suddenly, making Reilly jump. She raised the gun toward her. 'Turn around!'

'Jess—'

'Turn around!'

Realizing that there was no arguing, Reilly did as she was told and turned slowly to face the wall. 'Jess, I—'

Jess flipped the gun around in her hand and with a swift strike, clubbed Reilly behind the ear with the barrel.

Reilly dropped like a stone, searing pain flashing through her brain and sending a wave of nausea racing through her body. She hit the deck, crumpled in a heap.

Jess looked down at her and smiled softly. 'I'll be right back.'

45

C hris had searched the back of the house but found no way in, at least not one where he could gain access unnoticed. The place was locked down tight, no windows even halfway open. His best bet seemed to be the back door – it was old and made of wood and would probably pry open if he had the right tools. He just needed to stay as quiet as possible and hope that Reilly was keeping her sister occupied. In the meantime, he'd alerted Kennedy who'd automatically called out the Bray unit. With any luck they should be here within minutes.

Chris wiped the rain from his face and looked around. He was already soaking wet and cold but he ignored his discomfort. Reilly was in there alone with her mentally ill and very dangerous sister; this was no time to think about himself.

He looked around for something to prise the door open with. There was nothing useful lying around but the neighbors had a garden shed. Trying not to make a sound, he hopped the low wooden fence and landed softly in a flowerbed, his joints groaning afresh. He crept toward the shed – there was no padlock so he slipped the door open.

Peering into the darkness he saw the vague outline of some gardening tools propped against the wall. He felt around and found a small shovel, a hoe, then finally a fork – those might work.

He grabbed the shovel and the fork and headed back next door. Creeping up to the back door, he peered inside. Although visibility was poor, he could at least see that it led straight into the kitchen. A dim light shone from the front of the house, down the hall and into the kitchen. He could see plain white cabinets, a ladder and some workbenches – and over on the windowsill, a tool box. He set the fork against the door and tried jamming it between the door and the frame. After two or three attempts, he managed to get some purchase and slipped the prongs in between, forcing the door inwards a little.

With the fork jammed in place, Chris reached for the spade. He slid it into the crack, lined it up against the lock and shoved. Nothing.

The rain was still falling in sheets, running down into his eyes. He wiped his hand across his face. A couple more attempts, and then he'd just smash the glass, noise be dammed – he had to get in.

He positioned the shovel again and pushed with all his might – almost falling straight inside as the door opened. Then, cocking his gun, he stepped into the kitchen, and paused, listening. The house was silent – no voices, nothing. He tiptoed forward toward the front of the house, creeping softly. Suddenly a shadow filled the hallway, blocking the light.

'Hello, Detective.' Before Chris could react there was a quick flash and a burning pain in his shoulder.

'This is a private party,' Jess said, her voice cold, biting. 'No crashers allowed without an invitation.'

The force of the bullet drove him backward into the doorway. He stumbled over the doorstep, landed in the mud and the rain. He tried to turn over but the wheezing in his punctured lung sucked all the life out of him.

Jess reached down and picked up the gun that had fallen out of his hand. 'You know, it would never have worked out between you and Reilly,' she informed him. He looked up. She was standing over him, his own gun pointing right at him.

His breath was ragged, hard to control, the pain and the dizziness already threatening to overwhelm him. 'She wants to help you, Jess,' he gasped.

'Of course she does.'

The gun fired for a second time.

REILLY WOKE UP SLOWLY. Her head was on fire, a searing pain pulsed down the back of her head and into her neck. She tried to sit up but a wave of uncontrollable nausea swept over her. She leaned forward and retched onto the pale carpet, a short dry heave of bile and pain that left her feeling worse than ever.

Unwilling to move, she gazed at the carpet. It was vaguely familiar but right now it didn't seem to be important. Something else was much more important – but what?

'I hope you're going to clear that up.' A voice came to her.

Reilly tried to focus – the stars swirling in front of her eyes were doing nothing for her nausea. She slowly pushed herself upright, fought off another wave, and took several deep breaths. The pain was concentrated on the back of her head – she reached up, slid her fingers in through her hair, and found a moist, painful spot. She quickly pulled her hand away – it was too sensitive to touch – and found her fingertips were sticky with blood.

'Come on, Reilly, pull yourself together.'

Reilly looked around. The small room, the smell of paint – suddenly it all came back. She turned her head, another wave of nausea, and saw Jess sitting calmly on an old battered sofa. And in the chair beside her was Mike. He was unconscious, held upright in the chair by several thick bands of duct tape wrapped around his chest.

'Dad ...' Reilly struggled to her feet, still dizzy, but gaining strength by the minute. She stood steadily for a moment, caught her breath and looked around.

Jess sat very still, watching her. She seemed calm, composed, the most serene Reilly had ever seen her.

'Is he ...?' Reilly croaked.

'Dead?' Jess gave a sad smile. 'No. I just bought him a nice bottle of Jameson and encouraged him to finish it.'

As if to verify Jess's words, Mike gave a drunken snore and moved slightly against his bonds.

Reilly exhaled. At least her dad was OK. But what did Jess intend? Then she remembered something else.

'Chris – what did you do to him?'

Jess remained cool as ever. 'I simply reminded him that this was a private family gathering and he had no business interfering.'

Reilly's heart sank. Was Chris OK? Had she hurt him, or worse ...?

Mindful that she was most likely in this on her own, Reilly tried to regain some kind of composure.

Suddenly, her gaze was caught by something she had missed before – she had been so focused on Jess and her father that she hadn't noticed another chair situated in the archway between the two rooms. Sitting on top of it was another gun.

Reilly quickly withdrew her gaze, not wanting Jess to realize what she seen. If she could just get there without Jess noticing – talk, distract her, anything, while she slowly moved toward the gun.

She put a hand up, held her aching head, and took another tentative step toward the archway 'So, what happens now?' she asked.

'That's for you.'

Reilly paused, realizing she was referring to the gun. She looked at her questioningly.

'It's for you,' Jess repeated. 'Go ahead, pick it up.'

Reilly looked again at the gun and then at Jess as if to ask her permission. She chose her steps carefully, fully expecting some kind of trick, but Jess sat silently watching her. She darted forward and grabbed the gun up from the chair. It felt light.

She exhaled, disappointment flooding through her. 'No ammo.'

'Nope, there's ammo all right.'

'But—'

'One bullet.'

Reilly's brain tried to take in the significance of this. She opened the gun to find that Jess was indeed telling the truth – the magazine was empty but there was one in the chamber. She flipped it closed and automatically trained it on her sister, worried why this seemed so easy.

'Stand up.'

Jess shook her head. 'It doesn't work like that, Reilly.'

'I said stand up! I *will* shoot you, Jess, if I have to.'

A slight smile. 'Oh please, don't ruin the suspense ...'

Then, before Reilly could react, Jess produced a syringe from behind her back, and pressed it against Mike's neck.

'Don't—'

'I presume you know what's in this.'

'Pentobarbital,' Reilly snapped, breathing heavily. She moved closer.

'Stop right there.' The hypodermic pricked Mike's neck, causing him to twitch slightly. 'It's a lethal dose,' Jess informed her. 'Not like the little shots you and the others got.'

Reilly shuddered, remembering all too well the damage that stuff could do. 'Put it down, Jess, or I will shoot you.' Her hand shook as she tried to aim carefully at her sister.

'Do you know why I went to see Mom that day?' Jess asked, suddenly as if they were having a normal, run-of-mill conversation.

Reilly still felt nauseous, weak; it was taking everything she had to remain upright. Clear thinking was almost beyond her. She shook her head. 'No – why?'

'She called me up, invited me over.'

'I didn't know that. I thought—'

'Do you know what she wanted?' Jess seemed to grimace at the memory. 'She wanted to tell me that Mike wasn't my dad – that that deadbeat she'd shacked up with was my father.' She examined the tips of her nails as if assessing them for a manicure.

Reilly stood utterly still, unsure what to believe. Was this true, or just another one of Jess's weird mind games? Either way, Reilly decided to play along. 'That must have been horrible for you. Why didn't you tell me?'

Jess continued as if she hadn't spoken. 'Can you imagine what finding something like that out does to a poor confused teenager?' she asked turning those once-innocent but now deathly blue eyes on Reilly. 'Can you?'

'I can only imagine. I'm so sorry.' She moved an inch closer.

'I wondered why she would want to tell me that. Why she would want to mess with my mind and break my heart like that. But that was Mom all over, wasn't it?' Jess gave a bitter laugh. 'She offered me a choice, Reilly. Come and live with them – my *real* parents she called them – or stay with you two.' She shook her head. 'I was fourteen years old and totally confused – how was I supposed to make that choice?'

'You shouldn't have had to,' Reilly said, softly.

Jess looked up at her, the beginnings of a smile on her face. 'Are you trying to *understand* me, sis?'

Reilly nodded. 'I've always tried to understand you. I've tried so hard to imagine what you must have gone through, what it must have been like for you to—'

'To have killed my own mother,' Jess finished.

'Yes.'

She looked at Reilly carefully. 'It's the ultimate taboo, isn't it, sis? That's what Freud reckoned – I read all about it on the inside. Killing your own mother – your own parent – is the ultimate taboo. Do you think that you finally understand that now?'

Reilly nodded. 'I do understand, Jess.' She started to move closer. 'Look, please put down the syringe ...'

'And if I'm capable of something like that, then maybe you are too.'

Something in her voice froze Reilly. That momentary softness that had briefly surfaced was gone and the cold, calculating Jess was back. Now, she was toying with Reilly, preying on her insecurities, targeting her weak spot.

'So now, it's time for you to make *your* choice.' As she said it, Jess jabbed the needle deep into Mike's neck, stopping just short of pressing the plunger. He twitched and muttered something incoherent.

Reilly stared in horror. 'Jess, no!'

Jess's finger hovered atop the plunger. 'You want me to stop?' she shouted.

There were tears in Reilly's eyes. 'Yes ... please, Jess ...'

'Then make me.'

'What?'

'One bullet, Reilly. You have one bullet. You kill me and you save your father. We both know he isn't mine, so hell if I care. Make your choice – see once and for all if you're capable.'

'Jess, no, I don't want to kill you,' Reilly protested. 'No matter what ... you're still my sister.'

Jess laughed, a deep throaty laugh that sent shivers down Reilly's spine. 'Christ, you're so predictable. After all this you're still trying to play the happy families card?' Then her finger twitched, moving dangerous close to the plunger. 'So like I said, him or me?'

Reilly wavered on her feet, a combination of nausea, fear and confusion. 'I ... I can't—'

'Choose – now!' Jess looked up at her with that same demanding face Reilly recognized from their childhood. 'Clock's ticking, Reilly. Your cop boyfriend is lying outside bleeding to death in the rain – he would probably appreciate you making up your mind sooner rather than later ...'

Reilly tried to steady herself. She saw it all now, saw that this was where Jess had been heading all along – the taboos, the murder, the kidnap of Mike, all designed to bring them to this point, the point where Reilly also had to face the ultimate taboo, had to face killing a member of her own family, had to face the realization that she too was capable of something unimaginable.

'Time's up,' Jess said, suddenly, and Reilly saw her thumb twitch against the syringe. The instinct she'd so carefully honed ... all those years of Quantico training suddenly meant nothing as her finger hovered above the trigger. 'For God's sake, please—'

The bullet hit Jess somewhere above the eyes, hurled her backward and out of her seat.

Reilly gasped, the loud crack of the shot still ringing in her ears, and turned to see a rain-soaked Pete Kennedy standing behind her, gun in hand.

'Looks like I got here just in time,' he said, his face pale.

Just then Mike stirred, grunting and twitching at the hypo-dermic still jammed into his neck. Reilly covered the gap between them in three strides and quickly snatched the needle out, her heart beating almost out of her chest. 'Dad, are you OK? *Dad.*'

Mike spluttered and briefly opened his eyes. He seemed to have trouble focusing but from what Reilly could tell the drug hadn't actually entered his system. Then, just as quickly, his eyelids closed shut and he passed out, most likely from the alcohol, she guessed.

Relief and pain washed over her in equal measures. Eventually, she dropped the gun and fell to her knees alongside him – and face to face with Jess.

Her little sister stared unseeingly at her, her bright blue eyes wide open, a single hole in the front of her head and blood oozing into her soft blond hair.

Instinctively, Reilly stroked her cheek. 'I'm so sorry, Jess,' she whispered. 'So sorry it had to end this way.'

She gently closed her sister's eyes and sat back on her heels, still dizzy and nauseous. She leaned on the sofa for support and turned again to face Kennedy. But he was nowhere to be seen.

She got up and rushed out toward the back of the house where, to her horror, she saw him tending to Chris who was lying on the ground just outside the door. He was bleeding heavily from his midsection. Jess hadn't been playing mind games; she had indeed shot him, twice by the looks of it.

'Oh my God,' she gasped, her hand moving to her mouth. 'Is he ...?'

'It's not good,' Kennedy said, his face pale with worry. 'Not good at all. The ambulance is on its way, but he's bleeding out, fast.'

'Chris ...' Reilly moved to him and shook his body gently. His head rolled back, a trickle of blood running down from the corner of his mouth. She shook him again, her voice small and desperate. 'Please, Chris, don't give up on us now,' she pleaded. 'Not now, when everything's finally over.'

EPILOGUE
SIX MONTHS LATER

The bay was wide, a sweeping curve of sand backed by low rolling sand dunes. The golden sand was almost deserted, just a couple of families with kids playing in the surf.

Waves rolled in to break in steady patterns just offshore.

Her board under her arm, Reilly jogged easily across the soft sand toward the waves, her blue eyes trained on the water, reading the surf with an expert's eye.

She turned to her companion, pointing out at the waves with one arm. 'The offshore wind is northerly and the waves are spilling down, right to left.' She grinned. 'The perfect spot for a novice.'

Chris shaded his eyes from the bright sunshine and tried to see what she was seeing. He looked uncomfortable carrying the large board and despite his sallow skin, a large purple scar splotched his upper midsection. 'Those waves look pretty big,' he observed, nervously.

'Big?' Reilly teased, glancing sideways at him. 'These are tiny!' She took a tentative step out into the edge of the surf.

'Water's cold though – you might regret that decision not to wear a wet suit.'

'I'm an Irishman, born and bred,' he called after her, 'and I'm not afraid of a bit of cold water.'

He picked up his board and strode out through the surf to join her. Reilly stood in waist-deep water, her own board in the sea beside her. 'So, are you ready for your first lesson, Detective?' she asked.

He gulped. 'I think so.'

'Chris Delaney – you're not getting all scared on me, are you?'

He grinned. 'I have Kennedy for a partner, remember? Nothing scares me. Anyway, don't they always say that what doesn't kill you only makes you stronger.'

And for some reason, Reilly remembered, the massive blood loss he'd suffered in the aftermath of Jess's attack didn't kill him either. The doctors at the ER had been at a loss to understand why the bleeding hadn't weakened him more and since then the pain he'd been suffering had stopped and he'd been right as rain. As far as Chris was concerned that was the end of it but Reilly wasn't so sure. There had definitely been something off about those initial blood tests, and it might only be a matter of time before whatever it was flared up again.

Still, on Chris's request, she was resigned to letting him deal with it as and when he saw fit, and as things stood the mystery remained unsolved. Once it wasn't affecting his job, Reilly had little choice but to let the issue remain unspoken.

Ditto for Mike Steel's recollection of that night in Greystones. While Reilly's father had been too inebriated to remember what transpired at the house, she'd also deliberately kept him in the dark about Jess's ultimate challenge and her willingness to use him as bait. There was little point in him knowing the whole truth.

Thankfully, the authorities had been happy about Reilly's role in finding their killer and, following a long and painfully in-depth internal police investigation, after which it emerged she'd done nothing wrong, she'd only recently been reinstated in her role at the GFU. Albeit with reluctance from Jack Gorman.

Now, Chris laid his board flat on the rolling water, threw himself on it and began paddling frantically out toward the breakers just like she'd told him. 'Come on then, California girl,' he challenged, 'show me what you've got.'

Reilly watched him for a moment, a smile on her face before following suit, and they both powered out toward deeper waters.

From the Author: Thank you for reading SERIAL - we hope you enjoyed it.

Read more. Read on for an excerpt of **VICTIM**, the next novel in the Reilly Steel series, available now in paperback and ebook.

VICTIM - CSI REILLY STEEL #2

EXCERPT

Read the clues. Decode the science. Reveal the murderer.

That's Reilly Steel's mantra. Find the answers, solve the crime.

But the Quantico-trained forensic investigator is finding her skills aren't enough when a ferociously intelligent killer strikes Dublin. The modus operandi is as perplexing as it is macabre. What connects two seemingly disparate, high-profile victims?

Their corpses refuse to give up their secrets and the crime scenes prove a forensic investigator's worst nightmare. Reilly soon suspects that she may be dealing with a killer - or killers - who know all about crime scene investigation.

It's only when a third murder occurs - equally graphic and elaborate in its execution - that they discover that this particular killer is using a very specific blueprint for his crimes. Who is the killer's next victim, the real target? And what's his endgame?

1

Sandra Coffey was desperately struggling to breathe.

The smell - an over-ripe suffocating stench - completely overwhelmed her, making her nauseous and dizzy. She shook her head in panic, suppressing an urge to gag, thinking she wouldn't be able to hold out for much longer.

Suddenly she heard the crunch of tires on the gravel outside, and through the window she saw drawing to a halt a white van with familiar blue writing on its side.

At last, help had arrived.

Thank God, thank God ...

Sandra stood up, smoothed down her trousers, and trying to regain her poise, headed quickly for the front door.

'Morning Mrs Coffey,' Paddy Murphy the local plumber, greeted her amiably. He had a round red face, long white mutton-chop sideburns and his bulky frame filled every inch of his extra-large, navy-blue boiler suit. He looked up at her, a frown of concern on his face. 'Toilet backing up, you said?'

'Not just one, Paddy. All of them. The smell ... it's unbearable.'

His frown deepened. 'Probably your septic tank then.' The

plumber removed his cap to reveal his shiny bald head and scratched at it thoughtfully. 'Sounds unusual. Maybe a rat or something found its way in there. Only way we'll know for sure is to go and have a look.'

Paddy set his toolbox down, loosened the cap of the inspection pipe, then stood back and averted his face. He didn't want to be hammered by the acrid funk he knew would rush his nostrils when the system was opened.

He rummaged in his toolbox and came up with a large industrial torch. Tapping it on the heel of his hand, he flicked it on, aimed it down the tank and peered into the murky depths.

The inspection pipe was narrow – maybe sixty centimeters across – and didn't show much of the tank itself. He moved the torch around and peered in as far as he could to see if he could identify a blockage, but all he saw was the layer of scum that floated on top of the mottled and putrid grays and browns. Instinctively he held his breath. Helluva of a way to make a living …

'Can you see anything?'

Paddy jumped, startled.

Unheard, Mrs Coffey had come up behind him, her feet in a pair of patterned Wellington boots, a Barbour jacket draped across her shoulders.

He grunted as he stood up, trying to regain his composure. The woman was standing very close and her proximity was unaccountably disconcerting.

'You can never really see much down these. Reckon I'll just have to open up the manhole cover.' He sighed as he recapped the pipe.

What a pain in the arse – digging around in a heap of shite was not what Paddy had in mind just before lunchtime on a

Friday morning, especially with yer woman over his shoulder watching his every move.

He grabbed his toolbox and trudged across the sloping lawn and around a line of low-growing shrubs, Mrs Coffey hard on his heels. Then he stopped so suddenly that she almost stumbled into the back of him.

'What is it?'

He turned and looked at her, puzzled. 'Have you had someone else in to check the system lately?'

'No. Why do you ask?'

'Someone seems to have been digging for the manhole cover, but from the looks of that mess, they didn't know exactly where to find it.'

They both observed the turned-over soil, dark and rich from the recent rain.

'Maybe Tony noticed it was backing up before he left and tried to fix it, though he didn't mention anything ...'

The plumber approached the metal manhole cover. 'Someone's been at this for sure.'

He kneeled down, slipped a small crowbar from his toolbox, and placed it under one edge of the cover. He glanced over his shoulder at Mrs Coffey. 'You might want to stand back a bit – these things reek to high heaven when opened.'

She duly took a couple of steps back and pulled her jacket tightly around her. Paddy flipped the cover off, and once again averted his nose to evade the malodorous stink racing up to greet him.

Waiting for the air to clear a little, he was reaching for his torch when a horrified cry from behind stopped him short. He shook his head. Serves her right for standing over him – this was no place for a—

But Paddy quickly realized that it wasn't merely the stench that had affected Mrs Coffey.

Once, twice, three times her high-pitched screams split the cold, damp air, before she finally clamped her hand across her mouth, her eyes wide with horror.

What the ...? Paddy stared at her, puzzled, before slowly turning back to the tank to see what had so affected her.

Floating up to greet him was the bloated, distorted face of a man, his eyes protruding, skin purple with putrefaction, sewage spilling from his open mouth as he bobbed in the effluent pool.

Frozen with shock, the plumber just stared, unable to take his eyes away. The dead man's deeply veined, bloodshot eyes seemed be staring back at him in mute accusation.

Behind him, Mrs Coffey was whimpering little sobs of pure animal fear and horror.

Finally Paddy Murphy gagged and fell backwards onto the damp grass.

'Jesus Christ Almighty ...'

2

'Can you please state your name and occupation for the benefit of the Court?' the lawyer asked.

The oak-paneled courtroom was still, all eyes on the woman sitting in the witness stand.

She sat upright, her piercing blue eyes fixed on the man who was questioning her. Patrick Masterton was a picture-perfect lawyer in his immaculate dark suit, crisp white shirt and just enough gray in his hair to make him appear distinguished.

As Masterton referred to his notes, a court artist worked quickly to capture the scene. He had already finished drawing Masterton – he looked elegant, determined, powerful, even – and was now working on the witness.

With quick strokes he portrayed the shape of her head, the sheet of blond hair falling onto her shoulders, her high cheekbones and strong jaw line. Her eyes were an unusual shade of deep blue and her strongest feature. In just a few strokes he managed to capture the fierce light of intelligence – defiance almost - that shone through. She wore an elegant charcoal skirt and jacket, her shirt a complimentary pale pink. The only adornment was a small brooch in her lapel, shaped like a dragon.

'Reilly Steel, GFU investigator,' she replied, in a strong American accent.

'GFU?'

'Garda Forensic Unit,' she clarified. 'We collect and analyze evidence from crime scenes.'

'And how long have you been in this profession, Ms Steel?'

'I've been employed by the GFU for approximately thirteen months. Before that, I led an ERT – Evidence Response Team – out of the FBI San Francisco field office for almost seven years. Throughout this time, my Office carried out extensive crime scene investigative work with contacts in local, state, federal and international law enforcement agencies.'

Her answers were clear. Absolutely no hesitation – just statements of fact.

'And your qualifications?'

'In 2003 I graduated in Crime Scene Investigation from the FBI National Academy in Quantico, Virginia.'

'Impressive credentials, I'm sure the Court will agree,' Masterson said.

He smoothed his tie, and looked from the jury back to Reilly. 'Ms Steel, can you tell us about the evidence you found at Elizabeth Walker's house on the night of the 15th of August last?' the lawyer asked, pointing to a nearby projector screen, upon which two photographs were displayed side by side. The first photo showed the head of a bed, a heavy bloodstain on a pillow against the wooden slatted headboard. The second was a close-up of the same image, displaying a dark, frizzy hair wedged between the pillow and the headboard.

Reilly's voice was even. 'The hair was collected from the victim's bed.'

Masterton moved a step closer, once again focusing the

jury's attention on her. 'What can you tell us about it, based on your forensic analysis?'

'It's male, Caucasian.'

'You were able to extract DNA from it?' Masterson had his notes behind his back, but he had no need to refer to them.

'Yes. The follicle was attached, so we were able to extract primary DNA from the sample.'

'And you compared this with a saliva sample obtained from the accused?' He nodded towards a young man with dark curly hair, who sat slouched between two guards, his ill-fitting suit making him appear uncomfortable, out of place in these formal surroundings.

'Correct.'

'The hair was a match?'

'It was.'

Masterton moved towards the jury, making sure he had their full attention before asking the key question. 'Ms Steel, what would you estimate as the likelihood that the hair you found on the pillow belongs to the accused?'

Reilly sat up even straighter. This was her world – forensic evidence, scientific certainties. She could answer with complete confidence. 'The likelihood that the hair we found on that pillow belongs to the accused is 99.97 percent.'

A small murmur went through the courtroom. One or two members of the jury gave slight involuntary nods. This type of evidence – precise, cold, scientific – always hit home hard, and helped sway wavering minds.

Masterton resumed his questions. 'Ms Steel, could you now please tell the Court what you found beneath the victim's fingernails?'

'Samples of blood and skin tissue.'

'These are typically evidence of a struggle?'

'That's correct,' Reilly replied.

A photo of the female victim's upturned hand appeared on the projector, the woman's elegant fingernails darkened by the blood beneath them. The jury's gaze turned towards the image – there was something brutal about those cold, lifeless hands, the blood-flecked nails mute testimony to just how hard Elizabeth Walker had fought for her life.

The artist glanced quickly at the jury – faces were hardening, decisions were being made, and cold glances flashed across the room at the accused, Danny Doyle.

Masterton continued, relentless now that he was closing in on his prey. 'Ms Steel, you were able to extract DNA from these samples also?'

'We were.'

'And the DNA matched that of the accused, Daniel Doyle? Matched that of the hair sample, as well the saliva sample you obtained from the accused?'

'Correct.'

The word hung heavily in the air, and rolled around the courtroom with a resounding air of finality. Whatever else the defense might say, whatever tricks or stratagems they might come up with, the science had spoken – clearly and incontrovertibly. Danny Doyle had been in Elizabeth Walker's bed the night she died; his hair was on her pillow, his skin and blood beneath her battered, broken fingernails.

Masterton allowed himself a smile. 'Thank you, Ms Steel.' He turned to the defense. 'Your witness.'

The defense lawyer wore a tired, defeated look. In his late fifties, with a thousand tough cases behind him, Michael Liston knew when to attack, or when to regroup and look for a weak point elsewhere.

Reilly Steel, GFU investigator, had revealed no chinks in her armor. She had a rock-solid chain of evidence, unimpeachable scientific credibility, unshakeable conclusions, and a manner that spoke of unquestionable competence. Experience told him there was no value in pursuing her – what he needed was to get her off the witness stand as quickly as possible. Liston shook his head. 'No further questions, Your Honor.'

The judge nodded to Reilly. 'Thank you Ms Steel, that will be all.'

As the GFU investigator stood and walked quickly back to her seat, the artist noticed that all eyes were on her. She had delivered her evidence with such certainty, such an air of confidence, that it was hard not to feel admiration for her.

Even as the next witness was called to the stand, he began a second sketch of her, his quick strokes filling in the details that had been hidden while Steel sat in the witness stand – her slim figure, long legs, elegant way of walking ...

It was on days like this that he loved his job.

As she exited the courthouse, Reilly exhaled, finally able to release some of the tension, the strain of being the key witness. The entire trial hinged upon her evidence, and she had come through.

With Doyle's denial of guilt blown out of the water, the case should proceed smoothly towards a conviction.

Did the system always convict the right person? Of course not – Reilly wasn't naïve enough to believe that – but she did believe that most of time, if there was sufficient incontrovertible evidence, the correct decision would be reached.

In this instance it had all come together. Doyle had pleaded not guilty, and had denied even knowing Elizabeth Walker, but Reilly's evidence – the evidence so carefully collected and analyzed by her team at the GFU – had placed him at the scene of the murder, in Elizabeth Walker's bed.

Justice was about to be served.

Making a mental note to thank her team for their Trojan work in preparing for the case, Reilly pulled out her iPhone to type a reminder to herself, and also to check her messages. There were a few, but one in particular caught her attention: a text message from Detective Chris Delaney. He rarely texted unless it was important. Reilly opened the message.

'*Hope the trial's going well and you nail Doyle to the wall. Call when you're finished? We've got a weird one.*'

Reilly arched an eyebrow. A weird one?

Exactly how she liked them.

End of excerpt

Continue reading VICTIM, out now

ALSO BY CASEY HILL

ABOUT THE AUTHOR

Casey Hill is the pseudonym of husband and wife writing team, Kevin and Melissa Hill. They live in Dublin, Ireland.

Translation rights to the USA Today bestselling CSI Reilly Steel series have been sold in multiple languages including Russian, Turkish and Japanese.

Subscribe to the mailing list: enter the following link into your browser to be notified of new Casey Hill releases: http://eepurl.com/FFE2D

Made in the USA
Monee, IL
23 July 2022

10174836R00225